ZATAA
The Fang
The Bay of Innisjour
Hazut
Wrultho
The Sheets
Innisjour
he Sanguine River
Loursevain Gap
The Iron Peaks
The Iron Bay
Mekës
ASTERYA
N
W
E
S

THE SERPENT AND THE WOLF

THE SERPENT AND THE WOLF

REBECCA ROBINSON

LONDON SYDNEY NEW YORK TORONTO NEW DELHI

1230 AVENUE OF THE AMERICAS, NEW YORK, NEW YORK 10020

This book is a work of fiction. Any references to historical events, real people, or real places are used fictitiously. Other names, characters, places, and events are products of the author's imagination, and any resemblance to actual events or places or persons, living or dead, is entirely coincidental.

First Saga Press hardcover edition November 2024

SAGA PRESS and colophon are trademarks of Simon & Schuster, LLC

Simon & Schuster: Celebrating 100 Years of Publishing in 2024

For information about special discounts for bulk purchases, please contact Simon & Schuster Special Sales at 1-866-506-1949 or business@simonandschuster.com.

The Simon & Schuster Speakers Bureau can bring authors to your live event. For more information or to book an event, contact the Simon & Schuster Speakers Bureau at 1-866-248-3049 or visit our website at www.simonspeakers.com.

Interior design by Lewelin Polanco

Manufactured in the United States of America

1 3 5 7 9 10 8 6 4 2

Library of Congress Cataloging-in-Publication Data

Names: Robinson, Rebecca, 1995- author. Title: The serpent and the wolf / Rebecca Robinson. Description: First Saga Press hardcover edition. | London; New York : Saga Press, 2024. | Series: The serpent and the wolf ; 1 Identifiers: LCCN 2024033025 (print) | LCCN 2024033026 (ebook) | ISBN 9781668052488 (hardcover) | ISBN 9781668074671 (paperback) | ISBN 9781668052495 (ebook) Subjects: LCGFT: Fantasy fiction. | Romance fiction. | Novels. Classification: LCC PS3618.O33366 S47 2024 (print) | LCC PS3618.O33366 (ebook) | DDC 813/.6—dc23/eng/20240729 LC record available at https://lccn.loc.gov/2024033025 LC ebook record available at https://lccn.loc.gov/2024033026

ISBN 978-1-6680-5248-8

ISBN 978-1-6680-5249-5 (ebook)

For Ben, who held my hand in the darkness as I discovered my own magic.
You are still the kindest thing that's ever happened to me.

CHAPTER 1

With rope tied under one pillow and a tiny blade hidden beneath another, Vaasalisa Kozár scurried around a dimly lit room in the High Temple of Mireh.

She would not be here when the sun came up.

The people dancing in the downstairs hall of this enormous temple were the perfect distraction, with their aggravatingly loud music and communal dances, absorbed in themselves and their honeyed wine without a care for the bride or groom.

She despised each and every person in that great hall. Every person who had attended this fraud of a ceremony.

Her brother, Dominik, especially, with his serpentine smile and glinting raven hair. As she peeled off her ugly white marriage gown, violent images of ripping that hair from his head and silencing his audacious laugh pulsed in her mind.

But his death was not at the forefront of her priorities. He had already slithered back to his palace and his pretty women in their home empire of Asterya anyway. Whatever reasons Vaasa's viper of a brother had to arrange her marriage only months after their father's death, only *weeks* after their mother's, didn't matter. It was unforgivable. It was the sort of thing someone lost their life over.

Vaasa didn't know if death would be Dominik's fate, but she had decided this marriage would not be hers.

She only had minutes before her unfortunate new husband came for her.

Reid of Mireh was a brutal mountain of a warrior—the youngest foreman Icruria had ever seen, and by far the most notorious. *The Wolf of Mireh.* He had looked upon her white dress as if he detested its absence of color—detested her, perhaps. This nation exalted bright colors and brilliant hues, so she shoved away the white nightgown she'd planned to wear and traded it for a red one, which only fell to midthigh and had a slit up to her right hip. The cool silk glided over her body. Setting her bags inconspicuously near the window, she sank into silk sheets and crossed her legs in a way she thought made them look longer. In a way she hoped would ensnare Reid of Mireh.

Vaasa had studied this nation extensively—just as much as any other threat to her family's reign. While no one had managed to infiltrate western Icruria and come back alive, violence plagued the eastern territories, which were on the verge of an all-out war with Asterya. The republic of Icruria had begun as six independent city-states, united generations ago. Vaasa's tutors had emphasized its unusual political structure: Icruria's elected ruler, called a headman, changed every ten years. The headman was chosen from among the foremen of the six major territories. The five who weren't elected became the headman's councilors. They advised the headman, and it was eventually their votes that selected the next one. Vaasa's new husband was said to be the most obvious next choice to rule Icruria—a dangerous, violent warlord known for his lack of mercy.

If that was true, the little slit in her nightgown might be her best advantage—it fell to either side of her leg as she adjusted her weight upon the bed. Even warlords were men, after all, and men were almost always their own downfall.

Her fingers itched for the rope beneath the pillow. For the blade.

The foreman of Mireh would probably expect a demure, well-poised woman of the heiress of Asterya. Not the murderous thing Vaasa's father had turned her into—the callous, manipulative daughter he had demanded. Asterya's eldest would not be some useless bride—she would be a weapon.

Upon their parents' deaths, Dominik became the emperor, solely because of what dangled between his legs.

All Vaasa got was Reid of Mireh.

Approaching footsteps sounded upon the stone floors outside the door.

Unease threaded in her stomach for only a moment, and she shoved it down with the force of a blow. Fear was the most dangerous emotion she felt—one that summoned the infectious curse crawling beneath her skin. A serpent was how she pictured it, coiled in her gut, and prepared to strike. She might very well kill all the people in this temple if she let the force out. Might kill herself, too. It was far easier to remain angry—anger was not vulnerability.

Anger was the only emotion the curse seemed to listen to.

The door swung open and the foreman of Mireh padded through, taking up a majority of the doorframe with his far-too-broad shoulders.

Their eyes met.

Vaasa would not be terrified of this man, no matter the strength she saw there.

But there was a whisper behind that strength, a surprise or confusion at the sight of her sitting like this on his bed.

Then the foreman of Mireh morphed into someone diligent and duty-bound, pragmatic and calm. His clean-shaven face made her question what she might find attached to such a rigid jaw—fangs or some other atrocious feature, something like the magic and monsters whispered to roam Icruria.

Yet he only looked human, just like her, a thought that had haunted her since their brief and hollow exchange of vows. Young, poised. He was dressed in rich black and purple, dark hair pulled back with a leather strap, and his curious eyes roved over the image of her waiting patiently upon the bed for him. Vaasa softened her gaze and let her mouth tip into a struck grin. Golden eyes flicking down to take in that mouth, the foreman of Mireh was a fly in a web, something carnal ticking in the corner of his jaw. He looked nothing short of a conqueror.

Vaasa would make a meal of her escape.

Curling from the bed, long legs carrying her weight as she folded upright, she crossed the distance between them. Reid didn't move. He watched each step she took until she slithered to the space just in front of him.

"Red suits you." His western accent floated between them in the commerce tongue of the Icrurians, his eyes raising to meet the ocean of hers.

"You didn't seem to like the white," she said.

His lips pursed before sliding into a genuine grin. "I suspect you could stop my heart in any color."

Such pretty words. Lifting her hand to his chest, to the space right above his heart, she splayed her fingers and pressed her palm against the silk of his draped wedding attire. Instead of words, which hardly ever did a situation justice anyway, Vaasa slid her hands to the buttons of his cloak, right at the curve of his neck, and began to undo them. Carefully, she pulled the cool fabric from his shoulders and exposed more of his bare chest.

He took it from her hands and placed it delicately upon the chair to their left.

She moved for the cross-body drape, tucking her fingers into the fabric.

Reid watched her silently, eyes a little wary, but his breathing had quickened, too.

She worked him out of his ceremonial drape and gave herself one long glance at the plane of his bare chest—all corded muscle and covered in intricate ink that threaded across the light brown skin of his right shoulder and down his arm. The subtle fragrance of salt and amber wafted under her nose, a little sweet and earthy. In any other situation, she would have described the smell as irresistible. Admitted that his candlelit, brown body covered in black ink was more enticing than she wanted to give him credit for.

But that was not why she was here.

With reckless abandon, she dragged one finger to his waistline, and then guided him toward the bed until the backs of his knees pressed to the mattress.

Surprise and excitement flickered in his eyes, and he wrapped his fingers around her own, gently lifting her knuckles to his lips. "I hoped we would get along," Reid of Mireh said.

Vaasa released her bottom lip from between her teeth. "I would like that."

Hands gripping her waist, Reid spun them until he could guide her onto the soft blankets, gesturing with his head that she should lie down for him. Keeping her gaze locked with his, she lay back onto the bed and pushed just far enough up to place her hands within reach of the rope and the blade.

The bed dipped with his knees, and he crawled up her body. This position wouldn't work the way she needed, though.

She reached for his pants.

He caught her wrist. "Have you done this before, Vaasalisa?"

She paused. Did he expect chastity? Had that been a part of his agreement with her brother?

"The truth," he said, one of his hands lifting to brush a piece of long black hair from her cheek and trailing to her shoulder, "will always serve us best."

The truth was that men could not tell a virgin from a hole in a tree, no matter what lies they told themselves. She doubted this man could, either. Still, she wanted him to think her innocent. Wanted him to think her meek. "I have not," she lied. "But I have heard it's easier for the woman if she is above you. If she can control the speed."

"And you want to do this?"

The question could have paralyzed her, the severity of his taut mouth and furrowed brow, if she'd let it. "Yes, I want to do this."

Had he really just asked her that?

Nodding, thrill returning to his easy eyes and loosened shoulders, he slid his hand to the small of her back and rolled, placing himself beneath her. Right at her mercy. Gentle were his hands as they trailed up the sides of her legs, which were positioned around his hips. "Then by all means, carry on," he whispered.

This was the man who would rule all of the city-states of Icruria for an entire cycle?

Beneath her was no wolf—only a fool.

Running was for the best, then; he would be crushed beneath the boots of Asterya. Her brother had no interest in trade negotiations with a mere foreman, no matter the assurances she'd received that Reid would rise to headman within the year. Reid was one of six foremen of Icruria, and by the looks of it, the territory of Mireh was as far as he would go.

Vaasa dipped her mouth to his cheek, brushing her lips over the smooth, freshly shaved skin. She would have preferred the grit of a beard—a thought she kept low in her stomach. She proceeded downward, her hands passing softly over his shoulders, trailing her nails along his skin, raising bumps in her wake. Her lips moved to his chest. When she looked up through her lashes at him, his breath caught a little.

Rising, she kissed his neck again, one hand slipping from his shoulder and beneath the pillow.

In one strike, she snatched the blade and pressed it to his throat. Right where her lips had been.

"Lift your hands above your head."

Freezing, eyes seeming to flash on and alert, Reid of Mireh did not move.

Until he did.

He spun with an assassin's focus, they tumbled, and Vaasa barely held on to the knife with the force. Reid's leg slipped between hers and held the vantage until she dragged her blade down his thigh. He grunted at the slice, and she heaved his weight off her. Using her own momentum to push herself on top of him again, Vaasa pressed the knife into the skin of his jugular and her knee onto his groin, poised to strike.

This time, Reid of Mireh froze.

Vaasa pressed the blade harder, digging into the bloody skin. "Do as I say, or these white sheets will run red."

With slow precision, he did as she had told him. He raised his arms and pressed them into the sheets above his head, and she felt him tense as her knee dipped harder into his groin. She used her free hand to snake the hidden rope about his wrists and pull it taut, securing the rope to the headboard behind him. The entire process took a breath, something she'd planned for before he walked in the door. The single vulnerable moment was past, and she again rebelled against her rising panic.

The curse in her gut hissed, reminding her that even if she could control the man beneath her, she could not control the infection in her bones.

"Tell me," Reid said with lethal calm. "Did you intend to kill me from the beginning, or did you see me and decide I was not a handsome enough choice for you?"

Chances were not a soul would interrupt them tonight. His body wouldn't be found until morning, and by then, she'd be long gone.

She would start a war with the most brutal nation on the continent, let Dominik pay the price.

She pressed the knife a little harder.

With wide eyes, he gasped, "You don't have to."

His words haunted her now, coiling in her stomach. They mixed with magic and adrenaline and urgency.

And you want to do this?

Why should that matter? One act of kindness didn't erase the things she'd heard of him, the savage tales that had kept her awake with an ever-present fear since the announcement of their impending marriage. The youngest foreman, one who rose to his rank all before his third decade. No one secured power so quickly without evil.

But something about it tugged at her. Changed the way he looked beneath her.

Did brutality ask for permission?

Black mist began to swirl at her fingertips, to lick at the skin beneath his jaw. Her magic.

She was losing control.

Heart lurching, she nicked his throat. "Don't come after me, or I will finish what I've started."

Leaping from the bed, Vaasa hid her hands and the blade, stepping into her boots and pulling on the thick fur-lined cloak he'd presented to her at dinner as a wedding gift. She slid off the slim golden wedding ring and set it on the dresser. Faint sounds of his struggle emanated from behind her, but Vaasa knew damn well how to tie a knot. She slung her pack over her shoulders—the one she'd left near the window. In it she stuffed his silks and anything else remotely valuable left in the room. Tying the cloak closed, she turned to find Reid watching her in astonishment, fiery anger coiling each of his muscles as his arms tugged at the rope.

If he had been truly brutal, if he had been anything like the tales people in her empire whispered, she would have killed him and not thought twice about it.

And you want to do this?

Just words, though in a way, an action, too.

One that had saved his life.

"These knots are well done," he informed her, eyes not dropping from hers, that clipped accent turning into an angry snarl. "You'll have to teach me so we can switch places next time."

The cocky bastard smiled. He *smiled*, like he found something about her amusing. Like he found anything about being tied half naked to a bed on his wedding night humorous.

It made the curse in her gut and on her hands begin to tingle. Begin to dance with the thrill of his demons. Hiding her hands from Reid's view, Vaasa bolted to the window and opened it. Turning, she saw the red trickle of blood down his throat. "There will be no next time, Your Highness."

She slipped out of the opening and clicked it quietly closed. Through the glass, she took one second to watch him fight with the knots on the bed. To gaze at the black mist that overtook her hands and threatened to steal every inch of life from her shaking body.

She could not let it.

She scurried off the roof of the High Temple of Mireh, the hood of the cloak up to cover her features, and into the darkness below.

First, she'd find a sodality: an Icrurian school. It was not knowledge of history or arithmetic that she sought, though. No magic pulsed in Asterya, but the magic here was rare and had been craved by her father—now by her brother, who had taken his throne with equal cruelty.

Some people had called her father a snake.

He had called Vaasa his chameleon.

Blending in like she'd been born to do, Vaasa fled the glittering city of Mireh, selling Reid's silk for passage to another city-state. If there was a place she could learn of the curse that inflicted her bones, it was Dihrah, the City of Scholars.

CHAPTER 2

Night after night, with a stolen after-hours pass in hand, Vaasa entered the Library of Una.

Normally, this seven-story tower was filled to the brim with robed acolytes. They covered all seven floors and draped themselves along the upholstered chairs and circular tables, taking up as much room as they wanted, their noses in books or at least pretending to be. Some acolytes took their studies at this sodality seriously, others not so much, and Vaasa had quickly learned to distinguish between the two. And how to act like the first.

In the three months since she'd fled Mireh, only this ancient library had brought her any semblance of solace. It was the quietest place in the sodality.

She had grown to appreciate silence.

Dihrah, she'd learned, was known not only for its scholarship, but for this exact library. The rectangular atheneum plunged underground, all seven floors growing closer to the core of the world, only illuminated by the golden lights flickering upon each level and dangling down the center of the tower. Covered in polished brown-and-red marble floors, the mystical library was one of Vaasa's greatest imaginations. The first time she'd laid her eyes upon it, she had almost gaped. Nothing in Asterya was this magnificent, despite what her prideful people wanted to believe.

The more she explored this library, the more she understood why western Icruria was so isolated—its westernmost territories guarded their cities as a secret. This was only one of Icruria's six sodalities. Her father's spies had infiltrated the two in the east, but none of the men he sent into the west had returned. Vaasa had not stayed long enough in Mireh to see its city. She'd cut her hair short and enrolled in this sodality with forged identification, and it was the only reason she had access to this ancient library. Only Dihrah's students saw the inside.

Lanterns were strung down the center of the tower, hanging at various heights, fueled by the tiny spark of magic the descendants of Una carried with them. As Vaasa kept her head down and the hood of her robe up, she walked as casually as she could in the shadows cast by the golden glow.

The best place to hide was in plain sight.

If she was recognized or remembered, Reid of Mireh—and her own brother, too—would come for her head.

She shot down to the sixth floor, past the western side, where the bare section on magic was organized. She'd expected their collection to be larger, more fruitful, with updated texts. In the weeks she'd scoured it, she couldn't escape the feeling that she was missing something. Like a truth was hidden in this library somewhere and she had yet to uncover it. So far, magic had not been openly discussed by the acolytes. Almost as if it was so sacred, so misunderstood, it could not be shared even among their own.

Padding down one of the many rows of leather-bound books, she plucked the next set of texts off the shelf—authors with the last name beginning with V. In lieu of tomes about magic itself, she'd resorted to ancient texts on the Icrurian gods and goddesses. The books were stacked up along the table she'd chosen closest to the stone wall, as they were every time she had the freedom to read whatever she wanted. And she planned to sit until the waning hours of the morning and search. She often arrived at her early classes bleary-eyed and yawning, but with a few cups of tea, she found herself again. Down here in the library, Vaasa could breathe. No one would get too suspicious at seeing her here, if they did see her at all, and most people who stayed this late were too busy with their own tasks to care about her.

Vaasa dove in, completely losing track of time.

She'd already learned of the gods and goddesses these Icrurian sodalities inherited their names from, how the magic that pulsed in Icruria was said to come from those deities themselves. She'd read about the healers and the manipulators of elements, even some historical texts about the time before Icruria's unification, when wars over magic and bloodlines turned their rivers red. Most books detailed Una, the god this particular library was named after.

But he manipulated light, not creeping black mist and death.

She skimmed the pages in search of a description, the image of it in her mind distinct and haunting. Like a serpent. The curse felt like venom and teeth, like scales and anguish. Scanning, scanning, scanning, she came upon a word she had never read before: *Veragi*.

The goddess of witchcraft herself.

Most of it was an innocuous story about her love affair with Setar, the god of language and writings. But partway through the paragraph, her heart skipped.

Black mist. A senseless void with no sight or sound or smell, where only darkness does not shiver.

Vaasa's cold fingers began to shake upon the dusty page. Ashen skin and sunken cheeks flashed in her mind, paired with eyes devoid of their irises and swallowed whole by ink. Raven hair turned gray and limp, as if the color had been taken from each crevice and pore, like the woman's soul had been drained from her very core.

Her mother.

The empress of Asterya had been little but skin and bones when the black mist was finished with her, green silk gown flowing around her like a swimming pool.

Not a trace of blood.

Only oily black mist swirling around her skin, the rancid scent of dying flesh stuffing itself into Vaasa's nostrils.

It was this *thing* that Vaasa could feel. It had choked the air from the room and clawed its way out of her throat in the form of a curdling scream, one that echoed off each corridor and breezeway. That was the first time she felt the serpent in her stomach. The guards had appeared, the world had bent and blurred with the razor-sharp passing of time, and before she could even begin to process the tragedy, her newly minted emperor of a brother had her shipped off to Icruria to marry Reid of Mireh.

They said grief had taken her mother.

Dominik swore that not a soul could know the truth, or they would know it had infected Vaasa, too. Then they would question him. Magic would not be tolerated in Asterya, and certainly not in its emperor. The Asteryan lords would turn on him. Their father's closest advisor, Ozik, had snuffed out any word of what had happened before Vaasa emerged from her mother's rooms. If a guard had seen any of it, they'd died quietly.

Silence, Ozik had warned her. *Thrones are as precarious as one's humanity.*

The series of events made no sense. If she had never married, she'd never have been a threat to Dominik. A daughter could not take the Asteryan throne alone—only if she was married and the last living heiress could her husband become emperor. Dominik had spent a lifetime removing every threat to his ascension, then subsequently created one. Though this way, when Vaasa died in the same way their mother had, he would at least get *something* for her existence.

Salt, Mireh's most precious resource.

Her hand and her life had been worth salt.

Vaasa's heart tightened. The Icrurian spring she now lived in could not chase the cold away. That *thing* still coursed through her veins when the intrusive thoughts sank their claws into her mind and burrowed into her chest.

It fed on her.

She swore she could feel it there, sliding nails across her muscles and tendons, gurgling in her veins. As if the force itself was sentient, it went in her body where it wanted. For long moments, Vaasa focused on her breathing. She tried to dismiss the sense that something crawled beneath her skin. Tried to push it all away. If she died here, it would start a war and give Dominik everything he had ever hoped for.

She slammed the book shut.

"Aneta?" a trilling voice asked as the sound of robes swishing along the floor rounded the stacks. A simply dressed dark-haired woman appeared, her soft smile already full and her kohl-less brown eyes sparkling. So different from Vaasa's home, this lack of adornment and makeup.

Aneta. Not even her name. A fake one she had scribbled upon the folded parchment she submitted for entrance into the sodality.

Vaasa dove into her mind for a name, a *name*, of the woman she remembered from her morning instruction on the first wars of Icruria—of which there were seven. "Brielle," Vaasa remembered, pulling her lips into a smile as she shoved her hands into the folds of her robes beneath the table to hide any possible trace of black mist.

Go away, she commanded the choleric force as it drained from her fingertips and ducked back down somewhere in the twisting of her organs and tissues. Still present, still there, but willing to hide. Coiling back into her belly like a cobra, the magic lay in wait.

Brielle placed her hands upon the book nearest Vaasa, her dark brown skin richening beneath the flickering lanterns strung from the ceiling and placed along each wooden tabletop. "I didn't realize you'd found your way into a night pass so quickly."

She hadn't. Vaasa grinned, flashing the silver pass as if it was just as surprising to her. She didn't elaborate further or invite more conversation, hoping Brielle would bid her goodbye quickly.

The woman did no such thing. Brielle slid into the chair across from Vaasa and scanned the books upon the table, taking note of each one. Vaasa got the distinct impression that despite Brielle's warm demeanor, she possessed a wicked intelligence. She wouldn't be likely to forget a single title of the books she'd seen.

"Are you excited?" Brielle asked suddenly.

Vaasa's brow furrowed. "Excited?"

"For the foreman?" Brielle tilted her head. "He's visiting tomorrow. Isn't that why you left class a few days ago? Aren't you going to escort him? That's the rumor, anyway."

Vaasa's heart leapt into her throat. "Which foreman?"

"Koen?" Brielle said as if it was obvious. It should have been. "He's here for the guest lecture in a few days."

The foreman of Dihrah. Not Vaasa's unfortunate husband, the one she'd conveniently, albeit violently, escaped. Images of him sprawled upon the bed, hands bound and throat bleeding, pulsed in her head. Vaasa let out a breath and shrugged. "No, actually, I just wasn't feeling well. I'm having a hard time adjusting."

This should be interpreted as a weakness, an embarrassment. She silently hoped it would make Brielle uncomfortable enough to leave.

"Oh! I can help you. Now that you have the pass, we can meet here after our classes and study together."

"Oh, that's really not—"

"I insist. Someone helped me when I first came here; I'm only passing along the favor. It must have been so hard to come to this place. Someday, you can help someone, too."

Vaasa's head whirled, her sacred alone time slipping between her fingers and out of her reach. Where were the brutal, evil monsters her father had cursed? The unforgiving leviathans her brother had whispered about? Vaasa had met and negotiated with others from the east—ill-mannered and easy to burst. Was western Icruria so different?

All she had met were warm people with their happy smiles and contented ways.

The acrid taste of resentment and frustration washed along Vaasa's tongue, spilling out of her in a snap. "I do not require your assistance, Brielle."

The woman's eyes widened just a fraction, hurt flashing in them, and then they reverted to a neutral simmer. "Forgive me for offering."

Brielle pushed to a stand and plodded to the end of the stacks, then looked over her shoulder. "The books on magic aren't kept in the main library," she told Vaasa, eyes flicking to the table where Vaasa kept all of her texts. How had she put together what Vaasa was searching for?

Shit. Vaasa started to speak, but Brielle sauntered off without another word. Vaasa didn't blame her, not for a moment. It was Vaasa who had ruined the first opportunity she'd had at insight—of course there were tomes missing. Where was this hidden section of the library? If she didn't find it, she was dead.

The sharp pang of guilt and fear in Vaasa's chest forced her to look down at her shaking hands.

The unholy force skittered around her fingertips in a mist of glittering black. It seemed to swallow her hands the more Vaasa's fear rose—the more she felt. Feeding.

Vaasa stuffed her hands into her robes again, eyes darting around, but Brielle had disappeared behind the wooden shelves of books. It was just Vaasa, alone.

She had always been this way—sharp. Maybe that was why the magic had made a home in her.

Vaasa's chair gave an awful squawk along the stone floor as she stumbled backward, shaking her hands. Tears began to prick at her eyes. The mist only grew. It devoured her wrists and forearms, panic searing down her spine, and she pressed against the wall and into a corner as if she could sink into the shadows and never be seen again.

Did it have something to do with the goddess she'd just read about? Veragi?

It was her one lead. Her only lead in months.

She wasn't making any progress. The only way to get to the truth was through the help of someone else, but there wasn't a soul she could get close enough to trust. Maybe Dihrah wasn't where she could find answers, after all.

Behind her eyes, her brother's face twisted into a grimace. She could hear herself begging, being so forlorn she was willing to *beg*, that he not sentence her to death in this nation. She'd always known her family was cruel, but Dominik's proclivity for torture extended far past that of their parents.

Vaasa and her father had a deal. For all the awful things she'd borne witness to, this was never to be her fate. But now she was a threat to Dominik's succession, and there was no force in the world that could convince her this marriage wasn't his doing.

The demonic magic began to creep along the wall Vaasa pushed herself against, shadows licking the stone and devouring any light. As if it had a life of its own, it hissed and whispered in a language unfamiliar to Vaasa's ear.

Through gritted teeth she whimpered, begging the force to dissipate, begging it to leave her and never come back.

It grew and grew and grew.

Would this be the moment it took her? Would she look as her mother had, drained and colorless on the floor?

Her eyes squeezed shut and she forced herself to breathe. To think of anything else.

She pictured the books. She lent herself to the task of learning with every fiber of her fractured heart. Reminded herself that there was work to do.

It snapped back into her skin with a fiery hiss.

She stumbled backward a few steps as nausea overcame her, threatening her already tightening throat. Vaasa doubled over and gripped her knees through the sweeping red acolyte robes.

Slamming all the books shut, she hauled them back into their proper spaces on the shelves she'd diligently marked—not upon the rolling carts the strict librarians used to track use of each tome. She carried them one by one, her back groaning with the effort, until the table had no trace of her at all. Even in her sickness, she memorized the title of the tome with her only lead.

Her robes whispered against the stone floor and her leaden feet dragged up the stairs, stomach turning and thighs straining, until she reached the main floor. Avoiding each pair of eyes around her, she rushed for the exit.

One pair caught her, though, the darkest and warmest ebony, coated in sadness.

Brielle, who watched Vaasa with pity as she coasted out of the library and into the nearest latrine.

Vaasa's knees cracked against stone. That foul smell of rotten flesh and burning hair swirled into the bowl and crept along her gagging face. The same scent that had surrounded her dead mother. That had haunted her dreams and her waking hours.

Vaasa expelled the contents of her stomach. Twice. Three times.

And when the hurling finally ceased, when breath rushed back into her lungs and all she had left was the awful taste in her mouth, the sight of her vomit caught her eyes.

Black.

Like the mist.

Like the final color of her mother's eyes.

CHAPTER 3

Acolytes crowded around Vaasa as she made her way into the enormous lecture hall.

Upon the stage at the front of the room stood a podium, a small glass of water settled on it. The sages all marched with chins to the sky as they filed into the grand room, walking down the nine levels of black velvet stairs to the front section of the hall reserved for them. The acolytes all took their respective seats in the other sections. Most carried notebooks and pens, some graphite pencils, all tucked between their fingers or behind their ears as they found their friends and waved to each other. Smiles were in abundance, and not a soul said a word to Vaasa.

She sat alone in the shadowy corner without a clue as to the name of the acolyte who took the seat next to her. With short brown hair and mannerisms much like everyone else, the boy didn't even bother to look her way.

Heads turned as the high sage stood beneath the doorway and each acolyte shot to their feet, eyes raised in respect for the sharp-shouldered and even sharper-tongued woman. Her distinguished robes, made of silk the color of orange clay, trailed behind her as she stepped fully into the room. "Please be seated," she said, and immediately the sea of acolytes sat down. "And do not bother with greeting the foremen."

Foremen?

Behind the high sage stood a man not clothed in robes, but rather in distinguished fabrics of red and gold that swept over one shoulder and down his torso, the same shimmering fabric cut in a sharp triangle that hung from his waist and stopped just before his knees. Black pants covered his legs. He stood taller than the high sage, with chestnut hair and his light brown face covered in a closely shaved beard. Calculating eyes traveled along the rows of acolytes, and Vaasa noticed the sheer lack of weapons upon him. He didn't resemble a warrior, not in the ways Vaasa had expected or known. Rather, his long arms and legs reminded her of roots plunging into the firm ground. Coupled with his wire-frame glasses, the foreman of Dihrah did not appear a foreman at all.

Not like the one she'd known.

All of the acolytes followed instructions, returning their attention to the visiting sage at the front of the room, whose hooded robes gave away his stature and tenure as he glided across the stage to the podium. Stripes of every color ran up the black fabric covering his arms.

Another person walked through the door.

Every ounce of breath in Vaasa's lungs caught in her throat.

There, in silken black and purple, stood Reid of Mireh.

The room bustled, his reputation enough to make every acolyte sit up and stare.

Unlike the foreman of Dihrah, this broad-shouldered mountain of a man *did* look every inch the warrior, from his tighter garb to the arsenal of weapons hanging from his hips. Just as she remembered. Sharp daggers and an unforgiving onyx-metal blade seemed to wink at her. Visions of her spread over him, blade in hand and running it along the left underside of his chin, flashed behind Vaasa's eyes, and her back locked.

Wearing similar sweeping fabric across his shoulder and between his knees, Reid took up almost the entirety of the doorframe. Upturned eyes scanned the room. His face was no longer clean-shaven—not as it had been the night of their wedding. Now, a dark beard hid the scar she was certain she'd left, and his deep brown hair was pulled back from his face, highlighting the rigid line of his jaw. He reminded her of a predator with his terribly keen eyes and even more terrible mass of muscle along every inch of him. That night, she had worried she would discover fangs or some other monstrous feature beneath his deceptive mouth—she hadn't. A part of her knew he'd let her swipe the blade near his throat, smiled as she did it, really, as if he thought the idea of a woman from Asterya with a knife was funny.

She could, and would, do far worse things with a knife if he came near her.

Adrenaline threatening to summon the magic, she threaded the ink pen between her fingers and closed a fist beneath the attached wooden desk.

Control. She could control this.

If he were here for her, he would be moving already. He would not care if it made a scene or if it made him look like a brute—powerful people took what they wanted and were often praised for it. No, if he knew she was here, he would not have let her remain in her seat.

With her head tilting down at her notes and a little twist of her neck, her now-short raven hair swept over her cheek and eyes and concealed him entirely from her view.

She needed to leave. She had to run far away from here, barter whatever else she had left to go somewhere new. She had failed enormously in Dihrah—had found nearly nothing that would serve her purpose anyway.

It was time to start over. Again.

But she couldn't very well flee in this moment, or even in the ones following. She hung in a delicate balance; they already wondered whether she belonged here, so if she disappeared, no one would question it. In fact, they would expect it. She would be written off as just another failed scholar.

Though it was new for her, she realized she would rather be a failure than dead.

But if she left too quickly, she might raise suspicions. The foreman of Mireh might find her again.

Vaasa wondered if this was what her life would be—forever on the run from undeserving men more powerful than her, this curse rattling her bones until she made it to a shallow grave.

She'd always wanted to see the world. To make a home in her heart instead of within a border.

Vaasa moved only a few inches at a time, inconspicuous as could be, casual as any other acolyte in a room with not one but two foremen. To her dismay, they didn't make to leave. Looming against the left wall as if anything this instructor said could be considered interesting, the high sage and foremen remained planted in their seats of honor.

Vaasa had the extraordinary talent of closely watching the lips of those in front of her, pretending to hang on to every word without hearing a single one. She could spend a lifetime in her head and need nothing outside of it to keep her attention. To everyone else, she looked engaged, enthralled even, with the lesson given by this ancient sage.

She did not even know the topic.

The moment the three hours were up, she slid her parchment closed and tucked her pen into her robes, filing past the enormous group of acolytes who swarmed around the foremen. They all vied for the opportunity to speak to them, to prove themselves important and intelligent, and Vaasa knew she needed to prove neither of those things.

She ducked out into the hallway and raced back to her room. She couldn't stay for long—being holed up in one space would be an awful choice. She would need to hide through dinner, hope diligently that he had not noticed her or, if he had, that he had not been able to figure out her false name and room. Then she would have to find a way out of this city.

Hell, maybe leave this nation altogether.

But not without that tome.

Vaasa snuck down the stairs, a leather satchel hidden beneath the enormous folds of her robes. She hoped no one would find her between the dusty stacks of the library stealing a book that she had no right to.

Foolish. She was absolutely foolish.

The book was the only answer she'd gotten thus far, and she couldn't bring herself to leave it behind. It wasn't heavy enough to weigh her down or make it impossible to flee—it would fit in her satchel, which barely had a damn thing in it. And maybe once she'd gotten what she needed from it, she could sell it.

The library was empty this evening, everyone gathered in the great hall to break bread with the two foremen, and Vaasa bet it would be the only time she could swipe the book. By the end of the sixth set of stairs, her thighs rebelled, but she pushed forward until she slid around the corner of the western side, fifth row over, moving seventeen books in. And there it was.

Bound in cracking leather and secured with only a single string, the book looked like salvation. Vaasa plucked it from the shelf, thrust her robes aside, and unbuckled the satchel.

"That is an awful idea," a smoky, too-familiar voice sounded from the right. The flat vowels and clipped endings curled down her spine, which she promptly straightened.

There, leaning against her table, hands splayed along the wood as if he owned everything in his sight, was the foreman of Mireh.

Neither made an attempt to move, though Vaasa shifted her weight in such a way that she was prepared to spin and run. Death loomed right in front of her; he would kill her for what she'd done to him, for both the embarrassment and the wound. That shallow grave had found its way to her, and everything in her heart rebelled against it.

"Your Highness—" she muttered instinctively.

"We do not refer to our chosen leaders as 'Your Highness' here," he informed her with ease, still not moving, though his eyes did trail down from the top of her head to her toes. He paused on the way back up at her pulse, the one she swore he could see and feel from where he leaned, but then locked his bright eyes with her gaze.

And just as he'd done on that bed, he *moved*.

Vaasa twisted right and ran, but he was too fast. She made it halfway to the end of the dusty stacks before his arm wound around her waist and lifted her clean from the floor, setting her down with her back against a bookcase. Neither her strength nor her thrashing had done anything to hinder him; the bastard's execution was flawless. Bookshelves lined the passageway, leaving exits only to the left and right. A table obstructed the left, and stuck between him and a long shelf, she was at least ten paces from the main corridor to her right. She stared straight ahead over his shoulder, eyes focused on the bookshelf opposite her as the chance to escape disappeared.

"I would have told you, had you said goodbye properly, that you should call me by my name," he said, looming above her and practically daring her to try to run again. His body covered hers. Too close—he was too close.

Fire and rage spread in her belly, and she narrowed her eyes, finally looking up at him. "Would you have? We met so briefly."

His lips pursed—amusement or displeasure, she couldn't entirely be sure—and then he leaned back, giving her a little more breadth. "Husband will do, given it's my other title."

Vaasa sneered, her upper lip curling. "We are not married."

"Respectfully, I disagree."

"Respectfully, I don't care what you agree or disagree with."

At that he grinned outright, gazing momentarily at the tome that now lay half open on the ground. "If you steal that, I'll have no choice but to report it to the high sage. Her punishment is one I have no interest in discovering."

Could she leave it here? Did she even have a chance of escape? She just needed a way out, a way to freedom and choice, for as long as she could manage it. "And if I don't steal it?"

"Then it's one less thing we'll have to argue about. Marital spats are no fun, or so I've heard. Not that my wife has been around long enough for me to discover their level of joy."

Vaasa's eyes glittered with rage, and Reid seemed to soak it in. Seemed to want to drink it all up. Was this what he got off on, then? The threats and the control?

She'd let him live because she thought him the exact opposite.

"Let me leave," she demanded.

"Not until we've properly discussed your options."

"My options?" Vaasa hissed. "We should instead discuss yours. Step out of my way, or we can relive the last time you found yourself on the wrong end of my knife."

He raised a full brow at the exact moment she pressed the blade hidden in her robes to his stomach. She'd slid it into her hand while he'd glanced down at the book.

The same dagger she'd hidden under their pillows.

Surprise and a small spark of approval flitted through his eyes, dancing in the bits of orange and black that sewed the gold together. He took one step back, then another. Vaasa trailed him closely, pushing with her blade until he backed up against the bookshelf opposite her. Until it was her body controlling the movement of his. Until it was him with no escape.

She dragged the knife up and over his chest, stopping at his throat.

To her shock, he lifted his square chin, baring his neck to her. "Do it."

Anxiety pumped into her stomach, and she stared wildly at him, their faces a hairbreadth apart, him peering down at her.

"You won't, will you?" he asked, throat still bared, turning it just a little so the underside of his jaw became visible. The right side now. "Give me another one to match, Wild One."

Vaasa's lips parted.

Just as quickly as he'd moved before, his hand curled around her hand holding the knife, fingers tightening on her wrist and pushing her hard. He slid his foot behind her calf to throw her off balance and she started to fall. With one large step, he dragged her against the bookshelf she'd just barely escaped, her own weight doing all the work for him. Wood dug into her back. A yelp of pain threatened to escape, but she bit it down.

"I didn't think so," he growled, anger leaking into his words as her knife clanged against the floor. His face pressed closer to hers, no longer giving her the space he'd given before, as if she'd lost the right. "Now shall we speak as humans, or would you rather we continue to dance?"

"Ass," she snapped back.

"Maybe I do prefer *Your Highness*."

Vaasa struggled against the grip he had on her wrists, rage the likes of which she'd hardly known pounding in her head. In her chest. The serpent in her stomach began to slither upward into her throat, and she knew she had moments before it gave her away. "Let me go," she demanded. "Let me—"

"Listen to me for *one* moment and I will," he said.

Her lips pressed shut. Surveying the planes of his face and deciding he meant what he said, she nodded, her restless resistance fading and the curse humming just under the surface.

The foreman of Mireh took a breath, straightening his spine and taking the smallest step back so she had enough room to gulp down air. Unruffled, he relaxed his shoulders like the entire exchange had taken little effort, one hand still pressed to the bookshelf next to her left ear, the other hanging at his side as if he wanted to emphasize the space he gave her. She rolled her wrists and considered an exit strategy, eyeing where the hallway of bookshelves opened into the main corridor.

"Where have you been?" he finally asked.

Vaasa didn't answer. Instead, she stared at him coldly, waiting to hear these so-called options.

He seemed to understand her thought process, because he changed his approach. With a tilt of his head, he asked, "Has the magic gotten the better of you yet?"

Her heart dropped into her stomach, but she didn't allow a muscle in her face to twitch. Didn't allow herself to shift and reveal her hand. "I don't know what you mean."

"It covered your hands the night you almost slit my throat. Did you think I wouldn't notice?"

Vaasa couldn't move, didn't have time to deliberate or calculate a new strategy. Instead, she kept her voice intentionally even. "What do you know about the magic?"

"Plenty." He offered that one word and nothing more.

Silence coursed between them as Vaasa weighed her options and tried to pretend as though she wouldn't beg, barter, or steal for the information he kept to himself. "What do you want?" she finally asked.

Knowing he had her right where he wanted her, the foreman of Mireh lifted his hand from the bookshelf and took two wide steps back, giving her all the space she desired. Needed. She could run now; she'd make it to the end of the stacks.

Arms crossing in front of his chest, he said, "I believe we can be of use to each other."

Vaasa's brows rose. He wanted to make a deal? What could she possibly have to offer a foreman?

The bookshelf across from her groaned as Reid leaned back against it, the two staring each other down. "Do you know anything about our exchange of power?"

She lied. "I know little."

He chuckled, crossing his large arms. "Liar."

Pursing her lips, she shrugged. It was there in his eyes, the harsh glimmer of desire for a title and a sense of importance. Vaasa had spent a lifetime around power-hungry men—she could sniff one out with ease. "I know you're most likely going to be elected."

"And could lose a great deal of my reputation, should people learn my Asteryan bride fled after tying me to our wedding bed."

Vaasa realized it then. What purpose she served him. She knew it with such certainty it shredded itself down her spine, even if it shouldn't have mattered. "To conquer me would deem you worthy of their votes, then?"

Reid's eyes glimmered with amusement as he tucked away the growing corners of his lips. "To conquer you would surely leave me dead, Wild One. But you have gravely bruised my ego."

"Is that so?"

"I made an agreement with your brother in hopes of proving I could solidify an alliance between our people. Your absence threatens to shatter it. I've avoided telling him for long enough."

Dominik didn't know she'd run away?

"You don't want an alliance with my brother," Vaasa warned.

"You're right. But several of the salt lords do, and I figure if someone is walking into the lion's den, I'm most qualified."

Resisting the urge to roll her eyes, Vaasa leaned a little further into the wooden bookshelf at her back. He wasn't the most qualified, though she didn't say so. She wasn't unfamiliar with the precarious balance between a ruler and the people who kept their economy going. The difference was that in Asterya, her father had always brought the lords and merchants to heel. Could he not handle the men who harvested and sold his salt? "I thought you said your ego was bruised."

"Bruised, not broken."

She let out a small snort. "I don't understand what you want from me. You must know I can't convince my brother to do anything he doesn't want to do."

"I don't need you for your brother." He frowned, looking like he couldn't decide how much to reveal. "No one has taken the headmanship without an equally strong high consort. I need a wife of Asterya who does not renege on our agreement. What does it say about my potential to lead Icruria into an era of trade agreements if I can't maintain my relationship with your empire?"

Vaasa wanted to say that she wasn't capable of changing the truth, but instead said, "I don't want to be married."

"I've gathered that."

"Then I'm not sure what I can give you other than advice: Being the ruler of anything is a corrupting job, and no man walks out of it the same as when he walked into it. If you value anything about yourself, which I gather you do, given the seeming resilience of your ego, you'll settle for being a councilor and mind your own."

Reid mulled over her words with a careful consideration she didn't expect him to possess. "I may need your wisdom as well, it seems, though I wonder if your pessimistic outlook on leadership derives from an example different from mine."

"I wonder if every man who steps into a crown thinks the same thing."

"Good thing there are no crowns involved."

She snorted again. It didn't matter if the foremen and headman didn't don a formal crown—they played God, no matter the metal on their heads or the different titles they gave themselves.

"Plus," Reid said, "it seems that you, too, need something. If you do not learn to control your magic soon, it will undoubtedly kill you."

She knew little about what ran beneath her skin, but she knew it wasn't a gift. It was only a parasite that possessed her. Still, the thought of imminent death sent a shiver down her spine. "It's a curse. I intend to get rid of it."

With a strange, disbelieving look, he said, "The black mist leaking on the tips of your fingers originates from my home of Mireh. It is Veragi magic, and I know a master of it."

Vaasa stared blankly at him, forcing her face to remain neutral despite the pounding in her chest. It was the very word she'd read in that tome, though she'd never heard it aloud.

And he knew someone who had mastered it? In *Mireh*?

She believed in many things—even magic and monsters—but she had never believed in coincidence.

"And, of course, I offer shelter, food, and clothing. I might even be willing to replace that fur-lined cloak I gifted you that somehow ended up on the shoulders of a man in the Surmeny Peaks."

Something in Vaasa's stomach clenched in embarrassment, though she dismissed the feeling and tried to square her shoulders as if she didn't have any guilt about the incident. She shouldn't. He'd bought and bartered for her like cattle, just as every other man who sought power would inevitably do. She was a means to an end. "What is your proposal, then?"

Relief, small yet noticeable, crossed Reid's features. "I propose the following: You act as my wife for a time, and I will help you discover all you wish to know about Veragi magic."

Tempting, Vaasa had to admit. And relatively easy. It would mean no more running, and possibly answers.

But it would also mean putting herself directly in Dominik's path.

"And when do we part ways?" she asked.

He took her matter-of-fact demeanor in stride, not missing a beat. "After the election cycle has settled and you have learned to confidently control or erase the magic—say three years?—I will offer you a legal separation and relocate you to anywhere you desire."

Her jaw could have dropped to the floor. If they were legally separated, she would no longer give Reid claim to the Asteryan throne. She could run, make a new life elsewhere, and Dominik would not be threatened enough to chase her. "And you'll deal with the consequences of that? A separation?" Wouldn't that be counterintuitive to the same image he hoped to cultivate?

"There are few things I fear, Wild One."

Wild One. If they were to do this, she would have to put a stop to that. Running her tongue along her teeth, she leaned a little easier against the bookshelf. "If I say no, will you let me leave?"

Darkness clouded his eyes as if even the insinuation was absurd. "You are no captive, even if you agree to this. If you are to trust one thing about me, let it be that I will never make you do something against your will."

"You married me against my will."

"I was not aware of your objections."

"Would it have mattered?"

"It would have changed everything."

The world shifted at those simple words. *It would have changed everything.*

"If we are to do this," he said, "then I would expect a willing and engaged accomplice, one I could depend on. I need Icruria to believe that we are taken with each other. That our union is strong enough to represent them."

Vaasa wanted to remind him that she'd put a knife to his throat twice now, though the words felt like a step backward. She couldn't read him, couldn't see past the simmering hope and hunger in his eyes, past the determination to do whatever it took to obtain the one thing he'd ever wanted.

She hated every man who had put the world beneath their feet and decided they had a right to own it. Decided people were nothing but pawns crafted to achieve that very goal.

Yet he did not look at her as a pawn tonight. He looked at her like a partner.

To go with him was the quickest and safest option, the one with the most fruitful benefits. If emotion was taken out, the decision was easy.

"I leave tomorrow," Reid muttered, "at sunrise. I'll be in the high sage's office awaiting your presence, if that is what you so choose."

He turned on his heel, kicking her knife back toward her as he swaggered to the end of the corridor.

"And if I don't come?" Vaasa dared to ask, watching his shoulders go taut at her question.

He stopped, turned his head to the side to peer at her. "Then I will assume that is your answer and offer you a legal divorce whenever you ask for it."

Vaasa let out a deep breath.

And the foreman of Mireh disappeared around the stacks, leaving her alone with nothing but her stunned breath and her confusion.

CHAPTER 4

As the sun rose over the City of Scholars, Vaasa's fingers shook as she reached for the high sage's iron door knocker.

Pounding twice with metal against wood, Vaasa got one second before the door swung open to reveal a hulking figure who commanded every inch of her vision.

Reid and she locked eyes, and Vaasa could have sworn he shuddered in relief.

His mahogany hair was pulled back in a leather strap, and he wore the same signature purple and black sashes he'd worn at their wedding. The warm brown skin along his exposed chest richened with the morning light, which further brought out the burnt-gold tones of his hair. As he turned his broad shoulders back to the room, Vaasa had to catch herself from inspecting him closer, from swallowing every new detail instead of facing the others.

Vaasa had avoided this office for weeks now. Decorated exclusively in green and brown, the sun-drenched room held scrolls and tomes all neatly settled in their proper spots. The bookshelves against two of the four walls were each decorated with trinkets and baubles resembling the ancient artifacts this particular sodality was best known for.

Looming along the back wall was a marble statue of Una, the Icrurian god of history, justice, and wisdom. He held an enormous shield in one hand and a book in the other, piercing eyes sharply sculpted of red clay. Eyes that seemed to stare directly into Vaasa's soul and whisper *liar, liar, liar.*

Stepping a little to the left, Reid moved enough so Vaasa could finally see inside to the two others.

The high sage froze at the intrusion, and the foreman of Dihrah, wearing the same formal adornments as the day prior, looked up. Through his wire-frame spectacles, he looked up and down at Vaasa and smirked.

Hands clenched tightly, the ornery woman shot up—

"Cliona," Reid said, addressing the high sage by her first name. "May I introduce my wife, Vaasalisa, heiress of Asterya and consort of Mireh."

Shock tumbled briefly along Cliona's face, her pale skin going ghost white, but her expression contorted to humiliation and rage by the next second. Without a doubt, the extent of Vaasa's lie must have crossed the woman's mind; she'd managed to enroll in the sodality and study for weeks without anyone realizing who she was. Without Cliona knowing another foreman's consort lived beneath her roof. Standing erect and pinching her brows, she said, "Reid, I—" She stopped and narrowed her eyes at Vaasa.

A slew of options pulsed through Vaasa—to apologize, and seem weak; to hold confident, and appear sneaky; to be honest, and therefore vulnerable. Vaasa raised her chin, choosing sneaky and in control over anything else. Yet she didn't have the opportunity to speak.

"I wanted my wife to know everything she needs to in order to lead confidently at my side," Reid said as he placed his hand upon Vaasa's back, their eyes meeting only briefly enough to indicate that she should follow his lead.

Unconvinced, or so it seemed, Cliona looked between Vaasa and Reid as if measuring their distance.

"I was told there would be no better place," Vaasa said as he watched her every twitch. "But I felt I would not see reality if anyone knew who I was. I wanted to earn my knowledge, as the rest of you do. That is why I kept my identity a secret."

Knowing what she knew about these people—their pride in their academics and deep-rooted belief in merit—Vaasa knew she'd struck home. Particularly when the high sage's hands unclenched. Gray hair braided around her head in a coronet, the birdlike woman pushed back a falling tendril and pinched her lips.

Koen of Sigguth, the foreman of Dihrah, intercepted the woman's attention, pulling it away from Vaasa and Reid, sealing their excuse. "It was under my suggestion and protection, Cliona, that Vaasalisa came here to see for herself the way all people are given the opportunity to learn," the smooth talker said with an ever-so-innocent push of his glasses up his nose and a little tilt of his easy grin. "It is so different from her upbringing, you see, and I only wanted her to experience firsthand what our people feel under your tutelage—autonomy, trust, and possibility."

Cliona raised her chin with pride. "Well, I assure you that is what she experienced here under my close supervision," the high sage said. Then, turning sharply to Vaasa: "Isn't that correct?"

Vaasa nodded, looking up at Reid as if she was attentive to him, and then back to the high sage and the sprawling desk behind her, the bookshelves and locked tomes. "Of course it is correct. I have truly enjoyed my time here. Thank you."

This was the first time she'd ever met the woman, but what was one more lie?

Reid, with such gentleness she could almost believe it real, said, "I am glad to hear of it." Looking up and away from her, he commanded the attention of the room once more in a way that scraped against Vaasa's nerves. "I'm afraid I must ask Vaasalisa to return to Mireh now. I've had weeks without my wife, and it's time she fulfills her role at my side."

Vaasa wanted to laugh, or perhaps puke, but she smiled like she didn't want anything else in the world. "I'll need to retrieve my things."

The foreman of Dihrah dipped at the waist to honor the high sage, and then started through the door. "I'll be back soon. Thank you again."

"An honor," Reid told the woman, and Vaasa repeated the sentiment, clinging to Reid's side as if she felt some sort of safety there. Regardless of the discussion they'd just had, Vaasa felt Cliona's burning gaze as she stepped out of the room.

Reid didn't say a thing to her as he bid the foreman of Dihrah goodbye, the two seeming friendlier than Vaasa expected of two competing politicians. Koen stepped forward and they gripped each other's forearms, then embraced.

That was unusual.

She swore she heard Koen whisper, "Good luck."

Turning to meet Vaasa's gaze, the foreman of Dihrah stood tall and proud. "Consort." He dipped his head before disappearing around the corner and leaving the two of them alone.

Koen could have easily outed them both just then—why hadn't he?

Perhaps Reid could hear her thoughts, because he muttered, "My mother and his father were raised together. He is the closest thing I have to a brother."

"Be wary of brothers," she muttered before turning to plunge deep into the dormitories.

Acolytes stared wildly at her as the foreman followed each of her footsteps. Reid walked close behind her back, defensive or maybe in fear she would run again.

She wouldn't.

Sliding into her room, she clicked the door behind her shut, leaving him to wait outside.

What was she doing?

Back against the wall, she took one calming breath and feared if she let herself get too out of control, she might unleash the consequences.

Two breaths.

Three breaths.

Rushing to her bed, she pulled out the only clean clothing she had suitable enough to arrive in Mireh and began to change.

The door next to her pushed open, and Reid, with his giant body and graceful prowl, slipped into the room.

Vaasa's spine straightened, and she hissed as she covered herself with the robes.

Back against the door, Reid stared at her, and luckily, no one else had followed him inside.

"Was I not willing and engaged enough for you?" Vaasa asked, remembering his demand of her in the library last night and trying to pretend she hadn't just been lost in a bit of panic. That she wasn't half naked underneath this fabric.

That same infuriating amusement danced in his eyes—the ones she'd looked upon as he lay sprawled in that damn bed. "Good morning to you as well, wife."

"I am not your wife."

"In the eyes of my gods, you are."

Vaasa gripped the robes to her chest tighter. "We never consummated our union."

"What an outdated Asteryan concept."

Vaasa paused. If their ceremonies were not dependent upon a consummation, what were they dependent on?

Reading her expression, his wolfish smile grew with his victory. Prowling forward and into her space, the two of them near her tiny mattress, he asked, "Is that what you need, Wild One? To be in my bed?"

"Enough."

"Will you bring the knife?" he mused.

"It is the *only* way you'd get me there," Vaasa snarled, stepping up to his chest as a reminder that she did not fear the space his body took. She figured he already knew exactly the threat he bargained with, but if he needed a reminder, she'd give him one.

Brows rising, Reid chuckled at her audacity. The ire that pulsed through Vaasa at the curve of his goddamn mouth could level mountains. "Hmmm," he murmured, turning and ceding space, or maybe telling her that he had no foul intentions. Regardless, she could breathe correctly again.

"I'm not done," she barked. "Can you wait outside?"

Making sure his back was to her, he reached out his left hand and rolled it in a circle, gesturing for her to continue.

Fine.

Slipping into a lightweight pair of olive breeches and a beige shirt, she tucked the flowing top in and tried to look presentable. She went as quickly as she could, buckling a leather strap around the breeches so they held up and slipping her knife into its sheath. Around her thigh, she secured two more blades.

"Finished?" he asked.

"Finished."

Leaning up against her empty dresser, he tilted his head and took in her appearance, only lingering upon the knives for a moment. "You cut your hair."

Refusing to lift her hand to the wavy black locks that now barely brushed her shoulders, she nodded.

"I like it."

"I don't care what you like."

He snorted. "You're going to have to pretend to like me when others are around."

"I'm a fantastic liar."

"You don't say?"

Vaasa stared him down.

Displaying the intelligence she knew he possessed, Reid of Mireh once again reined in his amusement. He moved closer, body just in front of hers, forcing her to lift her eyes to look at him. He spoke low, like he was scared someone would hear. "You want this arrangement?"

There it was again. Choice on a silver platter. The damn thing that had saved his life.

Maybe she should have killed him. Maybe she'd be screwed if she had.

She breezed past him, aiming for her satchel on the dresser. "You haven't told my brother?"

Brow slightly furrowed, he shook his head.

"Three years," Vaasa said. "Enough time for me to expel whatever this magic is and for you to win a nation. When we both deem it acceptable, we'll dissolve this marriage."

"Agreed."

"You will not take me in your bed or expect anything from me, other than what we give to others in public."

"I do prefer my head attached to my body."

"Then do not give me a reason to remove it."

Grinning, he stepped forward. "We could be friends, you know. There is no requirement that you hate me."

Vaasa had no interest in friends. They would only complicate the swirling emotions in her chest and make the magic that much more palpable. It was easier to feel anger than to feel anything else at all. She stuffed the last of her belongings into her satchel, right over the tome she had stolen, and clasped it shut. "I don't need friends."

"Very well. You take your time coming to the conclusion I already have."

Stepping toward the door, desperate for this discussion to be over, Vaasa asked, "And what's that?"

Reid beat her to the door, placing his hand upon the knob to open it first. "That we are well matched."

She gaped at him. "Well matched?"

The door swung open, and Reid winked, taking the two blades that she'd secured around her thigh from his own arsenal at his belt.

Surprise and, admittedly, respect welled in her. She hadn't even felt him steal them.

Dipping to his knees in front of her, he wrapped his hands around her thigh, fingers pressed to the golden buckles on the leather strap. Her heart started to pound. "I told you. You underestimate just how much I enjoy a good game of blades."

He slid the knives back into their holsters, hands consciously holding steady against her breeches. They wrapped to the back of her thighs.

"I have missed you, wife," he murmured, just in time for her to see two sages and a small group of acolytes, all with jaws dropped at the sight of the foreman of Mireh and his apparent consort.

With a wicked grin, Vaasa ran her hand over his cheek and then dipped to the underside of his jaw, the pad of her finger scraping against the bump of his scar. The one she'd given him. "Take me home," she said.

His eyes may have shuttered at the audacity of her words—to claim his home as hers in mockery—but she didn't care an ounce for his feelings or sensitivities.

A game of blades he had asked for, and a game of blades he would receive.

Rising to his feet directly in front of her, he whispered, "Pretend you love me, Wild One. And make it convincing."

CHAPTER 5

Vaasa spent the entirety of the trip back to the City of Salt on a remarkably fast ship, refusing to let awe strike across her features. She'd heard of these sorts of vessels, ones that could cross the mighty Settara in a day, but she never expected to be on one. The salt lake spanned miles, splitting the west like a book's spine. Built above the compact captain's quarters, this small lookout deck only covered a quarter of the vessel. She sat on a bench bolted to the wooden ledge of the upper deck, legs to her chest. She could look over the edge and see the men and women at work on the deck below.

People could say what they wanted about Icruria, about Mireh, but they were hard workers. It made sense that their forces were notoriously vanquishing. On the tumultuous waters of the Settara, less experienced men would drown.

If this vessel could withstand the salinity of the Settara, the icy ocean Vaasa grew up next to could be theirs to roam, if the Icrurians ever dared take it.

They propelled the boat themselves, rowing as one, and much to Vaasa's surprise, Reid spent his time with the workers at the oars. He moved in shifts like the rest of them did, resting and then continuing the push-pull motion like he wasn't tired. Every so often, her eyes would drift down to him, then pop back up before he could catch her watching and assume her interested.

Vaasa was thankful for the reprieve—both from the prying eyes of the guards and from her supposed husband. He often looked at her as if she were a puzzle, and she didn't like the idea of being solved.

After the first few hours, she fell into the beauty of the Settara and forgot the rest of the world. Few Asteryans would ever see this side of the continent. Though Vaasa had studied ancient maps drawn in the days before Icrurian unification, so few people had survived the web of rivers that branched from this lake and toward her home empire that the maps were outdated at best. Those rivers acted as a shield against the rest of the world. The only vessels that could navigate the waters were those of the Icrurians, and it was only at Reid's direction that one had been waiting to bring Vaasa to Mireh for their wedding. The emerald waters of the lake eventually bled to turquoise. Layers of white folded around the shoreline their vessel followed, and she could smell it in the crisp air and taste it on her tongue. Salt.

All around them were rolling hills of green and yellow wildflowers, beige stalks of some heat-resistant plant poking up in places nature could not keep out. Trees didn't dot the landscape the way they did in her home. In Mekës, the capital city of Asterya, where Vaasa had grown up, the landscape was swathed in nothing but snow-covered mountains and trees. Here, in this hilly alternate universe, she found herself sinking into the way the sun felt on her skin and how it reflected off turquoise waters.

She had never seen Icruria this way before.

Resentment flooded her veins, and she straightened her back, remembering who she was and why she was here. No amount of freshness would erase what she would have to endure just to win her life back.

For the remainder of their travels, she kept her lips shut and her eyes focused on the horizon. When the sun set and night reigned in the sky, Vaasa fought the part of her that wanted to slip into a wary sleep. She'd always been used to the cold, and while the frigid air of the night made her skin pucker, spring had swept over western Icruria in a tolerable chill.

Mireh finally appeared under a blood moon, red and ringed in fire, in the late hours of the night. Multicolored buildings lined the expansive docks the men and women now tied their vessel to, lanterns hanging in the windows and illuminating the domed tops of many of the buildings. Stars speckled the sky and swayed upon the salt-capped waves. Eyes trailing up the one winding river that broke the city in two, she pinched her lips and looked away. She'd navigated her way out of this city in nothing but a cloak and a nightgown three months ago when winter still reigned. Had stripped down naked in an alley to shove on pants and an unassuming blouse.

She'd seen enough of this city.

Instead, she listened to the croaking of frogs, a chorus in the air that melded with the sounds of wolves howling along the distant shoreline. She'd only ever seen the solid white ones of the mountains, not the gray and red ones that roamed the shores of the salt lake.

"Vaasalisa," Reid's voice called to her from behind. The Wolf.

Turning, she found him watching her with tense shoulders that betrayed his easy grin and relaxed expression. Perhaps he was only sore from such hard work and truly was at ease now that he was home. Not that she'd yet seen him appear anything other than at ease.

"We're here."

Vaasa's eyes stung with fatigue, threatening to close, and her limbs felt like lead. Standing and trying out her legs again, she only wobbled a little before she forced herself to find her composure. Still, he lurched forward and tried to help.

She backed away from him.

With a furrowed brow, he took a step back and gave her the space she needed. "Have you turned it off since leaving me?"

"What?"

"Your instinct to run."

Her eyes narrowed. No one intelligent ever turned off that instinct.

"You are safe here," he said, as if it was obvious.

There wasn't a place in the world where Vaasa was safe. "I put a knife to your throat."

Extending a hand to beckon her forward, Reid said, "I'm not the vengeful type."

Vaasa could have laughed had she felt the need to react to him. Reid rested his hand on the small of her back to guide her off the ship and past his corps. A foreman with his consort, defensive of her very being, even if it was all a lie. When the warriors looked at her, sizing her up, Reid's fingers tightened in her now too-thin beige shirt. Bumps rose on her arms as she walked, and a small shiver trailed down her spine. The heat was blistering during the day, but nights here were formidable.

Much to her dismay, Reid of Mireh slung off his black cloak and draped it around her shoulders. Warmth rushed over her, and she took a small breath. "I was born on the ice," she reminded him.

"That doesn't mean you deserve to be cold."

Insecurity lanced through her, enough to make her tear her eyes away and stare at the black boots upon her feet. Affection such as this made her want to squirm—she didn't understand it like he did. Still, she spoke before realizing she was going to. "Thank you."

He grinned.

Waiting on the floating dock that threatened to toss Vaasa into the current was a small group of people, all on horseback. One in particular did not look happy to see them as she broke from the crowd and rode forward.

Swinging from her dark horse, a tall woman stalked up to them, removing her crested helmet and tucking it under her arm. Blond hair was pulled back to reveal the sharp angles of a pale face, tangerine mouth forming a frown. As the woman's blue eyes fell upon Vaasa, they narrowed as if assessing a threat.

Smart woman.

The coils in Vaasa's muscles clenched tighter. Just south of the line between this stranger's eyebrows lived an ice—in her gaze, in the pull of her mouth.

Reid's arm wrapped around Vaasa's waist, and she froze for a moment—and then melted into his warmth as if on instinct. *Pretend you love me*, he'd said.

"You found her?" the woman asked flatly. She appeared to gauge the lack of distance between Reid and Vaasa, the sight causing the line between her eyebrows to grow more prominent.

"Vaasalisa, you remember Kosana, my commander of arms," Reid said with conviction. "Kos, surely you remember my wife."

Wife. What a claim.

"Who could forget her?" Kosana said just as begrudgingly as before, though this time with the vicious smile of a warrior.

No way this woman didn't know what occurred on their pseudo wedding night. Perhaps Kosana was the unfortunate soul to have found Reid of Mireh tied to the bed, half dressed and bleeding. Noticing the protective glint in her eyes, Vaasa wondered if Reid's commander had enjoyed that sight more than she let on. Daring a glance at Reid, she found a stern expression. He was no longer at ease. A possessiveness shone in his eyes, and Vaasa knew better than to assume that was reserved for her.

Kosana was important to him in one way or another, then.

Vaasa gave a wicked smile, and something pulsed between her and the commander, as if their own wills fought for dominance in the little space. Life bloomed once again in Vaasa's stomach, false as it might have been, at the challenge.

Reid shifted his weight.

Another man, older than the rest and not dressed in the armor of Reid's corps, swung down from his horse and dusted off the length of his pristine black coat. His fair skin had been delicately touched by the sun in these early spring days. Astute and well put together, much like the foreman of Dihrah had been, the silver-haired man sauntered up to their little crowd with a peek between Vaasa and Kosana. He didn't smile or show much emotion at all, and something about that made him the most comfortable person Vaasa had yet to meet. "Vaasalisa, it is a pleasure to make your acquaintance. I'm afraid we never got the opportunity to speak the night of your wedding. I'm Mathjin, Reid's advisor."

He met her gaze directly with focused gray eyes.

How exactly did Reid intend to navigate this? Neither of these people—important people, she suspected—would believe the two of them to have a happy union. What did he intend to say in order to explain away her absence?

"Pleasure to meet you," she said, dipping her head as she'd learned was customary for the people in Icruria. They did not bow like the Zataarians did. Did not shake hands like the Asteryans. If they touched at all, it was on the forearm, and embraces were reserved for only the closest of companions.

"Well taught, this one," Mathjin said with a practical calm.

"Shall we?" Kosana asked Reid, pointedly writing off Vaasa.

Ugly magic stirred in Vaasa's veins, lit by the pulsing need she felt to run or hide or defend herself. Teeth gritting, she punched it down. Poison played upon her tongue, but she swallowed it and followed them all to the waiting horses. One in particular was a stunning Icrurian horse with a silky fawn coat and a mane and tail the color of ink. That same jet color crawled up the horse's legs and snout, and with a shake of its head, it adjusted into a natural intimacy with the foreman of Mireh. Hand landing upon the animal's chin, he pressed his own forehead delicately to the horse's.

"Duch is his name," Reid told her, peering over his shoulder to grin. "Bought his mother when I was seventeen; he came along about five years later."

"How old are you?" Vaasa asked, realizing she didn't even know that much about him.

"Twenty-seven."

"Young for a foreman."

"I thought you knew little of Icruria," Reid said, hand still resting on Duch.

Vaasa didn't say another word.

He gestured for her to mount the horse, and the moment she did so, he slid his foot into the leather stirrup. With languid movements too graceful for a mountain like him, Reid lifted into the space behind her, so close his chest brushed against her back.

"One horse?" she said.

"You can ride with Kosana, if you prefer."

Vaasa went rigid. "No, thank you."

Reid chuckled. Arrogant bastard.

On the ride back to his home, exhaustion once again slammed against Vaasa's mind. She felt on the brink of losing control. No matter. She kept upright, eyes alert, and scanned the streets they trotted through. Some people waved, others smiled and tipped their heads, but no one crowded the foreman and his escorts. Instead, they went back to whatever they were doing before. Some people ate at eateries and drank from copper glasses against the backdrop of strung lanterns and jewel-colored awnings. Even this late at night, the city of Mireh pulsed with an energy unlike any other place Vaasa had been. Even in Dihrah, they did not spend so much time outdoors. Never mind the frozen landscape Mekës became for nine out of the twelve months of the year.

Passing through a busy square, Vaasa watched as people danced in the streets to fast-paced music from drums and stringed guitars. Laughter floated around them, couples embraced, and people seemed to be drinking together or sharing their food. *Community* was the first word that came to mind, and the entire thing made something in Vaasa's heart lurch. Made her stomach tighten and her eyes drift back down to the horse.

People did not share their food with their neighbors where she was from.

They kept to themselves, bowed their heads before early dinners, and didn't have much to dance about. Would they ever flood the streets? Would they have even been allowed to?

She'd spent most of her days in the fortress grounds. Studying, reading, trying to avoid Dominik or sitting obediently at her father's side, translating. For that, she took the brunt of Dominik's jealousy and insecurity—always afraid she would somehow usurp him.

My chameleon, so good at blending in, her father would praise. *You will do great things for this empire.*

And so she would study harder, practice her languages longer, because she knew what could happen if she didn't. Ozik had warned her over and over about the fate of a useless daughter: becoming someone's miserable wife, and in turn, someone's miserable mother. So when he taught her a new language, she did as the advisor demanded. Every single time. And with each nation those languages helped her father conquer, she knew the cost was her morality.

Vaasa had never danced in the streets. Would *never* dance in the streets.

A waste of time, she decided, and stopped watching. She only looked up when they passed the High Temple of Mireh, with its reflective white stone steps that glowed pink under the red-tinged moon. On the back side of the multiple-story stone building was a window, one she knew, even if she couldn't see it. Her memory of slipping out of it brought the smallest of rebellious grins.

Looming on the skyline of the city was a taller, pointed building complete with a clocktower and bells. The Sodality of Setar, named for the god of language and writing. Something in Vaasa tugged toward the sky-kissing stone, some deeply entrenched thing in her gut she didn't understand. The enormous campus called to her.

The sodality disappeared as they rounded another corner, and with it, the instinct to follow.

Their small parade of three horses passed through two more districts, both quieter than the first one they'd ridden through. And the farther they went, the fewer people were around. As they trotted up a winding walkway, the buildings disappeared, and they began to make their way up a road lined in gangly trees and yellow grass. It hugged the coastline, just outside of the bustle of the city, and she could see the dark waters of the Settara poking through the trees.

They turned a corner and entered the grounds of a small estate.

Before them stood a villa against the backdrop of the open lake, settled perfectly upon a sloping hill that would lead directly to the water. The same wildflowers and yellow grasses Vaasa had seen along the other edges of the Settara dotted the hill. Those flowers trailed up a modest home and hung from wooden trellises at the entrance. Made exclusively of red and orange stones, the villa was neither grand nor simple, complete with a few stories marked by the glow of lantern-filled windows. What looked to be a garden sprawled in a small courtyard she could just make out through the single stone archway.

"Where are we?" Vaasa asked low.

"Home," Reid said from behind her. Vaasa could only bristle a moment before he swung himself off the horse and offered a hand. He helped her down from the sturdy horse and guided her forward again.

"We'll speak tomorrow," Reid told his commander.

"Reid, I—" Kosana said, anxious eyes darting to Vaasa.

"Tomorrow," he said again, no room for negotiation in his tone.

Dipping her head, Kosana took her leave without another word.

Reid led them both under the archway without explaining himself or the situation. Vaasa knew that the commander had intended for them to be separated, for her to be kept under watch. Gazing around, she took in each vulnerability of the villa, a warning biting at her heels.

No gates? No guards?

Nothing about this place made sense. Didn't Reid wish to protect himself? Didn't he want to be left alone? They were so close to the rest of the city, so accessible. Someone could just walk along the salt-covered shore and climb the hill.

Was this how he did things, then?

Vaasa made a quick mental map of the home as they entered. There was no receiving area, but instead a well-furnished living space complete with brown couches and a wooden table. Bookshelves and a liquor cabinet stood tall against the warm terra-cotta walls. Three hallways trailed off the main room, and they took one down a wide corridor. After they passed a few rooms, the rush of cold air hit them again as they traveled across a small breezeway, the lake on the right side. Through the stained-glass double doors, they entered a room.

Simple was again the first word that came to mind. The beige walls were mostly bare, save for two dark oak dressers and a floor-to-ceiling mirror. A forest-green couch graced one wall, a white dressing screen next to it. Off to the side, sheer curtains led into a bathing chamber that Vaasa didn't get a good look at. Instead, she stared at the expanse of the view, framed by two floor-to-ceiling glass doors with panels that covered an entire wall.

The Settara lay beyond those doors, beyond the stone veranda. Yellow and orange wildflowers hung from a wooden trellis, just like the main entrance. There were no other homes, no other prying eyes, through those windows. Just the reflection of the bloodred moon off midnight waters.

Did he consider this safe? Couldn't someone find their way in?

Reid leaned against the doorframe behind her, and when Vaasa turned, she found him looking tense for the first time since he'd found her. Jaw tight, he tilted his head and strands of his hair fell from the leather strap he used to pull it back.

"Thoughts?" he asked.

It's probably the most beautiful room I've ever been in.

I've never lived with doors, only windows.

"It's a room," she replied. "Where are you sleeping?"

Moving to slip off his coat, Reid gestured with his hand to the four-poster bed, the one draped in cream sheets and russet animal furs, facing the enormous panels of glass.

Something dropped in Vaasa's stomach. Why show her this room if it wasn't for her? She hated asking about things like this—accommodations, food, access to basic necessities. The weakness of it made her skin itch, and this late in the night her skin felt thin. Gripping her bag a little tighter, she said, "All right. And where am I sleeping?"

Nimble fingers at the back of his head undoing the leather strap in his hair, Reid used his chin to gesture at the very same bed.

And then he had the audacity to turn and amble into the bathing chamber as if he hadn't just implied what he had implied.

Infuriated, Vaasa dropped her bag on the floor and stormed after him through billowing white curtains into the attached room. Prepared to spit some choice words, she slid to a stop when she gazed upon the setup.

The entire left half of the chamber was inlaid stone reminiscent of opal, complete with an enormous showerhead and a claw-foot bathing tub behind glass doors. Leafy vines hung from the ceiling, spilling over pots, and a little wooden bench was settled just next to the tub.

Her home city was far too cold for this sort of infrastructure—in the snowy mountains, water brought into homes would freeze and cause the vessels to burst. She'd seen showers such as these in other areas of Asterya, in Zataar, too, but not in Mekës.

Shaking off her curiosity, she tossed her hand to her hip. "I thought I made myself clear: You will not take me to your bed."

"I will not take you *in* my bed," Reid said as he pulled at the center of his sashes and tugged the fabric over his head, dropping it to the floor without a care. His hair spilled to his broad shoulders, his inked chest entirely exposed to her once again. "But I do have members of my corps who live in this home, and if they are to believe we mean this, I can't very well have you sleeping in another room."

"Husbands and wives sleep in separate rooms all the time," she argued back.

"Sure, in Asterya, where husbands and wives hate each other."

"Oh, and we're just great friends."

"You don't hate me, and I certainly don't hate you."

She tossed her arms into the air. "I almost killed you on our wedding night."

"As I told you, you underestimate how much I enjoyed that."

"You're sick."

He just shrugged, then moved his hands for his breeches. “Would you like to stay? This shower is big enough for two, and it isn’t a bed, so if we’re going by the aforementioned rule, it wouldn’t technically be breaking our agreement if I took you in here.”

Mouth gaping, Vaasa cried out in frustration and stormed out of the bathing chamber, flinging the curtains closed behind her.

He roared with laughter and said something about blades.

Oh, he might not hate her, but she *hated* him. She would never be alone again. Never be able to sleep peacefully, to do what she needed and wanted in her own space. She’d have to share every waking moment with this asshole.

Magic stirred along her fingertips, and Vaasa shook her hands and stumbled until the backs of her knees hit the bed. The stupid, *useless* bed.

She could sleep on the couch.

No—*he* could sleep on the couch.

The sound of water running emanated past the closed curtains and Vaasa hurried behind the dressing screen, diving into her bag. She had a long shirt, her stupid acolyte robes, and—

The red nightgown. It was one of the few things she hadn’t sold on her escape to Dihrah.

Inspiration and power flared in her chest and Vaasa put the thing on, waiting behind the screen for him to finish. Within just a minute or so, Reid turned off the water and she heard him stepping along the stone in the bathroom. The curtains parted.

She slid from behind the screen, and Reid, with only a towel hanging from his waist, stopped suddenly. By the looks of it, he stopped breathing. Eyes dragging up and down her, he said, “I thought I’d have to work much harder to get you back into that.”

Running a hand through her short hair, Vaasa glided to the bed and pulled back the furs, her hands trailing along the same silken sheets their wedding bed had been dressed in. Arching her back just slightly, she peered up at him. “Husband and wife, yes?”

Tentatively, Reid nodded.

"Then what's yours is mine." She gestured toward the couch. "You can sleep there tonight."

He snorted. "You can sleep on the couch, Wild One. I've worked all day, and I'll be damned if I sleep anywhere but my bed."

"I will not sleep in the same bed as you."

Shrugging, Reid moved to his dresser. "Like I said, the couch is there. It's yours if you want it."

Like a damn child, Vaasa slid onto the bed, the *center* of the bed, and crossed her arms.

Reid stopped. Stared.

Then he prowled across the room.

Landing at the bottom of the mattress, he crawled forward until he came close, and Vaasa started to press into the headboard. Fire blazed in his eyes, and he wouldn't drop them from hers. Hands falling to either side of her, he moved his face closer until he loomed above her, his chest covering her torso, just as he had done the night of their wedding. "I *will* be sleeping in this bed," he drawled, and Vaasa started to breathe heavier. "Out of respect for your wishes, I'll at least wear pants when I do. Out of respect for mine"—he flicked his gaze up and down the length of her—"change. I will not have you in that damned thing unless you intend to let me take it off you."

Vaasa's lips parted at about the same time the fire in her chest burned hotter. Anger filled every empty crevice of her mind, and the tight leash she kept on the wicked magic strained. "And if I do intend to let you take it off me?"

"You will not win this game, Wild One." The bed dipped as Reid separated from her, once again padding back to his dresser. "Despite your assertions, you are not nearly as good a liar as you think."

"Didn't seem to pose a problem on our wedding night."

He looked over his shoulder as he plucked out a shirt. "I underestimated you. I will not be making the same mistake again." He threw the shirt into her lap. "Now, change and decide where you wish to sleep."

The dark mist at her fingers whispered with violence and cruelty.

It purred encouragements of anger and bloodshed and tugged at her sensibilities.

His eyes flicked down to it, and Vaasa could have sworn he scowled at the way the magic curled around her hands. Something about that look from him lit some deep, insecure part of her that wanted to hide under the sheets and never be seen again.

She knew it was hideous. Knew it was disgusting.

Balling the shirt into her hands, Vaasa considered each angle she had. Continue to argue and lose. Keep trying to win the way she'd won their wedding night and potentially piss him off more. All roads led back to one thing: the shirt in her hands.

Silently, she stood and walked behind the dressing screen, stepping out of the red nightgown and tucking it back into her bag. The shirt he gave her was practically a gown by itself, reaching to her midthighs. After dressing, she stood behind the screen for a moment longer and seethed.

Three years.

Just three years of this, and she would be free. She could go wherever she wanted; the magic would be gone. That was why she was here. No bed, no room, no damn view of a lake could be more important than that.

Reid's voice floated from the other side of the screen. "Your brother sent this some weeks ago."

All thoughts of timelines and freedom disappeared.

A letter fell from the top of the screen, dry parchment landing on the floor in front of her bare feet.

Quickly she bent and opened it, back pressing to the wall and eyes skimming the smoothly written Asteryan words.

Her heart leapt into her throat.

To anyone else, it would seem harmless. Concern for her well-being, even.

But to her, the message was clear: he wanted an update on how she was doing—not in her marriage, the election, or anything else surrounding Reid.

He wanted an update on the curse.

Which meant she had to break it before Dominik arrived to do the job himself. And when she did, she wouldn't need Reid of Mireh a moment longer.

The violence and rage and magic drained from her limbs and curled into a terrified ball in her stomach. Fear was a poison on her tongue and in her throat, but she swallowed despite the dryness.

When Vaasa walked out from behind the screen, Reid was dressed in gray pants like he had said he would be, and she didn't let herself look at him for more than a second. Not as he moved under the animal furs on the right side of the bed. "What does your brother want?"

She lied. "To know how I'm settling in," she said as she approached the bed.

Reid looked at her. He made no attempt to hide the carnal glint in his eyes as they landed upon the peaks of her breasts pressed against his shirt.

Hands folding into the warm furs, Vaasa tugged.

The blanket slid from the bed and onto the floor. Reid sighed in annoyance as she gathered the furs in her arms and marched to the couch. She lay down upon the cold leather and folded the blankets around herself, tucking them all the way around so he'd have to physically lift her to get them back.

"Just sleep in the damned bed, Vaasalisa," he growled.

Turning so she wasn't facing him, she said with casual cruelty, "Why would I? I don't have to pretend I love you in this room."

Silence.

Then Reid of Mireh blew out the lamp at his bedside, and the room went dark.

CHAPTER 6

The Sodality of Setar jutted up into the sky with pointed spires and two large symmetrical domes across from each other on either side of the property. Fashioned of white bricks and red roofs, the building sat along the watercourse with small floating docks of its own.

"Why are we here?" Vaasa asked, arching her back so it didn't rest upon Reid's chest.

Sitting behind her and seeming smug for a man who'd slept without blankets, he shifted his weight in the horse's saddle. "My end of our deal, Wild One."

No guards hovered around them, no prying ears that could spin tales of their lies. The horse trotted through the wrought iron gates of the looming building, and Vaasa counted a total of nine towers with red spires of their own. Windows dotted each of the many levels and a bell tower sat at the center of the campus with a clock so large she could see the curving details of the arms. Archways lined the entire perimeter of the bottom level, through which Vaasa could make out the expanse of brightly colored gardens.

Once inside the iron gates, Reid fluidly dismounted from behind her. Looking down into his cocky golden eyes, Vaasa was tempted to steal the horse and leave him here. Every moment with him was a trial of her patience and control.

Still, she dismounted and handed him the reins, resigned to face whatever awaited inside of this sodality. Knowledge lived in these structures, and it was a lack of information that haunted Vaasa more than anything.

After handing off the horse to an acolyte wearing amethyst robes, she and Reid plunged down one of the arching tunnels and took an immediate left through double doors into a grand entry room. Cool air flittered over the back of her neck and Vaasa let out a small breath of relief. They ascended the steps upon a curving staircase that led to a mezzanine of white marble, lined by more filigreed ironwork.

And then six more staircases, because apparently the people in Icrurian sodalities all had legs of iron.

Reid didn't look the least bit winded, but given his display yesterday on that boat, it wasn't unexpected. He outmatched her physically, something she didn't like to think about.

At the top of the stairs waited another hallway framed by the forest greens and burnt browns of the entryway floor. At the right end, three doors down, Reid opened the door without waiting for an invitation, dragging Vaasa through the threshold with him.

Black walls emptied into an enormous chamber covered in walnut bookshelves. Vaulted ceilings revealed one of the many spires of this building, the intricate iron filigree breathtaking from this lower angle. There had to be at least three floors to this room, giant ladders attached to each wall. The entire far side was glass panels, revealing the city and letting in enough light to glimmer off the mosaic floor of oranges, blues, and grays. Lanterns hung from the ceiling, carrying that same incandescent spark she'd seen at the Sodality of Una, next to vining plants that resembled waterfalls of green. On the far wall sat a daybed the size of a mattress.

Perched upon it was a stunning brunette girl, only a few years older than Vaasa, wearing amethyst robes that contrasted beautifully with her olive-toned skin, her hands clinging to the corners of a book.

She looked up immediately at their entrance and her face split into a smile, revealing pearl-white teeth. Just as her book snapped closed, another woman came around one of the bookshelves.

Blond hair threaded with silver fell into the stranger's face as she looked up, revealing wrinkle-kissed amber eyes. Smiling with the broadness of a sky, the older woman set down her enormous leather tome, her onyx robes swishing behind her. "You're back," she said with the same western accent as Reid, and then flicked her eyes to Vaasa.

The woman blinked twice like she didn't believe what she saw.

"We are," Reid said, finally moving away from Vaasa and crossing the room in four large steps. As he embraced the strange woman, who melted into his arms, Vaasa could have sworn she heard Reid mumble something.

The two made eye contact as the woman inspected him, hand grabbing at his jaw and looking him over, and then she gazed back at Vaasa.

"This is Melisina Le Torneau," Reid said, turning to face Vaasa once more. "The high witch of Veragi."

"The most powerful of us all," the other woman, the one with brown hair, teased.

Another body rounded the bookshelf and stopped abruptly, almost dropping her clay mug. Salt-and-pepper hair framed her light brown, wrinkled face and her eyes resembled spilled coffee.

"Vaasalisa," Melisina said, "this is Suma. I see you've already met Amalie."

She hadn't actually met anyone.

The young one—Amalie, apparently—bolted upright from the couch. "It's so lovely to meet you, Consort."

A pair of women walked through the door just then and straightened their backs in surprise. Both seemed to be in their fifth or sixth decade. One had long black braids and deep umber skin, dark eyes rimmed by purple cat-eye glasses; the other had pale white skin and hair so platinum it rivaled the floors downstairs. The one with purple glasses looked at the other and said, "We have company? We never have company."

The other snorted a laugh.

"Hush," Amalie said, and the women glanced at each other, then back at Amalie, and the platinum-haired woman stuck out her tongue.

Vaasa got the distinct impression no one told those two women what to do and walked away with their heads intact. Especially when Reid gave a chuckle and returned to her, his proximity now itching down her side.

"Don't worry about them," Melisina said, then leaned a little closer. "Trouble, if you ask me."

"No one did," one of them sang, her purple glasses falling down her nose as she breezed past them all to the daybed Amalie had been sitting on. Instantly, Amalie protested, but the woman swished her voluptuous hips down into the spot and kicked up her legs. After she propped open her book, the world no longer existed to her.

"She's an asshole," the other said before going over to that very daybed and tossing herself onto it, too. The two women giggled, then went silent as they each began to read their own books.

Vaasa took a step back. Who the hell were these people?

"You're Veragi?" Suma asked, brown eyes trailing up and down Vaasa as if she didn't entirely believe her.

"I—" Vaasa stopped, fear striking her stomach and cramping. "I am not anything. It's a curse, it's—"

"Show us," Melisina said.

Fingers shaking, Vaasa raised her wrist. With a little indulgence in the nasty emotions forever coiled in her gut, the pressure moved into her palm. Into her fingers. Dancing on the tips, black mist sputtered into existence and twirled playfully about her skin. *A void*, the stolen leather tome had described it.

Amalie caught a small breath, and, much to Vaasa's dismay, Melisina smiled as if Vaasa had shown her the sun.

The sight of it made Vaasa sick, and she shook her fingers before shoving them into the pockets of her tan breeches. She looked at the floor.

"You're afraid of it," Melisina said.

Words caught in her throat, and Vaasa's eyes darted to Reid. He was already looking at her, assessing. She swore it was disdain that now laced the way he gazed at her. Regardless, Reid gestured her on.

"I . . . ," Vaasa started, then snapped her lips shut.

She couldn't. Reid probably saw exactly what she did—this evil had made a home inside of her, and it leaked into her expressions and onto her tongue.

He probably thought it had chosen wisely.

He didn't need to know anything real about her—how she'd found her mother, how she had felt the awful invasion of this force in her stomach and her chest. The way it ruthlessly stole her breath, crashed down on her like a wave.

How it was strangling her from the inside out.

She could not give him another ounce of ammunition against her.

Throat increasingly tighter, magic increasingly heavier, Vaasa shook her head.

"Leave," Melisina said suddenly.

Of course. Nodding in resignation, Vaasa looked up.

To find Melisina looking squarely at Reid.

He started to argue, but Melisina gave one good shake of her head. "She will not speak with you in the room, so you must go."

"She is my wife. I need to know if—"

"And you will be a widower in a matter of months if she will not speak," one of the women on the couch said, slamming her book shut and standing. The other joined her. "You can walk us to our classrooms."

Something in Reid's jaw ticked, and he glanced at Vaasa. Softened, even if just for a moment. "I'll be waiting downstairs."

"You will come back in five hours," Melisina said with a wave to brush him off. "Surely you have more important things to do than supervise us. You're a foreman, for goddess's sake."

Vaasa . . . might like this woman? Especially when Melisina walked to the door herself and swung it open.

Grumbling, yet entirely outmatched, Reid of Mireh stomped out of the room.

The two women winked, then scampered after him. Amalie giggled like wind chimes and Suma just walked away as if she was bored of the whole thing.

Vaasa might have gawked, had she not wanted to puke from nervousness. "We . . . we need five hours?"

"No," Melisina said. "I just assume you haven't had a moment to yourself since Dihrah."

Vaasa's brows slammed together. How did this woman know she'd been in Dihrah?

She watched as Melisina clicked the door shut and began to walk back to her table, unfazed by the slight anger she'd just drawn from her foreman. "Has the vomiting begun?"

Vaasa's lips parted in shock.

"I'll take that as a yes." She gestured to the seat across from her as she picked up her black robes and settled into her chair. Vaasa took the seat and tried to appear comfortable. She wasn't.

Amalie helped herself to a seat at the table, too. Unafraid, this one. "What do you like to be called? Sometimes Melisina calls you Vaasalisa, other times it's Vaasa."

Melisina had talked about her? To these women?

"Vaasa is fine. Are you both sages here?"

"Melisina is," Amalie said with pride laced in her tone. "I will be one day. But more important, we are Veragi witches."

Brow threading, Vaasa looked to Melisina for answers.

"Veragi are best in groups," Melisina said. "All covens are."

"One witch is trouble," Amalie said.

"A coven is a nightmare," Melisina added.

Vaasa awkwardly shifted her weight, the wooden chair beneath her groaning. Motherly bonds often put her off, and that was the only way to describe what flowed between her two tablemates. Despite the pulsing instinct she felt to hide or run, Vaasa also craved the approval of at least one person. She needed answers; she couldn't ruin this. "I don't understand."

"Each sodality in Icruria houses one particular coven," Melisina explained. "A place to study safely, to contribute to the literature and research surrounding magic, and to be a home for witches who don't have one. Ours takes its name from Veragi, the goddess whose magic pulses through your veins."

"We are lucky to have found you," Amalie said. "So few bloodlines still exist with a connection to Veragi."

Turning to Melisina, Vaasa raised her eyebrows. "Bloodlines?"

"What do you know of Veragi magic?" Melisina asked, lifting a hand to Amalie as if to ask her to be quiet.

Nothing. Nothing real, at least. "I . . ." It had been so long since Vaasa had been like this—unable to speak. She had often chosen not to, had waited for the opportune moment to let the perfect sentence roll off her tongue, but for the words simply not to be there? She felt the intimate caress of vulnerability and wanted to pry it from her nerves. "I know nothing. All I know is that it infected me when . . ." She looked down at the walnut table. Swallowed.

Silence remained in the room, as if Melisina and Amalie were simply waiting for Vaasa to decide she was ready to speak. It wasn't pressure she felt, just the neutrality of two choices: *Speak and find out, don't and learn nothing.*

"It infected me when I found my mother's body," Vaasa finally said.

Amalie's mouth curved into a frown. Melisina shook her head, a small *tsk* rolling from her lips. "It did not infect you. Veragi magic is generational, passed down from a mother to her eldest daughter. It only passes upon the witch's death."

Vaasa's heart skipped, her chest constricted, and something about it made her want to double over. To cry. "What?"

"It would have passed almost instantly. I'm so sorry."

Vaasa dug her nails into her palm, angry with herself for not being as sad as Melisina wanted her to be. Instead, her confusion melded with resentment. "She . . . she always had this?"

"After her mother died, yes."

"No."

Melisina frowned. "I cannot change what is."

Then . . . had her mother known this would happen to her? Had she been through it herself, yet denied Vaasa the knowledge? Had she condemned Vaasa to death? The cruelty of her family really knew no bounds.

"My mother was a *witch*?"

Melisina nodded. "The very same as me. As you."

"As all of us in this coven," Amalie added.

"Who even was she, then?" Vaasa asked. "She was born in Asterya, she married an emperor—"

"That's a big question," Melisina said without a raise or dip in her tone. "Let's focus on what is possible."

Something about the words silenced the voices in Vaasa's head. What could be more important than the answers she had spent *months* searching for? Than the opportunity to leave this place and start somewhere new?

Melisina rested her palms against the table. "Sometimes, the world is too big and the questions too difficult for any one person to face. Focus on what you know with certainty. What do you know right now?"

By the look on Melisina's face, Vaasa wondered if she wanted to know the answers at all. If maybe a revelation like that might be the thing that finally broke her. "I want it to stop," she replied.

"It will not do that. The magic is a part of you, just like any organ or blood."

Bile crawled into Vaasa's throat, burning at the back of her teeth. The implications of it . . . She couldn't look at either of them. "Then I want to know how to turn it off when I need."

"Fine. Today, you will learn to move the magic by sheer force of will."

Could this magic even *be* willed? What was it made of, and why had it chosen her? Vaasa had a hundred more questions, each one stinging in her stomach and at her fingertips—

Focus on what is possible.

"You . . . you're going to teach me how to use it?" Vaasa croaked.

Grinning, Melisina said, "If you let us, we can teach you far more than that."

Five hours later, for the first time in months, Vaasa felt empty.

A good sort of empty. Not the aching, lonely, everything-hurts sort of drained, but rather the constant coil of anguish and upset had disappeared from her gut. Perhaps it was still there, but it was muted enough to feel dormant.

None of the women asked any further questions—they didn't prod, poke, or search for answers that Vaasa didn't have. Leaving the subject entirely alone, Vaasa had freed herself of the aching vulnerability and found a sliver of success.

Melisina and Amalie had been the only two who'd spent time with her, and as much as Vaasa didn't understand it, she'd come to respect both of them. Amalie was wickedly smart and compassionate, and clearly a hard worker. It was she who taught Vaasa how to direct her magic: back and forth, over and under, she could guide where the feeling went in her gut.

The magic still felt wily and resistant, yet when she accepted and focused on it, rather than trying to tamp it down, it would snake up her wrists or between her fingers. The sight of it still turned her stomach, though. But despite the impending sickness, the exhaustion pounding against her temples, it felt good to be this tired. To have done something worth doing.

When not working on controlling Vaasa's magic, the three women spoke about nothing important. For an hour, they'd left her to a book on the history of Veragi magic and its many uses. In that book, she'd gleaned what the stolen tome had meant by *a void*. The magic was exactly that—a force of raw power, one that smothered air and light and sound. Smothered any sense at all.

The coven's tower, which housed the witches' quarters, was filled with the sorts of books Vaasa had been searching Dihrah for, and she wondered if it was the same there. Were all the books on magic hidden away in the witches' quarters at the Library of Una, too? Had that been what Brielle meant?

For their final hour, Amalie had given Vaasa something unrelated to Veragi magic. Something simply to enjoy, to ease the weight of heavy things, and the girl's face had lit up at the thought of recommending something worth reading. Much to Vaasa's surprise, she found herself falling into easy conversation with Amalie. She had never been around women her age before, at least not for long. It was unnerving and somehow special, which only raised Vaasa's guard.

Upon leaving, they'd asked her to identify three things she was grateful for. It may have been one of the hardest things she'd done that day, and admitting that to herself bothered her.

She said the blanket she'd had last night, the cool temperature of the sodality, and the color green. Their names were the first things to pop into her head, but she couldn't manage to speak those out loud.

Still, those hours were the first she'd had of complete calm, and it took every ounce of her willpower to leave the sodality.

Couldn't she just sleep here?

"The fact that you have held on to this magic for so long is a testament to your power," Melisina said as she walked Vaasa back downstairs. "You have acknowledged it today. The pain should ease, at least for a little while. If it comes back, don't be afraid to sit in that discomfort. The magic isn't inherently bad. But if it feels out of control, do not let it take over you. In violence, you will lose your air."

While the thought of this senseless void suffocating her did nothing good for her nerves, to hear someone else mention the splintering agony, to have it simply validated, seemed to shift everything for Vaasa. It was the first time they had discussed how Vaasa had been holding this magic inside of herself without an outlet.

But to sit with it? She didn't think herself capable of that.

"Tomorrow, same time?" Melisina asked.

"I . . . I don't know how to thank you."

Melisina raised her hand. "There is no need for thanks. Tomorrow, same time."

This time, it wasn't a question.

Something brilliant began to simmer inside of Vaasa as she descended the marble staircase that would lead her back to the first floor of their secluded tower.

Perhaps it was pride.

The fleeting happiness drained from her when she hit the bottom and found Reid standing there. He waited patiently for her with his body halfway turned and eyes on the horizon through the panels of windows. His hair was pulled back, much like it always was, but tonight he wasn't dressed in the ceremonial garb Vaasa had grown accustomed to in the past few days. Instead, he wore dark pants with no shirt at all, though a brown drape slashed across one shoulder and over his chest. A lightweight cloak covered the other shoulder, falling to the center of his calves. Bands circled his formidable arms, and over one, he'd draped a bundle of fabric. Extra clothing. The moment he saw her, he took that fabric within his hand. "You're alive."

"Yes, well, they're much better company. Didn't feel the need to jump out of any windows this time."

Reid tipped his head back and laughed. "Gods, my conversations were infinitely more boring without you, Wild One."

How did he manage to pick at each and every one of her nerves? Peering at the witches who now descended the stairs, Vaasa stepped forward as if his proximity didn't bother her. "Can we go?"

Looking back to her, he confessed, "They know. You don't need to pretend here."

Her lips parted, and a bit of humiliation sparked within her. Taking a small step back, she nodded.

"Will you allow me to show you Mireh tonight?" he asked.

Show her Mireh? "What do you mean?"

"The Lower Garden comes alive at night. I'd like to show you off. I've waited months to do so."

Would this be their life, then? Putting on a show whenever he requested it of her?

It was exactly what she'd signed up for, actually. Reid probably needed to convince his people first that their union was real and his relationship with Asterya was assured. She looked down at herself and said, "Are those clothes for me?" Her tan breeches and now-dingy white blouse wouldn't be how he wanted his consort to appear to the rest of the world.

"They are," he confirmed, gesturing for her to go and change.

Sighing, Vaasa swiped the clothing out of his hands and marched to the left side of the first floor, cursing under her breath as Amalie watched her. Quickly, she ducked into the attached bathing chamber and changed, tugging her fingers through her hair and growling another curse at the clothing he'd chosen.

Breezy, olive-colored breeches and a sleeveless white top, one made of tight material that came all the way to her neck. She furrowed her brow. It hardly covered her torso. It was never warm enough in Mekës to wear anything this thin, or with her midriff showing, let alone without sleeves. To her luck, he'd included a cloak.

Amalie's jaw dropped as Vaasa ducked out of the bathing chamber and she stood next to Reid, who was exchanging words again with Melisina. Both turned to look at her at once, and Reid straightened his back.

"You're actually wearing them."

"Was I not supposed to?"

"Well, yes." He scrubbed at his jaw. "I just thought you'd put up a fight first."

"I'm sure I can find something for us to fight about, if you'd like."

The right corner of his lips turned up, a crooked half smile, and he said, "I think I like you agreeable."

"Don't push your luck," she muttered, bidding the witches goodbye once more.

She tried to ignore her irritation at his laughter as he followed her.

"I wouldn't dream of it, Wild One," he said as he guided her through the door.

CHAPTER 7

Once inside the heart of the city, the two of them made their way to what must have been the Lower Garden. This was the same place Vaasa had seen all the people dancing and sharing food just yesterday. Though it wasn't technically a garden, but was named thus because most fabric awnings were decorated with hanging plants of every color—blues, purples, reds, and greens seemed to light up the orange, red, and white buildings. They edged the Settara, white stone arching to give a view of the starlight on the lake. Inside the circular quad, settled in the epicenter of the busy area, were musicians. Notes from guitars and steel drums floated around them.

Beautiful.

The entire place was breathtaking, and if Vaasa let herself, she could have thought it was the most welcoming place she'd ever laid eyes on. Her father and her brother had been so scornful of this nation . . . but of what? The only difference between their people was that the Mirehans were happy. People roamed, most of them danced, and all laughed just as she'd seen before. The inviting sound of steel drums and guitar twisted something in her chest. What had these people done to deserve such happiness that her people had not?

As the bitter thought floated across her mind, so did the quick stab of regret. To like anything about this place was a waste—she would be gone the moment she could be.

Reid worked her out of her cloak and tossed it over a table near them. Threading his hand in hers, he tugged, heading into the thick of people in the middle. All eyes seemed to follow them, and heat crawled up her cheeks.

"What are we doing?" Vaasa asked, her earlier bitterness slipping into her tone as she scampered after him. Quickly, she smiled as if it had meant nothing and silently scolded herself.

Using his hand to force Vaasa into a turn, Reid glided them around a group of people and then placed that hand on her waist. He pulled her up against his broad chest and shifted his eyes to the surrounding crowd. "Dancing."

What?

It felt as if every person in the quad was watching them.

The music hummed and people danced in communal circles, some groups tossing their partners around and weaving through the other dancers. Couples clung to each other. One drifted a hand over another's torso and pulled her back against his chest. She pressed her body to him and leaned forward, swaying her backside on his hips.

Reid watched the way Vaasa inspected the couple, how her eyes trailed to the places the two touched, and he rumbled a low laugh.

Did he expect to touch her like that?

Tentatively, he reached for her hand. "It's quite easy. Touch me here." His hand slowly lifted hers along his torso, past the drapes so her nails skimmed his bare skin and settled it against his chest. "And here." Keeping their gazes locked, he did the same with the other, this time placing her fingers just beneath the hair at the nape of his neck. "Good." His hand pressed into the curve of her hip, flirting with the waistline of the higher-cut breeches. "Swing your hips for me."

He moved slowly, giving her the time to step away if she preferred, but she held firm in their contact. He'd more than fulfilled his half of their deal today, and with the eyes of his city on them, she felt a low tightening in her abdomen. A surprising willingness to be what he needed her to be. To the tune of the drums, she moved left and then right, and he guided her with his hand, the other raising to twine his fingers with hers at his chest.

A small smile started to creep along her lips, and his eyes flicked down to it.

Spinning and then pulling her back, Reid moved his hands from her waist and up and down her sides, moving her to the music in a way she had never been moved before. He led her through the echoes of steel drums without effort, looking irritatingly damned graceful while he did it. He guided her into each step, so all she had to do was follow him. With his guidance, there wasn't a single moment she missed.

Something in her gut twisted, not magic this time as Reid gripped her hand and tossed her from him just far enough to spin, as if displaying her for the crowd. His fingers trailed on her waist and caught her side, gripping and tugging until her back pressed to his chest—just like that couple had been.

She froze, missed a step. He wrapped his arm all the way around her waist to make her misstep seem intentional. Warm breath coasted to her ear. "Dance with me like lovers do."

Bending his head forward, he let his lips brush her neck.

People noticed. Some of them whispered.

Most likely about her recent absence. Or maybe about the way they looked right now.

I need Icruria to believe that we are taken with each other. That our union is strong enough to represent them.

On the edge of the circle, Vaasa noticed Kosana standing with an unfamiliar group of people. The blonde took a long sip of her wine, though even from afar, Vaasa thought the poor goblet was stuck in a death grip.

Vaasa had to sell this. To make everyone around them believe this mattered, that it was real. That when the time came, it would be the two of them working for the betterment of Asterya and Icruria.

Together.

So she raised her arm the way she'd seen another woman do and curled it around his head, fingers sliding into the mass of his hair. Reid laughed against her skin and slid his hand over her stomach, whispering, "Just like that."

The music lilted and sped, and she matched the pace, loosening the way she danced beneath his hands and giving in. He pulled her closer, their bodies pressed together, until he moved her forward and she ground against his hips. His hands guided her back into the motions, swinging in unison. And out of the corner of her eye, she watched Kosana plunge into the crowd.

The tempo shifted, and he seamlessly spun her once more, so she was pinned to his chest, having no option but to tilt her head up to look at him. "Would you like a glass of wine?" he asked, hands pushing Vaasa's back into his hair like he enjoyed the feel. Strands had come loose and now hung in his face, framing his sturdy jawline.

Throat dry, probably from the heat and the exercise, Vaasa nodded.

Reid led her from the center of the quad and through the massive groups of people, all greeting them or watching her closely, until they reached an outdoor pub. Plenty of people were strewn along chairs and tables, all wearing clothes like Vaasa's and Reid's and deep in conversation. She picked up bits and pieces of what they said but didn't focus on much—not past how tightly Reid gripped her hand as they moved through the crowd.

After Reid retrieved two glasses of wine, Kosana appeared, not looking particularly happy. The commander of Mireh's forces wore one side of her long hair braided back, sun-kissed white skin on display down her neck and chest. Sheer, powder-blue pants covered her hips, split, and then met again at her knees, where they split once more before bunching at her ankles. This breezy Icrurian fashion was foreign to Vaasa, but admittedly, it did wonders for Kosana's muscular legs.

She looked nothing like a guard, though. Was that not her role this evening? Vaasa enjoyed the sour pinch of the commander's lips, so she took a sip of the sweet wine and followed Reid to a table, where he sat without regard for how much space his body took up. Legs a little bit apart, arm draped casually over the wooden top, he looked like some strange mix between an irreverent god and a decorated warrior.

With mischievous eyes, Reid tugged at Vaasa's waist and dragged her into his lap, laughing at her rigidity and how she almost spilled her wine. "Like lovers," he reminded her on a whisper, his lips at her ear.

Vaasa's breath hitched, but then she settled into his chest like she belonged there.

His hand rested against her stomach as he looked beyond her, nodding at a few people who walked by and said hello in greeting. Kosana slid into the chair opposite him and looked out at the crowd, taking another long gulp of her wine, eyes falling to other couples who seemed just as closely embraced as them.

"Commander," Reid teased her.

"Foreman," she grumbled back.

Reid made Vaasa adjust her weight and kick up her long legs, folding them over one of his and settling her into his lap more naturally. One arm around his neck, she slid her fingers into his hair again, and like the fantastic performer he was, he leaned into her touch.

"How long have you known each other?" Vaasa asked Kosana, flicking her eyes to Reid. "You two seem quite familiar."

Swallowing her wine, Kosana said, "Since we were children. Melisina was practically my mother, too. I heard you met her today."

Mother?

Everything in Vaasa's chest constricted. "What?"

Reid froze, the glass at his lips, and then lowered it. "She didn't tell you."

Eyes steady, Vaasa peered around the outdoor tables. Some people watched, and it should have made her a little afraid, but it was the amused smugness of Kosana that lit a fire in Vaasa's chest. "Melisina Le Torneau is your mother?" she demanded of Reid.

His mother would know what she had done to him. Would know that she had almost *killed*—

"Yes," he said. "I thought she would tell you. Certainly, one of the witches would have said something."

Fingers gripping tightly around her glass, Vaasa said, "It didn't come up."

How could she ever go back now? Just when she thought she'd found the one place in the universe that Reid of Mireh didn't seem to have a hold on—

With good reason, Melisina Le Torneau should have hated Vaasa.

Why had she been so *kind*?

"Don't worry, Vaasalisa," Kosana said then, flicking a strand of her hair from her shoulder and spinning sugar in her tone, a falsehood that practically swelled with distaste. "Melisina is *forgiving.*"

Reid froze for a moment, the undertones of the comment not missing their mark.

Could Melisina really forgive Vaasa for what she'd done to Reid on their wedding night? For taking the chance at a true, blissful marriage from her son?

Kosana clearly hadn't.

But those were questions only Melisina could answer.

Milking it for all it was worth, Vaasa grinned and pulled Reid's hand down to rest upon her thigh. Threading their fingers, she took a much-needed sip of her wine. "Good. I think I like the Sodality of Setar better than Una. It matches the temple Reid and I were married in." Blushing and shrugging her shoulder, she mocked Kosana's tone. "In fact, it matches our bedroom."

Kosana flinched.

"Is all this normal?" Vaasa gestured to the three of them, trudging past it like she didn't know she had upset the commander. "For the foreman to just be out and about?"

"He does whatever he wants," Kosana muttered.

"It's normal," Reid said, eyeing both women as if he expected a brawl. "Kosana commands my forces, but she is also the closest thing to a guard I have allowed."

"He should consider allowing me to assign him real protection," Kosana said. "Especially given his recent choices."

Vaasa started to sit up, but Reid gripped her tighter. "I don't need protection," he said.

"You will when you are headman."

"I thought he did whatever he wanted," Vaasa prodded.

The commander narrowed her eyes, looking Vaasa up and down much like an ornery hawk prepared to dive at the surface of the Settara with claws outstretched.

Reid looked between the two women, lips pursing and then turning up into a satisfied grin. The sort that meant he had an idea. "Perhaps. Which is why you, Vaasalisa, will start combat training with Kosana tomorrow."

Vaasa's stomach dropped at about the same time Kosana sat straight up. "What?" the blond woman asked.

"No," Vaasa objected.

"I thought I did whatever I wanted," Reid muttered, taking another sip of his wine.

Kosana scoffed in frustration, and it might be the only thing she and Vaasa agreed on. Turning to look at him, her fingers still in his hair, Vaasa asked, "Do you really believe I cannot defend myself?"

Those haunting images—her, him, knives—seemed to course between them.

Reid smiled like the devil, his thumb beginning to do lazy circles along her abdomen. "Oh, I am quite familiar with your propensity for a blade, Wild One."

"None of this is necessary," Kosana said.

Turning to look at his commander, Reid didn't relent, his circles on Vaasa only going lower, causing knots in her stomach to form. "You are one of the most skilled warriors in Icruria, perhaps the continent, and you are my best friend. She is my wife. I don't want a guard around all the time, so train her like you would a Mirehan, please."

A look passed between the two of them—a deep-seated familiarity Vaasa neither understood nor cared to understand. Dripping with incredulity, Kosana sighed and nodded her concession.

"Reid." Vaasa tried to dissuade him, though she almost croaked as his hand dipped lower. Almost pulled herself from his touch.

He shook his head. Met her eyes, entirely uncompromising. "You can meet with Kosana before you go to the sodality when it's still cool outside, or you can try your luck in the heat."

The boldness of this man. The *audacity*. She started to speak again, but he leaned forward and nipped at her ear.

Vaasa's fingers tightened ruthlessly in his hair.

Something hardened beneath her.

Vaasa froze.

Grinning against her skin, he whispered, "Care to try that again?"

She could slap him. Could turn fully around and strangle him. But Kosana watched them with such anger and unrelenting coldness that Vaasa found herself crossing her ankles and taking a restrained sip of her wine. Looking directly at the commander, *not* at Reid, she said, "Does the morning work for you?"

She and Reid would discuss this later, in private, with the rest of her opinions. When she couldn't feel him pressed against her backside.

Kosana's fingers tightened on her goblet, but she jerked a nod and looked back out at the rest of the crowd.

No one said anything else of consequence, and when Reid seemed convinced the world believed their little game, he lifted her with ease back to her feet. "Let's get home," he said, and as they walked, they parted the ever-watching crowd.

"This is absurd," Vaasa snapped from across the room.

Reid only gave an amused smile, watching her pace in front of the couch while he leaned back on his headboard, hands behind his head. *Infuriating* was the only word Vaasa could use to describe how smug he looked.

"Learn to get along, and you two will be fine," he suggested.

"Learn to get along?" Kosana and she were not capable of such a thing. Stopping her pacing, Vaasa ducked behind the dressing screen and started dropping garments. "Is she in love with you?"

He barked a laugh. "She's married. You'll probably meet her wife tomorrow."

All right, so Vaasa had read that entirely wrong. But not unfairly so—did friends defend each other the way Kosana defended Reid? And he had called her his *best* friend. "Was she the one who found you?"

"When?"

She walked out just then, reduced to wearing his damn shirt again. "Tied to your wedding bed, alone and bleeding."

The little quirk of his mouth made Vaasa's fingers twitch. "She did untie me, yes."

Why did they have to pretend to be anything of importance to each other in front of Kosana, then? Vaasa looked away, settling herself upon the couch and curling the blankets around her shoulders again. He didn't need to put on some show about caring for her safety. "She knows this is just an arrangement. We don't have to pretend in front of her."

"Insisting you can defend yourself isn't pretending," Reid remarked as if it were obvious.

"What do you mean?"

Lifting from the bed, Reid sat up and put his elbows on his knees. "I won my title honorably, but there are those who don't like my position of authority. Those who would see me, and by extension, you, taken out before we can win the headmanship."

"I'm not defenseless."

"I know that well enough."

"Then why?"

"Because while you are smart, cunning, and wickedly resourceful, you are not a warrior. That isn't how your father trained you."

The mention of her father, of her training, awoke violence in her gut. "What would you know of my *training*?"

Eyes flicking up and down her body, he said, "I know you speak four languages, and that men threw themselves at your father to get you in their homes and their beds. Never once did he concede. Which means you were useful, and that he honed you no differently than a blade."

Six. She spoke six languages. And the sort of versatility they'd taught her gave her a leg up on almost any dialect she encountered on this continent—roots remained the same, even if their context and slang changed. It came as no surprise that Reid had assumptions about what purpose she'd served her family's empire. Of the secrets and councils she'd been made privy to. But she only ever translated, and she hadn't been married off because to do so would leave someone alive who might kill her brother and take the throne. Tilting her head, she said, "Are you so certain of that?"

"I am," he insisted. "Though I do wonder what else he taught you. That, and what you did to no longer be useful to your brother."

Those words hit her like a blow to the stomach. "Perhaps I am more useful than you think."

That brought him pause. "You know what I think?"

"Not much beyond your lap and your blade."

Smirking at her jibe and slinging his legs off the bed, he admitted, "I do often consider my lap and blade. Particularly when you're around."

In a way, she'd brought that one upon herself. Rolling her eyes, she sank back further into the couch. Especially when he started to prowl across the room toward her.

"I have two theories. The first is that you know far less than you let on." He gestured up and down at her. "That this act you have is nothing but a defense."

Cocking her head, she let out one breathy laugh. "You think baiting me will get me to reveal my secrets to you?"

"People with the universe in their hands don't hide so much."

"People with the universe in their hands never show their palms."

Reid sank to his knees directly in front of her and Vaasa's breath caught. "Or second"—his hands curled into the blankets at her waist—"you know far more than you let me see. Perhaps your brother doesn't stand a chance with you at my side. Maybe you are more dangerous than him."

Vaasa didn't dare say a word. She stared down at his hands, then back at his eyes, which assessed her through long lashes. Her heart started to pound. Where did he believe this was going?

Leaning closer, never breaking their stare, Reid said, "And maybe it is you who will be cold tonight."

He hauled the blankets off her and she spun, tumbling off the couch and onto the floor with a wicked hiss. By the time the entire exchange registered and she whipped her head up, an Asteryan curse on her tongue, he was slipping back onto the bed and smoothing the blanket out.

He didn't care about her safety at all. She was a toy, a source of leverage. An investment he felt obligated to protect.

"You're an ass," she snapped.

"You are welcome in this bed anytime, Vaasalisa."

"Never."

"Never say never. The days here may be warm, but as you know, nights can be brutal."

She pushed herself off the floor with a faltering smile. "My father taught me to speak those languages because he intended to sell me to the highest bidder, and he didn't know who would arrive with the coin. Which is why it astounds me that somehow I ended up under your roof."

"He taught you Icrurian, didn't he?" Reid leaned a little forward, holding the blanket between his hands. "He must have known I would be in the running."

What an arrogant, foolish man. "Considering I'm only temporarily in your home and certainly not in your bed, I'd say you weren't in the running at all."

"You're sleeping half naked on my couch, so I'd argue I'm still in the game."

"What a feat, to only ever get a woman half undressed."

"Come over here and I'll rectify the situation," he purred.

Scoffing and pushing open the door to the veranda, she said, "I'd rather be eaten by wolves."

In the most audacious of tones she'd ever heard in her life, Reid blew out the candle next to the bed with a single sentence. "Call me a wolf whenever you'd like, Wild One."

Oh, those words lit a fire in her. She spun and bared her teeth. "You are the most arrogant, pompous—"

"And *you* are the most insincere woman I've ever laid eyes on."

It was like he'd thrown a brick with that sentence. But Vaasa only shrugged. "Like you said, it's all an act."

"Let me be clear. If Dominik wants something from my home, it would be in your best interest to share it. *Right now.* I walked into this prepared to defend you just as I would a consort I loved, but I would rather alienate the Asteryans and lose this election than allow you to risk the safety of my home."

Dominik wants me dead, and you are just collateral. Cocking her head, she murmured, "I thought I wasn't a good liar."

Springing from the bed, he crossed the room in a few steps and backed her into the wall. He didn't touch her, a choice, but his face was only a hairbreadth away. "What happened? Did we get too close? Did you *almost* enjoy yourself, and now you want to pick a fight?"

Silence. Angry breath pushed from her nose, but she kept her lips sealed.

"This is *my* line, Vaasalisa. Do not threaten my country."

At any moment, her brother would walk into this pretty city and burn it to the ground. He might already be on his way.

But she couldn't say that. Not if it meant Reid would send her away before she learned to control her magic—or worse, make a move for the Asteryan throne.

If he knew what their marriage really meant, he would never let her leave.

She met his shadowed stare through the darkness, the open windows the only source of light in the room as she lifted her body from the wall, stepping instead into his space. She was not afraid of him, and she never would be. "It isn't a threat, it's the truth. You don't want an alliance with my brother." And she didn't want Dominik any closer to them than he already was.

"Why?"

"Because he is nothing but a viper, one who disguises himself as an ally and turns on you when you're at your most vulnerable."

"And are you just like him?"

Vaasa couldn't say why, but the words struck her in the chest. They tore at all the scars she possessed, both on her skin and beneath it. The magic in her stomach yanked itself upright, coiled like the snake she accused her brother of being, ready to strike.

Of course she was just like him. Her father had *trained* her to be. He'd made her in his image, and this magic was only proof of that.

The most insincere woman he'd ever laid eyes on.

Arching her back and pressing her lips to his ear as he'd done to her earlier, she whispered, "Yes. You don't want to be involved with me, either."

And then shoved him off her.

He stumbled backward and gaped at her, hatred threading like gold in his eyes.

She scoffed. "If you think for one second that a trade agreement with Asterya is beneficial, you are a fool. If you let my brother close to this city, he will make you regret it."

Without another word, she grabbed her cloak and headed outside to sleep on an outdoor settee.

Let the wolves come and find her. Let them tear her limb from limb.

At least out here it was quiet, and she was finally alone.

CHAPTER 8

Two miles.

Every day for two weeks, Kosana forced her to run two miles on the perimeter of the Settara, and Vaasa wanted to hurl.

She had been active her whole life. Had been taught by a blades master, had sparred with him, even bested him sometimes in close fighting. She'd taken bruises, withstood soreness, and could normally run two miles without much issue.

In the *cold.*

Here, with the morning sun causing every inch of her to sweat, Vaasa came to terms with the fact that she was outmatched. That perhaps Reid had been correct in asserting she learn to use her body in this temperature and humidity.

The only thing worse than admitting she was wrong was having to spend the morning with Kosana, who barely spoke a word to her. And when she did deign to speak, Kosana's distrust and resentment dripped into each of her words. After their two miles were up, they would stop near a group of Kosana's corps, and even though all of those warriors would be granted the opportunity to spar, Vaasa would be haughtily dismissed.

Vaasa knew it was a dig. Knew her body was strong enough to endure more than a run. That she could probably keep up with at least some of the maneuvers and sparring these warriors engaged in.

But why prove anything?

If they wanted to see her as a spoiled, helpless heiress, that was their mistake to make. So she would smile sweetly at Kosana and trot off to the villa and not exchange a word with Reid. The only time the two of them spoke was when they were around others, which was often—salt lords, merchants, and advocates from their workers' guild. In front of them, she was the devoted wife and potential high consort. She'd do whatever it took to keep returning to the sodality day after day.

The second day she'd arrived, Amalie had said when they were alone, *You look terrified. He must have told you who Melisina is.*

She doesn't hate me?

You didn't kill him, that must count for something.

It seemed Amalie was privy to the entire story, so she was one of the only people Vaasa didn't have to lie to. The young witch taught her to summon tendrils of the void and wrap them around things. Melisina taught her how to dismiss the magic when it became unruly. Even Suma had joined their lessons. She'd swiftly learned the name of the two rebellious women who'd stolen Amalie's daybed: Mariana and Romana. Not sisters, but they should have been.

Each witch was different in how they used the raw magic granted to them by Veragi, but they could all generally do the same things. They all summoned tendrils of the power, could form entire shapes and walls made of glittering black. Vaasa had watched in wonder as Suma created a ring of magic around her, never smothering her own senses, but casting a barrier that only a fool would cross. Something about their shared looks made Vaasa wonder what they weren't revealing to her.

But the limits, the *dangers*, of the magic were clear: within that void, someone could easily lose their life. They could not manipulate anything outside of the magic—which, apparently, could be done by the witches of Imros in Sigguth, who could manipulate metal the same way the witches of Una had manipulated light. It explained why their weapons were so precise, their boats so well crafted. The witches of Zohar in Irhu could move the tides. And there were healers in Wrultho. The more they taught her about the covens, the more she understood why magic was kept in the shadows: before Icruria's unification, wars between the six territories had decimated the magical population. Supposedly, even long before that, it was not the territories that had defined Icruria—it was the bloodlines that wielded magic. Ancient, cruel families ruled various estates along the coastline of the Settara. They had wiped each other from the face of the continent in their quest to own more land. It was a wicked, disastrous time, and now magic felt too precarious to share. Even separate covens did not typically work together or allow access to their histories. It was a scale that balanced on a razor blade; on one hand, it prevented the witches from consolidating their power, and on the other, it prevented them from fully understanding it.

I would like to someday unite them, the way the territories were united for the greater good, Amalie told her. Vaasa had never seen such a clear dream in the eyes of another—a worthwhile ambition. But almost all of the witches across the continent were in their sixth or seventh decade, sometimes far later, when they gained their magic. Suma believed it was the gods and goddesses punishing them. Melisina said it was an ambiguity even she could not understand. Magic only lived in one generation at a time.

Young witches, while powerful, were a tragedy.

One morning, when Vaasa went to sit down at her usual table and observe some of them quietly, Melisina put her hand up. "Don't. We have something to do."

"What are we doing?"

"Getting you a notebook."

"A notebook?"

Melisina walked to the door and gestured for Vaasa to follow. Amalie grinned like she knew something Vaasa didn't.

Melisina plunged down the stairs Vaasa had just walked up, and even though she wanted to curse Melisina for forcing her to use her sore muscles, they felt more flexible after the effort. On the main floor of the Sodality of Setar, they walked down a string of hallways and through the center courtyard. Acolytes in purple robes swished around them to their morning classes, and the routine was familiar—just as she had done in Dihrah. For a moment, she missed the small purpose she felt in a routine schedule such as that.

To learn for learning's sake was a privilege.

Melisina led her into a large room filled with parchments—papers and notebooks and books lined every shelf.

"Pick one you like," Melisina said. "But do not open them. You must choose from the cover alone."

The cover alone?

Vaasa crept forward and plucked a random notebook from the shelf, a gray cover with a sturdy spine and what appeared to be plenty of paper within. Turning to Melisina once again, she was met with a scowl.

"What?" Vaasa asked.

"Pick one you love," the woman said. "For if you don't love it, it will mean nothing to you, and it must mean something to you."

"Do notebooks have to mean something to us?"

"They do, otherwise we will not use them. I will be back in an hour."

Vaasa gaped. An hour? Who would need so much time? But Melisina grinned, just like Amalie had, and disappeared behind the door.

As she glanced around, she wondered if these women even used the notebooks they loved.

There were hundreds.

But she did exactly as Melisina instructed—she did not open them. Some were plain with only color to adorn, and others were so gilded Vaasa wanted to scrunch her nose. None particularly spoke to her, though, so she just kept moving down the shelf.

When Melisina returned exactly an hour later, she crossed her arms and laughed.

Vaasa sat on the floor in the center of the room with a disorganized spread of notebooks, her nose pressed against the cover of one while another sat heavy in her hand.

"I tasked you to find *one*," Melisina said.

"Well, I found twelve, and I would like to take them all," Vaasa declared.

Laughter flooded the room, and Vaasa curled her legs to her chest, her back against one of the stacks as Melisina slid into the spot next to her. "One. Only pick one."

One? She pouted as she looked at her options and then met the amber of Melisina's eyes. With that particular hue, she really should have known Reid and Melisina were related. "How do I pick?"

Shrugging, Melisina said, "Follow your intuition."

Vaasa didn't know much about her intuition anymore. Her whole life she'd depended on it to guide her. It had been the driving force behind the negotiations she'd translated, the tabletop battlefields that happened behind closed doors in her father's fortress. While his military men had might, and many of them could outmaneuver forces and weapons, she had known how to get in people's heads. How to communicate with them and win their trust. She'd done so by listening to that voice in her mind that told her what people wanted and how to give it to them.

Everything she had done, all she had borne witness to, was so she could remain in her father's good graces. To ensure that she never ended up exactly where she was now—married. Out of control. A threat to her brother. If she proved herself more useful at his side than as a bargaining chip, she thought Dominik would never have to hunt her down.

"I can't," she admitted.

"And why is that?"

Magic seemed to rattle in her bones. Instead of answering, she looked down at her feet.

But Melisina did not waver. She didn't answer for her and did not move on. She sat silently and waited. Vaasa realized she expected an answer, and she wasn't likely to let her off without one.

"I can't tell the difference between the magic and my intuition," she whispered.

"Hmm." Melisina shifted her weight. "That is because there is no difference. The magic is your intuition, and you will never learn to wield it if you do not learn to listen to it."

Those words settled somewhere in Vaasa, twisted with the power in her veins. Lifted something in her chest.

"Now, look and listen."

Peering down at the books, Vaasa took a deep breath. As she gazed upon the spectrum of colors, she pressed down into herself, down to where the magic reigned. Like an entity all on its own, she could feel its misty presence coating her insides. As if she could touch it. Smell it.

It roared to life and Vaasa retracted from herself, doing what she always did—focusing on something outside of her to take the attention away.

Melisina tsked. "You must face this discomfort someday. Why not today?"

Her first instinct was to take a notebook and throw it across the room. Her second was to run without a look back.

But she gazed at the notebooks once more, and some little voice inside of her told her to do something tremendously stupid: try.

So she did.

Nothing else had worked thus far.

She felt it again in her gut, the way the magic roared to life and slithered in her veins, writhing and dark and furious. She wanted to smother it. It looked and felt like hatred. Like the pounding pulse of horror.

Tears pricked at her eyes and she shook her head, using the back of her hand to wipe away a stray tear.

"Good," Melisina said. "Perhaps it's time you feel whatever that emotion is."

Was that what Vaasa had been doing? Hiding from her emotions and calling it survival?

Melisina was right, though—someday she would have to face it, and she would rather do so surrounded by parchment than by people. So she reached for it. She tried to listen.

Her fingers brushed the books, and she felt the texture of each one. Rough. Soft. Some like suede, some like gravel. Eyes running over the menagerie of colors, she almost stopped on an orange one, but her hand kept going.

Her touch landed upon a smooth leather cover that seemed to spark the magic. Beneath her hand was a pitch-black notebook with purple leafed etchings along the borders in whorls and curved lines and swirls carved down the sturdy spine. She'd plucked it off the furthest shelf about three rows down. It was nothing particularly special, except that it was. When she held it in her hands, she could feel the . . . rightness of it. At first she couldn't hear it, but the longer she sat with the slithering tangles in her gut, the more she heard the soft hum of the snake. Like it whispered its approval.

"This one," Vaasa asserted.

Melisina grinned. "Open it."

Flipping the cover, she found two words written at the bottom of the first page in unfamiliar handwriting.

It was her name.

Vaasa squeezed the notebook between her fingers. Melisina must have placed the notebook on the shelf, and of the hundreds in this room, Vaasa had somehow managed to find it.

"Weapons that are misunderstood cannot be used," Melisina said. "So that is where we will begin. This is hard work, listening to our intuition and not allowing our mind to make a mess of our heart."

"Did you know I would pick this one?"

"No," Melisina admitted. She stood up with effortless grace and extended Vaasa a hand. "But now that you have it, it's time to use it."

She didn't know if that was a justification in Melisina's eyes, or simply an explanation. It was the first time in two weeks that she didn't feel like laying waste to every person in a room. The first time her chest let go, and her throat opened for a full breath.

Honesty could be had in this room, and she reveled in it.

That day, she stayed long past nightfall.

To master Veragi magic often meant sitting uncomfortably, either with the entire coven or just with Melisina. Often, it was Amalie who sat beside her, quiet and entangled in her own work, but always there. She had grown slowly used to the woman's presence. Had even begun to take comfort in it. But in the wake of that comfort, worry haunted her. Images of Dominik destroying the sodality were sometimes so overwhelming Vaasa could hardly breathe. She didn't particularly like the introspective exercises—especially when it forced her to reflect upon the choices she'd made that night with Reid. Her veiled threats and how she let the worst parts of herself escalate a situation perhaps beyond mending. How when she felt hurt, she struck.

It was the first time she acknowledged how ashamed she was.

That feeling particularly weighed on her as she ran her two miles down the shoreline of the Settara and once again Kosana refused to speak to her. The blond warrior had not dared allow more than one sentence a day to pass between them.

Not that Vaasa truly minded or didn't find her coldness justified.

When this was over, she would steal away to the veranda and spend the little time she had to herself reading a book written in Zataarian. If she didn't use the language, she would lose it.

Around the bend of the shoreline, they came upon the same circle of warriors who always trained together at this time. Fluid movements and graceful leaps caught Vaasa's eye, and she pictured them as mountain cats. As a child, she'd been warned to avoid the stealthy creature that slunk through the mountains and into the gardens when night fell upon Mekës. The only time Vaasa ever got close enough to one to feel the softness of its thick, snow-colored fur was when a mountain cat broke into their coop and demolished a group of chickens. One of the guards sent an arrow directly through its head, and her father had made a pelt from the furs. He'd forced her and Dominik to watch as he skinned the extraordinarily thin creature.

This is the natural way of things, he said. *The strong outlive the weak.*

The warriors in front of her did not use arrows, but their knives were sharp enough to cut. Plenty of them threw their blades with greater precision than a bow.

Kosana made off to go spar with the circle and shouted over her shoulder, "Go run another two."

"Teach me something that matters," Vaasa shot back, the image of the lifeless mountain cat haunting her and chasing away her common sense. "I think I've mastered *run*."

Members of their group went rigid, and some averted their eyes entirely. One, a raven-haired warrior who'd just forced someone into surrender, stifled a chuckle when she stood up from the ground and wiped the dirt off her clothing.

Kosana narrowed her eyes.

"We're next," the commander announced to the group. Her blue eyes dragged over Vaasa and the murderous curl of her mouth set off warning bells.

The circle of warriors backed up a few inches to make room, and Kosana prowled into the center as if the entire thing was a show. Vaasa assumed it was, one where she would lose and look as weak as Kosana had made her out to be.

Still, the only thing worse than getting her ass kicked would be to refuse the offer.

So Vaasa stepped forward on tentative, tired feet and took a long, deep breath.

The raven-haired woman gave a low warning to Kosana, but the commander waved her off. So the warrior handed Vaasa a blade, and then began to strap one to her bare forearm. Vaasa furrowed her brow at it, having never utilized a sheath this way. Kosana silently slung a similar sheath around her own forearm and tightened the leather straps. The smallest of blades gleamed in the morning sun as the warrior rolled her shoulders and picked up her second knife. "First to force the other into surrender wins. Signal by tapping twice," the raven-haired woman told her. When Vaasa met the woman's hooded brown eyes, they appeared wary, as though she was concerned about what was going to happen but had no intention of saying a word.

Vaasa stepped forward, the unfamiliar pommel of the short knife pressed in her palm, the straps on her forearm itching a little.

Kosana crouched into a fighter's stance, and without so much as a warning, pounced.

Vaasa spun to dodge the attack, barely passing the commander. Kosana was quicker than the other two Vaasa had watched, moved with more agility and intention than anyone Vaasa had known, and the thought kick-started her body into action.

Heart pounding, Vaasa avoided most of Kosana's advances, but could never once get the lead on her. Dust flew around them, and it bit at Vaasa's eyes. Her muscles strained as she rolled over her own head and sprang to her feet, sliding into a crouch and then dodging again.

"I knew he underestimated you," Kosana spat as they circled.

"He learned that lesson first, though," Vaasa said with far more audacity than she truly possessed.

That murderous glint in Kosana's eyes returned. Would Kosana really hurt her?

It'd be one way to get rid of her.

Vaasa knew she had something to atone for with this woman. Knew that when Kosana had found Reid, it sealed their fate. The anger and resentment flooded the warrior's eyes, and the next time Kosana pounced, Vaasa didn't escape so quickly. Kosana's knee dug into Vaasa's stomach and she grunted. She didn't have the skill, or the energy, left to do much against the mighty woman. Though she had always been able to at least hold her own, Kosana outmatched her in all the ways that mattered.

It hit her then what she lacked: endurance.

Kosana would survive her any day.

This is the natural way of things. The strong outlive the weak.

Vicious pride roared to life and Vaasa threw herself at the warrior.

Flying through the air, Vaasa slammed into the ground with a harsh bite of her lip and Kosana dragged her blade in a short burst along Vaasa's upper chest. Vaasa didn't even see Kosana's movements. Her stomach coiled and the magic burst to life in her gut. Vaasa tensed and spun, maneuvering her legs into a tangle with Kosana's enough to gain leverage. The two women scratched at each other as they tumbled. Kosana pressed her knife down the inside of Vaasa's arm, and panic seared at the feel of her skin splitting.

"Surrender," Kosana commanded.

Vaasa's response was to spin them and drag her own blade down Kosana's thigh. The warrior hissed with her anger and slammed the pommel of her blade into Vaasa's cheek, *hard*. Color burst behind Vaasa's eyes and she cried out, losing any leverage she had.

Kosana swung herself up and on top of Vaasa, knife moving, and Vaasa caught the woman's wrist. With a twist, she forced her to release the blade and it fell to the ground near them.

Confidence bloomed in Vaasa and—

Kosana twisted her other arm in a swift, admittedly graceful motion, and before Vaasa could understand what happened, the tiny blade it contained was suddenly at Vaasa's jugular.

Vaasa slammed the ground twice in defeat.

But Kosana pressed her blade harder and spat, "This is for his wedding night," before slicing a shallow nick beneath Vaasa's chin.

Pain spiked down her throat, and Vaasa choked on her own fear, the unintentional, visceral response to a knife so close to her lifeline.

Just then, the commander was torn from her place by the raven-haired warrior, curses flying through the air. "She conceded!" the woman yelled when Kosana fought back.

The nasty threat of losing control stung against Vaasa's fingertips and she could no longer focus on Kosana. Slipping. The magic was slipping. All she knew was the power, the way it reared inside of her and threatened to explode. Darkness flooded down her arms and fingertips, the snake suddenly growing in size and pushing against her lungs. It took every ounce of strength Vaasa had to bite it back. To keep it contained within herself. It crawled into her throat, and she didn't know what it would do. Didn't know if she could control it.

"Whatever wound you inflict upon him, *I will give you one to match*!" Kosana bellowed, as two more of her corps slung arms around their commander.

Vaasa's breath came in pants, slipping through parted lips as tears stung her eyes.

Fight back, fight back, fight back.

She only nodded.

Kosana spat into the dirt next to Vaasa and dropped the blade, wiping off the dust from her leggings and shirt; she threatened something unintelligible at the warriors who tried to approach her.

Vaasa rolled to keep her hands hidden. The people around her probably thought she was weak, probably thought her a sniveling coward, but Vaasa forced breaths the way Melisina had taught her. She willed the magic down her wrists and to swirl in patterns around her fingertips. To listen instead of detonating.

Then she willed it to snap back inside of her, and the threat extinguished.

Vaasa choked out a sob.

Someone tried to touch her, to help her, and she cursed at them in Asteryan. Perhaps it was the first moment they realized she hadn't been speaking her native language since she arrived. That she knew theirs well enough to understand each word they said, to edit her own output—Every. Single. Day.

The blood from her neck, chest, and arm trickled in slow streams. Not enough to do any real damage. Even her cheek hadn't shattered, which Vaasa assumed was a calculated angle by the commander. If Kosana had wanted to, she could have made it far worse. And if Vaasa sat curled in this dirt any longer, the cuts might get infected.

She hauled herself up from the ground, limbs shaking, and watched as the raven-haired warrior forced Kosana to walk away. She tore the leather sheath off her wrist and threw it in the dirt.

Vaasa, in all her pride and anger, lifted her bleeding chin and met the eyes of each person in the circle.

Silently, she turned on her heel and limped back to the villa. Reid had already left for the day, and Vaasa thanked each of Icruria's gods for the reprieve as she slid to the floor of the shower and burned.

She let the wave of magic shake the stone floor and turn the water black.

Melisina Le Torneau sprang to her feet at the sight of Vaasa walking in the door.

Black robes swishing, she sprinted across the mosaic floor. "Dear girl, what has happened to you?"

Vaasa's face was swollen and had already begun to shadow over with the impending bruise of Kosana's bone pommel against her cheekbone. Her lip was split. The three wounds she'd sustained stopped bleeding in the shower, and in a few days, they would scab over. There were no broken bones, no fractures, not even a sprain.

All of this would disappear.

"Nothing," Vaasa said, voice low as she slid past Melisina and took a seat at the table closest to the bookshelf.

Amalie stood slowly, flanked by Suma, Mariana, and Romana.

Of course they were all here this morning. She'd considered not coming at all, but each day she wasted was another she'd have to spend married to Reid of Mirch.

Melisina didn't move. Standing at least twenty feet from Vaasa, she slowly turned. "Does he know this happened?"

"Your son?" Vaasa asked, pointedly raising her eyes but being careful not to lift her chin and aggravate the wound.

"Yes, my *son*," Melisina snapped as she closed their distance and began to inspect Vaasa's bruised face. At that moment, all five women bent over her like pigeons over breadcrumbs. Vaasa shooed them away with a few waves of her hands, forcing the women to give her space.

Too close, they were too close.

Eyes bulging at the cut beneath Vaasa's chin, Amalie's voice dropped. "Who did this to you?"

"I almost killed them," Vaasa said instead of answering the question. She looked at her hands, which showed no trace of mist any longer. "I almost lost control of this magic and obliterated an entire circle of people."

Melisina's lips tightened and not a soul in the room spoke.

"Is it always going to be like that?" Vaasa asked flatly.

Apparently Melisina had seen enough of Vaasa's wounds, because she rose to her full height. "No."

"All it does is *build*. All day it builds."

"I know."

Vaasa's hand slammed against the table. "*How do I get rid of it?*"

Pity covered each of their faces, so raw and full of familiarity that it made Vaasa's stomach churn.

"You do not," Melisina said.

"I want you to cut it from me!" Vaasa stood with her anger and urgency, her hands wrapping to her stomach, where she pictured the coiled serpent. Over the manipulative, evil, easy-to-anger void that would strangle her insides and anyone who came too close. Nails digging into her stomach, she wished she could reach inside and smother the force. Strangle it. Eviscerate it with a blade. No part of her felt like her own—her body had been stolen by this thing she had never asked for.

Just like her future. Her safety. All because of things she had *never asked for*.

Tears stung her eyes, her voice cracking. "I don't want this."

She didn't know if she was only talking about the magic now. It could be the chokehold of her brother. Of a life fated to the whims of a throne that she neither wanted nor loved. A marriage no one had asked her consent or desire for.

Romana stepped forward, but Vaasa launched back and almost slammed into the bookshelf. Once again, she couldn't maintain control, couldn't calm the slithering force and push it down. Icy fear pulsed at the idea of what this magic would do. "Don't." She tried to push past the anger and fear in her chest, but the snake would not rest. It hissed and consumed her, crawling up her throat and biting her tongue.

She wouldn't let it out again. She would rather it kill her than touch any of them.

Maybe she was better off dead anyway.

As if it heard her and wanted to grant such a wish, the magic strangled Vaasa's airway and she gasped, hands on her throat and eyes bulging. She couldn't breathe, couldn't breathe, couldn't breathe—

"It is water," Melisina said as she stepped forward, mist bleeding from her hands and swirling up her arms. "Whatever form the magic takes right now, picture it as water. It is trickling and flowing, slipping back down to its home."

"I . . . can't," Vaasa said, choking, hot tears welling in her eyes.

"You can," Mariana insisted, stepping forward, too. The rest of the coven flanked her.

As if they trusted her.

As if they believed in her.

"Try," Melisina demanded. "Please try."

As if they wanted her to live.

Water. Vaasa thought of rivers and seas, pushed back against the snake that wanted to harm. Wanted to bite and coil and suffocate. That wanted violence so tremendously it was willing to take her when there were no other options.

Water.

Vaasa thought of the Settara, of its glittering turquoise depths and the color it looked under moonlight. How the waves lapped at sand and churned beneath the sun.

Water.

The serpent in her throat cooled and melted, liquid on a hot day, and she felt the icy movement of it down her chest like a full glass into an empty stomach. Just as the Settara did at night, it swayed with her emotions. It lapped at her insides.

Vaasa gasped for air and tears burst from her eyes.

She fell to her knees and whimpered as the cut along her arm split open.

They could all see her on the ground, breaking. It was too much, to peel back each of these layers in front of any other soul. Like a child, she crawled beneath the table so she could hide, knees pressing to her chest as the world closed in on her. Sobs burst from the back of her throat. Humiliation tore at her insides.

Melisina was there in the pool of her robes, climbing under the table.

Vaasa tried to pull back, but Melisina softly begged her not to. "Just cry. Let it out."

Suddenly, all five witches were on their knees and crawling beneath the table, too. The sight of grace and understanding on their faces forced a miserable wail from the back of Vaasa's throat. She hid her head in her knees.

But she did as Melisina asked, and she wept. She wept until her eyes burned and she couldn't breathe through her nose. She wept for what her life should have been. For what her marriage should have been. She wept for the children she would never be safe to have, the home she could never grow old in, the family she could never return to.

Somewhere in the haze, Romana began to speak. "When my mother died, all I saw was flames, and they burned me from the inside out. I hated that part of me, the one that lit everything on fire—even the things I loved. Even the things I wanted. Especially those. But look."

She held out her hand, and upon the mosaic floor, her mist started to take shape. It folded in on itself and grew until there was an ever-so-small bear, edges trembling as it took a few steps and then disappeared.

Vaasa's breath caught.

Suma scooted closer, but she didn't try to touch Vaasa. "It came to me as nothing but long, sharp cramps. Now it is a hawk."

"Mine began as a cat," Amalie whispered, "that wouldn't retract its claws. But now, it is a fox."

"Mine was a bull, big and horned and angry," Mariana said. "But now it is a tiger that prowls."

"What do you see?" Melisina prodded.

How could she ever say it out loud? To cut open her chest and put her shame on display was the one thing she was incapable of.

These figures they spoke of, they were beautiful and strong. Hers was conniving and cruel.

But then Amalie whispered, "Just because this is all you have ever known, it does not mean it is all you will ever be."

Shaking, Vaasa lifted her eyes. Met the familiarity of Melisina's gaze, the calm severity of her sharp features. Then to Romana, to the wisdom carved in the brown of her irises; to Mariana, whose power didn't topple others over; Suma, with her few words that often meant more than everyone else's; and finally, to Amalie, who wore her strength quietly, cloaked in grace and compassion.

They had each mastered what they first saw in themselves. And when she gazed upon them, all she found was how they could choose who they wanted to be.

She wanted that. To choose.

"It is a snake," Vaasa confessed through her tears. "I see a snake."

She was no chameleon. She had become exactly what her father had, and it served as no surprise that what she saw in herself was exactly what others had seen in him. "That is what people called my father," she whispered. "The Serpent of Asterya. And I do not believe my brother is the only one who inherited his cruelty."

Suma shook her head. "You can inherit someone's eyes, or their hair or their nose, but you cannot inherit their faults. You learn them. Which means you can unlearn them, too."

Melisina placed a hand upon her shoulder, and Vaasa latched on to the warmth. Leaned into it. "You call it anger, you call it fear, but it is none of those things. What lies inside of you is pain. The kind that burns worlds to the ground."

Pain.

It speared through her, and she choked again, the anger peeling back in bloody red to show the deepest feeling of blue. The inescapable coldness racked her like she'd been buried in ice.

The magic in Vaasa's stomach hissed, once again a snake. But this time quietly, like it wanted to be heard, like it was begging her to listen.

And when she did, she could hear what her own self was trying to say.

They'd told her from the day Dominik was born that she was second. That her life was worth less than his. That the only way she could survive was if she behaved, if she was useful.

And in the end, no one had protected her from him.

The anger and fear fell away.

And Melisina was right—all Vaasa had left was the pain.

But she didn't know how to get rid of it. How to conquer the emptiness and the anger.

Exhaustion weighed down upon her shoulders, bending them with its force. "It's not going away," she repeated.

Melisina leaned back on her knees, but this time she did not add any further truths or explanations. Silence threaded the air of the Sodality of Setar, and in it, tears began to stream softly down Vaasa's cheeks.

Beneath this table was the safest she had felt in months.

"Teach me," she whispered as she swatted the liquid falling from her eyes, forcing herself to take a deep breath. "Please, will you teach me?"

And for the first time, it wasn't because it was the only way to escape.

It was because it was the only way to have the choice.

Amalie smiled like the sun, and Mariana laughed like it was a foolish question. Voice like a wind chime, Amalie said, "You are not alone, and you never will be again."

At those words, Mariana started to stand, and a small thud reverberated under the table. "Ow," she said, rubbing her head.

Romana roared with laughter, and then Mariana did, too.

Amalie giggled and Vaasa couldn't fight the grin that grew upon her own lips.

Careful to avoid the table, Melisina got to her feet, dusting off her robes and extending Vaasa a hand.

It all felt like too much, their affection. She'd done nothing to earn it.

But she took Melisina's outstretched hand anyway.

"Today, you will learn about grounding. About where in the world you can plant your feet firmly and come back to yourself, no matter how out of control you feel."

CHAPTER 9

When Vaasa arrived back at the villa alone, she crawled into the bed and immediately fell asleep, despite the sunlight that filtered through the windows. She didn't know the last time she'd slept in the middle of the day.

Curled on her side, she wasn't drawn from her slumber until the door creaked open. Reid's heavy footsteps padded across the floor. Their harsh words and silent mornings pulsed between her eyes in a headache. Vaasa rolled and watched as Reid shuffled through his dresser, his accent floating between them when he said, "Oh, now you want the bed."

She turned and let her hair slide over her face before he could see her, hoping he would just think her asleep and leave.

He didn't.

Instead, she heard his purposefully quieter footsteps on the wooden floor as he approached the bed, fingers carefully adjusting the blankets so she would be warm.

She kept her eyes closed.

He paused then, gingerly sweeping a piece of her hair back from her face. And she could feel his eyes inspecting her.

"Vaasa." He touched her shoulder to wake her, urgency riding his tone. "Wake up."

She knew he'd seen the bruises.

"Wake up," he said again, shaking her shoulder.

It made her wince.

Silence.

Then, low and dark, Reid demanded, "What happened?"

Vaasa pulled the blanket higher and hid her bruised face, wincing at the cut beneath her jaw. The ones along her arm and chest didn't hurt nearly as bad as that one. "Training accident. It'll clear up in a few days."

"That is no accident."

"It was."

Suddenly, his hand was on her shoulder, and he tugged the blankets back.

Vaasa cried out at the stretch of skin as he stumbled, eyes going wide at the bandages on her chest and arm that Romana had carefully placed. "What the *fuck* happened?"

"Leave it alone, Reid," she snapped at him, pulling the blankets back. Luckily, the bandages covered up most of the damage. They'd left the cut under her jaw exposed, knowing a bandage would only prevent her from moving. But if Reid saw that wound, the twin to the one she'd given him, he'd know damn well who had cut her.

"Like hell." Suddenly he was looming above her, both knees dipping into the bed as he invaded her space. "Sit up."

"Stop."

"Sit up."

Sighing in frustration, Vaasa sucked down air before lifting on the exhale. Her first instinct told her to tuck her chin, to keep that wound to herself for as long as she could manage it. The others she had been complicit in.

All of them she deserved.

His eyes went wide, dipping to her split lip and the black and blue along her cheekbone.

Reid scooted closer, his massive body shadowing out all the early evening sun. Amber and salt wafted under her nose and Vaasa tucked her chin a little more, letting her hair fall in her face. "I can handle myself."

"I'm well aware of that," Reid said as he continued to inspect her. His eyes locked on the bandage wrapped around her arm and then trailed past her shoulder to the space below her collarbone. Tentative hands reached forward, and Vaasa winced as he peeled back the gauze on her chest and exposed the smooth red slice.

His hand froze. "Tell me who did this to you."

He knew this wasn't an accident—she'd been fooling herself to think she could convince him otherwise. The slices were every bit as intentional as the wound on her cheek.

But that didn't mean she hadn't earned them.

"Mistakes happen during training," Vaasa said, shooing his hands away as she scooted back. "Just leave it alone. It'll heal."

"Look at me."

She didn't.

"*Look* at me."

She raised her eyes, and Reid scanned her face. He was too close for it ever to be acceptable, but something about the intensity of his gaze made her keep that thought to herself. And then, his gaze dropped a little. He extended a hand forward and brushed back the hair at her neck, his fingers light on her jawline as he tried to get a better look at the bruising on her cheek, but then his eyes flicked down—

He gritted his teeth.

He'd seen the cut beneath her jaw.

"Reid—"

Shooting up from the bed, he burst through the door.

"Reid!" Vaasa yelled as she winced and forced herself up. "Where are you going?"

"Kosana!" Reid bellowed out for his commander as he slammed down the breezeway. Everything in Vaasa's stomach dropped.

For Kosana's safety, she hoped the commander had chosen to be somewhere else this afternoon.

Vaasa tugged on boots and followed him through the breezeway into the main part of the house, cursing under her breath at the effort. Had she not done enough today? Every muscle ached, the cuts throbbing right along with her swollen cheek.

Reid barreled into the back gardens and Vaasa called for him, her voice coming out more like a choke when she launched herself onto the stone pathway leading to the Settara. He turned, anger and panic swirling on his face and watched as she struggled to catch up.

"Don't!" Vaasa exclaimed. "You'll only make it worse."

"How could it be worse than this?"

"I could have killed them. We were in one of those training rings, and I almost lost control of the mag—"

"This happened in a trial combat?"

Vaasa paused. "Yes."

"Did you concede?"

Breath caught in her throat. "No. I pushed her. I—"

"You're lying."

"I'm not."

Stalking forward and meeting her gaze, Reid firmly stated, "If you had killed a single soul, the blood would have been on her hands."

"Reid—"

He spotted Kosana at the same time Vaasa did, down next to the lake with a group of her corps. He didn't even bother to use a regular path. Less like a mountain cat and more like an angry bear, he leapt over the wall and trudged through the yellow grass, smashing wildflowers under his feet.

Vaasa cursed and darted down the pathway he created. Dry grass rubbed at her leggings and foxtails stuck to the fabric, but the downhill momentum propelled her forward, so her thigh muscles didn't have to. Her calves, however, screamed.

Almost as loud as the indiscernible raised voices that echoed below.

At the bottom of the hill, Vaasa stumbled onto the sand and adrenaline spiked as she watched Reid pounce on and drag Kosana to the ground. The two tumbled, and when Vaasa finally arrived, Kosana yelped, pinned beneath Reid and effectively trapped. It had taken Reid mere moments. Vaasa had never heard such a sound come out of Kosana.

"You were *explicitly* instructed not to put her in a fucking combat ring," Reid snarled as he pushed Kosana into the sand. What? As Vaasa looked around, the six or seven members of Reid's corps avoided her gaze. Vaasa had been beneath Kosana's grip, so she knew the strength of that woman; if Reid held her so effortlessly, then the world's frightened assessment of him held truth.

"I know," Kosana admitted, dragging Vaasa's attention back to her and Reid.

"Did she concede?"

Kosana sucked down air and looked for a moment at Vaasa, who barely caught her breath. "Yes." Kosana squarely faced Reid. "I dealt one wound after."

"Which one?"

"The one on her neck."

Reid dug her into the sand harder. "Tell me why I shouldn't do to you *exactly* what you did to her."

"Reid, stop—" Vaasa tried.

"You should," Kosana said.

Vaasa snapped her lips shut and held her breath. He wouldn't do that, would he? She was nothing in comparison to Kosana, a small scratch mark in his life compared to the commander's presence.

Reid turned over his shoulder to peer at her, and Vaasa pleaded silently. His eyes locked on her black-and-blue cheek, the split of her lip, then dragged to the cut at her jaw.

"Don't," Vaasa begged.

But it was too late. Grabbing one of the three blades at his hip, he cut beneath Kosana's jawline in one shallow, two-inch drag.

The commander did not utter a single sound.

"Stand," Reid commanded as he released Kosana and straightened his back.

No one around them said a word. None of them moved to intervene. In the corner of the group was the raven-haired warrior, who gazed upon the scene as if this was exactly what she expected. Most mirrored her expression.

Vaasa didn't know what to feel—to be angry at either of them, or if she had a right to feel anything at all.

Kosana did as she was instructed, coming to her full height and forcing her eyes up to meet Reid's. Trickles of blood ran down her neck. The two held their stares and Reid said, "What is the punishment for a member of your corps who disrespects our trial combat rules?"

Kosana's body shook, but she refused to divert her gaze or escape his wrath. It took Vaasa a moment to realize it wasn't pride on Kosana's face, it was accountability. "Demotion," she said.

Vaasa's stomach dropped. Things between the two of them were about to get significantly worse.

"And what is the punishment for a member of your corps who harms your foreman or consort?"

Everyone froze—except Kosana. As if she had already considered this, she said, "Dismissal."

Reid's jaw tightened again, but he nodded through his visible upset. "So be it."

Vaasa lurched forward. "Reid—"

"Do not interfere," Kosana warned.

Vaasa balled her fists as she faced the commander. Magic roared to life, sensitive in her exhaustion, and grew on her hands and up her elbows. As the black mist swirled around Vaasa, everyone else took a step back.

"*You* should not interfere," Vaasa insisted.

Irritable. The snake felt irritable and easily flustered, like the smallest of nudges would set it off.

The realization that she was slipping into exactly the same position she'd been in earlier skittered across her mind. It would be easy to respond in anger, to let the magic make a mess of them all.

That wasn't what she wanted from this situation.

Vaasa beat down the serpent in her belly and thought of water once more. Churning and cool, following the rhythm of the tides. *Grounding*, Vaasa reminded herself. *Focus on what you feel around you—the way the wind sweeps across your skin. How the air smells dry in the back of your throat. Your toes in your boots.*

Cold water replaced the angry swirling of before.

The magic extinguished.

Kosana's eyes went wide as she took another step back and others in the group did, too.

"Do you see what you could have done?" Reid warned Kosana, stepping closer to Vaasa, something unfamiliar in his stature as he loomed next to her. "You put yourself and every person here in danger."

That was why he'd told Kosana not to put her in the training ring—he knew she couldn't control the magic.

That she was a liability.

Humiliation threaded through Vaasa. It wasn't Kosana's responsibility to manage her magic, or her inability to manage it herself. Vaasa had *asked* to be put in that fight. So she squared her shoulders through her soreness. "I started this, Reid. Don't punish her. Just assign someone else to teach me."

Reid turned to look at her, one thick brow raising.

Through it all, the loyalty that pulsed in Kosana's veins was something Vaasa recognized; it was the way the coven had looked at her today. She had no intention of smothering it. Besides, it was unwise to isolate his commander in the middle of an election.

She turned squarely to the warrior. The two locked eyes and Vaasa gazed over the hard set of Kosana's mouth. "I know we aren't even, but are we done here?"

Kosana let out a breath.

Reid rubbed at his jaw. "Vaasalisa—"

"I asked you a question, Kosana."

The commander dragged her tongue over her teeth, but Vaasa could have sworn a small spark of respect flittered across her face. "We're done here."

She wondered for a moment if Reid would undermine her. If this would be the moment he went back on the image he wanted them to display. She looked up at him and dared him to do so.

Reid turned to the crowd and observed their hard stares—to the six other warriors standing behind Kosana with a mix of wonder and fear in their observant looks.

"She is my wife," Reid said suddenly, and everyone at once seemed to turn to him. Still, his attention sat plainly upon Kosana, the cords of anger and friendship vibrating between them. As if he no longer spoke to her as a foreman, or anything but a friend. "That inevitability is not subject to your judgment or your approval. It is simply what she is."

Something cracked on Kosana's face. And for the second time, Vaasa questioned her understanding of the woman. It was not longing or grief there. Vaasa could only describe the downcast set of Kosana's eyes as guilt.

She didn't think she'd ever had a friend like Kosana.

"You walked away alive," Reid said as he returned to his previous stature and position, tone dropping to that of the foreman. "You should be grateful she has learned enough self-control to leash the magic. If you ever forget who we are, what this corps stands for again, I won't hesitate to remove you."

Kosana forced her ashamed eyes to meet his, her throat bobbing, but she nodded.

"Since you are taking the lead on this, Vaasalisa, please choose her replacement."

Once again, Vaasa froze. How was she to know who best to choose? All eyes fell on her as she turned to the small group, and Vaasa met the gaze of the raven-haired warrior. "You," Vaasa asserted, remembering how the woman had pulled Kosana off her. How she'd moved with more agility than just about anyone Vaasa had ever seen spar. If Vaasa learned to fight like that, she'd be better off.

Kosana's face twisted and she looked at Reid.

"Esoti," he said, and the warrior stepped forward. Anger still burned in his eyes, especially when he said to Kosana, "You intervened in my marriage, why shouldn't we intervene in yours?"

What? Oh *no.*

Esoti—presumably Kosana's wife—nodded at Reid sternly before turning her full attention to Vaasa. Meeting her eyes with the strength of mountains, the warrior nodded once more.

It was only a small sign of mutual respect, or perhaps it meant nothing at all, but Vaasa decided to take it that way. She nodded back.

"I will see you in a week's time, Consort. Until then, it is best you rest," the woman said before turning to Reid and Kosana. "Foreman, *Commander.*"

Vaasa wanted to hide as a few members of the small group stifled chuckles before turning to follow Vaasa's new teacher back down the beach.

Reid and Kosana exchanged quiet words before he cut her off and ended the discussion. Silently, the commander tried to hold her head up as she walked down the edge of the Settara.

Vaasa slumped forward a little, and then gazed around at their suddenly empty surroundings.

That wasn't a victory. She may have destroyed any ground she gained by choosing Kosana's wife to take her place. However would she navigate that?

Vaasa turned to gaze up the steep slopes of the treacherous hill. Of all the frustrations and thoughts in her head, the biggest one was walking back up. She'd have to climb it or walk all the way around.

Every inch of her hurt.

Letting out a frustrated breath, she started through the dry grass.

"Are we going to discuss your newfound control?" Reid asked from behind her.

"Your mother is a better teacher than Kosana," Vaasa said over her shoulder as she plunged into the wildflowers.

"Vaasalisa—"

"I am not like my brother," she said suddenly, turning back to face him. He stopped just short of the flowers, the breeze blowing through his hair and the anger draining from his face.

"I know," he said in the softest tone she'd yet heard from him. "I shouldn't have said—"

"You should have," she asserted. "You don't know me, not really. And I don't expect you to trust me. I am the eldest daughter of the most ruthless man on the continent. A man who is now dead, along with my mother. I wouldn't trust me, either."

Reid watched her closely for the moment she remained facing him, and it was as if for the first time he considered there might be more than anger inside of her.

"But I am not like my brother," she repeated.

Dominik had looked upon the world and decided it was his, and Vaasa knew nothing belonged to her at all.

She spun on her heel and trudged up the hill. Aching muscles forced her forward, if only to be done with the task and finally able to sleep. Her breath came in hot pants as she made it halfway, but she stumbled over her own feet and let out a small cry at the pain of using her hands to catch herself in the flowers. Something seared along the inside of her arm, and she knew she'd reopened the wound.

After everything today, a pathetic sadness burst forward in the form of stinging tears. They bit at her eyes, which she closed and wiped quickly. Would Reid see her like this? He couldn't. A strange and hypocritical grief overcame her, one she didn't believe she would ever put words to, and she didn't want him and all his prying tendencies to ask. She forced herself up and started forward again. With each step, she felt her energy drain further.

She was *not* like Dominik.

Suddenly, her feet lifted off the ground and she landed against a hard chest—*Reid's* hard chest—as he curled his arms beneath her legs and back. Without a word, he trudged up the hill. She started to fight him, but he whispered, "Will you just stop?"

Her muscles went slack, and she didn't know why the words mattered, but they did. She clung to him. He carried her all the way to the villa and didn't let go, maneuvering the door open and then waltzing through the breezeway as if she weighed nothing at all.

Once inside his bedroom, he set her down on the bed and made for the bathing chamber, leaving her to curl her legs up to her chest as she leaned against the headboard.

He appeared once more with supplies in his hands—bandages, gauze, a wound-cleaning solution, and ointment. The bed sank with his weight, and he reached for the sodden bandages beneath her shoulder.

As she recoiled, his hands paused in the air, as if asking permission.

She leaned forward. His touch was warm from the sun as he carefully peeled back the bandage on the inside of her arm. Wincing, her breath came in short bursts as he meticulously cleaned the wound. It stung with each press of his bloody rag, but soon enough he moved on to the cut beneath her collarbone. Watching him work was both fascinating and strange. It reeked of vulnerability, and she was too tired to pretend to be anything but.

Once that wound was clean, he said, "Lift your chin."

Vaasa bared her neck, and he inched forward and pressed the solution to the cut, causing Vaasa to grit her teeth. Reid paused again for a moment. Deliberating, perhaps.

Before he could speak, she whispered, "I once heard someone say that you eat human hearts."

A small snort escaped his lips, and when she opened her eyes, that smug amusement returned to his mouth. "That's vile."

"Despite what Asteryans choose to say, I believe you scare them."

He pressed the solution to her neck again and she closed her eyes once more, trying not to wince too overtly.

"Do I scare *you*?" he asked.

What a question. "There are many stories told about Icruria, about the Wolf of Mireh, but I can't say which are rooted in truth and which are rooted in fear."

He paused. Pressed the rag once more. "Perhaps you should find out for yourself."

"Maybe that's what I'm doing."

His touch disappeared and she didn't open her eyes, but she could hear him fumbling with a bandage. Without warning, he asked, "Do your allegiances lie with your brother, Vaasalisa?"

No. They could never. When she thought of Dominik, she thought of everything she had lost. Everything she would never have. A face flashed behind her eyes, soft-eyed and kind, the face of a soldier she'd managed to keep secret from even her father. Roman Katayev, with his brown eyes and easy smile, and how when he was near, the harshness of the world had disappeared for her. Just a soldier, but one who'd taught her to hold a knife and how to touch in the dark.

Until Dominik had found them together.

It didn't matter that she'd promised not to marry. It didn't matter that she swore she'd never see him again.

Roman was sent to his death on Asterya's northern border, the one it shared with Icruria.

Love is a useless thing, her father had said.

Dominik had watched. He had rejoiced in her heartbreak, because he knew that for her to love would always be a threat to him, and he reveled in her misery. The thought of Roman was a knife to her core, but she had learned to live with this grief years ago. Had buried it as deeply as she buried everything else.

"No, my allegiances do not lie with him," she whispered. A once-unutterable truth. "And if he ever knew I said that, he'd put my head on a pike."

Her neck was bared, her cheeks tearstained. What was one more piece of her soul?

"Look at me," he said again, just as he had earlier in the day.

Vaasa opened her eyes. Met the severity of his.

He let out a long breath. "I am not foolish enough to believe myself safe from your brother's ambitions. He wants to conquer the continent, and if it does not happen immediately, everything he does is a stepping-stone toward it."

Vaasa conceded with a nod.

"But are you one of those stepping-stones?" he asked.

Such a simple question. So direct. Reid held her with his gaze, and for the first time, he seemed more cunning than she'd ever given him credit for—as though he could drag truths out of people with the same ferocity that she could spin lies.

We are well matched, Wild One. Not until this moment had she believed him.

She wondered how Melisina had taught him goodness. How she had shown him to balance trust with his loyalty to himself and his country. She understood without a doubt why these people had elected him, and it hadn't been for brutality or cunning.

But there were things she could never show him. Truths she could never tell him about the dangers Dominik presented, or the opportunities Reid had gained because Dominik had been foolish enough to bargain Vaasa off into a marriage.

Reid wanted a headmanship, but what if he saw an opportunity for an empire? Who would he become then?

She would never give another person the opportunity to steal her chance at freedom.

So she told him the truths that mattered. "My brother believes this magic is a curse. He assumed I would die in a matter of months, and so I suspect he was hoping to wage war. If I die here, it will give him the leverage he needs to escalate further with Wrultho. To escalate with you directly. I do not believe Dominik's intentions are good, and I urge you not to bargain any longer with him."

Reid's brow furrowed, confusion tumbling once again over his hard features. "Your mother made this arrangement, Vaasalisa, not your brother. She spoke directly with my own mother. While I made the formal request of our councilors, it wasn't your brother's idea, or mine."

Vaasa's gut twisted and her throat closed. Her *mother* had chosen this? Had bargained for it, with Melisina?

Everything she thought she knew about her mother flipped in Vaasa's stomach. The cold, aloof woman who'd doted on Dominik and shunned Vaasa suddenly looked different in Vaasa's eyes. It wasn't so much cold as it was calculating.

Did her mother send her into this marriage to keep her safe, or to put her directly in harm's way?

"I don't understand," Vaasa whispered.

"When your mother died, Dominik made an obvious effort to sever our agreement. I refused his efforts at my mother's instructions."

She hadn't a clue what any of that truly meant, or if it meant anything at all. Maybe her mother was simply sick of her, or she thought it would be funny to watch her children hunt each other down. But Dominik assumed she would die, which was probably why he didn't waste his time arguing. He'd seen an opening and he'd taken it.

Reid leaned back, settling his hands in his lap. "Do you want his throne, Vaasalisa? Is that your ultimate goal?"

"No," she answered immediately.

"Then what do you want?"

She spoke six languages, had memorized and studied cultures to communicate with the ambassadors and visitors from surrounding nations. So she could twist words in their slang when they believed her facade of familiarity. Her father was a master of conquest—of making nations dependent on him in some way, and then turning around and burning them to the ground.

But she had never seen those nations, not as she had seen Icruria. Mireh. She had always longed to, and she thought if she just behaved long enough, she would.

And now she thought everything the witches said was true—it was possible to choose a different outcome. To pave the road to a life she crafted for herself.

"I want to live, Reid. I want to live long enough to see more of the world before Dominik erases all the color from it." Her body unfolded just a bit. She owed him more than that answer. More than only acknowledging what *she* wanted. "I never should have spoken to you the way I did. You have done more than enough. And I will never threaten Icruria. I will never do anything to harm you or Mireh. I will do whatever I can to get you elected, and in three years, I will go."

She meant what she said—if it was in her control, she would give him the three years she promised.

Lips pursed, he offered a strong nod. A nod that seemed to mean something more—something like trust. Reid of Mireh confused her, and yet he might have been the most transparent person she'd ever known.

"I know you're tired, too," she said. "But can I please have the bed tonight?"

It stung to feel as though she was begging, but she needed to sleep. She needed to know she wouldn't roll off in the middle of the night and reopen all of these wounds. And he'd offered his home to her, bargain or not.

She'd done an awful job of treating him well.

"Of course, Vaasalisa. Of course." He stood from the bed and padded toward the door, his hand landing on the handle. "I know this is my fault. I'm sorry I forced you into something you didn't want to do. I know I told you I wasn't going to do that."

Something in her chest squeezed at the sheer affability of those words, at the willingness to bear the burden of something he was truly only on the perimeter of. "Believe it or not," she said, "I did egg her on."

"Oh, I believe that."

She grinned a little.

He looked at the upturn of her lips for a second longer than was acceptable, but she didn't say anything. Not as he turned the handle and disappeared into the breezeway.

He returned less than a minute later with another blanket in his hands.

Vaasa's jaw dropped. "You had that the whole time?"

It earned her a small shrug as he set the blanket down on the couch and then went back to the door. "Can you eat?" he asked. "Do you feel well enough for that?"

"Yeah." She leaned back against the headboard, curling her legs to her chest again. "I could eat."

Hesitating, Reid dropped his hand from the door and leaned against it. She met his eyes, where the amusement was replaced by a calm that made her skin itch. "Your father underestimated the weapon he built. And through his cruelty, he forced you to play for yourself and yourself alone. But I will play for you, if you will play for me, too."

She stared at him silently. Who was this man standing before her now? The one who cleaned her wounds and had been willing to dismiss his oldest friend out of a respect for an honor she had never seen in another's actions?

He had proven himself arrogant yet steadfast. Proven himself heavy-handed yet gentle.

"There is much I don't know about you, isn't there?" she asked.

He shook his head. Opened the door. "I'll tell you anything you want to know. All you need to do is ask."

And then he disappeared into the breezeway to find them food, leaving her alone to contend with the discomfort of such transparency.

CHAPTER 10

It took about a week before Esoti gave Vaasa the okay to start running with her. They did not speak about Kosana, did not spar with others, but Esoti was kind and forthcoming. She told her about her childhood, about growing up here in Mireh, and how there was never a time in her life when she didn't want to join the corps.

Her father was a long-retired member, an extraordinary warrior, apparently.

On day one, she asked Esoti to show her how to use that sheath they all seemed to keep attached to their arms.

"It is a secret weapon," Esoti said with a glittering smile as she strapped on a practice sheath—one holding a blunt blade. "But mostly, it is simple. If you catch the blade, aim for the throat."

Vaasa had yet to catch the blade. She cut her fingers a few times, though, much to the warrior's chagrin.

In the three weeks that passed, she said little to Kosana and spent the majority of her time with the coven. They focused primarily on balance and grounding, though she had begun delving into the mythos surrounding Veragi and discerning truth from whispers. She learned more about the inheritance of magic; each coven was a little different, if their sources could be trusted. Veragi witches only passed their magic through the maternal line, but others passed their magic through both the maternal and paternal lines. Vaasa took particular interest in the eastern sodalities in Hazut and Wrultho. The one in Hazut was named after Umir, the god of peace, while the sodality in Wrultho was named after Unir, the goddess of war. Their respective consorts, Zuheia—the goddess of life and healing—and Zetyr—the god of bargains and souls—were whispered to be lovers.

Zuheia witches could heal miraculously, while Zetyr witches filtered a dark, deadly magic. She'd read about them in Dihrah. They summoned demon-like creatures and did incredible things—until they were wiped from Icruria altogether. Their magic depended on bargains with mortals, which made them cunning and maniacal, as it was only through those twisted bargains that the Zetyr could access their power. Ultimately, they were hunted and slaughtered for their transgressions. Shivers ran down her back every time they discussed the Zetyrs' mistakes. Something about them felt close to Vaasa, like she was inching on their fate. She, too, felt as though she'd made a bargain with Reid and would surely be killed for it.

Which was why, over and over, Vaasa asked the same question: *Can you tell me more about my mother?*

And each time, Melisina's answer was the same: *Focus on what you do know.*

Biting her tongue, Vaasa waited patiently.

Until one day, with tentative words, Melisina stood from the table and said, "Come with me."

The two women began climbing the stairs to the third floor. Black walls lined the space as they passed by the windows, light flooding onto the mosaic floors and bouncing off the ivy strung from the ceilings. Iron hooks held the many lanterns, though none of them were lit with the sun so bright. She'd learned they were powered by the witches of Una, sparks of light that grew only in darkness. It was the sole coven that the Veragi were close with, and they shared many of their secrets.

As they made it to the back of the third floor, Vaasa found a gallery of paintings from floor to ceiling, all mounted on the enormous wall. She'd often glanced at it, though she had yet to delve this far into the coven's vaulted room.

Women, flowers, landscapes, children, and animals adorned the matted canvases in different sizes and shapes. A few immediately caught Vaasa's eye for their use of color—every hue of the rainbow taking form to create something more lifelike than Vaasa had ever been able to put to paper. One was just swipes of gray and black, an animal Vaasa thought was only found in Zataar. An elephant.

"It's time you learn about your great-grandmother," Melisina said. "My mentor, and a founder of this very coven."

Hands falling strangely at her side, Vaasa did not speak for at least three breaths.

Did not blink.

"What?" she finally said.

"Her name was Freya."

That was the moment she noticed the signatures along the bottoms of each painting. They matched that name—Freya. Her great-grandmother? Her mother did not speak of their extended family, not ever.

Looking up, her throat tightened. "She . . . painted these?" For a moment, Vaasa wondered if she'd been the one who'd written her name in the notebook she'd chosen. She studied the small signature, a haunting anxiety growing within her.

What else could she not see coming?

Melisina nodded, gazing at each one with a smile. Nostalgia made a home in the lines of her face, but it didn't appear to be a painful one. Rather, it radiated a sense of calm. Peace. Like perhaps Melisina had lost something more significant than could ever be named, but grief could not snuff out the love anymore.

Yet there was something in Vaasa's bones that rattled. That reached. Once again, she gazed up at the gallery wall; her eyes couldn't settle on any painting in particular.

Until she saw something that stole the air from the room.

Glittering water of red and orange, the sun setting over the peak of a distant hill, drying grass and yellow wildflowers dotting the rock-covered slope. There, on the right side, was a weeping tree with falling white blooms.

It was the view from Reid's veranda.

There were at least seven paintings with that same tree—different seasons and times of day. One was a depiction of the tree at night, which glowed like its own form of moonlight on the reflection of the water.

Vaasa stepped forward and then spun to Melisina, mouth agape.

"The villa once belonged to Freya, and she passed it down to me. Now it belongs to my son," Melisina said.

"She lived here?"

"Freya fled Asterya at fifteen after her mother died, and she searched high and low for an explanation to the magic she had inherited. She found that explanation in my own grandmother. They started this coven, and both of them had their daughters together, here."

At first, Vaasa denied the idea altogether. She fought against it with the veracity of a warrior. Her own great-grandmother was one of the witches who founded the coven of Veragi? *No*, she thought as she took a step back. *No, that can't be.*

Melisina continued. "My own mother died while giving birth to me, and the magic passed down. I shouldn't have survived it, but I suppose Veragi was not ready to lose my bloodline. So Freya took me in and raised me as her own. Her daughter—your grandmother Esme—left Icruria for her ancestral home in Asterya. She gave birth to your mother there and never brought her back to Mireh."

Silvery hair and a wretchedly bitter face passed in Vaasa's memories. Vaasa had known her grandmother, a woman who had been married to one of the lords of Asterya, but hardly ever saw her. She died when Vaasa was barely ten, and she never visited the castle. Not after Vaasa's father had begun his conquests. If what Melisina said was true . . .

"My grandmother left Mireh? Why?"

A melancholy look flashed across Melisina's features. "Esme did not see the magic as a blessing—not in the way I do. Not in the way I hope you will someday. In her own words, she wanted to live her life normally for as long as she could, and she didn't see that as a possibility in Icruria. She wanted what she believed Freya had given up."

Vaasa got the sudden urge to sit down or at least lean up against something, but after gazing back at the paintings, she didn't think it possible to move. She thought back to what she could recall from her younger age, but it was fuzzy at best. She remembered her mother disappearing in grief after Esme died, remembered Ozik making excuses as to why the empress was often unavailable for dinner, the advisor always knowing where everyone in their family was. "My mother must not have known she would inherit the magic," she whispered. Why had she never thought of that before? That her own mother may have been just as shocked at the arrival of the magic? If Esme had shunned the Veragi altogether . . .

Her grandmother had stolen an entire existence from Vaasa and her mother. Had ripped this coven right from their hands.

But she supposed Esme felt that way about her own fate, too. About her own mother. Perhaps in Esme's eyes, Freya had chosen Icruria, chosen the magic and the coven, over her. It was as if the women in her family inherited more than magic—their line was fraught with resentment. Freya to Esme, Esme to Vaasa's own mother, and Vaasa's mother to her.

"I first heard from your mother two years ago," Melisina admitted. Reid's tidbit of information tumbled through Vaasa's mind—that her mother had sent her here. That Melisina had instructed him not to dissolve their marriage agreement.

"Is that why you insisted Reid keep our marriage agreement?" Vaasa finally asked. "Because my mother asked you to?"

Melisina pursed her lips. Nodded. "Esme never told your mother what would happen to her. Instead, she let her go off and become an empress of a nation, all the while knowing she would reach a stage in her life where the magic would appear. She let her have a daughter of her own and never once whispered an ounce of the truth."

The cruelty. The blatant *selfishness.* "My mother did no differently," Vaasa asserted, a bit of bitterness on her tongue.

"Vena spent a summer here," Melisina corrected, and the sound of her mother's name made Vaasa's chest hurt in such an unexpected way. "Just after we first made contact. Do you remember that?"

Vaasa thought back on the past few years, and . . . yes. Nodding, she distinctly remembered those few months when her mother had visited extended family up north. *To escape the cold for a while*, she'd told them. Ozik and her father had practically dragged Vena back by force, claiming the violence along the shared Icrurian and Asteryan border was too great to allow her to stay any longer in northern Asterya. Vena had been flighty and cold for those months after. Vaasa hadn't thought much of it—she was concerned with studying and a brown-haired guard five years her junior she only let in her bed for a few months and never let herself care for. Not after what had been done to the first soldier she'd loved. Instead, she had been deepening her understanding of the language of Zataar, where she wanted to go the moment she was able.

"Vena was not evil," Melisina explained. "She was . . . lost. And confused. Most Veragi witches don't inherit their propensity for magic until late in their lives. We are much better equipped to handle it then, the anger and impulsivity from youth having faded. Those who inherit this gift at a younger age are often killed by the force itself or led astray by some terrible influence looking to profit off what a young, powerful Veragi witch can do."

"Are we more powerful when we're young?" Vaasa asked.

Melisina shook her head. "It isn't the age that matters. It's the time you have with the magic to master it and help it take shape. Being only in your midtwenties, you will be extraordinary when you are older."

"But you . . . you've had your magic since birth?" Vaasa asked.

"She is the most powerful Veragi witch to have ever existed," a voice said from the side. Amalie moved from around the bookshelf then, arms crossed as she leaned against it, holding her books like she had just returned from one of her many classes. "You and I will be legends, too."

"I am frightening," Melisina confirmed, either reading the look on Vaasa's face or plain reading her mind. Settling her hand affectionately on Amalie's shoulder, Melisina looked at the beautiful girl and let out a breath. "But there are greedy people in this world, and magic is already a rare enough commodity, once threatened to be bought and sold among territories. I do not know what your father knew, or if he knew anything at all. I know with certainty that your mother spent years trying to trace her own ancestry back here. That summer, we began making plans for your betrothal to my son. She thought if you were in close proximity to us, you would be better prepared than she was when she eventually passed."

Why, after everything she'd taught and promised her, had she jumped to marriage instead of an ambassadorship? Her mother's coldness flashed behind Vaasa's eyes. Her absence. Her explosive nature and the way she could become so overwhelmed by her own emotions that she fell apart . . .

Had that always been the magic, then? Had she struggled in silence? Had she even known what it was when it first appeared?

Vaasa always thought her mother hated her life. Hated her husband and her foolish fortress. But what if her mother had been just another desperate victim of Asterya? A lost witch, as consumed as Vaasa had been just months ago?

To send Vaasa here must have cost her mother *something*.

The heaviness in Vaasa's chest grew at the horrifying thought of what she'd stumbled upon that night. "She lost control," Vaasa realized, eyes flicking between the softness of Amalie's face and the calm neutrality of Melisina's. "The void, it consumed her, didn't it?"

Melisina paused for a moment, but then sighed. "It is possible."

Far too many moving pieces shuffled in her head.

If her father had known . . . would he have protected her mother? Or would he have exploited her? *Had* he exploited her?

Would he have exploited Vaasa, too?

Of course he would have. He'd used her every day of his life, magic or not.

Which begged the question of what truly happened to them both. Had it been a flu that took her father, or a vengeful woman with the power of a goddess in her veins? Her father's sickness had looked real. He'd gone quickly, and no one questioned the cause. Poison? Perhaps he really was just sick. She didn't think Veragi magic could do that.

But what had her mother been through? So much so that she would bargain Vaasa into a marriage she had to have known would give her a claim to the Asteryan Empire?

Had that been her mother's goal?

Anger coursed through Vaasa. It stole her peace and replaced it with something vicious. Vaasa saw a clear option, one she swore to herself she would have taken—her mother should have told her the truth. Should have armed her for the life she would live. At least then, this all would have felt like a choice.

Perhaps she wouldn't have run from Reid that night at all. Maybe she would have left years ago. Married him willingly. Learned of the streak of gentleness under his skin and maybe even grown to love him. She could have lived happily, safely, here in Mireh.

The water in her gut transformed into a silvery fish that grew teeth, long and jagged, and she swore the magic would feast on her insides.

"I've had enough for today," Vaasa said coolly, lifting her chin and turning.

"Please don't go," Amalie said from behind her. "We can do something else, maybe read another book together?"

A deep longing burrowed into Vaasa, mirroring what she swore she saw in Amalie's eyes. She hated that part of herself, the one that wanted exactly what Amalie offered. The truth was that Vaasa didn't want to be alone, but she'd learned that being alone was the best way to keep everyone else safe. "I'm going," was all she managed.

A moment of silence treaded on the heels of her decision. Then Melisina followed her silently but didn't add another word. Amalie moved out of their way, though her doe eyes seemed to shutter with disappointment.

Vaasa didn't say goodbye to anyone in the room before she slammed into the Icrurian heat and loaded her horse. Not even bothering to enjoy the beauty of the Lower Garden at midday, she rode back to the villa.

The chosen home of her maternal ancestor.

The one that didn't belong to Vaasa at all.

She knew what Melisina would say. Knew that she held the answer in her hands: to acknowledge the pain and to take control of the cycle.

It was too much. This was all too much.

Anger took everything she had with it, and nothing else would sit comfortably in her hands.

Irritability picked at Vaasa as she sat upon the veranda and stared out at the landscape she'd seen in that painting. Glittering turquoise waters, yellow swaying grass, and that large tree at the top of the hill.

It all seemed to taunt her.

She did as Melisina taught her: sat quietly and erased her thoughts, only focusing on the feeling of the magic in her stomach. How it felt as it pulsed through her veins and along her skin. She thought of it like water, thought of it like air, thought of it like a damn hawk with gliding wings and a white belly.

No matter how hard she tried, she had yet to find a sense of calm.

Sometimes she felt violence—it became a jungle cat, scratching at her insides. Other times she felt panic—that was when the snake returned.

The worst was when she felt nothing at all.

But she did not explode. The mist didn't dance on her fingers or crawl across the stone veranda. It stayed put inside of her, fangs digging in softly as a constant reminder.

No amount of blankets or Icrurian heat seemed to ebb the shaking of her wrists and hands. Even in the very early evening, they were already sore from the magic and the clenching of her fists, much like how her jaw felt tight. She tried to release her shoulders from her neck—

Someone burst through the patio doors, and on instinct, Vaasa hid her notebook under her right leg.

"Vaasalisa," Reid said as he stormed out onto the veranda, looking overwhelmed when he found her. "We have company."

Her stomach dropped at the thought of any social interaction while her magic felt this reactive. But by the severe cut of Reid's mouth, she thought he may be just as distressed as her. Had she ever seen him so . . . frazzled? "Who is here?"

"Who isn't?" He raked a hand through his hair and began to pace. "The councilors."

"All of them?"

"The ones that matter. Galen. Kenen." His eyes shuttered just slightly. "Marc."

Galen of Irhu. Kenen of Sigguth. The two councilors reigned from the coastal territories to the west, Sigguth building the quick-as-wind ships that could navigate the Settara and Irhu holding one of the most notorious naval forces on the continent. Inextricably linked, these two territories depended upon each other principally. Both of these men were invariably important—their two votes could determine the outcome of this election—yet it was that last name that seemed to dig claws into Reid's skin.

Marc, the councilor from Mireh.

Each territory had its own election cycles and terms—in Mireh, a foreman served for five years, with a two-term limit, and only those elected in a headman term were eligible to run for the highest position in the land. Reid had bested the incumbent and stolen that man's opportunity to be headman. Marc, however, had served two full terms before becoming a councilor. He'd spent the last decade in Dihrah.

Something about the way Reid paced told Vaasa it wasn't just Marc's vote that mattered.

Perhaps it was his approval.

Immediately, Vaasa stood. Her mind raced at the discomfort in her stomach, but she pressed down upon the magic and squared her shoulders. This was what their deal had been built upon, and she'd be damned if she let what happened today interfere. A thousand questions flew through her mind, but Vaasa started with, "What does the visit entail? How much time do we need to account for?"

If she couldn't master the despair and anger, at least she could master this.

Reid kept pacing near the door. "The formal thing to do would be to host a dinner in Marc's honor at the High Temple, but he gave me *no fucking notice*, and there's no way I can pull something like that together in the matter of an hour."

Vaasa took a small breath. Considered. "Why the High Temple?"

"Historically, it is where the foreman has lived. I declined the housing."

Apparently, this villa meant something to everyone. "So that's why you have very few staff, only members of the corps, here in the villa?"

"Correct. The usual staff still lives and works at the High Temple, and it's reserved for special occasions or city-sanctioned events. Events like this one *would* have been, had he given me ample notice. Three councilors, Vaasa. *Three*."

Vaasa fought the small grin threatening to grow. No, she'd never seen him frazzled before, and she rather liked it. "You are the youngest foreman ever elected to Mireh. Surely a little political roughhousing is nothing new to you."

"That isn't what Marc cares for," he said, still pacing as he dragged his hand through his hair. "He was elected on authenticity. He will smell it out if there is any lying, any schmoozing—"

"Reid."

He stopped pacing and stared at her. Tendrils of his dark hair lifted with the breeze and in that moment, she saw through any facade of amusement he'd once worn.

Reid respected this man, and that made it all the worse.

"What would you like me to wear?"

Reid parted his lips, then ran his tongue over his teeth. "I . . . You aren't going to argue with me?"

Unfortunately, she couldn't blame him for that assumption. "Of course not, this is our deal." Though she did question the irony of his authenticity remark, given the nature of their relationship. She walked into his room and headed to the bathing chamber. There, she brushed her fingers through her short black hair and applied a few cosmetics, trying to brighten her tired eyes and bring color to her cheeks and lips. As she did so, she walked herself through her thoughts—she could balance this. She could push the magic down.

Reid leaned against the curtained doorframe, watching closely.

By the cautious furrow of his brow, she assumed he knew something about what she'd learned this afternoon.

Vaasa asked, "Normally, would the High Temple host a celebration similar to that of our wedding night? Large dinner, important merchants and members of your corps invited?"

He nodded, a small, disbelieving grin coming to his face. "Yes, but with fewer knives under pillows and wives who jump off the roof."

Vaasa snorted at his brazen humor, side-eying him as she finished applying the color to her lips. The wheels in her head kept turning. "The staff would have needed much longer to put something like that together. If we do, it will seem disorganized. Half-assed."

"I suspect that was his purpose, yes."

"So he's a difficult man?"

"Extraordinarily. His wife is the only friendly thing about him, though she's friendly enough for them both. He's a damned economic genius, though."

Vaasa nodded, leaning up against the counter. "Marc used to be foreman of Mireh. He grew up here, yes?"

"Yes."

"So he knows what would be expected of a foreman when their councilor shows up? That he should have given you proper notice?"

Fists clenching, Reid muttered, "Like I said, he's a difficult man."

This didn't seem like an intentional undermine. A surprise, sure, but not purposeful harm. If Marc had been born and raised in Mireh, had risen to power here and spent the past ten years of his life living in

Dihrah, perhaps he had a reason for showing up unannounced. "Have you considered he has no interest in a formal party?"

Reid's brows slammed together. "No, I hadn't considered that. This feels like a test."

"Self-important men give plenty of notice. They want a party in their name, and they want it to be big. The sort of thing you would stress over for days, because if they really didn't like you, that is when they would disapprove. When you had worked hard, and they could make a wreckage of your effort. That isn't what's happening here."

"What are you getting at?"

"*Authenticity*. What if you didn't host anything formal at the High Temple at all?"

Running his hand along his jaw, he said, "I'm listening."

"What if we took them all to see Mireh, to truly see the city Marc grew up in, and see how much it has thrived? Have dinner at Neil's restaurant on the Settara, where we can handle most of the conversation. Then we can dance in the Lower Garden, where it's too loud for either of us to say the wrong thing. With less pomp, you will seem more secure, and perhaps they will enjoy a return to their youth."

Reid's lips parted as he gaped at her. "That could work."

"I know." Vaasa lifted herself from the counter and breezed through the curtains back into the main room, the idea playing out in her head. She stopped when she noticed the clothing already laid out on the bed. She'd missed that on the way in.

Reid's formal attire with its sweeping purple and black fabric, which she'd seen back in Dihrah, came as no surprise. But the matching outfit sitting to the right was for her, and she tilted her head.

"What?" Reid asked.

"I don't know how to put it on."

Fighting a grin, he gestured toward the changing screen and said, "I'll guide you through it."

She almost protested, but his pacing had stopped, and he was coming back to himself. His humor. He'd need that to survive the evening, and she'd need to feed it to survive herself. With a sigh, she glided past the changing screen and held out one hand. "What's first?"

He started by tossing her a pair of skintight black pants much like what his corps wore during training. Then she layered on a black bustier that wrapped up to her neck, much like the shirt she'd worn her first night here. The hem fell just below her breasts. She couldn't lace up the back by herself. Turning and stepping out from the screen, she used one hand to hold up her hair and the other to raise the fabric, eyes meeting his.

Apparently, Reid had done this before, because he had the damn thing laced in under a minute.

Next was a sheer, glimmering purple piece of fabric she didn't know what the hell to do with.

"Come here," he insisted when she stepped out from the screen with a dumbfounded look on her face. He took the fabric from her hands and stepped far too close, wrapping it around her waist so the panel fell over one hip. Salt and amber filled her air, and she turned her face away, so he wasn't overwhelming. So she could think. With nimble fingers, he tied it off, chuckling as she looked down at the peculiar knot he tied.

"These boots," he said, holding out sturdy leather things that would go up over her knees.

Eyes taking in the thick material, she felt sweat bead on her legs already. "It's almost summer. In Mireh."

"I thought you weren't going to argue with me."

Begrudgingly, she grabbed the boots from his hands and sat on the bed to lace them up. As she did, he retreated into the bathing chamber to put on his own garb. Once he came out, she stood, faced him, and lifted her arms. "Good enough?"

Crossing the room, he plucked a set of gold threaded chains from a drawer and draped them over her head, attaching them nimbly just below her breasts and once again behind her back. Still too close, his arms were all the way around her until he finally backed up.

That dripping amusement—the in-control look she hated—made her want to take all of it off and shove both him and the councilors into the Settara for good measure. "Turn," he instructed, inspecting her thoroughly.

She raised a brow.

He wiggled a finger in a circular motion. Not even stress could crack this part of Reid's personality.

Muttering a curse, she did one single turn before placing her hand on her hip and locking eyes with him.

He smiled. "I have it on good authority that I fell ass-backward into the most striking consort in all of Icruria."

"Who's the good authority?" she asked.

"Me."

"Not good enough," she said, though a held-back laugh came out as a smile, and she took the compliment as an opportunity for pleasantness between them. "Though I don't believe you fell ass-backward into it. From what I remember, it was quite intentional."

She started out the door.

"Vaasalisa," he called. When she met his eyes, he took a breath and seemed to plead with her. "This is important. I don't know why, but I feel there's a purpose behind his visit. To show up unannounced is an intention in itself. If I don't get his vote, I don't see how I could get any others."

The undertone of his words settled between them, and a small part of her retreated. "Do you believe I would do something to harm your chances?"

"No," he asserted suddenly, stepping closer with worry carved into his expression and his drapes a bit askew. "My mother spoke with me about . . . today. And—wait, please don't be upset."

Swiftly, she corrected the scowl on her face she hadn't realized she'd let through.

"My point is that I didn't realize the connection you had to this city or to this home." Awkwardly, he shifted his weight. "She's worried about you. Are you all right?"

The force in her rumbled, but she swallowed and pushed the intrusive thoughts down again.

"Don't use my full name," she said as she reached out and adjusted his fabrics, focusing on the things she knew for certain, just as Melisina had told her to do the first time they met. "It makes us sound more familiar. At dinner, do not cede the head of the table, but do wait for Marc to begin eating first. Be sure I am seated at your left. After the Lower Garden, place him and his wife in the room normally reserved for the foreman, about an hour before it would be generally expected, and have no one disturb them. The other councilors should be honored, but peripheral."

He paused, eyes assessing her close work at his chest, and then asked, "Why?"

Vaasa stood up straight, letting her hands fall to her sides. "Because you will make Marc feel honored without making him feel powerful. Because you eat with your right hand, and I cannot tap your wrist below the table to tell you to be quiet if it's holding a fork. And you will end the evening early because it gives them all an hour they didn't expect, and a powerful man who has drunk wine all night and watched strangers dance with his wife will want her in his bed. And men who get properly laid are much more agreeable."

Reid's lips parted again as he gazed at her, and a small bit of pride bloomed in her at finally rendering him speechless.

"Don't talk to me about what happened today, and we'll be fine," she asserted, lifting her chin as she stepped away without bothering to wait for his reaction. This wasn't negotiable.

"Vaasa," he said, utilizing that little nickname like somehow it had always belonged to him. "Thank you."

Was this what the two of them were like when they worked together? "You're welcome."

She watched in awe as Reid took a deep breath, centering himself in the way Vaasa often saw Melisina do. And then his face returned to that calm, natural smirk. Without another word, he swaggered to the door like a headman in his own right, and Vaasa followed at his side down the breezeway.

CHAPTER 11

In the Lower Garden, Reid returned to a sense of comfort and normalcy at Vaasa's side.

Vaasa led the small talk in a way Reid didn't seem capable of and he filled in the gaps whenever she pressed his wrist beneath the table. To the people sitting across from them, they probably looked like lovers who couldn't keep their hands off each other.

Marc of Mireh didn't look a day over fifty, with his salt-and-pepper beard on deep, rich brown skin. Perhaps the taut nature of his face remained so youthful because he never gave any indication of emotion. Stoic as a statue, his features only lightened when he looked to the woman sitting at his right.

Isabel, his consort, had grown up in the home next door to him. A perfect other half, Isabel was boisterous and wild, her tumbling black hair framing a petite body that always seemed to be moving. The other two at the table were less welcoming than her—both councilors, both a little strange.

Kenen of Sigguth reminded Vaasa of a tree, with lengthy arms ending in long fingers that curled as Vaasa took note of them. He looked the sort to gamble, if assumptions could be made, with an ever-present mischievous glint in his narrow eyes. Vaasa pictured him swiping cards and turning coins between his fingers. Still, something about the tilt of his smile was reassuring.

Or perhaps difficult-to-read people didn't confuse her the way the rest of these transparent Icrurians did.

Galen of Irhu, however, was the antithesis of his counterpart. Bulky like Reid and more of a boulder than Kenen's swaying tree, Galen stood perceptibly closer than Kenen. Galen had the air of someone more self-important than the rest. He may have enjoyed a large party. He was, as the rest of them, transparent. She could picture big emotions in the wrinkles around his eyes. Most notably, she saw a faint distrust woven there. But just because she couldn't see it in Kenen's expression didn't mean it wasn't there.

Reid's hand rested on her thigh, her own fingers wrapped around his wrist, and she tapped with her index each time she needed to. He listened as if he could read her thoughts.

Were they truly so capable of partnership?

For the first time since she'd been here, she wondered if three years would be so bad. Sure, she could survive them—she could survive anything—but perhaps it would be more than surviving. Maybe she and Reid of Mireh would fall into a comfortable friendship, one that served them both, like he had suggested.

Too soon to tell, yet not too soon to hope for.

Neil, a man she'd met a few weeks back on one of the many nights Reid had forced her to dine here with someone he considered important, came shuffling out of the kitchen and onto the stone veranda with a broad smile, his round belly almost preventing him from cutting between two tables. He squeezed through with a wooden tray firmly pressed to his palm. Wisdom and expertise shone as he served each order with perfection, winking at Reid as he glided to his side.

"I missed your cooking," Isabel gushed as she dug into her fat, sauced chicken leg. Somehow, the bites didn't smudge the deep red rouge on her lips.

Vaasa mimicked Isabel's comfortable demeanor. "You two used to come here?"

"This is where Marc and I had our first true romantic outing," Isabel confirmed.

Marc's lips twitched for the second time that evening and Vaasa glanced through her peripheral vision at Reid. He was already looking at her, a wolfish grin on his face. "One of ours was here, too."

Lies.

"Neil's father used to own this place, and his father before him," Marc said, dragging Vaasa's attention from Reid.

"Oh?"

"We almost lost it last year during the food shortage," Neil remarked with an obvious spin. "And we would have, had Reid not subsidized this business and many others along the Settara. I do believe he learned that strategy from you, Marc."

Vaasa tapped Reid's wrist—three times to disagree.

"Neil," Reid scolded humorously. "You don't need to sing my praises."

"We already know why he was elected," Isabel added, waving her fork. She pointed across the table at Galen and Kenen, grinning. "They do, too."

Making assurances that forced the men to outwardly disagree, which placed the responsibility upon the two councilors to stir conflict if they wanted to correct her, was done so fluidly that someone raised with more integrity and righteousness might just think it harmless.

Vaasa was raised with neither of those things, so it didn't look harmless at all.

The light above Isabel stirred, as if Vaasa was seeing her for the first time.

Isabel wanted something. To their luck, it seemed Reid earning Galen's and Kenen's votes was a piece of that puzzle.

"I don't," Vaasa suddenly interjected, taking the opportunity to lean forward and capitalize on this conversation. Reid didn't look boastful, and she could still milk this for what it was worth. "What happened?"

"There was a particularly dry summer in the east," Neil said, and Vaasa smoothly took bites of her chicken while she listened. "There was no way to trade meats and produce, not enough to keep us up and running. Reid tried to establish something with Zataar, but they levied such a tax that our businesses couldn't manage. We'd have gone under if it hadn't been for Reid. He gave quite the write-off to the salt lords for each shipment they sent to Zataar. Suddenly, our taxes lowered, and we withstood the shortage. Benefited every territory, not just our own."

The way Neil boasted had Isabel laughing and Marc succumbing to at least a proud nod.

"It was well thought out," Kenen commented. Those mischievous eyes danced to Vaasa, inspecting her as if she spoke a language only he understood.

Not to be underestimated, Vaasa thought. Apparently, he lived up to his whispered nickname: the Dagger of Sigguth.

"Had you gone under, that would have been a shame," Vaasa said sincerely, gazing around at the stunning lantern-lit patio and the gorgeous view of the Settara. She found her own words to be honest, and suddenly she saw the reason Reid had been so successful in his role so far, and why they were as opposite as night and day. Reid didn't see opportunity; he just saw people.

Vaasa felt a flicker of shame. For a moment, she thought she and Kenen did share a language, one she had never asked to learn.

"Which is why a partnership with Asterya is key to keeping food on our tables," Marc finally interjected, eyeing Vaasa as Neil squeezed Reid's shoulder and then darted back into the kitchens.

Taking a sip of her water, Vaasa leaned back a little and forced herself into the political angle she'd already considered for this conversation, though a deep-rooted lie. "I couldn't agree more. I've only spent a few months here, but in doing so, I've seen plenty that would enrich the lives of the Asteryans. If my brother were to have ships built like the ones used to trade between the territories, perhaps he would be able to navigate the Loursevain Gap."

This would provide a key contract for Sigguth and Irhu, one of greater economic possibility. If they were enlisted to build the ships and train the men who would navigate the terrifying river that passed through the Iron Peaks where Mekës was built, they'd solidify their own importance on the continent.

"They say the Loursevain Gap is full of creatures," Galen said.

"If it were, wouldn't the Settara be as well? The Sanguine connects them," Marc asked, and suddenly Vaasa and Isabel were on the outside of a political conversation among councilors, one Vaasa assumed they should be having behind closed doors in the capital. Her leg moved beneath the table and Reid's fingers tightened.

Suddenly, she was more alert.

"Maybe those creatures are too large to fit through the passage of the Sanguine," Kenen said. The Sanguine River wound through eastern Icruria until it broke the border of Asterya, then snaked down the continent all the way to Mekës. The Sanguine was unnavigable for the Asteryans, though, with its labyrinthine curves and hundreds of fingers. It was part of what made western Icruria so impenetrable, and one of the only reasons Vaasa's father had never been able to sustain a proper war. His legions and spies couldn't make it past Wrultho and Hazut due to the treacherous waterways.

"I have never sailed the Loursevain Gap, nor would I like to," Reid said confidently, securing his place in their discussion. He slipped into a tone of what Vaasa assumed a counselor or headman would sound like. "But Asteryan trade with Zaatar is impossible without Icrurian vessels, especially with the pirates who keep sacking their merchant ships. I believe offering a solution will be the key to solidifying our trade agreements."

Whether they actually had that discussion with Dominik was an entirely different conversation. Still, she tapped his hand once to indicate a yes, a little praise that caused the edges of his lips to twitch.

"Which you intend to do, correct? The councilors have yet to hear word of Dominik's intent to visit Mireh again," Galen said.

Though her hand curled instinctually on top of Reid's, Vaasa kept her face as smooth as Marc's.

"Yes," Reid said. Vaasa's magic lurched at confirmation of a visit from her brother, but Reid slid his hand to the inside of her thigh, securing her leg in his grasp. "I thought we could discuss that tomorrow morning with my advisor, as he's been maintaining frequent contact with Dominik's advisor."

Was it a lie? Had Mathjin been talking with Ozik? Vaasa couldn't tell, but with the grip Reid maintained, she thought he might have realized what a suggestion like that could bring out in her.

"Perhaps," Marc suggested, "if the goal is to save lives, we could end the constant warring with the east."

Such a subtle veil of his opinion—that Galen's and Kenen's votes would be the difference between life and death. The territory of Wrultho was Reid's greatest threat as of now. And given its proximity to the violence with Asterya, this entire election would be decided by this issue. War was likely profitable for the western ship makers; their votes were up for grabs.

Galen seemed noticeably irritated, but it was Kenen who said smoothly, "How rude we're being to your consorts. We'll save the rest of this discussion for where it belongs."

Marc gritted his teeth, but Reid smoothly nodded.

Isabel and Vaasa met eyes across the table, and much to Vaasa's confusion, Isabel winked.

On the smooth stone ground of the Lower Garden, Vaasa gazed with awe as Marc and Isabel lit up the bustling quad.

Everyone seemed to watch them. Plenty of people cheered and welcomed them home, vying for a chance to swing with Isabel's gorgeous hips or fall into Marc's arms. He was smooth and put together in the crowd, greeting each person with the same stoic nature that everyone seemed to remember fondly. The younger crowd furrowed their brows as they watched Reid and Vaasa, who kept to the side beneath one of the many dangling planters of wildflowers. Maybe they hadn't been old enough to relate to Marc's tenure; the foreman of their young adult lives was Reid.

Kenen approached and dipped his head at Vaasa, offering his hand. His long blond hair was tied behind his head much like Reid kept his, and out here in the dim light, he looked younger than he had in the restaurant. With a glance at Reid, she took off into the crowd with the councilor. Something she'd grown to love about Mireh was the way no one asked Reid if she could dance with them. Back in Asterya, they would have needed her father's or brother's permission.

Isabel bolted to them before more than casual conversation could be exchanged, and something about it felt intentional. Isabel showed Vaasa some of the steps she hadn't been able to keep up with, the two gathering a crowd as the music changed, and Kenen scurried off with a stranger.

"I don't know this one," Vaasa admitted as she tried to bow out.

Isabel grabbed Vaasa's wrist and pulled her back, brown eyes more full of life than any other moment thus far. "Come, we'll teach you!"

"We?" Vaasa asked.

Three or four women surrounded them, and much to Vaasa's surprise, one of them was Amalie. Fear and embarrassment washed over Vaasa as she considered how she'd left this afternoon, but when Amalie smiled with the light of a thousand lanterns, Vaasa's own heart lurched. It wasn't until that moment she'd realized how uncomfortable she'd become this evening. Amalie was the most familiar thing she knew.

Without a whisper of Vaasa's unceremonious exit that afternoon, Amalie gripped Vaasa's other hand and said, "Come on, this is my favorite song."

And the group began to dance.

It took about three tries before Vaasa could successfully lift and switch her foot the way others did, but the moment she got it, they all cheered and circled, pulling her into their larger group. Seeing Kenen and Galen on the periphery, she wondered if they watched or if it was important at all if they did.

Everyone in the crowd seemed to move together. Isabel held one of her hands while Amalie held the other, as if the women had known Vaasa for more than just a few hours or months—like they had known her for a lifetime. The lines of people spun in interwoven circles, friends making room for anyone and everyone who wanted to join. Each time Vaasa fell off rhythm, Amalie would patiently show her how to dance, smiling with every note.

Vaasa had never danced like this, without a partner and just for the joy of movement—in a *community*—and it sank its claws into her chest and tugged. Gazing around as she made the foot switch successfully again, she threw her head back and laughed when Isabel cheered once more.

Was this what happy people did?

Was she one of those happy people? Had her great-grandmother been?

Her insides rumbled with the threat of today and she silenced the creature inside of her, refusing to allow it a single inch of space. Not now.

Spinning, she took in the entirety of the Lower Garden. The song started to shift as people paired off, Isabel running to her husband and tossing herself into his arms. Steel drums echoed around her and Amalie gripped her wrist, spinning her around so she flew to the left. She rammed into someone's chest.

Reid.

He nodded a quiet appreciation to Amalie before she plunged back into the crowd. He held his hands on Vaasa's upper arms and gazed down at her, smiling wider than she was. His dark hair fell in strands from his leather tie, the light of the fire bringing out the golden undertones of his brown skin peeking out from his disheveled drapes.

She lost her breath.

Dipping his mouth to her ear, he whispered, "The councilors will be won. Focus on me instead."

Her lips parted. "I don't know how."

Warmth pressed to her cheek as his lips did. Low, he whispered, "Like lovers, remember?"

This time, the urge to smack him was faint. Instead, she felt bumps on her skin rise and lifted her hands, letting her fingers slide into his hair and curl.

And she tugged.

Throwing his head back, he roared with laughter and spun her for the crowd to see, hand gliding across her waist like he had the first time they'd danced. Taking her back in his arms, he fell into a step she did know. She lifted her eyes to his.

Real happiness spread across his face, and she realized she could tell the difference—it wasn't that dripping amusement any longer, but a contentedness in the way both sides of his mouth lifted instead of just one.

And it was true. Thoughts of the councilors were lost.

This time, she turned herself and pressed her back to his chest, his hands gliding to her abdomen. Her heart raced as his fingers pressed into the tiny chains he'd tied around her. She felt the swing of his hips with her own, the music a chanting crowd of encouragement, and a foreign courage washed over her. Without reservation, her hands guided his downward, skimming over the tops of her thighs as she pressed back into him.

"Careful, Wild One," he warned low and wicked, tugging lightly at those chains before swiping the tips of his fingers just under her waistline. "Don't forget what you said about powerful men."

Muscles in her stomach tightened and she told herself it was because everyone was watching. Because they were putting on a show and she was merely doing a fantastic job. "You'll have to remind me."

Reid stepped back just far enough to spin her around. To let his leg slip between hers as they faced each other once more. He dipped her back, not allowing any room between where their hips pressed, and then with the music, hauled her up to his chest so she had no choice but to breathe against him. No choice but to feel the press of his body each time she inhaled. His lips coasted over her neck, barely touching, until he reached the curve of her ear. "I believe you said a powerful man who has drunk wine all night and watched strangers dance with his wife will want her in his bed."

Their eyes met, and he held her there for a moment, one hand in her hair and her heart in her throat.

And then he tossed her into the arms of one of those strangers, winking at her as he did so. The man, who was closer to Marc's age, quickly tossed her off to another. She spun and smiled, eyes falling to Reid and finding him still watching every place someone put their hands upon her. Daring her to come back, his implication just hanging in the air of the Lower Garden.

Surely that was all for show. To make them look like Isabel and Marc, who were so desperately in love it leaked into the pulse of the night.

Isabel grabbed her hand, pulling her away to the edge of the dance floor, and Vaasa finally caught her breath. The crowd parted for them, and they stopped walking next to the little corner of the outdoor bar, shadows covering them. Alone. Raising her brows, Isabel said, "That husband of yours cannot keep his hands or his eyes off you."

Warmth crept up Vaasa's neck. Apparently, his acting was just as good as his tax code.

"I see you've become friends with the heir of Veragi," Isabel continued, and Vaasa realized she was talking about Amalie.

Vaasa paused. How much did Isabel know? The existence of Veragi magic was no secret in Mireh, but Melisina had warned Vaasa not to speak too openly about their capabilities. Their mystery was half of their protection. Yet Isabel was married to a former foreman. By the looks of it, she probably knew more about Icruria than most of the councilors themselves; she had a keen familiarity about her, a talent for prying into the heart of people. "Yes," Vaasa said instinctually, unsure how to fully incapsulate all the things Amalie was becoming, though certainly more than just the future high witch. "Though I wasn't aware you knew of my magic."

Isabel grinned like a fox. "It was one of Reid's selling points on the marriage. He claimed to be bringing another Veragi bloodline back to Mireh, and who were the councilors to deny him that?"

For whatever reason, that small tidbit of information shocked Vaasa. She'd known, of course, that Reid recognized her magic. But he'd known about it from the very beginning? Had used it as a justification for his marriage to her?

He'd known of her magic as she climbed out that window?

Of course he had.

Her mother had been here. Had trained with Melisina for an entire summer.

Isabel pulled her from her rambling thoughts. "Your daughters will be prodigies, will they not?"

"I . . ." Vaasa paused. Swallowed. "I never thought about that."

Everything she'd learned came roaring back. Reid could sire a Veragi witch without Vaasa, if the magic manifested from his mother's side and if the goddess willed it. But combined with hers?

Prodigy was one word for it.

Would a daughter like that inherit the magic even before Vaasa passed? Would she earn it from Melisina instead? What would happen if she bore two daughters? *Twins?*

That moment she realized none of it mattered.

She would never give Reid children.

Isabel leaned against the bar top. "May we speak candidly?"

Was that not what they'd been doing? Vaasa nodded.

"I believe he will make a good headman. Marc believes so, too. They all do. The challenge lies with swinging Sigguth, which it always does. All of our ships are built there, and that makes them quite pompous on the Icrurian stage. Their self-importance is comical."

"How is Wrultho a contender at all?" Vaasa inquired carefully. This she didn't understand—the eastern territories were so racked with violence, why would anyone put the capital for the next decade in a place like that?

"The eastern city-states tend to take issue with us more . . . globally interested. But they do want war, and their entire campaign is built on the benefits of proximity."

"There is no benefit to proximity."

"It'll be your job to prove that to Sigguth and Irhu. They are terrified of Asterya, have heard the stories of what your father—" She cut herself off, a bit of shame in her pursed lips. "I'm sorry. I shouldn't speak about your home in such a way."

"Please don't apologize." Vaasa looked out at the quad once more, the events from today playing on a loop in her mind. "The truth is . . . Asterya did not feel so much like home."

And she wasn't the only one from her bloodline who had thought so. Something else existed inside of her that she hadn't even known was there. And now that it had surfaced, she didn't really know who she was at all.

Isabel gave a knowing grin. "I have learned that home is seldom a place; it is people, the most unexpected of them, that give us roots."

Vaasa realized what Isabel thought—that as she gazed out at the groups of dancers, her eyes had been on Reid of Mireh instead of the complex horizon that suddenly looked so different through the lens of belonging.

It was best to let Isabel believe that.

"I would like us to do more than win this election," Isabel suddenly said.

Their eyes met once more, and Vaasa furrowed her brow.

"I hope that we can be friends," Isabel said. "I have not had many friends this past decade, and quite frankly, I'm sick of Dihrah. And as you ascend to high consort, you'll want an advisor and ally."

Vaasa's chest tightened, and she felt an irrational part of her want to leap from her throat and say that she would love that, that she would *need* that, and it all played in the back of her mind. A life here with nights in the Lower Garden and days at the sodality.

A coven.

A home.

A place where she was worth the love of someone like Reid, where she could give him those two little girls with her raven hair and his golden eyes.

The other part of her—the one that knew the truth—told her to hush. To be realistic. To consider that fleeing was her only option, and Vaasa could never morally bring more Kozár heirs into the world. "I would like that," Vaasa replied.

Not entirely a lie.

"Good," Isabel said.

Turning back, Vaasa watched as Marc and Reid found them, parting the crowd like a sea and emerging more prominent than the rest of the world, if only in her eyes. But as the people behind them closed like a zipper, Galen and Kenen were entirely out of sight.

Out of earshot.

And suddenly, Isabel's schemes played two roles. It was not just Vaasa she wanted to get alone; it was all of them.

Isabel might be the most strategic woman she'd ever met. Yet it seemed that her morals and actions were in the right place, which begged the question: Was it possible to have both?

"The other two seem content," Isabel said to the men as they arrived. "You need them to be content, Reid, if you intend to swing their votes."

"You believe their votes can be swung, then?" Reid asked outright, turning to Marc.

Yet the councilor didn't stand with as much ease as Isabel. It was as if the entire conversation made him uncomfortable. He was clearly not the schemer in their relationship, and Isabel raised her brows at her husband.

"Nothing is certain until the votes are cast," Marc said.

An air of awkwardness crawled over them all.

Reid nodded. "I apologize for my brazen question. I assumed you were here to provide guidance on the matter."

Just as stoic as before, Marc blinked once before saying, "Do you feel you need guidance?"

Looking between the four of them, Reid leaned back against the bar and dropped his other hand to Vaasa's, his fingers winding around hers and squeezing while the rest of him went lax. Pretending he was just as calm and assured as he always seemed to be, Reid said, "I think anyone in this position would need guidance . . ." He paused and looked to Vaasa for a moment, and then the corner of his mouth flicked up. "No man walks out of the position the same as he walked into it. To be the leader of anything can be a corrupting job."

Her words to him, deep in the catacombs of the Library of Una, seemed to rattle around the space as his self-assured eyes held Marc's.

He'd been listening, even through all that swagger.

Marc remained frozen for a moment. As if Reid had unlocked something in him, the councilor relaxed a bit. "I see you have remained too wise for your years."

"It's only been what, two years since you last visited?" Reid asked.

"I . . ." Marc looked down at Isabel and grinned, her mischievous brown eyes gazing up at him like the sun rose and set with that small crack of his composure. "I am very ready to come home."

With a strong dip of his head, Reid agreed. "We are ready to have you home."

That was a vote if Vaasa had ever seen one.

"Enough, enough." Isabel broke the tension with that effortless grace of hers. "Take me back to the temple, Marc."

Lust was the only undeniable emotion on Marc's face the entire evening, and it split his lips into a wicked grin. "I can depend on you to get the other two back?" he asked Reid.

Reid nodded, trying desperately not to laugh.

Without another word, Marc hauled Isabel into the crowd and out of their sight.

Reid's jaw dropped, though Vaasa only let out a breath she'd been holding. "He is, like most men, simpler than he seems," Vaasa said.

The gold of Reid's eyes turned to hers, the glitter of flames strung around them dancing in the depths as if they were catacombs. "I can't say I disagree with his motivations."

Her chest tightened, the heaviness of the day and the evening weighing more than she wanted to let on. She could see it there, the desire to be like them. To love like them. A craving for a soulmate seemed to make a home in him and, somehow, that was heavier than anything else she carried. "Go win your election," she whispered.

Reid's gaze stayed trained upon her for the length of a breath, but then he nodded sternly, determination still coating all of his mannerisms. Silently, she took his arm and let him lead her back through the crowd.

Galen and Kenen were waiting, and with a little coaxing, she managed to paste a smile upon her own face, too.

To push all of it away.

A serpent in chameleon's skin.

Vaasa remained silent for the entire ride back to the villa, taking the winding streets upon Duch's back without a single word.

But everything played like a carousel in her mind.

Back at the villa, the high of the evening seemed to close in on her and she hurried through the breezeway into Reid's room, searching for a way to calm.

"Vaasa, we need to discuss something." Reid spoke firmly, though with a strange nervous lilt at the back of his words. Her heart stuttered. "Marc and I spoke; he's insisting that we invite Dominik once more. That we trade more than salt to prove our relationship is ongoing."

Vaasa froze. "No."

"Vaasa—"

"Reid, no. You can't do that."

"I don't have a choice."

Everything she and Isabel had spoken about rattled in her bones, and she felt nauseous.

Dominik, here. What would he do when he learned she still lived? When he saw her pretend to be in love with this man? Dominik systematically removed all threats to his reign—she would be no exception.

Her stomach dropped.

Would he simply choose to kill Reid instead?

Reid didn't know the extent of the danger this would put them in.

"Why are you so afraid of him?" Reid finally asked.

She looked up at him and the words tingled on her tongue. She *wanted* to tell him. When had she let him get close enough for that?

He was willing to fake a marriage for this election. What else would he be willing to do?

As she stepped deeper into the room, the magic in her turned over like it could do flips. She balled her fists as she replayed each moment, choosing not to answer his question. "When will he be here?"

"I expect he'll arrive in a few weeks."

Her hands started to shake. The moment Dominik learned she had found control over this magic, had uncovered a semblance of happiness and potential . . .

Dancing. Laughing. Drinking.

Happiness.

That was what she had felt. *That* was how close to her Reid had gotten.

And how dare she? How stupid it was to like anything about this city. To bond herself to a single person.

Love is a useless thing.

Dominik's baleful grin flashed behind her eyes and her breathing became uneven. Ozik stood next to him, laughing like he had expected this all along. Her father tsked, lips curved downward in perpetual disappointment. But her mother's face was clearer than the others—now unreadable, foreign to her entirely. She had made a sacrifice for Vaasa to end up here.

It was about to be wasted. "Vaasa," Reid said, brow furrowing as he watched her.

She met his eyes.

Which dipped to her hands.

Black mist swirled between her fingers and Vaasa hissed, stepping back while tears welled in her eyes. She shook her hands and cursed wickedly. Weeks. She hadn't lost control in weeks, and she'd been able to keep it down all night and—

She spun.

Took in the view of the Settara coated in moonlight. The way it played upon the little waves and led the current. How it seemed to be born from that white tree at the top of the hill.

Her great-grandmother had lived here.

Had painted that very tree.

And yet she had no claim here. No claim of her own in Asterya, either. She had been born a pawn and it didn't matter which man she told the truth to—they both would use her to get what they wanted.

The magic grew.

"Vaasa." Reid started forward.

"Don't," she warned, frustration striking down her spine as she scuttled away from him and caught sight of the magic swirling up her arms. "Don't follow me," she gasped.

"Wait—"

Vaasa burst out the double doors and to the left of the veranda, diving into the dry grass and letting the steep hill guide her down. Consciously she knew it was treacherous to navigate at night, knew that any type of predator could be out here, but she needed to be away. Needed to be as far from this villa as she could before she lost control and brought it all down.

Faintly, she heard him following. Heard him calling for her. She turned and yelled, "I said don't follow!" Desperately, she slid onto the flat shoreline and sprinted, breath coming in hot pants.

The snake in her gut was no longer a snake. No longer a fish, or some soft-bellied creature with only teeth and poison to its name.

It was a volcano, smoke rising, molten rock ready to burn.

"Vaasa—" Reid tried.

She spun. Locked eyes with him. "Don't. Don't come closer. I don't want to hurt you, Reid, I don't want to—"

"You won't."

"I will!" she screamed, arms flying up and tendrils of glittering mist bursting into the full-mooned sky. The anger and fear inside of her bubbled as the dancing and the music and the smiles played over and over again.

She couldn't want this.

Dominik would smother the breath from the lungs of the city, would plunge a knife into the heart of the Lower Garden.

He would take this from her, too, just as everything else had been.

The magic in her crested, and this time she couldn't swallow it. Couldn't beat against it and win.

This time, it detonated.

Darkness shot out of her. Magic ripped through the air and slammed into knotted trees, leaves flying in every direction. A cracking boom burst through the small space and Vaasa could feel the edge of the tree, could sense like she was touching it all. The roughness of the bark, the delicate silk of the grass.

Reid.

She felt the magic touch him.

Felt the ripple of his hair and skin.

Such miserable panic sluiced through her.

She pulled it back as hard as she could.

It slammed into her chest, and she *screamed.*

The ground beneath her feet shook, black mist morphing into something she'd never seen it do before. It flew in every direction. Clattering louder than the scream ratcheting from her throat, the magic pierced the air and then dove down her throat and into every crevice of her body.

It grew into an arch and covered her with a dome, smooth curves banishing the moonlight and snuffing out everything else. Raw magic flowed out, climbing the walls and melding with them, adding to the void until there were no holes of scent or light or sound.

Black.

The void consumed her.

Vaasa sank to her knees, choking for a breath, but finding nothing but empty air. She burned. She burned and burned and burned and—

And then it stopped.

In the violence, there was peace.

The void swirled around her, and even though she couldn't breathe or smell or taste or see, for the first time since she'd come here, everything was quiet.

Faintly, she felt hot tears sliding down her cheeks.

All around her was black, glittering with specks of blue and purple and white.

Beautiful.

And it kept everything else out.

No one could touch her. No one could see her. She was in a cage of her own making, and it kept her safe. The magic did not seek to harm her—it sought to protect her. It knew this outcome was far better than the assured death that would arrive on the Mirehan docks.

She didn't care if she died here. She welcomed it. At least then it would not be by Dominik's hand.

Her fingers dug into the cool grass and she closed her eyes.

Tears watered the grass below for minutes. Hours. A lifetime.

No breath. No life.

Slipping.

She heard it then, the sound of a voice, perhaps her own or perhaps someone else's—Freya, or Esme, or her own mother.

Get up.

Get up.

Your life is still your own.

Something in her lurched and reached. The intimate caress of that voice fueled within her and then it *burned.* It burned and burned and burned—

The darkness she'd let out, the one that built into a home around her, leaked behind her eyes.

She swore she heard someone roaring her name. Swore that familiar accent cracked on desperation.

The last thing she remembered was the faint image of moonlight breaking through black and arms curling around her until her fingers unclenched the grass.

CHAPTER 12

Vaasa shook.

She shook and shook and shook.

Coldness racked her bones, and faintly she heard her own retching. Felt her knees crack against a stone floor. Smelled the atrocious scent of her own sickness, of her own memories: rotting flesh. Burning hair. First she pictured her lifeless mother, and then Ozik's twisted grimace, and then her brother. That smell followed her.

Consciousness came and went like the flow of water.

Still, she felt it again. The feeling of arms around her. Of warmth. Of the blackness smothering her as something soft consumed her body.

Vaasa shook.

She shook so hard she worried her teeth would shatter.

And then finally, she stopped.

When she sank into the warmth and buried her nose in it, she slept.

Rays of sunlight flooded through Vaasa's lids and she shifted, her body light and warm. Blankets up to her neck, she pulled herself deeper and curled her leg up. Like that she stayed, heat coating her bones.

Until she shifted and felt the rigid body of someone beside her.

She sprang to a sitting position, and soreness ripped down her sides and she released a small cry, hands flying to her ribs. At the same time, Reid popped up, his face racked with worry and sleeplessness, red eyes blinking a few times as if he couldn't believe he'd fallen asleep. He sat above the blankets in a pair of soft pants and no shirt, his inked chest glaring at her.

Vaasa looked down at herself, at the oversized shirt falling to her midthighs. Her bare legs breezed against the sheets she'd been tucked under.

Fury spiked in her chest and she opened her mouth to speak, but Reid lifted his hand. "Amalie undressed you, not me," he insisted. "Now, are you okay?"

Her lips parted and she let out a harsh breath, the events of the evening barreling back to her. The outburst. The sickness. The crippling lack of sleep he must be enduring. "You . . . you have a meeting with Marc and Mathjin—"

"Fuck the meeting. Answer my question."

"But you have to discuss the ships and—"

"Vaasa."

"I don't know if I'm okay!"

He finally closed his mouth, no trace of that amusement anywhere to be found. Just a harsh pull of his lips and tightness of his shoulders and jaw. "What do you need to be okay?"

What sort of question was that? How could anyone know the answer? Stumbling to her feet, she almost lost her balance and he lurched for her, hands on her waist. She pushed his touch away and backed up. "I . . ." She looked around at the sheets. "I slept in this bed, with you?"

He raised his brows and leaned back. "Well, I'd hardly say you slept, but that's a summary of about a tenth of your night, yes."

"What about the other nine parts?"

"The other nine parts you spent vomiting and shaking so hard you almost cracked your head on the marble in the bathing chamber. It took my mother hours before she decided you would not die."

Humiliation washed over her. Had she been that sick? The magic had given her some tough moments. Hours, even. But all night?

And he'd seen the entire thing?

"You could have slept on the couch," she snapped.

His jaw dropped.

Vaasa spun away from him. "Go to your meeting."

"Oh no," he growled. And right as Vaasa ducked behind the changing screen, she heard the harsh sounds of his feet hitting the floor. "You don't get to go back to this."

Go back to what? What did they even have to—

Reid came around the changing screen so fast Vaasa barely had time to blink before he was in her space. Looming above her, he practically had her pinned to the wall again.

His voice came low and angry. "If I hadn't been in that bed right next to you, you could have choked on your own vomit. You were shaking so badly you could hardly hold yourself up. You're lucky I broke your little rule about that *stupid* bed. So you are not going to go back to pretending I am your enemy."

"You're going to be late," she said.

Reid shook his head. "I got word from the High Temple that Isabel and Marc fucked so loud they could be heard until the early hours of the morning. I expect I have plenty of time to discuss this."

She wanted to be angry with him, but the realities of last night beat against her. He'd spent all night awake with her—he must be exhausted, too. His eyes were red and bleary, his breath uneven. She could grasp at bits and pieces of her consciousness, and much to her dismay, he was at the forefront of most. Holding her hair. His hand on her back. The only warmth she'd felt the entire night had been from his body.

Maybe she wasn't angry about them sleeping in the same bed at all. Tears welled in her eyes that she should have smacked away. But she couldn't bring herself to. She was exhausted from forcing herself to be neutral.

Wasn't that what Melisina had said? That these awful emotions were only pain, and she'd been disguising them for too long?

Vaasa looked away, finally wiping those escaped tears.

Reid straightened. "Why are you crying?"

Her voice barely above a whisper, she said, "I lost control."

Softness took the place of where his anger had been. Shaking his head, he reached for her tentatively, hand brushing her cheek. "But you didn't. You pulled it back into yourself. You didn't let it harm anyone but you."

That realization sat heavy in her chest as she stared up at him. He didn't have a scratch, not anywhere on his skin. She checked every inch of what she could see. Whatever she'd built from the raw magic had cocooned her and somehow left him alone?

"Good," she said, though she needed to pull away. To distance herself from him.

"Vaasa." Reid bit his lip, then let out a breath of resignation. "What did he do to you? Why are you so afraid of him?"

Her spine locked and a ball formed in her throat, expanding until barely any air could pass through.

She jerked her head away, shaking it only once.

Silence.

Then, "One of these days, I would like to hear what caused that sort of desperation. On your terms. When you're ready."

She would never speak it out loud—never hand him the keys that opened the door to either an empire or her freedom. They would stay in her hands, so she could choose when and how to use them for as long as she lived.

When she didn't speak, Reid sighed. "You are the only reason I made headway with Marc. I've spent half my life trying to break through to that man, and you accomplished it in one night."

"I didn't do anything," she said, giving in to his change of subject.

"You did. Your idea worked perfectly. Isabel told me as we left that she couldn't wait to come home so she could spend time with *you*. Which means Marc's vote is ours, otherwise you and I wouldn't be here when they returned. It was you who won them over, not me."

"She told me that, too."

"And that bothers you?"

"How is she going to react in three years, Reid?"

He paused. Then, voice lower than before, he said, "Is that what this is about?"

Vaasa didn't say another word. She'd already said too much. It didn't matter what any of them thought of her, what he thought of her, if she was just going to leave anyway. That she'd found herself wanting to be here at all was a vulnerability she would keep tucked to her chest until the day she died. The things she wanted had a way of slipping through her fingers.

Reid's hand snaked beneath her chin as he tilted her face up to his, forcing her to meet his gaze. Immediately, her heart leapt into her throat.

"I rather enjoy having you on my side." He paused. Smirked. "I'd like to do what I can to keep you here."

Keep her . . . where? Here by his side? Here in Mireh?

He must have seen the confusion on her face, because he straightened his spine and dropped his hand. "You're right. I'm going to be late," he said, stepping out from the changing screen and leaving her stranded in nothing but confusion and his shirt.

Ambling across the stone floor, he swept up his clothing and moved into the bathing chamber.

Vaasa took large breaths with the minute and a half she had alone.

What was she supposed to make of those words?

All she knew was that it was colder now. That her bones hadn't warmed nearly enough.

Reid emerged from the bathing chamber, and she heard his footsteps move toward the door. "My mother asked that you go see her when you woke up."

"Reid—" She lurched from behind the screen, stopping just outside of it and regaining her composure.

He raised his brows, waiting.

"Thank you," she managed. "For . . . for helping me last night."

She owed him that much. She owed him more.

His face softened just a touch, enough for her to want to fidget, but then he shrugged with such nonchalance she wondered if her thanks meant anything at all.

Until he said, "Dismissing your emotions doesn't make them disappear, it only gives them reason to rise later without your consent."

Vaasa blinked, and then crossed her arms. "You really are Melisina's son."

"Through and through," he agreed, pulling his hair up and securing it with one of his leather ties. Hand on the doorknob, he paused once more before opening it. "What I mean is this: here, with me, you don't need to hide anything at all. I promised you safety, and I intend to uphold my part of our bargain."

With that, he swung the door open and clicked it shut behind him.

Vaasa's hands dropped to her sides and she forced her shoulders to roll, trying to shrug off whatever feeling crawled down her spine. Tried to push the sound of his voice in Icrurian from her mind.

You don't need to hide anything at all.

I'd like to do what I can to keep you here.

Words like that would be the death of her, she decided, and resolved to go see Melisina.

Resolved to do anything but stand there half naked in his shirt, thinking on what he'd said.

Melisina did not let Vaasa use magic. When she'd tried to pull Romana and Mariana onto her side—a last-ditch effort and her ace of spades—even that failed.

Not an ounce of power could be exerted today, apparently, and Vaasa was silently grateful for the reprieve. Much to her surprise, the group didn't focus on her outburst for more than an introductory two minutes. Amalie often disappeared after lunch, but this time she asked if Vaasa wanted to join her.

"Where are you going?"

Amalie smiled with a bit of mischief and gestured for Vaasa to pick up her notebook and pencil. "Trust me."

The two women entered the main halls of the Sodality of Setar, and Vaasa felt out of place in her soft brown breeches and sheer white blouse while everyone else who scurried past them wore sweeping amethyst robes. Still, as they ascended the main hall stairs past the artists' wing, a place she wondered if her own great-grandmother had frequented, Vaasa settled into Amalie's side. Through the gardens, the familiar smell of salt wafted around them. Chocolate lilies and black hollyhock swept through the olive- and forest-green vines. Plunging through a set of enormous oak doors, they entered one of the cathedrals Vaasa had yet to explore. Oak and indigo decorated every wall, iron curling in over itself in filigrees upon the wooden banisters and staircases.

"Sage Vaughan," Amalie greeted a kind-looking older woman in ink-black robes as they approached a lecture hall. "I was hoping our consort could observe your class today."

Vaasa's back straightened at the same time the sage's eyes darted to her. Smiling with more openness than she expected, the silvery-blond-haired teacher gave a wide sweep of her arm as she gestured into the room. "Of course, it would be an honor."

"The honor would be mine," Vaasa replied. "I apologize for my lack of dress." At the Sodality of Una, they'd have turned her away.

Yet Sage Vaughan only winked. "You have a writing utensil, it's a good place to begin."

Amalie chuckled as she threaded her arm through Vaasa's, pulling her into the enormous lecture hall. Three rows of tables, each at least twenty desks long, took up the entirety of the marble floor, while stained glass covered the far wall. A lectern sat at the front with papers strewn along it. Chandeliers strung from the ceiling emitted soft light upon each of the shiny, light brown desks. People turned over their shoulders to watch them, and Vaasa immediately thought of the sodality in Dihrah. She'd spent her time there hidden, hoping to avoid stares such as these, and the scholars had been content to ignore her.

But Amalie walked as though it brought her pride to be standing next to Vaasa, and warmth bloomed in her chest.

No one had ever loved her in the light.

"What are we learning today?" Vaasa whispered as they sat at conjoined desks.

"Linguistics. I'm studying the etymology of the first Icrurian languages, before we had the commerce tongue."

Letting out a little laugh, Vaasa opened up her notebook. "Hoping to learn another language?"

"I already speak three, what's one more?"

"You do?"

"Icrurian was my first, I speak the old tongue of Wrultho, and I speak Asteryan."

The pencil might have slipped from Vaasa's hand had she not gripped it tightly. "You speak Asteryan?"

Fluently, with precise pronunciation that may have put Vaasa to shame, Amalie slipped into Vaasa's first tongue. "Since I was ten years old. Today's lecture is on Hazut, though. Maybe you'll learn something we can use against their foreman."

"Amalie, I . . ." She paused, speaking Asteryan for the first time in months. She had to admit, it felt good to let the Asteryan out to play, to feel it roll off her tongue. "I didn't know."

It earned her a shrug. "I heard you speak four."

"Six," she said honestly—for the first time, she realized—and Amalie's brows rose. Vaasa muttered, "But that'll be our secret."

Letting out a soft chuckle, Amalie turned her attention forward as Sage Vaughan started to pace up the center of the room. In Icrurian, the lecture began, and Vaasa leaned back and listened.

The feeling of learning, that stunning moment when the world fell away and all Vaasa had was the thrill of new information, had been long lost to her in Icruria. It had evaded her for months, even in Dihrah, where she should have taken advantage of the opportunity.

But here, she gripped it between her fingers just as hard as she did a pencil.

Language was one of the most telling records of history—the words pointed to the people. Hazut was no different; they were inextricably linked to Wrultho, the two eastern territories trading among themselves long before Icruria united under a headman. In those years of trade, the commerce language took shape out of sheer necessity; the rest of Icruria had those two territories to thank for paving the way to the words spoken in this very sodality. But as she studied the familiar roots, she knew it wasn't so far removed from the other smaller nations that had existed before Asterya swept through the continent. Before her father had stolen that history in front of everyone's eyes. While Icruria united generations ago, Asterya had been nothing but a snow-trapped nation, steeped in tradition and ice before her father took the helm. It was under his rule that the empire took form: he'd conquered the smaller nations around him with ease, always playing the long game but never truly satisfied.

She thought back to the languages he had insisted she be taught. Each one was used purposefully, for the negotiations that brought those nations to their knees. But he'd focused on the words, never delving too far into the history. She realized now that the stories of others were a threat to him, greater than any weapon or fortress.

But for the first time, she wondered: Why her? Why *not* Dominik? Wouldn't it have been far more strategic on her father's part to arm his heir with this knowledge? Why would he spend so much of his life teaching her one of the most fundamental elements of survival: the ability to communicate?

Vaasa hadn't expected to take seven pages of notes or to hang on every word the sage said. She'd never jotted these questions down in the margins of a notebook, giving life to words simply by putting them on paper. It would have been too dangerous to write such thoughts. But within minutes, it was simply out of her control, and hours passed without Vaasa caring about the chime of the clocks.

When the sage finished her lecture, Amalie led Vaasa out onto one of the patios near the second dome. Mireh was a beating heart around them while they dug into their lunch. Green lettuce and pine nuts covered Vaasa's plate, the salad full of fresh vegetables and dark red beans. Lime burst on her tongue and she sighed, leaning back in her chair.

"I . . . I'm sorry you had to come to the villa last night. That you had to deal with that," Vaasa said.

Responding in turn with a smile, perhaps knowing the use of Asteryan was a pleasure Vaasa hadn't gotten in months, Amalie set down her fork. "Well, I once lost control and brought down an entire building, so I have no room to judge."

Vaasa relaxed just a touch. "A building?"

"Three stories—an entire tower of the Sodality of Unir. That was when Melisina and Romana came for me."

"You studied there?" Vaasa asked, considering all of the new information she had just learned about the region's languages. If Amalie had studied in Wrultho, she'd have been so close to the violence along the border.

"Um, no. I was born in Wrultho, but we couldn't afford for me to attend a sodality."

"I thought the sodalities were free to attend," Vaasa said.

"Well, they are, if your family can afford for you to take four or more years *not* working. That's the real catch. Most families in Wrultho can't."

It was foolish of her never to have considered that barrier. Of course it would be a factor. "Is that why you left Wrultho, then? The tower?"

Amalie paused, face tightening.

Insecurity threaded through Vaasa, but she knew better than to ask for answers that weren't voluntarily offered. Instinctually she reached for the witch, placing her hand on Amalie's hand. "You don't have to tell me anything you don't want to."

Shoulders rising, Amalie regained her composure. Practiced, intentional confidence shone in her eyes. "The choices of others are not a burden I carry any longer, and neither is their shame."

Those words settled in Vaasa's stomach, mixing with the prowling magic.

If she'd been born in Wrultho and been impoverished there, Amalie had lived through the violence. Had probably seen it firsthand.

The witch adjusted her weight, setting down her fork. "It's a long story, but in the east, magic is a commodity. And while it is illegal for witches to be forced into the armed forces or even a territory's personal corps, it doesn't stop people from finding other ways to barter and trade the poorest of us who happen to live through the acquisition of magic. While the bloodlines once ruled the land, the wars before unification scattered our ancestors, and many of them went into hiding. Wealth used to be passed down in tandem with magic, but now the bloodlines are no longer the wealthiest families in Icruria." Amalie ran her tongue along her teeth and then uncurled one leg to sit more solidly. "That was what Melisina and Romana saved me from. I . . . I was meant to marry Ton of Wrultho. To bring my magic to his bloodline."

Vaasa's lips parted, and her heart dropped into her stomach. The foreman of Wrultho. "What happened?"

"I was in love with someone else, a childhood friend, one of the guards. Eventually, Ton realized I was still seeing him, though he never learned who it was. He threatened to kill any man who got too close to me, and I couldn't control the magic. In the imbalance of it all, I destroyed part of their sodality. Ton wanted me gone, and Melisina gave him an out."

Visions of that couldn't form—Amalie, exploding so large she brought down a building. The girl had never so much as raised her voice. Yet Vaasa felt a deep sense of familiarity with her suddenly, in knowing that they faced the same questions.

But Reid had given Vaasa a way out, while Ton had sought to control Amalie.

She felt less and less guilty about the violence at the shared border. "Our magic, it's truly that rare?"

"Think about it. In all of Icruria, we only know of six Veragi witches. Only two of us under the age of thirty."

Vaasa awkwardly shifted her weight. "Melisina said young witches often die. But they are more powerful in the long run."

The past took the shape of grief as it coated Amalie's eyes. "That is true, and why we are grateful to have found you. Why I am especially grateful to have found you. There is . . ." She took a small breath and lifted her chin. "I've told you of selfish people, but there are equally desperate people, too. My mother was one of those people. She inherited her magic after never knowing her own mother, never knowing of our Veragi bloodline. But my mother was poor, and she lost my father to one of the many battles with Asterya."

Vaasa stayed entirely silent.

"She was sick, racked with an ever-present sadness that stole light from every corner of her world. She could not withstand the magic. She saw it as something that would give me a greater opportunity than she ever had the chance of finding. So she sacrificed her life and gave the magic to me."

Something inside of Vaasa fractured at the words, at the horrible memories playing upon Amalie's face. At everything this terribly young witch had been put through, for the burden of a magic that Vaasa had once sought to extinguish. "I . . ." Vaasa could hardly speak. "I'm so sorry."

"Thank you." Amalie took a breath and then lifted her eyes again, wiping the wetness from the corners. "I am still working on coming to terms with the weight of grief. But . . . so are you. In your own way, with your own story. And since I was privy to information you might not have wanted me to know yesterday, well, sharing only seems fair."

Vaasa didn't feel as though she could tell her story, could utter a word of it. To anyone. But when Amalie looked at her with such open brown eyes and the sort of kindness that she'd never encountered in a person, she thought if she could someday manage it, it would be with this woman. And she realized that she wanted Amalie's friendship, no matter how much she denied it. "I'm glad you asked me to come with you today," Vaasa confessed.

A lovely smile grew upon Amalie's lips, and her body relaxed in her chair. She picked up her fork and took another bite, chewed, and swallowed. "I know we've just met and that life for you is . . . complicated. But the truth is that you are the most honest friend I have. Can we be that? Friends?"

Hopefulness and longing rose up in Vaasa, and she didn't know how to say that it terrified her. That she didn't think she deserved Amalie's friendship at all, but that she wanted it more than she'd wanted just about anything. Vaasa dropped her gaze, a bit of shame rising. She could still hear the sound of her father's voice—the upward lilt of pride and legacy woven into warm Asteryan words. But she also remembered that *other* tone, the one that turned Asteryan into sharp consonants and mountains at the back of her throat.

Do you want to know the secret, Vaasalisa? Only ever depend upon yourself. The world does not treat kindness with a mirror; it treats kindness with a blade.

But Vaasa had been treating herself with a blade for months, and no matter how hard she tried to cut out the parts of her that wanted and wished and hoped, those parts still lived. Perhaps she should fuel them instead of smothering them. Perhaps she should treat Amalie's kindness with a mirror instead.

"I am afraid," she whispered.

Amalie tilted her head with inquisitive eyes, waiting patiently for Vaasa to continue.

"I . . ." Vaasa took a deep breath. "There is an ancient law in Asterya, one we have not seen enacted in generations. One that allows me, as long as I am married, to ascend the Asteryan throne. It gives the emperorship to my husband."

Amalie straightened her posture. "I don't understand."

"If my brother were to die, then Reid and I have the only viable claim to the Asteryan throne. And Reid doesn't know it."

Shock tumbled across Amalie's features, but she quickly schooled them. "You haven't told him?"

"I don't know how. But my brother will be visiting in a few weeks. I fear what he might do."

"Do you think he's going to harm you?"

"He sent me here because he believed I was dying. I'm afraid of what he'll do when he learns I haven't. Not just to me, but to Reid."

Amalie nodded slowly in understanding, leaning back in her chair.

"You can't tell anyone," Vaasa gasped, suddenly upset with herself for having said anything at all. How stupid was she? She'd only managed to make it a few months without putting her own safety on the line, all for what? For friendship?

But then Amalie said, "Vaasa, I promise not to tell a soul. Not Reid, not Melisina, not anyone."

And somehow, Vaasa believed her. She had never fully believed someone before.

"We must be prepared," Amalie asserted.

"Prepared?"

"There must be a way to throw your brother off your scent. What if we convinced him you *were* dying? Do you think he can be fooled?"

"You . . . you're going to help me? Even at risk of danger?"

"You're in our coven now." Amalie shrugged. "Your strength is my strength."

Warmth flooded Vaasa. She'd underestimated Amalie's soft strength. Her acceptance of something otherwise often brutal—the truth—was anything but. Resilience shone in all of Amalie's cracks, and Vaasa found herself wanting to be more like her.

"I think he can be fooled," Vaasa said, a plan starting to take shape in her mind.

Amalie grinned. "Then fool him we will. You're not going anywhere, Vaasa—one witch is a problem, but a coven is a nightmare."

A smile crept across Vaasa's lips. Upon hearing those words, on this little balcony, Vaasa suddenly thought her father may have been wrong about everything he ever told her.

CHAPTER 13

Vaasa stood at the edge of the city, having donned the same formal attire Reid had helped her with the day they met Isabel and Marc. To her side, Kosana loomed, eyes trained to the horizon, where they waited for Dominik's caravan to appear. Vaasa had been on edge for the two weeks since Dominik accepted Reid's invitation. Amalie had tried to join them, but with each day Vaasa spent with the girl, the less she wanted Dominik ever to lay eyes upon her.

Your strength is my strength, Amalie had said, but Vaasa had firmly denied her any chance to be near these negotiations.

Esoti had doubled down; had not let Vaasa leave their morning routines until she'd learned to catch that little blade and strike. The raven-haired warrior stood at Vaasa's side for this meeting armed to the teeth. The rolling hills and yellow grass blanketed the horizon, a few homes speckled here or there, but mostly farms and ranches for as far as she could see. Vaasa swallowed down her magic, which seemed to tap-dance along her nerves; the force again felt like a snake, coiled tight and afraid to bare its neck.

She wondered how Dominik was surviving in the heat. He couldn't pass through Wrultho and Hazut safely, which meant he had no opportunity to cross the Settara, nor did he have a vessel that could navigate the Loursevain Gap. He'd had to take the longer, less comfortable land route, navigating the labyrinth of rivers that made an invasion toward the west a foolish choice. Only through working with the current headman had this visit been possible; the Icrurian Central Forces had guided Dominik through, taking Reid's instructions about a confusing path that wouldn't grant Dominik more information about Icruria than he already knew. They'd traversed a heat-scorched valley, one that would be untenable for a large army, though Reid had promised her it was safe.

Hopefully, Dominik would dry up like a raisin in the sun.

Kosana shifted her weight as the caravan came into sight, blue eyes fixated on the road ahead. At least seven carts moved in lines, twenty horses on either side of the one leading the front. On instinct, Vaasa stepped closer to Reid, and he eyed her curiously in his peripheral vision.

Dominik's raven hair came into sight, cut close to his head on the sides and swept back on the top, a few loose strands placed exactly where he wanted them to be. She knew as he got closer she'd see his incredibly high cheekbones and pointed nose, only made more severe by the pronounced ridge of his brow and his pale ivory skin. Dominik looked harsher than her in every way, though their coloring remained alike, particularly their shared indigo eyes.

Reid's hand moved to the small of her back and his chin lifted. He wore his hair tied as he always did, the rigid line of his tense jaw cut like shards of salt. He looked remarkably strong at her side. The winking onyx blade at his hip only added to the effect.

Her brother had called men like him brutal, and despite the gentleness she knew of him now, she thought him capable of meeting that description should he need to. Something about it brought her comfort, and as they'd spent the entire week discussing how to approach this very visit, she felt like she knew some hidden secret about him that no one else did.

He was nervous about this. He was a warrior, a wolf, but he wasn't a courtier.

Good thing he had her.

Dominik's horse came to a stop about ten yards in front of them, his own carts and soldiers stopping in unison. To his left was Ozik, their father's oldest advisor, black cape blowing in the subtle summer breeze that lifted his long white hair in tandem. Something about him had always made Vaasa shiver; it was in his constant presence, how no matter where she went in the castle, he was always *there*.

The air seemed to spark.

And then Dominik gave a sugared smile.

"Sister," he said in Asteryan, dismounting from his white horse as if the two of them were friendly and he truly was pleased to see her.

Murderer, murderer, murderer, her magic seemed to hum. The twisting in her gut felt like a thousand blades.

Sauntering forward on long, lean legs, Dominik stopped just in front of her to pay traditional Asteryan respect to her husband.

"Foreman," Dominik said in the same smooth tone, only able to speak in Asteryan. "A pleasure to be back in Mireh."

Vaasa translated for the two of them, moving between Asteryan and Icrurian as easily as she breathed.

"A pleasure to host you, Your Grace," Reid replied, curling his hand a little tighter in Vaasa's clothing.

Dominik inspected the area between them before he crossed the threshold of her personal space, gathering her in his arms. "Far too long, Vaasalisa."

Never long enough, she thought. "Far too long," she said aloud, sliding her hands around his narrow waist affectionately, subtly prepared for a blade or some other trick. He was all bone in her arms and she thought for only a second about snapping him like a branch. The memory of her mother came flashing back, that putrid scent caressing beneath her nose, and she tried to fight it back. Tried to tell herself it wasn't real.

"Your carts will have to file as a single line through the city, or they may of course stay here," Kosana said. "Narrow passageways."

"Single file will be fine," Ozik assured her, speaking Icrurian with the same ease with which he'd taught it to Vaasa, as Dominik finally released her and stepped away.

She wanted to shake, but she gathered her composure and smiled with all her teeth. The nearer the advisor came, the more her magic dove deep inside of her, as if it, too, wanted to run away. She was nothing more to him than a tool. She analyzed him, expecting to see the bleak neutrality with which he had always gazed upon her. But when Ozik came to the emperor's side, his narrow golden eyes flicked over Vaasa's body with the same scrutiny before he turned to Reid, who had reclaimed his spot next to her. Inspecting her warrior husband, Ozik dipped his head. "Foreman."

"Advisor," Reid said.

"Inside, inside," Vaasa said, playing into Dominik's practiced tone. "I do believe we can call each other by our names, yes?"

"Always a pleasure, my dear," Ozik said.

"Still grumpy, is he, Dominik?" she asked her brother, as if Ozik didn't terrify her one bit.

"Still grumpy," he assured her. The gleam in Dominik's eye was telling—a rehearsed routine between the two of them of which the other knew the truth.

There was no family connection between them. No love or consideration.

Dominik was a snake in the grass.

But he wasn't the only one, a fact that the little slither in her belly affirmed. She, too, was a snake who could play as a friend.

"Inside," Vaasa said again, turning and leaning into Reid as he guided her back into the city of Mireh. They would only need to entertain him for one night, and then Dominik would turn back around and go visit the other *investments* he'd made in northern Asterya—beneath the Icrurian border. This was merely a short detour from his already-scheduled visits.

"You're doing well," Reid whispered. "Even if I only understood half of what was just said."

"Nothing of importance," she replied, eyes focused on the gates of Mireh. "At least not yet."

As Dominik got settled at the High Temple of Mireh, Vaasa waited in the second-floor room she expected her brother would arrive in at any moment. She'd never said so aloud, but she was grateful Reid hadn't chosen to live in the temple. They were surrounded by the constant eyes of the Mirehan temple acolytes, and the only privacy they found yet was behind this door.

While Kosana and Reid spoke in the corner, reviewing the movements of Dominik's men outside the city, Vaasa was sprawled upon the couch watching Esoti, who paced back and forth in front of the door. Mathjin sat casually upon another couch in the far corner, his head moving to follow Esoti's movements.

"Stop pacing," Vaasa begged.

"I don't like you all in here with them," Esoti growled.

Mathjin's lips quirked. "Kosana could slaughter Dominik before he could blink."

"Not him. He is merely a green bean. I worry about the advisor. His eyes are those of an eagle. He sees everything."

Green bean was the oddest way Vaasa had ever heard her brother described, though arguably one of the funniest. Yet Esoti had perceived a truth about Ozik; he did not miss much, even in his peripheral vision. Vaasa said, "As it stands, it isn't a smart investment to attack Mireh. Ozik wouldn't suggest that Dominik do so."

"How do you know this?" Mathjin asked.

Her father had trusted Ozik, but only as far as her father trusted anyone. His proselytization about love and friendship hadn't been for naught, and his advisor was no exception. The only member of Vaasa's family who seemed to openly trust Ozik had been her mother. But Ozik was, after all, human. Likely he had ambitions of his own, and a hasty attack on a single city was not necessarily a powerful statement if it had no teeth behind it. In all probability, the Asteryan lords were chomping at the bit to test their new young emperor. They'd sold her for salt, so she wasn't certain the lords would want to risk losing that trade opportunity over Dominik's ambitions. Ozik would not want Dominik to fail, because to do so would mean he, too, had fallen short, and surely there was a bold lord somewhere waiting to take the advisor's position. "An attack on Mireh would be far too expensive when they do not have a viable exit plan. No. Their assault will be slow and drawn out, likely with a death toll higher than a single city. I anticipate an offer for trade. They will sink their teeth in slowly."

Everyone turned to her, staring silently. Only Reid remained staring at his stack of notes, unsurprised by the frankness with which she discussed her family's cruel ambitions or how easily such machinations came to her.

"If Dominik decides not to heed his advisor's warnings?" Esoti asked.

"Then either Kosana or Reid will kill them both," Vaasa suggested.

"You speak with such ease about the slaughter of your brother and your family's oldest advisor," Mathjin said.

Reid lifted his head then, turning to watch them at the same time Esoti stopped pacing.

A bit of insecurity bloomed, but Vaasa kept her chin high. "Yes, well, they sold me to the foreman of Mireh three weeks after my mother's death. If you couldn't tell, there is little love between me and my brother."

Mathjin sat up straight. "What I said came across entirely wrong; I apologize."

"No need."

"There is one," Reid said from across the room.

"There isn't," Vaasa said louder, not moving her eyes from Mathjin. She didn't blame him for questioning her in the least; she respected it. Mathjin was a smart advisor, and she admired his tenacity. He would spend the day pretending he didn't speak Asteryan, the smallest of upper hands they could have in this meeting.

Still, Kosana side-eyed the Mirehan advisor, and Esoti curled her lip.

It was foolish to want to be here, but she felt as though a tether had tied around her heart and latched on to the part of the map labeled with their city name. Mireh. Like it belonged to her, too. Power threaded along her fingertips at the thought of someone harming it.

And then that someone rapped against the door.

Mathjin and Vaasa stood from their couches, both coming to the table. Reid gestured for Vaasa to sit at his left, just as they'd done the night Marc visited. Taking what suddenly felt like her rightful place at his side, she watched the door open.

Reid twined his fingers in hers.

Foolish, possessive man—or so anyone looking upon them would think. They'd gotten good at pretending.

Dominik entered, freshly bathed and changed into another green jacket the color of Mekës's treetops. He adjusted the lapels, smiling widely at them all. Ozik followed on Dominik's heels, golden eyes surveying the room with his cloak around his shoulders. Upon entering, the advisor swept it over his right shoulder and draped it upon a chair.

"I did not realize we would have such a large group this afternoon," Dominik said in Asteryan. Vaasa translated, speaking low and close to Reid. Ozik listened in, prepared to translate every word of their response in Icrurian. It was strange to be standing opposite Ozik, considering she only knew these languages because of him. She had spent her life on the other side of the table—on *Asterya's* side—and she didn't know if that made her a liability or a threat.

Reid did not hesitate to answer, a calm friendliness dripping from his lips. "I cannot convince my wife's guard to leave her side, no matter the company."

Dominik tilted his head and grasped the chair in front of him with long, bony fingers when Ozik whispered the translation. "Ah. Well, we will see you for dinner tonight, Vaasa, and I'm sorry I do not know your guard's name," he said as he settled into the chair across from Reid.

Vaasa translated, and Reid slid out her chair without dropping his gaze from Dominik's. "Her guard's name is Esoti, and though you are unfamiliar with our traditions, Your Grace, it is the custom that a consort remains with her husband. My wife will stay at my side."

Upon the words, Esoti took her spot against the wall, hand conveniently rested against her dagger.

Dominik's jaw ticked as Ozik translated. Then he looked to Vaasa. Gleaming on his finger was his signature clawed silver ring, one sharp enough to cut just like his words, and she swore it twitched. The black stone inside of it swallowed the light that touched him. "Good to see you settling in so nicely at his side. It seems this country suits you." He attempted to undermine Reid in the way he looked to her, though he probably didn't realize to respond directly to her wasn't an insult to Reid of Mireh.

Reid gestured for her to sit. When she did, he ran his fingers over her shoulder and down her arm, collecting her hand in his again before taking his own seat. "She has fit in better than I could have hoped," Reid said.

Ozik grinned as he relayed the message. Dominik kept his sickening smile plastered to his face. "I'm thrilled to see you're happy with our first transaction."

Transaction. The word was purposeful—as was the subtle tap of Vaasa's finger against Reid's wrist as she correctly contextualized his intentions; a signal to leave it alone, even though his palm twitched. Even though her own did, too.

"Perhaps these negotiations will be quick," Mathjin said in an even, unbothered tone, "given everyone is so happy with this arrangement."

"Perhaps," Dominik said a few moments after Ozik translated.

Vaasa wanted to throw herself across the table and rip his hair from his head, but she blinked away the violent images and kept her magic at bay. It sat in her stomach, coiled, prepared, and she licked her lips at the thought.

"What do you need from us?" Reid asked, giving Dominik the opportunity to start as she'd told him to do two nights ago when they discussed how to approach this very moment.

"As you know, the crossing of the Loursevain Gap is of paramount priority for Asterya. Trade with Zataar is practically impossible, given our little pest problem," Dominik said.

He referred to the pirates who ruled the bay Mekës was built upon. They'd haunted the area for centuries, and her father had only begun to temper the problem.

"So, you are in need of ships?" Reid asked.

Exactly what they expected.

"Ships . . ." Dominik rocked his hand back and forth with a pinch of his lips. "Ships, eventually. The issue with the pirates cannot be solved by any water vessel. No, we need to be able to travel by land *before* we travel the sea, which is currently impossible given the hostility of your eastern territories."

Vaasa's brow furrowed. "What are you asking for, then?" she asked, skipping the translation.

Reid didn't question her—something Dominik took note of.

Something she intended.

"I would like you to order the foremen of Wrultho and Hazut to remove their troops from the trade routes and allow us safe access to the Innisjour Fang," her brother said smoothly.

This time, she translated. Reid's hand froze beneath the table. "What do you need with the fang?"

"We would like to set up a trading post there, and for everyone's cooperation, we will fund the cost of erecting it," Dominik said. "The kingdom of Zataar has already expressed interest in opening up their ports for both of our use, which I believe all of us would benefit from."

A trading post at the edge of the fang? The single piece of land jutted out like a canine tooth from the Icrurian shores, creating the Warfell Strait that divided Icruria from Zataar. If any headman tried to establish trade with the nation, that would be the best place.

To give Dominik access to the fang meant giving him a stronghold in Icruria.

There was no way Reid could even consider it.

Regardless, Reid pursed his lips. "I cannot order any of my fellow foremen to do that."

"What is the use of being headman, then?" Dominik asked, sharpening his tongue. "Is that not what you will be? Not why I agreed to allow my sister to come here in the first place?"

"He will be headman," Vaasa snapped in Icrurian, being overt about her attention to Reid. She translated quickly.

Looking down at her, Reid grinned. "My wife is correct."

The guise of protectiveness in a language her so-called husband could understand must have registered with the Asteryan advisor, because Ozik gave a pleasured purse of his lips when he translated.

"Good," Dominik said, leaning back in his chair and glancing between the two of them. "Then it will be within your purview to call for a cease to the violence at the border."

"Is it not within *your* purview to call for a cease to the violence at the border?" Mathjin asked in stunning Icrurian, having waited for a translation, not letting a soul know that he could understand them.

Ozik shifted in his seat, looking squarely at Mathjin as he said, "Do you blame the Asteryans for the violence?"

"You built the dam along the Sanguine," Mathjin pointed out.

"It was *your* people who attacked. The lands around those areas were flooding," Dominik added, causing Reid's jaw to flicker as she translated the words.

Lies. All bald-faced mistruths strung in a tone of sweet desperation. To remove guilt from the Asteryans and make it seem like a choice made for survival . . . It was manipulative at best.

Ozik watched her, waiting. Testing her, she realized. To see if she would correct them, because she had been there when that war started. She had been in the very room.

Vaasa translated it word for word without a single correction—and Reid nodded like he believed her. Mathjin, too.

Ozik's lips slithered into a smile, speaking in Asteryan as he gazed upon her. "You look so much like a devoted wife; I forget you are the same chameleon your father raised."

What was Ozik up to?

"The nature of a person does not change, even if their surroundings do," Vaasa replied in Asteryan.

With pursed lips, Ozik swept a strand of his white hair off his shoulder. "Perhaps you and I should speak in private before this little visit is over."

Dominik flicked his eyes to her. Smiled with all of his teeth.

"About the *flooding*?" Vaasa asked, still in Asteryan.

"About the *flooding*," Ozik agreed.

Mirroring Dominik's smile, Vaasa coolly said, "Perhaps we should."

But her throat felt tight.

There was no flooding. There never had been.

The two of them were purposefully lying, just to see if she would go along with it.

Reid furrowed his brow as he looked between them all, his hand tightening in hers. She translated an entirely false discussion about how the flooding was so miserable in that area that the Asteryans had no choice. She made them out to be a victim, one in authentic search of an end to the violence, just like she suspected Dominik and Ozik were hoping she would.

"I do think I can negotiate with Wrultho," Reid said in Icrurian once more. "But that will be the cost—the dam. If you opted to take it down, they may be willing to free up an opportunity for trading in good faith. Perhaps we can come to an agreement about the infrastructure your people need."

"Would this negotiation harm your chances of election? Alienate the very people who will elect you?" Dominik asked outright.

Reid pursed his lips as Vaasa translated. Shook his head. "No, I believe it is the will of most of Icruria to build upon the foundations this marriage has laid. It is time our city-states trade openly."

Ozik translated each word with full fidelity. Dominik leaned back, gesturing widely with his hands. "Then let us build upon them. Show them what an alliance with Asterya looks like. I expect to have your people address my sister as high consort within the year."

Reid's hand tightened on hers as she translated. Still, she used her free hand to run it up and down Reid's arm, looking rather territorial in everyone's eyes.

Everyone's but Ozik's and Dominik's.

Especially when Reid beamed down at her and slid his own free hand to her cheek, turning his lips to her temple and saying, "That she will be."

If Ozik and Dominik wanted to speak with her in private, there was more than they were letting on. To so blatantly address *her* potential for upward movement . . .

From where she sat now, her placement could easily be construed as intentional. If she didn't know that they'd expected her to die, that they *wanted* her to die, she would say without a doubt it was. To seat her at the side of the man soon to be elected headman of all of Icruria?

She was in the prime position to gain Reid's affection and trust. She was as close to a queen in this territory as anyone could get.

The heiress of Asterya. Planted directly inside where they wanted to go.

And *that* was how conquerors schemed. Which immediately begged the question: Had her mother been a conqueror, too?

"Like my husband said, I believe we can bargain in good faith," Vaasa said in Asteryan.

She knew how Dominik would hear it—that she wasn't referring to her and the foreman of Wrultho. Rather, she was referring to her and him.

"Good faith is all I'm in search of," Dominik assured her.

That sugared tone and smile said otherwise, something she doubted slipped past Reid. Still, she tapped his wrist again, signaling him to agree. "Then bring down the dam."

"Provided you convince Wrultho to lay their weapons down," Dominik said.

Reid nodded. "We are in agreement."

"Shall we be done with this now?" Vaasa asked.

Dominik happily obliged, standing from the table and stretching his legs.

Ozik followed her brother out the door, the two headed for a walk around the grounds of the temple led by Kosana's corps, dressed as acolytes. The moment the door closed, Reid turned to look at her, eyebrow lifting.

"He wants to speak with me in private," Vaasa whispered.

"Is that what the advisor meant?" Mathjin asked. Undoubtedly, he had understood every Asteryan word. Would he trust her less now?

She nodded.

"No." Reid's eyes moved between her and the door. "Absolutely not."

"He won't harm me," she said. *At least not yet.* "He wants something, and it's in our best interest to find out what."

Reid shifted his weight uncomfortably but didn't argue again.

It was Mathjin who said, "You don't have a choice, do you?"

Vaasa shook her head. "No, not really."

CHAPTER 14

That night, while Reid and Kosana were engaged with one of Dominik's men discussing lodging for their carts and unit, Vaasa slipped into a first-floor room in the High Temple of Mireh. Knives strapped to her thigh, she tried not to be afraid.

Standing next to the large, purple-curtained window was Ozik, his cloak thrown over a distant chair, the lapels of his jacket neatly pressed. His elbow rested upon a stone banister jutting from the wall. At her entrance, he smiled and crossed one ankle over the other.

To his right, on a blue velvet chair with his long legs crossed, sat Dominik.

"Sister," Dominik said in smooth Asteryan, not deigning to rise but rather gesturing to the sibling blue chair placed across from him. Upon his middle finger was that ring, pointing for him. "Please, sit."

A very real part of her lifted at letting her Asteryan out to play again. Like her tongue stretched and sighed, she said, "Brother, Ozik," as she sat down.

"How are you settling into Mireh?" Dominik asked, eyes carefully gauging her response.

If she wanted to keep them all safe, it was imperative Dominik believe her slighted. A little unhinged. Out of control and unwilling to admit it. So she let the magic on her fingertips dance along the arm of the chair—random swipes of mist that to someone who hadn't spent every day with Amalie would look like a lack of control. "Are you asking if I enjoy being married against my will to a brute from Icruria?" She tilted her head and inspected him just as thoroughly. "Or if I am still on the verge of death?"

For a few moments, silence coursed between them. Would he buy her little tantrum? She'd already decided her best plan of attack was to make him think she was far closer to death than she really was. The best lies were rooted in truth, and as Ozik had already said, she could be anything in a room that she needed to be.

The advisor spoke from the window, gold eyes narrowed upon the black mist. The more she looked at him, the more she noticed his age. It had only been a few months, but he seemed to have lost years to Dominik. "So, you did master the magic?"

She summoned more of the power, but also dug her nails into the blue velvet like it caused her pain.

Golden eyes caught the movement. "How does it feel?"

"To have unknowingly inherited the very thing that killed my mother?"

"Perhaps you will control it better than she did," Ozik said, a bit of sadness dripping from his voice. Vaasa didn't believe it was genuine.

With each simmering word, the magic slithered along the chair a little further from Vaasa's control. Or so it seemed. Stubbornly, she held the advisor's eyes with all the unleashed fury she possessed. How long had he known of her mother's magic? His sheer comfort with it contrasted with Dominik's apparent disgust. While her brother wrinkled his nose, Ozik examined her with wonder.

"I didn't think you would be comfortable settling for this heat," Dominik said, revulsion thick in his tone as he eyed the places the magic touched.

Vaasa snapped her head to him. "And yet you sent me here anyway."

The black stone of his ring glared at her as Dominik lifted his wine goblet to his lips and drank. Setting it down, he shrugged his left shoulder. "You seem to have made him your bitch as quickly as I expected."

To speak that way about Reid . . . "I am Asteryan. These Icrurian men don't scare me."

"Hmmm." Dominik considered for a moment. "It seems even the hiccup on the night of your wedding could not discourage him from you. Did you enjoy Dihrah?"

The magic in Vaasa's gut roared a warning, snake coiling and hissing. His spies shouldn't have been able to reach this far—how did he know about her time at the sodality?

Raising his hand, he waved it casually. "There are no happenings on this continent I am not aware of. Not to worry, it has worked in your favor. Reid of Mireh is enthralled with you. It seems these Icrurian men enjoy a challenge."

Crossing her own legs and leaning back in her chair, she said, "That little *hiccup* is the reason I am alive."

Lies.

"It was always up to you whether you lived or died. It seems you wanted to live," Dominik said. The confidence in his eyes made her think he didn't believe a word that came out of his own mouth.

"What I wanted was to not be married."

Something wicked pierced his gaze. "You can blame Mother for that."

Was that . . . resentment?

Just as quickly as it was there, Dominik's fury folded neatly back into control. "The only reason you would stay here is because he offered you something to make it worthwhile. So, sister, what did he promise you?"

Dominik hadn't come here to pretend, then. She shook off what she'd just seen in his eyes. She could deny his assumptions about her, assumptions that were entirely true. That *was* why she'd come back to

Mireh. And it was working in her favor, so what was the use? "A legal divorce," Vaasa confessed after a moment. "And the arrangement to start somewhere new."

Brows rising, Dominik ran his tongue along his teeth. "In how long?"

"Three years, give or take."

"You can stand being in his bed for three years?"

Vaasa said, "He's giving."

"Has he won you over with his *giving* tendencies?"

"Do you believe a little curve to the left is all it takes to domesticate me?" she snapped, letting the magic circle her neck like it thought to choke her. As if she was scared of it, she visibly tried to dismiss the mist.

But she did not let it disappear entirely.

Dominik leaned back in his chair again, eyes glittering with amusement at her outburst. At her apparent lack of control. He took another sip from the goblet upon the wooden table next to him.

"Do you believe he will be elected?" Ozik asked, pushing a strand of his snow-white hair from his face.

Turning to face the advisor, she said, "Only if he can make them believe my presence is an advantage rather than a threat."

"But you don't want that?" Dominik asked. "You'd rather have this new life than be their high consort?"

"High consort of what? A nation with no water or influence?"

"Oh, it can't be that terrible."

"You weren't exiled here."

"Exiled!" Dominik laughed. "I gave you a nation; it is certainly not my fault you haven't chosen to claim it."

"With what forces, Dominik? I can fuck Reid of Mireh all I want, but that won't give me an army."

Dominik paused, looking to Ozik.

"If you're going to say it, Ozik, do so out loud," she growled.

Ozik chuckled by the window, toasting them both as if he found their sibling spats to be humorous. Yet when he looked upon her, it was with a slice of pity. "Your sister believes she was sold to Reid of

Mireh and sent here to die, and therefore her allegiances do not lie with you. He is proposing her freedom, Dominik, and unless you can beat that offer, she is not likely to bargain with you."

The goblet froze at Dominik's lips. "Freedom?"

"Yes, freedom," Vaasa confirmed.

"And if I offered you a life back in Asterya?" He said it with a casual neutrality that dragged nails down her spine. "An ambassadorship to any of the nations you studied so intently, and all the rights and privileges that came with it?"

At one time, that had been a dream of hers. Dominik knew the impact of those words—knew she would leap at such an opportunity.

"So you can kill me later?" she asked outright.

Dominik paused before drinking, lowering his glass to his knee. "I don't have to kill you if Reid of Mireh is dead."

Hatred sewed into the caverns of her chest, but she curled her lips like a starved animal smelling blood. Like her foot was caught in a trap and she was moments from chewing it off with her own teeth.

Dominik ate up her desperation. "I'm not foolish enough to underestimate what you can give me, sister. Mother may have wasted you on this foolish marriage, but I won't be making either of our parents' mistakes."

There it was again, that veiled resentment she'd never known existed in him. "That sounds a lot like freedom," she deigned to say.

"Is it better than what he's giving you?"

She stopped speaking for a moment, lips pursed, pretending to contemplate. "If I swear to never marry again, you'll let me live?"

He nodded. "There would be no reason to kill you."

Vaasa let herself flinch at the words, as if she were still scared.

Dominik seemed to revel in that. "Icruria will fall, and these people will bow to me. So if Reid of Mireh won't give you an army, perhaps I can."

Her magic bubbled in warning, her gut telling her not to trust a word that came out of Dominik's mouth. But she uncrossed her legs and leaned forward anyway. "I'm listening."

Like a predator gazing upon injured prey, Dominik's eyes glimmered with power and ambition. It must have been all he saw—he was drunk with it. "Get that husband of yours elected. Give my men half a year to establish what looks like peaceful trade along the route to the fang, and our commanders will take care of this *new* capital with your insight. Within the year, you will have your freedom and I will have Icruria."

Dominik's plan wouldn't work. The Icrurian forces were loyal to their nation based on principle, where the Asteryan forces were motivated by money alone. Hazut and Wrultho were already insurmountable to him without another angle, and the Icrurians would fight longer and harder than even Dominik's purse could maintain. Even if they did bring the capital closer to Asterya by Reid winning the election, Dominik would still have more military force to contend with than he understood.

The far smarter strategy would be to stay truthful to his first few bargains—to set up the trading post and wait a few years, so at least one or two of the territories were economically dependent on its existence. By then, at least a fraction of the population would consider war with Asterya to be foolish. Then he would have all the leverage in the world; to take their salt, steal their ships, and use their own reserves of steel against them in a swift and brutal attack.

But Dominik was greedy and brash, and by the whispers of resentment she'd seen, he had something to prove.

"One year?" Vaasa confirmed. "And I live?"

"One year and you live."

She looked to Ozik, raising a brow. The advisor nodded. She thought it odd that he'd advise such a brazen move, but by the look of the expensive fabrics draped over his shoulders, Vaasa wondered if Ozik cared for this particular endeavor at all.

"I will be in contact with you directly. If you have so much influence over your husband, be sure he does not translate the letters from your dear brother," Dominik instructed.

Vaasa snorted. "Is that all?"

"That is all. For now." Pouring her a goblet of wine from the tray between them, he passed it to her and lifted his own. "A toast, to family."

Cool metal fell into her fingertips and she raised it to her lips, sniffing carefully.

Like honey and wine, though with a tiny twinge of an acidic note.

So subtle, she may have never smelled it.

Her heart thudded against her ribs.

She paused.

Put the goblet down.

Leaning forward in his chair, Dominik gripped his own wine tighter, malice swimming in the ocean of his eyes. "I know you will do as our father raised you to, so I may do as he raised me to."

A threat, not at all veiled in subtlety, and an insult all wrapped into one. "Poison?" she dared to ask.

"Just seeing if you're still on your toes, sister."

Hatred, cold and glowing, grew bright within her. She hated them both—and in that moment, she hated Asterya, too. "Dancing on them."

"Good." Dominik tilted his head. "Because as it stands, there is no one better situated to bring about the fall of a nation than you. And no one with so much to lose."

He'd played the battle as their father had raised them, in true Asteryan fashion. By preying upon the things she wanted more than anything, he had done exactly as he'd been taught.

It was sickening.

Dominik smiled.

Running her tongue over her teeth, she nodded in understanding.

Sauntering out the door without a look over her shoulder, Vaasa waited until she was well down the hallway before she smiled to herself.

He had misjudged her loyalties, believing them to belong only to herself. Perhaps a few months ago, she would have taken his offer. A few months ago, she didn't have anything but her Asteryan name.

She'd since dropped that name and traded it for something new.

He still believed this city useless. Defenseless. Easy to conquer.

He did not know of their ships or their armies or their magic.

But he was right about one thing: there was no one better situated to bring about the fall of a nation than her.

Which, at the very least, bought her a semblance of time.

The moment she got to their room, Vaasa turned and faced Reid. "I was right. The trade route is only a way to clear the path to Mireh."

Reid went rigid, then seemed to force himself to relax. Leaning against the door, he asked, "What did he offer you?"

"A year and then an ambassadorship to any nation of my choosing."

This time he froze, all traces of comfort draining from his features.

"What?" Vaasa asked.

"That's a better offer."

Her brows knitted together. "Excuse me?"

"One year, and you could have more than what I offered to give you in three."

"Reid." She paused, took a small breath, and then turned to escape deeper into the bedroom; her footsteps echoed with the sounds of her pounding heart. "You are making the same mistake he did."

Silence.

When Vaasa finally turned, Reid was still leaning back against the door watching her. Insecurity threaded between them, and she wondered for a moment if that was fear she saw laced in his eyes.

"And what is that?"

His voice curled down her spine something fierce and jostled the already ill-tempered magic. It paced like a jungle cat again. It was too intense, the way he looked at her.

She slid behind the dressing screen. Took a long, deep breath.

Vaasa's jaw set as she looked down at her clenched fists—at the little stirring of mist there.

Footsteps padded along the floor and she froze. Reid didn't cross the threshold of the screen. Instead, he stood directly in front of it and out of her view. "You're hidden now. Talk to me."

The moment she saw Dominik dismount his horse, she knew she'd been a fool. How Reid had guarded her only confirmed what she should have realized the moment he found her in that library.

He was her best chance at survival. He always had been.

Hidden from anyone's view, truth seemed to slither along her tongue. She'd told Amalie, hadn't she? But knowing Reid could read her so easily, knowing that she needed him, lit up her nerves. She took the opportunity to untie the knot of fabric at her waist, ignoring his shadow on the screen's fabric. Stepping out and brushing the hair away from her neck, she looked over her shoulder and met his gaze.

With a flick of his eyes downward, he moved to the spot behind her and began unlacing the impractical bodice of her formal wear. They were entirely silent as he undid the last string.

She stepped behind the dressing screen and let the fabric fall to the floor. Next came the pants.

His shadow started to move.

Spine straightening, her breath hitched.

A drawer opened. Closed. Steps echoed on the hard stone. In a moment, his shadow returned, and soft gray fabric draped over the top of the screen.

It was another one of his shirts. He'd begun switching them out and laundering them himself, never once mentioning the routine. She should have gotten her own night clothing by now, but she hadn't, and . . . damn him. "Thank you," she said as she pulled his shirt over her torso and wiggled out of the constricting panties he'd never find out she wasn't wearing.

As she stepped out from the screen prepared to speak, he ducked through the curtains into the bathroom. What compelled her, she didn't know, but she followed. Leaning against the doorframe, she watched as he dragged his drapes up and over his arms. Her eyes scanned the plane of his chest, down the depiction of armor inked upon his shoulder. Dropping his hands to the buttons of his pants, he raised a brow. "You here for a show, Wild One?"

Her eyes snapped up. "I didn't think we'd finished our conversation."

"We haven't. I was just letting you decide when you're ready."

"I'm ready."

He spun his finger in a circle, a wicked, mocking grin stealing each of his features.

"Oh, now you care for modesty?" she asked.

"Two can play at this game."

With a heavy roll of her eyes, she turned around and stared out at the bedroom, her hip leaned against the doorframe. Faintly, she heard him balancing and changing out of his pants.

Something in her wanted to turn around, and she didn't know what that instinct was or where it came from. With a full breath, she pushed the thought away. This, she could do. The harmless flirtation was just how they got along.

"I think we should speak with Wrultho anyway," he finally said. "Persuade them to at least attempt a peace."

A plan like that was idealistic and foolish. "I think we should persuade them to move their army farther east and prepare to strike," Vaasa countered.

"That's awfully violent of you."

"It's practical of me."

"It's the opposite of peace."

"They should not leave themselves defenseless," she argued, staring at the wall in frustration. "Dominik will think his plan is working, and all the while we'll be building our forces under his nose."

With the sound of three steps, Reid sauntered up behind her. "I thought you were a courtier, not a war general."

"Who wouldn't want both in a wife?"

"A fool."

She grinned, even though he couldn't see it.

Suddenly, his body came a little closer, his bare chest hovering behind her back. "Why not take his deal and run?"

She still struggled to find the right words, to confess something that took any power and control directly from her hands. "I don't want his deal."

"Why?"

"Because it isn't real. When his soldiers march in, he will ensure I die in that conflict."

"And how do you know that?"

Bluntly, she confessed, "He tried to poison me tonight."

Every muscle Reid had must have frozen; she could feel his rigidity behind her. "He did *what*?"

"I smelled it before taking a sip of the wine. It was a threat, a reminder of what he intends to do if I don't behave."

There was the smallest of pauses, just a second. Enough for her to feel the charge of his anger.

And then the warmth of his chest against her back disappeared.

"Don't," she warned, but Reid didn't stop moving.

Her newly trained reflexes kicked in and she swept her leg out and caught the lift of his back foot. His steps stuttered just enough for her to leap in front of him. He grabbed at her shirt and she rocked her hip outward, skating just past the pads of his fingers on a spin. And then she threw her back against the door. Both hands grabbed at the handles behind her, and when she caught her balance, he was suddenly there.

The air turned warm as he looked up and down the length of her body. "You know I can move you, right?"

"You won't."

His jaw ticked like he contemplated proving her wrong. "This ends in his death. Give me one reason I shouldn't do it tonight."

"Because we are smarter than he is, and that would be an act of war. We would lose both countries."

Reid didn't uncoil, but he didn't try to come closer or move around her, either. "What do you mean *both* countries?"

Menace tingled on her tongue, a twisting anger stealing the parts of her that wanted peace. The parts of her that thought there was some way to avoid Dominik's ambitions.

But there was no way. For as long as he served on that throne, the world was in peril.

She was in peril.

She didn't know a thing about trust, but she thought if she had to put a name to it, it was whatever she felt when Reid looked at her just then. It was enough to give her a voice, one that spoke truth. "For years, my father killed off every distant member of our family. Few still survive, only cousins who keep the Kozár name because of the fear it strikes in the men they lead. He was obsessed with it, ensuring there would never be a legal challenge to his throne. Dominik has inherited that obsession, among other things."

Watching her carefully, Reid waited for her to continue.

Letting out a strong breath, she relaxed against the door. "There has never been a female monarch of Asterya, only male, regardless of bloodline. Generations ago, a man won his throne by marrying a Kozár daughter because she was the only sibling left. And while my father has changed every border and grown a kingdom into an empire, that is still, legally, how it works in Asterya."

"I don't understand," he said.

"A Kozár daughter cannot claim the throne alone. She must be married. She must be the only option left."

Shifting his weight in front of her, his large shoulders almost brushed hers. "You have claim to the Asteryan throne?"

"No, Reid. You do."

Confusion came first in the furrow of his brow, then understanding tumbled across his widening eyes. "What?"

"If Dominik dies, any husband of mine can take it."

"Then why did he make this arrangement? Why would he ever allow you to get married?"

"Because he didn't make this arrangement, he was only forced to live with it. My guess is that the lords who fund his border disputes and land expansions wanted your salt badly enough that he would have lost more by severing the agreement. He expected this magic to kill me."

"But it didn't."

"So now he will."

Reid's fingers curled into her shirt, low on her hip, and he stepped forward into her space. "Then let me make you an empress. Tonight."

Nervous heat rushed over her. She'd considered this already, but to do so would be detrimental to Reid's ambitions. "And explain to the voting councilors how you murdered the Asteryan emperor? I thought you wanted to win the election, not throw it away."

"Surely you don't believe he is the only one who can make death look like an accident."

"No, but if I know you like I think I know you, you'd look him in the eye as you killed him."

Reid's hand remained on her hip as he gritted his teeth. But he couldn't argue that point. He knew it. "Why am I only hearing of this now?"

"Because in three years, neither of us will have a claim to the throne." Her hands tightened on the golden door handles digging into her back. Would he believe her, or would he think she was only playing a game with him? "I told you the truth: I don't want it. So it didn't matter until Dominik waltzed in here and threatened Icruria. It isn't his to take."

"And now it matters?"

"Now it matters."

"You sound awfully defensive of Icruria."

"Should I not be?"

"Oh, you should. I just didn't realize how much I would enjoy watching you defend what is mine."

Charged silence coursed between them, and she forced her eyes away.

Reid paused for a moment, still not asking her to look at him, and not as angry as she suspected he may be. Slowly, the hand at her hip stroked her side as he considered what he wanted to say. As he, too, calmed himself. "Did you think I would force you to stay? That I would see the potential for an empire and renege on our deal?"

Her body went taut at that question. "Yes, I feared that at first."

"And now?"

Her eyes closed so she couldn't see his face, couldn't see the reaction to her words paint across it. "Now I think you are more worthy of the Asteryan throne than anyone else I have ever met. And if you want it, I will give it to you."

All sense of his breath seemed to stop. The hand upon her side stopped, too, and something about that absence of movement made her open her eyes.

He wanted her to look at him. "What are you suggesting?"

"I've already told you."

"You subtly hinted. Tell me with authority, Vaasa."

"Why?" she asked. "Why must you insist on making an event out of this?"

"Because I have learned not to make assumptions when it comes to you. Tell me exactly what you want, so I can stop guessing and just give it to you."

Letting out a frustrated sigh, she tipped her head back against the door. "My father consolidated power in his empire. I'm suggesting you disperse it once more. Put in place local foremen who will be honest and loyal to you as their headman, and whoever serves after you."

"You wish?"

Swallowing, she dove headfirst into her treason. "Yes."

"That—" He stopped. Faintly, she felt him shift his weight; it was in the way his fingers subtly rocked. "That land would change everything. Those resources."

"You'll solve a drought and prevent a war, all in one fell swoop."

"Where does that leave you?"

An answer glowed on the edges of her mind, distant like a horizon but visible nonetheless. "Free."

His body relaxed in front of hers. "That was the mistake Dominik made, assuming your mind hadn't changed about Mireh. About Icruria. About me."

"He asked if I could stand being in your bed for three years."

Reid grunted. "Now that's just insulting."

A small laugh slipped out of her.

Still not moving away like he should have, like she should have insisted he do, Reid tilted his head. For a moment, she wondered if he would speak at all or if he would ask some unanswerable, foolish question.

And then his accent floated between them, doing just that. "Why would you help me take everything your father built?"

He always found a way to pry straight to the root of things.

For some reason, she felt she owed him this truth, too. The one he had asked for weeks ago. She wanted him to understand. "Years ago, there was a man. His name was Roman. I loved him, and Dominik had him killed."

Reid froze, his fingers curling into her shirt. "Vaasa—"

"Don't. It's long over. The point is this; I hold no loyalty to Dominik. If you believe one thing about me, let it be that."

He loomed in front of her, close enough to give the unmistakable air of intimacy. Of the protection of her words, her secrets, because they were the only two in the world who could hear. "I believe you."

His words settled into a crevice of her chest that she didn't want to admit often felt empty. One that had started to feel so much fuller since coming here, in ways she didn't understand. "He'll be sending letters. I'm under strict instructions not to let you read them."

Reid only smirked. "I believe we can find a way around that rule."

Something about the way he said it caused the knots in her stomach to tighten. The skin beneath his fingers to rise. His words from the first night she'd followed him into the bathing chamber rolled through her mind.

It wouldn't technically be breaking our agreement if I took you in here.

She subtly squeezed her thighs together. That was somewhere she would never go, so she began to move, to create space so she could think properly.

But his arm shot out and blocked her path, his hand on her hip gathering in the fabric of her shirt to hold her there. "Sleep in the bed tonight."

Her breath caught.

Looking from his arm to his pleading gaze, she said, "If you get too close to me, Dominik will kill you, and he will make me watch."

"I am not afraid of your brother."

"You should be."

He shook his head. "I'm not asking you to love me. I'm asking you to sleep."

Refusing to drop her gaze, she said, "What if I like the couch?"

"You don't like the couch."

He was right, and her heart started to pound harder. "I don't like the couch."

Both corners of his mouth turned up and he dipped his voice to a whisper. "And if I say there are monsters under the bed and I am desperately afraid of the dark?"

Her lips threatened a smile. "It doesn't seem you're afraid of anything."

"I have fears, Wild One. You just don't know them yet."

She fought herself relentlessly, and yet with a flick of her eyes to the warm fur blankets of the bed, her resolve crumbled. They were walking a thin line.

It was only sleeping.

"All right," she conceded, wanting to be angry with herself and yet finding nothing but a contentedness in her belly. For once, her magic was silent. "But only because of the monsters."

He released the grip he held on her shirt, but his fingers crawled to the small of her back as he nodded slowly. "Only because of the monsters."

Desire formed deep in her abdomen. She didn't think she'd ever allowed someone to remain this close, not in years, if ever. The right thing to do would be to pull away.

Neither of them moved.

After a moment, Reid chuckled. Releasing her slowly, he dragged his touch down her arm again and curled his fingers inside of hers, leading her to the main room and gesturing toward the bed.

Months ago, she would have strangled him before obliging.

This time, she crawled beneath the sheets and pulled them up to her chin, letting their softness and warmth swallow her. As she blew out the lantern on his bedside table, darkness bathed the room. He slid into the spot next to her, his large body emanating warmth even as he kept a terrible, respectful distance.

Just as he had promised.

She tried to slow the beating of her heart.

"Why do I get the feeling you preferred us up against the door?" he whispered into the space between them.

With reckless abandon, she said, "Because I did."

The bed dipped once more as he turned, his body sprawled in front of her, their breath mingling. His touch returned to her hip. "Was it the proximity, or was it my hands?"

Looking up at his far-too-confident grin, she placed her own hands against his bare chest and curled her fingers just slightly against his skin. Leaning a little closer so their foreheads touched, she whispered, "I'm not going to answer that."

And then spun so her back was to him.

Pride washed over her at besting him, but then her breath stuttered as Reid slid his arms under and over her, dragging her waist against the crook of his body. As she froze there, she couldn't breathe, not as he started doing those damn circles on her abdomen that he'd done that first night in the Lower Garden.

He rumbled with a little bit of laughter. "Then I'll do both, and you can tell me when you're ready what you prefer."

No witty remark came to her, no clever rebuttal. In every language, she was out of answers. Even with his hand firmly above the shirt, with each pass that almost touched the sensitive lower curve of her breasts, her breathing became less even. The line between her instinct and her mind was muddled.

This was dangerous, but her body roared to push further.

Her back arched just a small bit and she told herself it was an accident, that she was merely adjusting her position. But when she brushed up against him, he went rigid.

"Sleep, Wild One," he breathed into her ear. "Or I won't let you."

It was an invitation. She knew it was.

She shouldn't do this.

She forced her eyes closed, the undercurrent of his words doing unfathomable things to the muscles in her stomach, and tried to center herself. Tried to control the foolish instinct she felt to ask him to make good on that promise.

She would never forgive herself if she messed this all up. If she started something she couldn't finish and ended up without a home or a dream again.

She would never give someone the power to leave her desperate.

So she evened her breathing and turned her magic to water, drifting to sleep with the rhythm of his hands.

CHAPTER 15

Each day, Vaasa trained her offensive magic relentlessly with Romana.

They had been right—one Veragi witch was a problem, a coven was a nightmare.

Working with Romana had changed Vaasa's offense twofold. Melisina was as flexible as water and as wise as an owl, and the cycles seemed to cater to her whims. With her, Vaasa learned balance and the importance of tensile strength. Romana, too, was as unmovable as a mountain, but unlike Melisina, she quaked like one, too. She taught Vaasa another piece of the cycle—release. Vaasa found their unique practice of magic to be curious, considering she hadn't realized how much she would benefit from the exposure. She had strong faith in the tenets they all lived by, but her excitement grew at the thought of what she would accomplish and who she may become.

If only she had the time.

Vaasa had slept in the bed each night since Dominik had left. Neither she nor Reid made a big deal of the occurrence, the foreman acting as though it was the most normal thing in the world. Some nights she slept soundly, and others, she couldn't breathe with his body pressed to hers.

Reid simply woke and padded off to his responsibilities, or sometimes joined the larger group for their exercises in the morning. He spent a vast amount of time with Kosana and Mathjin. Vaasa had never understood before how close the three of them were, and as they settled into her role and presence on their team, they began to frequent the villa more often.

They must have been like this before she'd arrived, she realized one evening, and the thought made her heart sink a little. She wondered what Reid did all day, but by the shuffle of papers he sometimes brought home and pored over on the veranda, she assumed it was mostly managerial. Was that what his life would be like as headman?

In times of peace, perhaps.

One hot afternoon, Reid took her to the vast salt flats and introduced her to the salt lords, the same rich men he'd negotiated with to keep restaurants like Neil's open. They looked at her strangely, and it took a few minutes for them to warm to her. Upon seeing Reid's affection for her, though, they softened. One even gave her a vial of purplish salt as a friendly gesture.

She kept that tucked in her pocket all day for a reason she couldn't name.

Two weeks later, Vaasa received Dominik's first letter.

She sat with Mathjin and he documented each word, writing down the exact translation and filing it away in a little box in his office. Scribbles across his brown ledger recorded the date and gave the letter its own serial number. Meticulously, he wrote down those numbers and placed the journal in that same box.

"I don't quite understand what he's saying," Vaasa told the advisor in Asteryan, who clung to each of her words with fidelity. It wasn't lost on her just how much trust all of this required, and she did her best to remain as open and forthcoming as she could be. "Most of this is small talk, though he mentions a gift. If there's a part of this that's meant to mean anything, it's that."

Nodding slowly, Mathjin pressed a pale hand to the table as his eyes scanned the letter once more. "Yet there's nothing about Wrultho."

"Nothing."

"I have thoughts on that, but I suspect you do as well," Mathjin said, speaking in her native tongue, if only to give her someone else to use it with.

"I want to propose they move soldiers farther east, that they take down the dam themselves. We can approach them during the conferences at the election."

Mathjin pursed his lips, looking older now than he usually did. He had this way about him, a stern tug of his mouth that spoke about all topics with a clinical neutrality, as if he had never learned to indulge in anything. Again, she wondered why he'd spent his life alone—why here, in this land of unfiltered possibility, he'd chosen not to seek partnership. "I think that is smart, and I think I know where we should send them."

Plucking a map from his stack of rolled parchment behind him, Mathjin laid out the four corners and weighed them down with chunks of obsidian salt stone. In front of them lay the entire continent, color coded with rivers bright blue. "They should move through this branch of waterways." Pointing to one of the many spidering webs of small rivers that crisscrossed the eastern lands, his finger trailed down one specific path that, as she narrowed her eyes, she realized wasn't the most convenient. It went all the way east, making the trip a bit more difficult, but certainly not impossible.

"That path is almost . . . random," she commented.

Mathjin winked.

A calculated choice, then, to take the road they wouldn't expect.

"Here"—she pointed to the little place where the dam lay—"is where the most people are. The city will suffer at the falling, probably be laid to waste."

Sadness passed over his face. "That's the thing about leadership. It's often a balancing of victims."

Even though Kosana often chuckled at Mathjin, and perhaps Reid didn't always understand him, Vaasa felt she did. He'd been a soldier himself once, supposedly for the Icrurian Central Forces, and he'd risen up enough ranks to serve one of the richest territories.

That didn't come without a level of moral culpability.

He had balanced victims, then, perhaps one of them being himself. She wondered what he had given up, and if it had been that splendor she had considered earlier.

"Reid will know the path," he continued. "It was his father who charted it."

Furrowing her brow, Vaasa leaned back. She'd never heard stories of Reid's father—only his mother.

"I served with him, actually," Mathjin told her. "I was his commanding officer in the ICF. He was born here in Mireh, though everyone thought he was nothing but a poor boy with a talent for the blade. He made a name for himself in our corps, married one of the most powerful witches on the continent, and sired a son who has his mother's penchant for books and his father's strength."

"How . . ." Vaasa looked down at the map, realizing what an invasive question she thought to ask.

"How did he die?" Mathjin said. At Vaasa's awkward, apologetic look, he didn't even flinch. The topics others usually considered off-limits Mathjin seemingly found to be the most interesting point of conversation. As if each detail about people was simply another item on a list of who they were, and not something he saw as taboo. For Mathjin, the world simply *was*. "It wasn't anything spectacular. He simply got sick, as some people do, and there was no cure—Zuheia or otherwise—that could have saved him. It was right before Reid was elected, actually."

The Zuheia witches were scattered throughout the east, their skill for healing in high demand. She couldn't picture Reid like that, desperate and breaking. Heart racing, Vaasa nodded. It had only been five years, then.

"You are no stranger to loss, either," Mathjin pointed out.

"No, I am not."

"Nor am I."

She wondered what Mathjin had lost, but he didn't add anything else. Even if he placed no weight on boundaries, Vaasa decided against asking further questions.

"Now, shall we discuss the economy?" he asked.

Laughter burst from her, and she sat up on her stool. "You want to teach an Asteryan the secrets of Icrurian trade?"

"How else are you supposed to serve as high consort?"

Guilt washed over her for a moment, and then she rolled her shoulders. "Mathjin, you and I both know I will hardly be serving in that role."

"Fine. How else are you supposed to pretend you will?"

She opened her mouth to argue, but practicality barreled through her. Even though it was crass, the man had a point. "All right, let's discuss the economy."

And they did, the sorts of things her father would have killed to know.

He detailed the salt lords and their inner workings with Sigguth and Dihrah, outlining the major trade routes and ports along the Settara. From the map, he showed her the passage into the narrow Sanguine, and all of the winding eastern rivers. The map was expansive, so much so that it would take an outsider like Dominik years to chart half of what they'd discovered.

So she listened.

She learned.

As he explained the election and the complex relationship between Dihrah, Sigguth, and Mireh, she realized how interwoven all three territories were. And in that bond, there was a weakness. If any side of the triangle were to shift, the already tenuous relationship between the formally independent city-states would fracture. For example, say, if Sigguth could find the wood used to build ships elsewhere. If Reid's men capitalized on their alliance with Dihrah and decided to build the vessels themselves. One wrong, selfish move, and the result could plummet hundreds—*thousands*—of people into joblessness.

But such was the way of power, and Vaasa knew that better than anyone else.

It was just *one* of the interlinked economic systems functioning in Icruria. Hazut and Wrultho were irrevocably intertwined, and Irhu depended on Sigguth's ships for their own fishing practices. Most important, each territory contributed something influential to the military: Dihrah and Mireh were the richest of the territories and could pay the ICF. Wrultho and Hazut supplied most of the men, and Irhu and Sigguth built ships and trained their naval corps. The only groups that couldn't seem to work together were the covens, each of them holding their history so close to their chests. They all knew the others existed, but how and to what limit was an uncertainty.

Suddenly, Vaasa understood the reasons places like Hazut and Wrultho were so against Icruria opening up to outsiders. For them, it was more than just their culture. The only thing that made them competitive was the food or soldiers they provided, and even that was being stolen from them by a dam. Even that required salt if they wanted to preserve it.

Mireh and Dihrah held more political power than the rest. *Of course* Reid was a front-runner for this election. His territory had the salt.

Immediately after leaving Mathjin, she wanted to review what they'd discussed with Reid.

The foreman stayed late at the High Temple that night, and she didn't know what compelled her, but she stopped by Neil's to get Reid some food. When she stuck her head into his office, she found Reid deeply focused on a pile of paperwork. Shooing away Esoti, who had lingered near her the entire way, Vaasa gazed at him for a moment longer than she should have.

Reid sat at his wide desk made of wood of different shades—apparently all found growing along the shore of the Settara. The ceremonial desk was passed from each Mirehan foreman to the next. Crystal vials of salt and clusters of paperweights peppered the work surface, and her chest tightened at the sight.

"Reid," she called from the doorway.

He looked up and his expression softened, accompanied by a tilt of his head. "Is everything all right?" Then his eyes dropped to the woven bag in her hands and a smile crossed his face. "Please say that's for me."

"I take it you're hungry, then?"

"Starving." Shuffling the paperwork and tucking it into a leather portfolio he placed behind him, he made room. She rummaged through the bag Neil had given her and picked out his food, then slid to the side of his desk and started on her own container. Reid immediately dug into his, covering his mouth as if he was embarrassed. Then he wiped his fingers on a cloth napkin he kept in his desk. "How did it go with Mathjin?"

She pursed her lips, recalling the one thing Mathjin didn't share, and a question that haunted her now. "Where is his family?"

Reid paused. Setting down his napkin, his gaze shadowed with grief. "They're dead. Killed by Asteryan forces in the east."

Vaasa looked down at her hands, more uncomfortable than she could contend with. "I see." There was nothing she could say and no further questions she was entitled to ask. All she wondered was how, in the face of all that anguish, Mathjin had never chosen to hate her.

"That's the difference we can make, you and I," he suggested softly.

Vaasa raised her eyes.

"To change their fates. To change everyone's fate." Reid adjusted how he sat, turning to face her more openly. "I spent some time in the east, too, and it was . . . brutal, to say the least. It was there I decided I would run for foreman. That I would be headman someday."

"How long were you there?" she asked.

"A few years."

She thought it odd he didn't elaborate, but by the ghosts painted in his features, she assumed he had a reason. "Is that where you learned to fight?"

He shook his head. "I learned to fight the first time someone pushed Koen to the ground. The east is where I learned how not to fight."

Koen, the foreman of Dihrah she had met when Reid found her at the sodality there. They had been close friends, she remembered. She wondered about Reid more in that moment than she'd yet allowed herself. Who was he, truly? He'd told her so little about his past that it felt almost ignorant to trust him; wasn't it information that faith should be built upon? Yet he'd given her something more valuable: action. The facts and figures of his past meant little compared to his actions of the present.

And if that was true of him, what did it mean about her?

"That's why you want to lead, then? Because more people need to learn when not to fight?" she asked.

The question earned just a small tilt of his lips. "I guess. Sometimes I sit and wonder how, after all these years, people can't seem to figure out how to get along."

"You and I are learning how to get along."

At that, he grinned completely. "Is that what we're doing?"

"I'd like to think so."

He frowned, as if unsure of his own confidence. But then he spoke. "By choosing to come back here, you have grown my capacity for hope."

Her lips parted, but she didn't have an answer. Not a good one. It didn't matter, though, because his eyes returned to his food, and he added, "There have been years I have felt none of it at all."

She could barely picture him so despondent; he always seemed to hide any pessimism. She didn't know how *she* had given him hope back when she'd had so little of it herself, but it didn't matter. Not truly. "You will win," she assured him.

He nodded, as if he, too, believed it.

Rolling her shoulders, Vaasa relayed the details of her discussion with Mathjin, reexamining everything the advisor had taught her, this time focusing on the economics of it all. On the parts that would solidify Reid's tenure as headman.

Leaning back in his chair, hands behind his head, Reid watched her. He relaxed slowly. Eased into their partnership. "Salt builds empires," he eventually said, reaching behind him for the folder he'd been working with and opening it. "That's what I'm working on right now, actually. Trying to see if there's a way to leverage it with Wrultho."

"Do you think the salt lords will go for that?"

"No." He shook his head, rubbing at his jaw and the dark beard that covered the scar she'd given him. "They don't understand why Wrultho started the violence with Asterya in the first place. To this day, their resentment of Ton runs deep."

"Ton didn't start the violence," she said. Didn't he know that?

Reid furrowed his brow.

"My father purposefully built the dam on the Sanguine. The foreman of Wrultho tried to negotiate at first. He sent his advisor. She started with peace—and by the look on your face, I suspect you didn't know that."

Dumbfounded, Reid dragged a hand through his hair. "That is not the Icrurian way. No territory may bargain with a foreign entity without permission from the headman."

"But imagine if one did," Vaasa suggested. "And saved the entire eastern half of Icruria. A man like that could win an election."

"But if Ton wanted to be headman, he wouldn't have given the order for an unsanctioned attack on the dam."

"They didn't attack the dam."

Reid paused, then let his hand fall against the desk. "What do you mean?"

Surely Ton had come forward about what her father had done. "The treaty only asked that they send the laborers to help take down the dam safely. When Ton of Wrultho made good on his promise, my father slaughtered each workman he sent."

Reid's lips parted. "What?"

"I always wondered if he would be too prideful to admit he'd gotten into bed with Asterya and lost, but I thought by now he would have asked for aid. Explained the situation."

"No, he hasn't said a word." Reid leaned back a little, trying to wipe the surprise off his mouth, but then sat up straight with his elbows on his desk. "But it wasn't a real treaty, not without the headman and councilors. As equally as your father manipulated Wrultho, they manipulated your father."

"Do you truly believe my father had any intention of following through?"

He shook his head. "No."

But that wasn't really all. Vaasa took a small breath, setting her container of food to the side and leaning forward, hands on her knees. "I speak six languages, not four. I read and write in them proficiently, too. *That* is how I was trained—to translate at his side. Which is why when you said that he honed me no differently than a blade, you were right."

Reid clung to each word she said, not even a phantom of amusement on his face. "Six?"

She nodded. "Few people other than his children were privy to his maneuvering. I wrote the treaty with Wrultho. I sat in the room and translated their negotiations. I suspected what my father would do, but if I said anything, if I did anything . . ." Looking down at her tangled hands, she stopped speaking and braced herself for his anger.

Yet that fury never took shape. Nodding slowly, Reid muttered, "I should expect you'll have a strained relationship with Ton, then?"

"You . . . you aren't upset?"

"I don't begrudge the ways you chose to survive, no."

As she looked down at him, she wondered if anyone had ever been so profoundly compassionate. That was the crux of who he was, and why he was often unfamiliar to her. "I would expect strained relations, yes."

With pursed lips, he leaned back in his chair once more. "We have three weeks before the election. Perhaps you can help me come up with a way to convince Wrultho to listen to us?"

"I know little of economics," she said.

"Anything you don't know, I can teach you."

Letting her dangling legs kick a little, she shrugged. "All right, let's scheme."

There was this little tug of his mouth again—not quite the amused look she so often saw from him, but a gentle comfort, as if the world wasn't so heavy.

It was dangerous to get used to. But Vaasa thought that if the world were different, if she had met Reid the way people should, it would have been very possible to rule a nation at his side.

To give him Asterya would be one of her life's greatest works.

Three weeks wasn't enough.

It wasn't enough silence, or no silence at all, or nights holed up in Reid's office as he taught her the inner workings of the foremanship and what she hoped eventually would be his headmanship. In that little office or even on the veranda, he'd taught her every detail of the election: the events that took place each day, what the dinners would be like, how she should pack. He even taught her the dances they'd do. There was an art gallery in Mireh, too, where they'd spent an evening. By the end of the three weeks, she could get herself around the city without any help, and people had begun to wave to her.

But as the day arrived for them to leave Mireh, peace felt like a tightrope that frayed at the edges, and she bristled at the idea of losing the city's skyline.

Vaasa watched the enormous ship from Dihrah approach. Built of a wood sourced from the west of the Settara, the ship was light enough to float through shallow waters, with four levels above the main deck for passenger quarters. Sanded down, the wood displayed veins of black and red. Clinker-built and as grand as could be, this particular ship was so different from the vessels she'd grown used to seeing in the bay her family's fortress was built upon. Those ships had enormous hulls that needed much deeper water. This one had only one level below the main deck—the oarsbank, where soldiers rowed. It was nowhere near as fast as the ship Reid had taken when he'd found her in Dihrah. That ship had been all business, no grandeur. This one was meant to make a statement, meant to carry large groups of people.

Which meant the trip would be overnight.

Waiting on the main deck was Marc of Mireh, Isabel standing at his side.

They boarded to meet them, and immediately Isabel rushed forward to embrace Vaasa. "Oh, it's happening!" The curvaceous woman pulled back just enough to gaze out at Mireh's many-level buildings. "We'll be back home soon."

"You will be," Vaasa assured her, though she wasn't so confident herself.

Marc set his hand down on Reid's shoulder, actually grinning as he gazed at the city. "We have much to catch up on. Come, help me get these men in line."

Leaving her with a brush of his hand upon hers, Reid plunged down the stairs into the oarsbank after Marc.

"Wait!" Amalie's voice came from behind her, and Vaasa turned to find the woman running down the dock, a leather bag slung over her shoulder.

Vaasa's heart rose. "I thought you weren't coming." Facing Ton and what felt like every person she'd known from Wrultho had been too much, and despite Vaasa's pleas, she had understood Amalie's choice to stay behind.

Amalie stopped in front of her, pulling back her shoulders and standing tall. She took a deep breath. "Your strength is my strength, right?"

A smile split Vaasa's face. "Your strength is my strength," she said.

Isabel looped her arms through both of the witches' arms, excitement thrumming around her. So much so that a little bit of it seeped into Vaasa, too. Isabel pulled Amalie and Vaasa across the dock to where the others waited. "Let's get that coven of yours boarded. I haven't seen Romana in years, and she owes me a game of poker."

CHAPTER 16

Every hue of gold rose in stripes along the hilly horizon. The glittering turquoise water of the Settara deepened to an emerald green as they sailed into the middle of the enormous salt lake. A peak here, a memorized jagged edge there. By the time the sun began to set, the water reflected the red and orange rays, colors glittering upon the surface and stealing Vaasa's breath.

Reid spent the day in the oarsbank with the soldiers, just like Kosana and Marc, drenched in sweat as they rowed. Located just below the main deck, Vaasa had avoided that part of the ship, opting to stay upon the upper deck above the captain's quarters.

Vaasa asked Esoti and Mathjin if she should go down there and join, and Mathjin shook his head. "Look," he said with an exhausted wipe of his squeezed-shut eyes. "Travel is boring. There is often nothing to do; that doesn't make you lazy."

Nodding slowly, she looked out upon the water once more and scanned the edges of the shoreline. They'd moved closer, opting for calmer waters. It shocked Vaasa how deep this part of the lake appeared, even this close to shore. Here, orange rock jutted into the sky and out into the lake, with plateaus dotting the towering cliffside. It was different from the soft hills she'd grown used to back in Mireh.

Isabel was entrenched in a heated game of poker with Melisina, Romana, Suma, and Mariana in the cool passenger quarters, while Amalie had stayed glued to Vaasa's side. The setting sun drenched them all in rays of golden light so bright she had to put her hand above her eyes to make it tolerable.

Onshore, movement caught her eye, and she leaned forward on the bench. Squinting, her vision bobbed up and down. There was nothing. Had she imagined it?

Her magic coiled and sprang, leaking down her arms, like it knew something she didn't. As if her intuition was blaring a warning.

Amalie sat up.

Panic started to rise.

"Draw your weapons," Vaasa cried, right as she unsheathed the dagger at her waist.

Voices burst from below.

Mathjin leapt up, his little leather satchel falling from his lap and slapping against the deck. Esoti was already on her feet and standing directly next to Vaasa, gleaming daggers in each hand.

Esoti spun.

"Down!" she screamed as she leapt for Vaasa, the two slamming onto the ship's deck as something whizzed past her ear.

There, jagged point piercing the wooden deck, was an arrow.

Vaasa whipped her head up. Studding the plateaus were soldiers, bows drawn and aimed.

Mathjin crawled to cover her as a shower of sharp, gleaming arrows began to fall like rain.

Instinct slammed through Vaasa's veins and coated her bones, black mist pouring from her hands. She crawled to the side of the deck with Esoti, Amalie ducking with them, arrows skittering across the deck.

To her left, the magic hissed as it moved, hovering over the upper deck like fog. Her heart beat wildly. The ship rocked and she was tossed with the force, slamming into the side of the deck with a grunt.

Arrows began to fly from their own ship, bodies falling from the plateaus and slapping against the water.

Still, the ship cut through the sun's reflection, and Vaasa pulled herself back to her knees.

Fewer arrows pierced the upper deck this time, but enough that one ripped through the billowing sleeves of Vaasa's blouse. It didn't cut her, though, and she tore off the fabric. "What the fuck is happening?" she shouted.

"We're under attack," Esoti snarled. "We need to get you in protected quarters."

"I am *not* going into a room."

The boat rocked again as voices shouted from below.

Something clanked against the boat, and Amalie lifted herself and bent over the side.

Immediately, she flung herself back down. "They're boarding from the water," she said, voice thick with concern.

Panic seared down Vaasa's spine. She demanded, "Where is Reid?"

"He's with Kosana. I'm sure they're in the oarsbank," Esoti said, though something about the way she spoke told Vaasa her guard wasn't so confident. "We should find both of you a safe room."

"Esoti," Vaasa said, and both the witch and the warrior turned to meet Vaasa's eyes. "I told you. We're not doing that."

One strong nod from Amalie, then a curse from Esoti, low and angry.

Vaasa sprang from where she sat and broke through the magic as it crept across the upper-deck floor. Just as quickly as she stood, Vaasa ran to the stairs and threw herself down them, Esoti and Amalie sprinting on her heels.

The main deck was covered in blood and arrows, and the door to the hull had been ripped open. Tiny boats surrounded their ship, each with at least four men, and a sailor near her slipped on the now-slick surface of the boat. Vaasa scanned the entire bow.

At least ten soldiers were down, and Reid and Kosana were nowhere to be seen.

Esoti hauled Vaasa back, just as another clanging noise beat against the side of the ship. A metal claw rested upon the edge, and one of their soldiers sliced vigorously into a connected rope to set it free.

An arrow slammed into the soldier's shoulder and she cried out, falling backward as the rope snapped. Amalie rushed forward.

Arrows rained down again.

Vaasa lurched and grabbed Amalie's wrist, hauling her away from the spray of blood. They all ducked beneath the overhang of the upper deck, the injured soldier crawling as far as she could from the edge. Concern for Mathjin was fleeting as he landed upon the deck and drew his sword. Vaasa noticed his hands shaking slightly, and didn't know if it was caused by age or by adrenaline. Esoti pushed him through the door, commanding that he needed to find Kosana and Reid.

On the other side of the vessel, a man in an unfamiliar green vest and black breeches swung himself onto the deck. The sigil on his chest in gold and white indicated his connection to Wrultho.

"We are from Mireh!" Esoti yelled.

Still, the man from Wrultho launched himself forward. He and Esoti each drew jagged blades as steel clashed with steel. From the ratlines, arrows pierced the men who tried to board the ship, and bodies fell back into the water.

"They're coming too fast," Esoti shouted as she disemboweled the soldier.

Vaasa jumped back to avoid the spatters of blood, trying to fight off the instinct to disappear. They had trained her, too—she could fight. She picked up an abandoned dagger from the floor and squeezed it between her fingers. "Why are they attacking?" she demanded.

Someone burst from the other side of the deck.

Vaasa could have shuddered with relief at the sight of her coven.

The bow swarmed with green, at least twelve enemy soldiers tossing themselves upon the boat, and Esoti cursed something wicked before diving into the battle. Mariana howled as she lifted her arms and blackness began to hiss along the water surrounding them. Amalie sprung after her, mist bathing her hands as she shot the magic toward a soldier, the void of Veragi power circling his eyes and mouth and nose, cutting off his senses.

Vaasa leapt, felt the resistance of tissue and bone against steel, and pushed through it. Ripping her dagger from a man's abdomen, she pushed him to the floor.

One arrow slid into the arm of a Mirehan near her, and he screamed as he hit the deck.

Any ounce of regret Vaasa felt at the death of the Wrultho Corps winked out.

Vaasa plunged into the fray, fear coating her tongue but her magic drawing her deeper and deeper onto the main deck. As Amalie expertly wielded magic, Vaasa finished the job, watching the life drain from the brown eyes of a stranger whose dead body she tossed to the deck. Soldier after soldier fell to the warriors and witches. The Veragi magic seemed to roar, twisting in Vaasa's gut as arrows rained from the sky, and she unleashed it upon the man nearest them.

All she saw in her mind was Reid—his dark hair and a gaze so gold it put the setting sun to shame. Her chest twisted with agonizing fear, and then rage hotter than any she'd known before. Was this her own panic playing tricks on her, or was her instinct trying to tell her something?

She needed to find him.

"Esoti—" Vaasa said, but the boat rocked once more and Vaasa lost her balance, falling to the deck as Esoti slammed into the side of the boat, nearly splintering wood.

A man pounced at her, angry blue eyes blinking out blood.

Before Vaasa could react, a knife hurled through the air and slammed into the man's chest. Red bloomed to soak the green of his shirt. He stumbled backward and lost all tension in his shoulders, knees buckling and cracking on the magic-coated deck.

When Vaasa turned, she found Marc, another knife at the ready.

Vaasa had barely a moment to gasp in relief before two more soldiers started in her direction. Eyes wide at the mist surrounding them all, they traced it back to her hands.

She lurched forward and pulled the knife from the fallen man, then sprang to her feet. The fear that washed through Vaasa lit a fire in her stomach, and her magic morphed from a fleeing mouse into a roaring jungle cat.

When the first man dared get close, she gave a feral snarl as she pounced. Her knife sank into his gut and she pushed him off her blade, spinning to the next one who dipped toward her. Black mist coated her hands and knife, tendrils of the magic flaring from her skin and wrapping around a man's neck, then plunging down his nose and throat.

She watched the life snuff out from his eyes after she'd stolen his air. As the magic ripped back from his mouth, he sank to the deck. She silently thanked Romana.

A man in green to her left took a step back, and he spat the word *witch*.

Vaasa froze.

Asteryan.

He'd said it in Asteryan.

It wasn't Wrultho they fought, but her own damned empire.

Everything Romana had taught her flexed in her muscles, and she let the tendrils out again, guiding the obliterating void around the heads of soldiers in green and letting them fall with the rock of the boat, just like Amalie did. As they collapsed, the Mirehans dealt the finishing blows. Two soldiers defended her front and back, so she could drain the balance and life from those in green. One by one, assailants slammed to the deck and lost their lives, some being hauled over the edge and dropped into the water.

More men spilled onto the deck, one after the other, in a never-ending waterfall.

Mirehan soldiers with their shields pushed forward, trying to form an enormous wall and block the invaders.

One point of a shield impaled an Asteryan as he tried to slide up over the wall, and his blood ran down the Mirehan black and purple sigil like a fountain.

Yet what caught her eye was just beyond him—the monstrosity of black mist that morphed along the green water.

It bent and twisted, hissing in a language Vaasa didn't understand, then rose from the depths. Water streamed from the shadowy creature as it formed a mane and tail, shadows feathering along the edges and snapping against its thick torso. A horse, made of shadows and wisps of darkness, with eyes so white they seemed to harness the moon.

And at the other end of the boat, Melisina, whose own eyes glowed.

The phantom horse glided over the water with a body as large as three sailboats, slamming into the clusters of assailing men who tried to row away. Screams pierced the air as they were hauled under the water, their lives forfeit to the depths of the Settara or the void of Veragi magic.

She'd seen these witches summon their power in the form of animals, but never one so great.

Would she ever be able to do such a thing?

Kosana emerged just then from the far left side of the deck, her own teeth bared, a dangerous thrill lacing her eyes. The warrior leapt at two others who spread out onto the deck, gripping someone's head and twisting to break his neck before somersaulting over his body and plunging her long-bladed knife into the other's groin. His piercing scream could be heard for a flash, and then she snarled at him and cut his throat.

Their eyes met.

Vaasa froze.

"What? You think I'll kill you?" Kosana spun and swept her blade up the chest of another, ripping directly through his sigil, and then kicked him to the floor so he could bleed out of her proximity while she closed the space between them. "Get over yourself."

Torn between amazement and fear, Vaasa clenched her knife in one hand and broke through the soldiers around her. "They speak Asteryan."

Another tried to climb over the wall of shields, and Kosana's knife rang true, piercing the spot directly between his eyes. "I know." Running, she gripped her dagger and kicked the man's stomach, sending him plummeting off the side of the boat, while Amalie's tendrils of magic burrowed down someone's throat and caused them to back up and fall, too. "Where is Reid?" Kosana demanded.

Everything in Vaasa dropped. "I—but he was with you."

"He left the oarsbank." Kosana paused, then continued scanning, eyes catching on the horse and blinking.

Vaasa didn't think—she only ran.

Esoti screamed after her as Vaasa barreled through at least three men and ducked around the side of the deck, plunging into the passenger quarters and immediately climbing the stairs.

Darkness bathed the narrow corridor as she climbed and Kosana's curses of protest echoed behind her. "I should have fucking killed you!"

The sounds of battle could still be heard on the main deck. Steel. The smacking of bodies. Screams. Awful, desperate panic washed over her and her hands began to shake. Vaasa called over her shoulder, "Help me find him and you can kill me after."

"Deal."

The boat rocked so hard she slammed into the wall and then slipped on a step. Kosana cursed as she helped lift Vaasa to her feet, and they scrambled through a doorway into a hall of passenger quarters.

If he'd left the oarsbank and hadn't made it to the bow, he would be in one of these rooms.

Kosana must have come to the same conclusion, because she started slamming doors open, cussing a storm each time she found an empty room. Vaasa sprinted toward the door at the end of the hall, the one that led to their personal quarters. She swung the door open.

Four men spun at her intrusion. In the corner, Mathjin lay unmoving, a small smear of blood in his silvery-blond hair. Vaasa's heart rose into her throat. One man stepped forward just enough that Vaasa could see the scene beyond them.

Reid was shirtless and on his knees in front of the bed, wrists bound by rope to either side of the footboard. His shoulders were tugged back and stretched, though no marks marred his skin.

Yet.

A lanky man with a wild, dark gaze smirked, holding a winking iron-toothed comb.

Vaasa's breath caught.

Those familiar blue eyes. The serpentine turn of his mouth. That *weapon*.

She knew this man—an Asteryan general.

And suddenly Dominik's letter, the mention of a *gift*, spun in her mind.

Kosana gave a battle cry as she ran into the room. Magic burst out of Vaasa on instinct, the glittering darkness whipping over the men and wrapping around the eyes and throat of the Asteryan general. Power constricted with her anger, strangling his airway and causing the comb to clatter to the floor. His mouth parted for a scream he couldn't make.

The other men pounced.

One tackled her to the floor while another grabbed her wrists, tugging at her arms. She bucked hard against the restraint, and the one who tackled her tried to catch her foot, which she promptly smashed into his nose. Gushing blood coated his mustache and lips. He screamed something vile in Asteryan and brought his fist down into her stomach.

Vaasa lurched upward in pain, but the one who held her wrists pressed down so she couldn't raise her arms. She gasped for air, and the man she'd kicked grabbed her ankles, blood dripping onto her pants. The gold and green emblem of Wrultho, right over his heart, mocked her.

He would kill her.

He raised his toothed knife.

Faintly, she heard Reid's horrified roar.

And then a jagged onyx blade rammed through the soldier's throat.

Blood spurted to cover her blouse and face and the man gurgled, his body immediately going slack as the life winked out of his eyes. The blade slid back, and when the man in green fell, Vaasa let out a desperate choke of her own.

Kosana snarled as she glided her knife across the neck of the man who held Vaasa's wrists.

The man fell backward and his jugular drained upon the floor.

One moment.

Vaasa shook for one single moment.

A hand appeared in front of hers. Kosana's.

The world sped up again, and Vaasa darted her hand to the commander's, finding the strength to rise. Immediately Kosana wiped the blood from Vaasa's face, dragging her own decorated jacket over her skin. "Thank you," she muttered.

They turned and saw the general writhing on the floor. Two feet away from him was his severed hand. Kosana laughed at her work, which she must have done while Vaasa had been on the floor. The snake in Vaasa's gut turned far fiercer, amusement entirely distant, morphing and growing into something it never had before. An animal she didn't recognize. Teeth and eyes so white they could rival the moon, much like the horse she had just seen Melisina conjure.

It stalked forward in tandem with her steps.

Slow.

One step.

Two.

Ruthless malice burned in the white of this creature's eyes. In her own. Ice froze in her veins, lip curling as she released the magic once more. It slid across the floor. "Please," he choked in Asteryan. "We are—" He choked again, unable to finish his sentence.

Her magic plunged down the general's throat. She knew what they were to each other. Comical, really, that he thought it would save him.

An idea, burning and bright, came to life. Vaasa's lips parted. She heaved the flow of magic until he lost consciousness.

Kosana raised her blade, but Vaasa said, "He's a general. You want him alive."

The commander lifted a brow but, much to Vaasa's surprise, did not argue. The creature within her faded, and Vaasa immediately slumped. Though she felt like falling onto the floor and sleeping for a lifetime, she dropped to her knees next to Reid. His hair hung loose, and sweat drenched his neck and chest. She refused to allow any emotion to beat through her as she reached for the ropes at his wrist. They looked like any other set of ropes, but there were fibers of black intricately woven into them.

The moment she touched them, something emptied in her stomach. The magic. Like it burned out. Gone. She cursed and pulled her hand back, the magic roaring back to life inside of her.

"What are these?" she whispered.

"Magic," Reid breathed. "They dull magic."

Vaasa felt nothing.

Everything.

All at once.

She held her breath through the process. The magic in her drained out miserably until she felt as though there were entire parts of her insides missing. Still, she sawed at the rope.

"How long have you been here?" Kosana demanded from the other side of the room, fingers taking Mathjin's pulse at the crease of his neck. Kosana gave a sharp nod. Mathjin was alive.

"He was only just starting." Reid gasped as one arm released and he tucked it to his chest, jaw gritting. "I saw him dart after Mathjin, so I followed."

Vaasa moved to the other rope, still unable to speak or to process what they'd tied to Reid. She cut through the tightly woven material, eyes fixed on the black threads. Her fingers burned slightly at the touch the longer she maintained contact.

The ropes frayed and broke, and Reid gasped again as he sank to the floor. Vaasa dropped her arms, shaking her hands out.

Kosana's boots echoed past Vaasa until she crouched in front of Reid, gripping his jaw and moving his head left and right, inspecting him. Apparently, she decided he was fine, because she let him slump back to the floor as she lifted to her full height. "You are so *fucking* lucky." Then, turning to Vaasa, Kosana dipped her head. "Your instinct was right. I take back our deal."

Vaasa nodded silently, realizing that was potentially the closest she'd ever get to a compliment from Kosana.

They all turned to the man crumpled on the floor. The Asteryan general, still bleeding. If they wanted him alive, he'd need that wound cauterized immediately.

With one look at the burns on her fingertips, she decided Dominik's "gift" had been just another warning.

"He's a general?" Kosana asked.

"His name is Ignac Kozár," Vaasa said. "One of the few members of my father's family who still lives. He is my cousin."

CHAPTER 17

The first thing Vaasa did was wash the blood from her skin.

The boat cleared the ambush. No unworkable damage was sustained to the ship, and it cut through the Settara as if nothing had ever slowed it down. Men scrubbed blood from the deck as Kosana ran from end to end, collecting as much information as she could about the attack.

Each body they found wore the same vest—the sigil and colors of Wrultho sewn into it. Apparently it was an old uniform, though, which meant Ignac and his men must have lifted it from some other battle.

They did not fight like Icrurians. They followed patterns and orders, whereas the Icrurians had been trained as terrifying militias. The unpredictable nature of Icrurian forces was what made them so deadly. Within minutes, the Mirehans had determined what their assailants intended to do, and they were able to block their attempts to damage the galley. The coven could pick them off the plateaus without so much as a hiccup, and Melisina . . .

Well, she'd taken more lives than all of them combined.

The first person Vaasa went to see was Ignac, the son of her father's youngest brother.

He'd only dared come to the castle a few times while her father was alive—he was smart enough to know that possessing the Kozár name was a threat. Undoubtedly, he knew it had been the very thing to put his own father in the ground. He'd done his duty, far away from Mekës, for as long as she'd known him.

Vaasa asked him only one question: what he wanted from Reid.

She already knew who'd sent him.

All Ignac did was plead. He spilled lies until Vaasa stepped forward and used that treacherous iron-toothed comb along the soft skin of his cheek. Still, she got no real answers; not about the rope, not about the questions he'd intended to ask Reid, nor whether her own death was the goal. Drenched in grime and blood, Kosana watched the entire interaction with a lazy tug of her brows. The Dihrah and Mirehan men had heard word of Wrultho forces in the area, but they'd assumed it was election related.

Vaasa eventually told the commander her idea about how to leverage the Asteryan general, and the blond woman lit up like one of the lanterns in the Sodality of Una.

"You are a formidable ally," Kosana said in response.

Leaving Ignac bound and bleeding, the two women moved to the overwhelmed brig, passing Mathjin as he limped into the general's holding room. Though Mathjin was worn, determination struck across his tightly pressed mouth. He instructed the two guards near them to prevent anyone from entering until he was finished, then closed the door behind him with a resounding slam.

Kosana remained by Vaasa's side as she went from prisoner to prisoner. They all spoke Asteryan, and while Mathjin was still with Ignac, Vaasa was one of the only people on board who could communicate with them. Which was why she executed the first one herself—to banish any doubt the Icrurians had about where her loyalties lay. A sliver of her own conscience punished her for the action, but she knew well enough these men would not have spared her, had they been given the chance.

That she had most likely been a target.

The Asteryans gave her no useful information. Most sneered about her magic or called her *invoque* (witch), or worse, *bonas* (traitor). One spit on the ground where she stood.

A Mirehan stepped forward immediately, his knife to the man's throat, and turned his attention to Vaasa, awaiting a command. One small jerk of her chin, and the Asteryan's life ended. It shouldn't have brought a grin to Vaasa's lips, but it did. Through this battle, she'd established herself among the Mirehan people as a strong choice for their high consort.

As she turned to leave, one of the men asked, "And the general?"

Vaasa pursed her lips. She peered at Kosana, and they shared a chuckle. "Leave that one alive."

No one questioned either of them.

Except, of course, Esoti and Amalie, who each had a bone to pick with her choice to descend into the hull. They finally relented after Marc and Isabel ushered them away to give Vaasa a moment of reprieve.

Stealing two minutes to herself, she gazed out at the starlight glimmering upon the Settara and curled her hands around the railing of the boat. Reid was fine; consciously she knew that, and yet violence clawed at her gut. This was the first battle she'd seen up close, the first one she'd ever been a part of.

The creature in her stomach wasn't entirely identifiable, but its presence was clear. Still unfamiliar, its white eyes glowed a little less than they had in that moment, but its teeth sharpened nonetheless.

There was no reason to avoid him. No good reason, at least.

On a long exhale, she turned away and ducked back into the hull of the ship.

Adrenaline seemed to spike in her veins as she walked down the corridor leading to their quarters. Vaasa pushed through the door to find Reid sitting upon the bed, no longer spattered in blood. He was only dressed from the waist down, his blood-soaked shirt nowhere in sight.

Her nails dug into her palm and her chest burned at the memory of how she'd found him here.

Reid looked up and furrowed his brow. "Are you all right?"

Silently, she clicked the door shut behind her and ambled to the space in front of him, inspecting the faint red lines on his wrists herself. She turned his palm over in her hand and tentatively touched.

"It doesn't hurt," he said softly. "I have no magic; they were a precaution at best."

The creature in her paced, her mind reviewing each detail of the fight, eyes trailing to the tattoos she rarely gave herself liberty to gaze upon. The ink traveled all the way over his left pectoral and beneath his collarbone, falling down his upper arm to his elbow. It looked to be a detailed depiction of Mirehan armor, the lines of their pauldron drawn with precision. On the curve of his shoulder was the Mirehan sigil: the wolf. The same ones that howled at the Settara at night. The one he was named after. It looked so vivid, so real, she couldn't help but run her fingers over it.

His skin pebbled at her touch.

Gazing up at her, he slid his hand over her own like he wanted to keep her there. "You aren't going to talk, are you?"

She didn't know how to say it—that she didn't have words to explain herself. That all she had was the remnant of a panic she didn't understand and this visceral fear she had never experienced for anyone but herself.

This *coldness*.

She'd dived into that hull without a second thought—into a fight that had almost gotten her killed. It was reckless and stupid, and she realized she never would have done that for someone before this.

And that thought absolutely terrified her. It was the opposite of what she was supposed to feel.

Holding his gaze, she remained silent.

"All right, then I'll speak." He rose from the bed and walked to the bolted-down dresser of their tiny room, where he plucked out one of his enormous shirts. No signs of pain crossed his features, and the fact that he only sustained minor injuries was a testament itself to her timing. He extended her his shirt. "Dominik is responsible for this, isn't he?"

She couldn't breathe. Or disagree.

So she looked away and tightened her jaw, running her tongue over her teeth and taking the shirt. Marching into the barely arms-length latrine chamber, she tried not to hit her elbows on any of the walls as she took off her bloodied blouse and trousers and changed into Reid's shirt.

Of course her brother had planned this. No matter how it ended, he came out on top—either he gave Vaasa a way to prove her loyalty to Icruria, or the only threat to his throne was eliminated.

Yet it wasn't herself that she feared for. She'd long come to terms with Dominik's desire to snuff her out of existence.

But *Reid*?

Months ago, she wouldn't have cared if he died, and now it was all she could focus on. She had to finally admit to herself how much it mattered.

The magic at her core morphed into the simmering embers of a flame, low and threatening and cracking with sputters. In the wake of the icy cold, this angry warmth was welcome.

"Why did you leave the oarsbank?" she demanded as she burst back into the room.

Silence.

Now sitting under ivory sheets, Reid leaned back into the headboard. No words fell from his lips; instead, he inspected her balled fists and taut shoulders.

Approaching the bed where he had made himself quite comfortable, her tone sharpened. "*Why* did you leave the oarsbank?"

If he'd have stayed, he never would've been caught.

Those men hadn't breached it.

But an awful thought sprang to life—perhaps it hadn't been breached because they'd already found what they were searching for.

"Answer me."

Lips pursed, he shrugged. "I was looking for you."

"You shouldn't have done that."

"I will never not do that."

It wasn't up for debate, judging by the strong hold of his jaw and his unwavering gaze. Or perhaps it was the way he snuffed out the lantern and left her standing in the darkness that assured her he had no intention of admitting his own stupidity.

"You're a fool," she snapped, turning and trying not to stumble through the dark to get to the other side of the bed.

"Why am I the fool, Wild One?"

Wild One. The way he said it dragged down her nerves, infuriating her to her bones. Scoffing, she finally managed to find an edge of the bed his body didn't cover. Crawling up it and under the blankets, she begged her magic to settle. To breathe. To stop clawing at her insides.

It didn't. Though she'd once considered herself ruthless and unmovable, her magic tightened around her throat. Legs curling up to her chest, she formed a ball to press down the low knots in her stomach.

Her hands began to shake.

Warmth coated her as Reid's body pressed against the back of hers, one arm falling over her waist to capture her hands. "*Breathe*, Wild One." The other hand searched for a way to wrap his arms around her. She was in too tight a ball, and she shifted away from him.

"I *am* breathing," she snarled.

"Slowly."

A small sigh of frustration made it past her lips.

His hands tightened on her wrists.

"You don't have to do that," she spat. "I don't need to be contained."

He froze for a fraction of a second and then tugged, forcing her to her back so he could kneel next to her, his large body leaning over hers, one leg slipping between her thighs. She went rigid. Then she forced herself to uncurl. Darkness bathed them both, but her eyes had begun to adjust, and she could see the angry line of his mouth. The narrowing of his eyes and the strands of his hair that almost covered them as he inspected her. "If you want to pick a fight, look at me while you're doing it."

"I'm not picking a fight."

"You are. You always pick a fight when you feel out of control."

Magic rose in her like bile. She wouldn't lose her grasp. She wouldn't. But this power needed an outlet, a way to course through her veins and leave her empty.

Shit. He was right.

He gestured with his chin toward where he held her, her arms bent with wrists almost pressed to her jaw. To the magic, growing on her hands locked between them. "What do you need?"

Torn between anger at such an observation and shame at it, too, she looked into the lightless room. "I just need a second."

She needed to come back to herself.

"Then take a second," he said, refusing to let go of his vise grip on her. Like he knew the magic was dangerously close to loosening and that here, on this ship, there was no place she could go.

Dipping her eyes to the incremental space between them, she gritted her teeth and tried to run herself through the cycle. To feel, to accept, and to release.

All she did was feel.

The magic riled and lifted. Her breath caught. She didn't know how to release a little without releasing it all.

"It hurts." Her eyes squeezed shut. "I can't."

"Control the release. I know you can."

On an exhale, the magic started to move. She felt it first on her fingers, consuming both of their hands in cold mist between them. Small trickles of power threaded from her. She tried to pull back, but he chastised her, squeezing her wrists harder. He was too close, seeing too much. Panic pressed to her chest at what he might think. "I don't want you to see this."

Yet Reid didn't flinch at the sight of her magic coating his skin.

Instead, he brought his lips down and ran them along the top of her mist-coated knuckles. Heat crawled up her neck, but her lips parted.

"Let it out," he insisted, mouth brushing past her wrist. "Turn the bed black."

Obstinance drained from her at the same time she had difficulty swallowing. He continued his downward descent, his breath coasting along her forearm. She let out another trickle of power, and this time it sighed with her. Dancing along the ivory sheets, the black mist crept across the pillows and down to where his knee pressed into the blankets.

The sting started to ebb.

He nipped at her skin, dragging his lower lip as bumps rose along her arms.

A bit more of the magic trickled out and she gripped it, stopping the release before it flooded. This was *working*.

"Good," he praised. "More?"

"More," she rasped.

Lifting her wrists above her head, he used one hand to push them into the pillows.

A thread of awareness rode her nerves, and she instinctually arched toward him.

At her invitation, he lowered his mouth to where the borrowed shirt covered her breast. He paused. The icy feel of his inhale caused her breasts to peak, and he ran his teeth over the new curve, licking the fabric of the shirt. Desire curled down her hips. On another sigh, she let the power out again, the pressure in her stomach subsiding.

He hovered over her covered breast, this time stopping to pull it into his mouth and suck.

Each cavern the slow release of magic created instantly flooded with yearning, which was easier to manage than the anger or the sadness or the fear. Her senses turned and bowed to where he knelt. To where he touched. She felt his skin against hers, felt the proximity of his broad chest and how when she took a deep breath, her wrists strained against his grip.

On her exhale, she directed it outward again, the magic slithering farther along the sheets.

His voice rose to linger directly above her. "More?"

As she opened her eyes, she found his gaze measuring the space between her parted lips.

"More."

He lowered and captured her mouth with his own, stealing the sound from the air as if he wanted to make sure it belonged to him and only him. His tongue immediately snaked between her lips, and she melted against him, the fire inside her becoming hotter as he swept into her mouth and tasted her.

At their lips' touch, the magic ebbed, then spread like steam from a boiling pot. It surrounded them, black mist smothering the bed and the floor in a hiss as it melded from an angry bird of prey to the surface of the Settara. Lapping against her insides, it was capable of great calm or immense storms.

When he released her wrists, her body chose storms.

Like a band snapped, she kissed him wildly, hands sliding into his hair and body lifting up to his. When he slid his hands behind her back and used them to spin her, she lost all sense of caution.

She wanted to forget anything that could ever harm him.

He moved her with grace as he landed with his back against the headboard, dismissing the darkness that crept along the bed. Gripping her thighs, he slid her legs to either side of him and settled her hard against his lap, his mouth only leaving hers to start a teasing descent. Teeth grazed the curve of her neck and he lifted his other hand higher, fingers toying with the bottom hem of her shirt. He slid his hand beneath the fabric and his fingers scraped over her bare hip.

He froze. She felt him harden at the same time he said, "You aren't wearing anything underneath that."

She never did. Vaasa started to pant. Started to tilt her hips up to him.

"Do you *ever* wear panties underneath my shirts?"

Biting the inside of her cheek, she shook her head.

A low sound emanated from the back of his throat as he kissed her mouth again, biting down on her lower lip. "I've clung to that barrier, Vaasa. Told myself it would be inappropriate to push them to the side and take you."

Desire shot down her spine, and she pressed harder into his lap, her own hips begging him to take it further. To do as he wanted. She had no resolve against these words—hearing them in Icrurian only burned hotter, like her ear bent to his language just as she did to his touch.

"All I needed was an excuse," he whispered. "And permission."

"Have you found one?" she dared ask.

His grip tightened. "We could pretend that it's because it'll help you fall asleep, that I'm selfless and altruistic."

"That's not the truth?"

"No, that's not the truth." His fingers curled against the crease of her leg, sliding to the inside of her thighs, dangerously close to where she wanted him. Stroking up and down. "The truth is that all I can think about is sliding my hand between your legs until you come so hard you forget you ever hated me."

Vaasa whimpered against his lips and lifted herself, so his hand slid closer to the wetness waiting for him. "You're being selfless, altruistic," she assured him.

"Good. That only leaves permission, Wild One."

There it was again—that question. This time, it wasn't the least bit disarming. "Please," she begged into his mouth.

He kissed her again, tongue brushing her lips, and then his fingers dipped and slid down her core.

Her breath caught and he groaned at the wetness he found, fingers finding a rhythm against her as she tried to kiss him back. Tried to retain some control. But then he released the grip he'd kept at the base of her hair and lowered that hand between her legs, too. As her hips rose, he slid two fingers inside of her. Pleasure jolted down her spine, and once again, her magic spun over itself into something new. Something she'd felt earlier—the white eyes and sharp teeth.

Her mouth opened against his, hips rocking up and down as she rode his hands. He pressed circles into her core, stroking her, letting her set the rhythm with how deep he went and how fast he got there.

The magic in her rose and tightened. Different now from anything else she'd ever felt. She hadn't dared finish herself with this unpredictable power, not with him so close. But he knew the force by now, and she knew with certainty that it knew him, too.

Knew herself.

She wouldn't hurt him.

The thought sent her barreling upward. Her mouth parted against his and he kept the pace. Didn't dare push further or change a single thing about the rhythm they'd found. He only captured her mouth and reveled in her parted lips and how she couldn't manage to kiss him completely through her sounds. Crying out, the last of her pent-up magic burst out of her in a wave of black that snuffed out any bit of light in the room. She came as hard as he'd wanted her to, her whole body tightening with the wave.

Reid kissed her, hands keeping the rhythm until her hips slowed.

Darkness bathed them both, and she could hardly tell the color of the bed any longer. Black mist floated through the entire room, coating each surface and hissing against the walls.

But she was empty—sated, no longer desperately containing the magic. It didn't claw at her insides or prowl back and forth. She laid her head against his shoulder. Took a deep breath, letting his scent fill her senses.

Salt. Amber.

The magic settled into the calm flow of water, as if it, too, could reflect the moonlight.

"Glad to see we found a solution," Reid whispered in her ear as he released her hips. Confusing as it was, he didn't ask for an explanation—or more. There was a part of her still desperately on fire and willing to go up in flames with him. To do anything he wanted for however long he wanted it.

But his quickness to rise made her stifle such words.

Vulnerability pulsed in her chest at the sight of his back when he walked into the bathing chamber.

Wrapping her arms around herself, she pushed it all down.

The magic. The wanting.

Quickly, he came back into the room and settled into the bed, giving her respectful space. "Sleep, Wild One. You need it."

She squeezed her eyes shut. The truth was that he wasn't the fool—she was. Against all rationale, she'd gone looking for him, too.

How could she ever admit that?

No language had given her the words she needed to explain herself. No language could quite convey the longing she felt in his presence, or the confusion that overrode her own assurances. But mostly there were no words to say how people, much like homes, would always be taken away.

And she had no clue how to let someone close enough for that to hurt.

Perhaps that was why he didn't take it further.

Perhaps he didn't know how to, either.

CHAPTER 18

By the time the sun rose, they prepared to disembark in the breathing city of Dihrah. Vaasa could hardly hold herself up. Exhaustion beat like a drum, and her magic stirred, unsettled again. It did not immediately coil into a snake, something she attributed to the release she'd been offered last night. But it wasn't quite dormant, either. It simmered just beneath her skin.

Before they joined the rest of the group, she discussed her intentions for the general. Not a word or indication of what had passed between them earlier. That was only another impossibility she needed to turn to water. There was far more on the line than just the election: the fragile balance between Dominik and Icruria sat upon a frayed rope that hung above her head—above all of their heads.

Dihrah was just as beautiful as she remembered it, though now awe pierced her heart where it hadn't had room before. Gazing upon it stirred something in Vaasa's magic—locations held memory, too. Dozens of waterways flowed through the enormous rainbow-toned city, curving bridges over the emerald-green water of the Settara. Arches and iron filigrees decorated the buildings dotting the skyline. And in the near distance, Vaasa spotted the giant spires of the Sodality of Una.

Crowds of people waited. Clusters of them lined the dock and the entire way to the High Temple of Dihrah. Their raucous cheers and hollers echoed all the way to the water, filling the chambers of the boat and Vaasa's ears. Their soldiers in ceremonial garb flooded the dock, forming an enormous parade in rows of ten. The men and women of the Mirehan Corps, led by Kosana herself, marched through the street with their swords drawn.

The infamous coven of Veragi witches disembarked next, clustered together in the sweeping amethyst robes worn by the sages of Setar. As they hit the docks of Dihrah, the women each let out their tendrils of magic, the mist creeping along the pathway and hovering over the bottoms of their robes.

The crowd seemed to draw a breath all at once.

Such a display of power for Icruria's favored foreman.

Isabel and Marc walked forward with their proud gazes sweeping over all they had helped rule for a decade, and then Marc turned with his palm open, sweeping up toward the opening in the hull.

To the Wolf of Mireh, his consort at his side.

The crowd's cheers echoed off the boat.

Reid truly looked like a headman in his own right. His purple-draped shoulder swept against Vaasa's when he looked down. "Ready?"

Vaasa nodded.

"Pretend you love me, Wild One," he murmured, and she elbowed him for good measure. He shook with laughter and settled his hand on the small of her back.

And then they descended into the crowd, which roared at Reid and Vaasalisa of Mireh.

At the edge of the dock stood each contender and their consort, accompanied by their councilor. Reid and Vaasa were the last to arrive, which didn't come as a surprise given the events of their last day. Vaasa first noticed Kenen and Galen, the two councilors each standing with their respective foremen. Their familiar faces were little comfort in this crowd, though. Koen, who hadn't changed a bit since he'd bid them both goodbye that fateful morning, stood with the headman.

The two seemed the friendliest of the bunch. The foreman of Hazut looked as though he believed they had a real chance at winning. But it was Ton of Wrultho who caught Vaasa's eye, accompanied by his councilor, Hunt.

Reid immediately approached the group, dipping his head in acknowledgment at each contender and councilor, and Vaasa did the same. They went one by one, introducing themselves. The foreman of Mireh sped his pace and Koen came forward, the two embracing and warmth radiating from them both.

"Consort," Koen said as he dipped his head to Vaasa, finally releasing Reid and minding the group. "Lovely to see you again."

The two had hardly exchanged a word when they'd found her in Dihrah. Koen obviously knew her marriage was a ruse, but much like Mathjin and Melisina, he didn't outwardly resent her for it. "You as well," Vaasa said.

"The foreman who won a Veragi witch for his wife," said an unfamiliar man who approached from behind the umber foreman of Dihrah. He appeared open and approachable, with dark skin highlighting the glimmers of gold and brown in his eyes.

"When did you start calling me by my title, Kier?" Reid asked with a friendly, laid-back laugh.

Kier. As in, *Headman* Kier of Icruria.

"An honor to meet you," Vaasa said with a heavy dip of her head. Kier grinned and bowed away, giving space for the contenders. Swiftly, they greeted their competition from Hazut, and Vaasa's heart started to pound.

As they approached, an enormous man sauntered forward with large swinging shoulders that looked like they might very well knock over anyone who stood in his way. The dock shook with his footsteps. Ink in the toothed markings of Icruria climbed the side of his face and onto his shaved scalp.

Ton of Wrultho. The current foreman of Wrultho.

Without bothering to gaze at Reid, eyes so orange they rivaled the sun settled harshly on Vaasa. Isabel suddenly slid to her side, lifting a hand and laying it protectively upon her arm. Marc shifted his weight next to Isabel but didn't utter a word—he'd told Reid he planned as much, ensuring Reid knew that he would look weak if he allowed Marc to pretend to be in charge.

Behind Ton, another man walked to meet them, and though she didn't think it possible, he looked even less friendly than Ton. Gazing at the enormous boat looming behind them all, the man straightened his back.

Hunt of Wrultho, the reigning councilor.

Reid had properly informed her of everything she'd need to know about this man before stepping onto this dock, starting with Hunt's close relationship to the advisor Vaasa bargained with all those years ago. To their luck, that particular woman didn't seem to be waiting for them.

Hunt's term as foreman ended when he lost the headman vote and became a councilor, and Ton had taken his place shortly after in a legendary display of skill and strength. While Mireh elected their foreman through a diverse tourney of strength in which the population voted, Wrultho had a far simpler way of choosing their leader.

A fight to the death.

Ton had claimed victory, and as Vaasa looked up and down his enormous body and withering gaze, she understood why. Though Mireh elected a foreman twice in the headman cycle, Wrultho did not. Ton had served since Hunt became a councilor, which meant his cycle, too, was almost up. What Hunt knew or didn't know about her history with Wrultho was a mystery to them all, given Reid didn't know the truth of Ton's broken treaty with Asterya.

The ire in Ton's eyes leashed as Hunt appeared at his side, as if Ton knew he could not let his history with Vaasa slip in front of the man he so desperately wanted to please.

"May I introduce Vaasalisa of Mireh?" Reid spoke as if he couldn't sense the dripping hatred in the man's gaze.

Again, her name attached to his. Attached now to Mireh; no longer a Kozár.

The corner of Ton's lip curled. "I have heard many things about you, Vaasalisa of Mireh."

There were plenty of ways Vaasa could play the situation—she'd considered a few before stepping off the boat. While they didn't need Hunt's vote, without a successful bargain with Ton, there would be no outmaneuvering Dominik. So Vaasa went with the only angle familiar to her: a scheme. Smirking, she said, "You may not like me, but I would like to wager that by the end of our time, you will."

Ton frowned as he looked to Reid, who stifled a small chuckle at her audacity and shrugged.

"You have your hands full," Hunt remarked.

"Only when she allows me," Reid responded smoothly.

Much to Vaasa's surprise, Hunt cracked a grin.

Vaasa fought her own amusement and the heat that threaded its way along her body. All this posturing was the least authentic thing she'd seen among Icrurians so far, but Reid's comment . . . well, that was nothing but truth. "Would you like to take my wager, Ton of Wrultho?"

The foreman of Wrultho wrinkled his nose at her directness and said, "Get to your point or stop wasting my time."

Apparently, that was a no. "Last chance," she offered.

Steam could have been flowing from Ton's ears. Especially when Hunt leaned back like he was actually interested in how this would all play out, and the other councilors and foremen began to take notice. "I think our nation has learned not to play games with Asteryans," Ton said with a sneer.

While Ton's hatred for Asterya was justified in many ways, his vitriol didn't provide any new insight as to what Hunt did or didn't know. Mathjin had warned her of the outright dislike many people would show her this week. "Allow me to express my sincere hopes for our relationship moving forward."

Then Ton peered up at the boat, of which the doors groaned open once again.

The entire crowd hushed.

The rattling of chains flooded the dock as steel links clanked against wood.

Being hauled down the walkway was the general from Asterya, terrified eyes squinting at the harsh sunlight.

The crowd on the dock all took a breath at once, not an eye on anything other than Reid and Vaasa and the long chains Esoti tugged harshly on. Ignac looked worse than when she'd left him, more bloodied, and she wondered silently what Mathjin had done to him.

The general fell to his knees.

Esoti placed those chains directly in Reid's hands.

"I'm not certain if you've formally met General Ignac Kozár, but we happened to stumble upon him wearing Wrultho's sigil on the Settara," Vaasa said loudly enough for the other contenders and councilors to hear. "He and his Asteryan legion attacked our ship. You can imagine our surprise when men who had donned *your* uniforms boarded our vessel in aggression."

Ton's stern lips parted, eyes darting between her and the general. Rage coated his already harsh features, and the vein at his temple throbbed. "Those uniforms must have been *stolen*. My men never would have attacked you."

Hunt stood up straight.

"Of course," Reid chimed in. "The Asteryans must have taken them. They've paid for their insolence."

Vaasa gave Ton her most saccharine smile. "They are all dead now, other than General Kozár. Consider him a gift."

Hunt of Wrultho curled his lips in utter delight, looking at her directly now with more surprise than she thought she'd receive.

"Is this man not related to you?" the councilor from Hazut asked. He looked at the scene as though he didn't believe his eyes, and she quickly realized he was capitalizing on the opportunity.

"This man assaulted my husband and my ship." Vaasa looked to Reid, then back to the councilor. "Any relation was left there in the water."

Galen and Kenen whispered to each other, both of their eyes wide at the scene in front of them. And Vaasa knew the display had done exactly what they'd wanted it to.

Hunt snorted in satisfaction, tipping his own inked head as he looked her up and down. "It is a good thing my successor did not take your wager, Vaasalisa of Mireh."

Reid clenched his fist. "I have learned quickly that people who bet against my wife often find themselves saddled with regret."

Ton grunted, trying not to look at the entire group of contenders who'd heard the comment. Yet Hunt raised his brows, looking between his successor and the incredibly confident foreman of Mireh as if observing two kings.

Reid lifted his chin, possessively sliding his other hand over Vaasa's shoulder as he aimed the full strike of his words at Ton. "In light of these events, I'd like to request a meeting, one where you'll get to decide which side you'd like to be on: ours, or the losing one."

Hunt's delighted smile twitched with the threat, but something about the way he let out a small hum told Vaasa he might respect them both more than he cared to admit.

"Then let's go inside," Ton said with poorly concealed ire. "We can discuss such things now."

"It's safe to assume no meeting will be held tonight," Hunt said, a note of command in his tone—a deep undermining of Ton's authority. Violence shimmered in the growing curve of his mouth. "Instead, you and I shall decide what to do with this gift. To use our sigil for his own end is a grave offense, one he will pay for."

Ton hesitated, and Vaasa almost laughed at the meaning behind their words. To give such a direct decree, especially to a man merely days away from completing a decade-long foremanship, one who would at minimum rise to a councilor . . .

Marc of Mireh would have never dared speak to Reid like that, no matter how much Reid sought the man's exaltation.

Hunt turned back to his wife without accepting an answer, because he already had one. Vaasa pointedly laid the chains in the hands of the guard Hunt sent to retrieve them. They rattled once more as

Ignac was dragged to where Hunt quietly instructed Ton's men to take him. With a frustrated scowl, Ton stomped off after the councilor, and Vaasa wondered how much faith Hunt had in his successor at all. How much responsibility he believed could be laid in the man's lap.

Given how close Wrultho was to Hazut, it was a dynamic she could certainly play off of.

The contenders and councilors descended into the clamoring crowd.

As they cleared out, Isabel muttered under her breath, "Hunt's lapdog. Sit, stay."

Reid's laughter threaded around them.

Despite herself, Vaasa grinned. Looking up at their small group, she whispered, "Shall we see if he can roll over?"

Against all odds, Marc of Mireh snorted a laugh before quickly regaining his composure. "Let's go win an election, shall we?"

Upon entering the High Temple of Dihrah, they were blasted with cool air pushed by large fans moving upon the vaulted ceiling. Flared edges went back and forth in unison, appearing sharp from Vaasa's angle. Coming immediately to her side, the five other Veragi witches crooned about their grand entrance and how the crowds had shaken with anticipation.

Koen found them in the main chamber immediately, metal spectacles highlighting the chocolate of his eyes and the enormous smile growing on his face as he spotted them. Koen's eyes traveled across the small coven, greeting each of them with a strange familiarity, until his piercing gaze settled upon Amalie at Vaasa's other side. He tilted his head. "I don't believe we've met."

Amalie seemed to freeze for a moment, but then she said, "I don't believe we have, either."

From behind Koen, Reid raised his brows.

"Koen of Dihrah," the other foreman introduced himself with a hefty bow of his head.

"Amalie McCray." The brown-haired witch shifted her feet a little.

"Melisina!" another voice called as a tall, thin man sauntered forward with the grace of a dancer, long limbs carrying him past the rest of the world and right into the woman's waiting arms.

"Elijah," Melisina greeted him, purple robes twisting around him. Vaasa swiftly realized he was high consort of Icruria. "You simply must meet my daughter-in-law."

"Another Veragi witch, you sneaky woman!" he said to her. "As if your bloodline needed any more magic."

Elijah of Icruria turned to greet Vaasa, stunning cornflower-blue eyes sliding up and down her. "Oh, I approve!" he trilled, stepping forward to grasp her forearm.

"Lovely to meet you, High Consort," Vaasa said as Reid returned to her side and placed a reassuring hand at her back.

"Elijah," he corrected. "Only ever Elijah. As I will call you Vaasalisa when you inevitably take my job."

Reid laughed in confident agreement, but Vaasa smiled through the tightening in her stomach. "Actually, you will call me Vaasa. It's what all my friends call me."

Hand smacking against his chest, Elijah gaped. "Oh, Reid, she's a smooth talker, all right."

"The smoothest," he said with a wink before pressing his lips affectionately to the side of her head.

"You have one hour," Kier told them, eyes trailing to Romana and Mariana. "Don't think about sneaking off to the sodality this year."

"Don't think your little title means you can boss us around," Romana reminded him.

Vaasa stifled her laugh, given his *little* title was headman of Icruria.

Rolling his eyes, Kier fought a smile. "Good luck, Reid. Perhaps you will finally be able to negotiate with them."

"Not likely," Mariana said as Kier plunged back into the crowded main hall.

Shaking her head, Vaasa spent that single hour escaping to their quarters and fixing the cosmetics on her eyes and lips, Amalie sitting on the counter and dangling her legs. Reid caught up with Koen on the patio, and, dressed in their finest, all four of them descended upon the traditional first dinner together.

The councilors observed the entire dinner smugly, taking note of each of Vaasa's gestures. Hunt of Wrultho clearly distrusted Vaasa after her earlier stunt. He often leaned over and whispered to his blond companion, the councilor from Hazut. But Hunt still managed to look more inviting than his successor, who had to bend over his table to fit. Ton of Wrultho's eyes went wide when he saw who took the seat directly to Vaasa's right.

Amalie.

The magic in Vaasa rumbled.

Regardless, they ate with ease, laughing at the jokes Reid made and smiling widely when Koen spoke. He'd taken the spot next to Amalie, which brought a smile to Vaasa's lips, though she minded her own business.

The crowded room was filled with tables upon tables, all laid out around a dance floor. Food was piled on two larger rectangular tables lining the edges. Lanterns lit by the coven of Una were strung from the ceiling in varying levels, much like the library, shimmering in pale gold. People filed in, most of whom Vaasa didn't recognize. Still, she ate her fill and joined the conversation where she could.

Brom of Hazut passed by their table, nodding at Reid and her while he regally promenaded his admittedly lovely wife around the room. The two presented as real contenders. Her dress fell gracefully from her shoulders and dragged a small train behind her. Swathed in all green, she looked like what Vaasa thought a high consort might. All lithe torso and long limbs, the woman elegantly looked over her shoulder at someone and smiled.

She must have practiced for this all her life.

Amalie chuckled, and Vaasa elbowed her.

Dancing began, Ton drank more honeyed mead than was or should ever be acceptable, and Vaasa rushed to dance with Reid. These steps were less unfamiliar to her, thanks to his lessons. But as he mastered each dance with the grace of an actor, Vaasa took the first excuse to slip out of his arms and to the edge of the circle in order not to embarrass herself any further.

Or to make herself look any less Icrurian.

Amalie stuck to her side, her only real saving grace in the unfamiliarity of the crowds. But just then, Koen extended her a hand. Amalie took it, garnering the attention of many around them as Koen took to the dance floor with her.

Finding Vaasa standing alone, Melisina took the opportunity to educate her on each major coven. Throughout the room were the witches who resided at each sodality, all with magic different from her own. Some could manipulate metal, others water, some were healers. While their blood could be passed down to any child regardless of sex, every coven was plagued with the same issue Veragi were: only one witch per bloodline lived at a time. Unlike Veragi, however, their power was not so overwhelming that it killed its untrained members. Yet most of them were prickly, closed off, and secretive. She supposed this was the issue Amalie had dreamed of fixing; imagine what they would be capable of, if only they worked together.

Melisina pointed out the coven Vaasa had sought all those months ago—the coven of Una. She scanned the faces of the large crowd of witches, all dressed in their ceremonial robes from the sodality.

Vaasa's heart dropped.

There, with a stemmed glass in her hand and a smile on her face, was Brielle.

The young woman had been the only person to offer her friendship at the Sodality of Una, and Vaasa had shunned it.

I do not require your assistance, Brielle.

Shame emerged, and regret, too. She'd been wrong then to assume that being alone was the only way to survive. Being alone was the most assured way to die.

Vaasa gripped her wineglass and averted her eyes.

"She is the one who told me where you were," Melisina said quietly, still at her side. "And I told Reid."

The world could have dropped from beneath her feet. She'd never understood how he'd found her. How he'd known exactly where in the library she would be.

Vaasa tried to focus on the twirling of those around her, on Amalie and Kosana and Esoti and the room full of beating hearts she could suddenly hear. She tried not to shake. Tried not to let her thoughts swirl out of control at the memories of her time in this city.

It terrified her that any moment she could be alone again.

As Vaasa turned, she found Reid standing in front of her, that cocky amusement painted on his lips. He stepped into Vaasa, the smell of him surrounding her senses and forcing her eyes to break from Brielle. The salt. The amber. She looked up at him, only to find him already inspecting her.

"A toast?" he asked, wolfish grin growing as people watched the two of them, assessing who might very well be their next headman and high consort. Voice booming with all the assurance of a ruler, Reid said, "To my wife, who will make one of the most brilliant high consorts this continent has ever known."

Quite a bold statement to make in the midst of an election.

But when Elijah raised his glass with a loud yowl of agreement, the room stirred with noise.

Ton watched them both, as did Hunt. Brom, too, along with his wife.

Vaasa's lips slithered into a smile only she and Reid would know wasn't real. Pretending to be perfectly flattered, she plucked the goblet from his hand and took a large gulp, toasting to the circle of people gathering around them. "To Icruria!"

They all cheered and laughed, raising their own glasses. Cheering for Reid of Mireh and his enthusiastic Asteryan bride.

She had a job to do. Though she would undoubtedly suffer for it later, she pushed down the magic and the awful tightening of her chest. She became what they all accused her of—a chameleon, melting into her surroundings and becoming whatever they needed her to be.

The world was watching, so Vaasa pressed her hands to Reid's chest.

Peering up through her lashes, her indigo eyes met the depth of his, and if she hadn't known any better, she'd have sworn he was caught there.

So she whispered, "Dance with me like lovers do."

His jaw twitched, and as soon as she'd asked it of him, Reid of Mireh obliged.

CHAPTER 19

After a night of broken sleep and a morning of political posturing, they moved through the city on the backs of rhinos, which bayed with great pleasure whenever Vaasa scratched behind their ears. In the afternoon light, the gray of their hides was lighter than she expected. People filled the streets with loud conversation. The bustle of the election had settled like dust on each pathway, people moving from place to place, some trying to rush forward to get a look at the contenders, the lines to enter the Dihrah colosseum wrapping around multiple blocks.

Vaasa took those opportunities to whisper to Reid, who sat behind her and kept an arm possessively wrapped around her waist. She wanted to say it was too hot for such games, but she kept the thought to herself—she was nervous about this event, even if he wasn't.

Today was the tourney of strength: the greatest show of physical prowess in the election, despite it being purely for show. The eastern foremen were favored to prevail.

Except that Reid would be fighting.

The heat of the summer kissed the dry sky, and in a great testament of willpower, Vaasa didn't throw herself into the Settara for relief.

Every inch they rode on the backs of the tough-hided rhinos, she understood with greater degree the purpose of her training with Esoti.

Rounded edges couldn't dull the sharpness of the hollering screams and echoes of pounding feet that emanated from the towering colosseum as they emerged onto the battleground. Filling each of the rows of stone benches were families and children, elders and young soldiers alike chanting their excitement at today's events. The music of it wrapped around them like a battle cry. Reid dismounted fluidly onto the sand and helped Vaasa down, pulling her into him as the crowd watched and screamed.

"They like how you look in my arms," Reid whispered, forcing her to tear her eyes from the clamor.

She tried to ignore the sound of her own thundering heartbeat. Stomach in knots, Vaasa knew his comment was only to maintain their little show, so she ran her fingers through the loose tendrils of his hair.

Mischievous eyes sparked, and Vaasa bit her lower lip, causing his gaze to drop down to her mouth. It reminded her of the first time they'd been this close, when it was only she who had been playing a game. Something about the memory of that moment kindled the dangerous closeness she felt to him. Their moment on the ship hadn't left her, though by the cool set of Reid's rigid jaw, she suspected it wasn't anywhere on his mind. "Are you nervous?" she asked, low enough that only they could hear.

At first it looked like he might deny it, but then he gave a small nod. "My father competed in this tourney once, before he married my mother."

Pushing the stray tendrils out of her way, she raised her lips to his ear. Another part of the show, though her words weren't. "You will make your father proud," she assured him. "You already have."

He pulled back and looked at her then, like he saw more of her—as if some puzzle piece he'd been struggling to place in his head had finally found a way to fit. Then, loud enough for the people surrounding them to note, he asked, "And if it were your pride I would like to earn today?"

She smiled wide. "Then you must win."

His finger settled beneath her chin and lifted her face upward, and though he had never done so in public before, he pressed his lips to hers. Her heart immediately slammed against her ribs.

"Very well, Wild One," he whispered against her mouth, then broke the contact with the same quickness with which he'd started it.

He sauntered off into the crowd, leaving her standing there with Amalie and Mathjin, plagued with questions.

Had all of that just been for show?

Amalie looped their arms and tugged, choosing wisely to remain quiet, and Mathjin stepped closely behind them. Vaasa shook it off, choosing to instead focus on what mattered. Over her shoulder, Mathjin held his hand upon the pommel of his sword. Kosana and Esoti had entered a partner match, and Reid was lining up, which left Mathjin as their guardian.

As they took their designated seats, wooden chairs instead of stone benches, Vaasa spotted Koen. "Are you not participating?"

The greatest warriors from each territory would fight until surrender, a bracket battle for the decade. Some of these men and women were contenders for the foremanship of their own territories, which added a sharpness in the way these competitors gazed at each other. Everyone wanted to prove themselves before returning home for their own local elections and tourneys. No group was sharper than the contenders for the headmanship, who were all gathered in the same place Reid was, except, apparently, Koen.

He laughed and pushed up his glasses. "I am not going to be headman; I see no reason to injure myself for it."

Koen had taken the opportunity to explain last night just how *uninterested* in the headmanship he was, mostly because Kier and Elijah were his adoptive parents. There would be no councilor who voted for a familial inheritance of power. Knowing his fathers had already won the headmanship and that Dihrah would likely not contend for it anyway, he'd stepped into the foremanship with eyes on being a councilor for Reid's tenure. They'd grown up together, both Reid's father and Kier having served together in the Icrurian Central Forces. While

Reid forwent the sodality for a long tenure in the ICF, Koen had studied endlessly in Dihrah. He was even close with Kosana, and all three had promised they would someday rise together.

"I think this is foolish," Amalie admitted, causing Koen to glance at her out of the side of his eye.

Hunt of Wrultho took his seat just then, gracing the stone balcony reserved for councilors. He sat near Isabel and Marc, who were chatting with Kenen. Hunt nodded at Vaasa, but then his eyes landed on Amalie.

He furrowed his brow, glancing at Ton, who Vaasa now realized inspected their every move from where he stood with the other contenders.

Upon Amalie's passing, he sneered.

Koen stood with graceful limbs and swept his fingers along the chair next to him. "Join me?" he asked Amalie, who had visibly bitten the inside of her cheek to keep from showing how much Ton's distaste affected her. All the woman's defenses were up, yet when Koen gestured for her to take the seat at his side, her shoulders dropped a touch.

By the subtle way that Koen pointedly directed his body toward Amalie, Vaasa wondered if Ton's fury was only a bonus to the foreman.

Mathjin calculatingly glanced between everyone and took the bench directly behind Vaasa. She felt safer knowing he was at her back and could rise at any moment if she needed him.

The first set of athletes came and went. Vaasa didn't even remember who won. Through the throwing of spears and hurdling over large obstacles, each athlete proved themselves more capable than the last. While the Mirehan corps made it a focus to outlast, something Kosana had proven to Vaasa the hard way, these warriors were so aggressively offensive that it made Vaasa's heart lurch into her throat at moments. Spears and axes made their brutal movements different, too, and she narrowed her eyes to take note of them. Swiftly, they were identified as soldiers from Wrultho and Hazut.

Sweat beaded at the base of Vaasa's neck, and the short black strands of her hair wouldn't stay put. Fight after fight was called. Blood spattered the sand as warriors were dragged off by the healers from the Sodality of Zuheia.

It took two hours to call the other brackets, each one leading to the grand event: the contenders. First to fight were Irhu and Hazut, which was hardly a battle at all. Brom quickly earned a surrender from Irhu. Reid was out next for his first fight, taking on the contender from Sigguth without much trouble. The bracket almost seemed like it had been set up to pit West against East, but after Reid won, it was suddenly a battle between Wrultho and Hazut.

Within a few minutes, and though it seemed as though he'd put up a good fight, Brom of Hazut surrendered.

Vaasa furrowed her brow. Had someone ordered him to do such a thing? Brom didn't strike her as the type of man to surrender so quickly.

"Planned," Mathjin confirmed as he leaned around the arms of Vaasa's chair. "The point is to pit Reid against the foreman of Wrultho."

"Why?"

"Because they are the two top contenders in the election," Koen said.

It seemed to have more to do with Icruria's economics than it did with the actual contenders. Which was more profitable: war or peace?

The rattling of chains snapped Vaasa out of reflection.

A spiked, barred gate lifted on one side and then Vaasa's breath caught. Stumbling through the gate into the blazing sun, eyes squinted painfully against the sudden brightness, was Ignac Kozár.

The sigil of Wrultho had been torn from his chest, bloody skin glaring through the hole. The amputation of his hand couldn't be inspected from this far, but it dripped blood in the sand. Parts of the crowd erupted in louder cheers than they'd given all day. The colosseum shook with their raucous screams and the pounding of their feet.

Yet other sections hushed.

Vaasa looked down at Reid, who had taken a few steps back. Everyone seemed to look at *her*.

The councilors, specifically.

Vaasa trained her features into neutrality, folding her hands in her lap and lifting her chin. If she reacted as though this bothered her, what damage could that do? Koen didn't pretend to stay objective—he stood up at the same time Elijah and Kier did, probably wondering the same thing.

How, in *their* city, had someone given an order like this?

Vaasa steeled herself, the stakes of this single string of moments beating in her chest. This was a plot, then. To remind the world of Asteryan aggression, right as Reid fought one of the eastern territories plagued by violence from his wife's homeland.

Men surrounded Ignac with spears as they chained him to a large wooden pole in the center of the makeshift battleground. He was hoisted onto a platform, the centerpiece to a table of bloodshed, raised high above the chaos below. He was meant to be looked at. Meant to be a sign—like a prized hog. One that would undoubtedly be slaughtered the moment someone became ravenous. Would they force the winner to murder him? Torture him into confessing his crimes or revealing who had sent him?

She didn't dare show an ounce of emotion.

The gauntlet was dropped, and the fight below rang out.

Reid wasn't as large as Ton of Wrultho, but instantly Vaasa could see that he was faster. The two men danced with more skill than even the warriors Kosana trained. The offensive eastern fighting caused Reid to move more than was perhaps strategic, but he held his balance. After dodging three of Ton's ax swings, Reid put enough space between them that Ton had no choice but to circle.

Ton charged at him and their iron clashed, echoing around the arena and causing people to jump out of their seats. Reid weaved, spinning in a full circle to avoid the might of Ton's ax. As the large blade swept past Reid's abdomen, Vaasa sucked in a breath. It missed—barely. Reid spun and kept his sword focused on blocking while Ton pushed forward with more strength than before.

If Vaasa had been watching this weeks ago, she'd have assumed Ton would win. The burly man had the momentum, the fire, and he seemed to be gaining ground. But Reid was very particular about where he planted his feet and how much energy he gave each motion. She knew this aspect of him, of his fighting—it was calculated, specific, and resilient.

Ton's blows came slower. Reid's blocks did not.

Reid spun in that full circle again, now far too quick for Ton to keep up, and the burly man stumbled.

An opening.

Vaasa slid to the edge of her seat, forgetting for a moment that anyone else existed.

It was there, in the way Reid stalked with a terrifying gait, strategy woven into even the smallest of twitches, that Vaasa saw what they had named him after—*the Wolf.* There was hunger in his prowl. Threat in his steps. Heart hammering in her chest, Vaasa couldn't entirely breathe when she watched him. Admiration filled her at the same time adrenaline did.

He was going to win this.

Wild, piercing sounds slammed off the stone corridors.

In an instant, everyone was on their feet, eyes wide at the scene unfolding directly to their left, and the magic gathered again in her limbs. People wailed, the crowd moving like waves along the rounded stadium seating.

Fleeing.

They were *fleeing*.

Black oil coated the benches and spilled over the stones, moving along the colosseum much like the mist from her own magic did, only shiny and slick. This wasn't Veragi magic. A miserable keening emanated around them, then it morphed into an angry and pained growl.

Vaasa's breath stopped as this *thing* curled over one of the sandstone pillars.

It jumped onto the benches with spindly legs and talons, its torso perpetually hunched over. Stone crumbled beneath the weight of it, plummeting to the seating below.

Dripping shadows and blackness, oily tendrils danced around the creature with arms so long it leaned forward upon its clawed hands for balance. One claw protruded like an elongated pointer finger that chipped bricks of stone beneath it, and its two front arms were coated in webbed wings. Two horns grew from its head and curled backward all the way to its sides.

Soldiers moved from every direction, screams filling the air. Reid and Ton were no longer engaged in fighting, and then Mathjin appeared at her side. Hands gripped Vaasa's forearm and tugged, and she was moving away, eyes still glued to the creature and the two contestants in the arena.

Mathjin tugged her back toward the stone archways.

The creature jumped, gliding unceremoniously on its wobbly, outstretched wings, and landed on the sand in the arena.

"Mathjin!" Vaasa cried, pulling against his grip.

"Don't you dare," he growled at her.

Vaasa tugged with all her might, and her arm slipped from Mathjin's grasp.

Then she was sprinting down the stone steps, Mathjin hollering behind her.

People moved on all sides of her, but Vaasa didn't notice anything outside her tunnel vision. She leapt down one of the rows of stone seating and dodged another group, eyes remaining on Reid. She didn't know where the instinct came from or how she could be so sure, but something told her with certainty that this was her brother's doing.

If this was how he killed Reid . . .

Screams grew louder as people fell over each other, the colosseum descending into madness. A thousand scenarios flooded her mind. Was this only the beginning of an attack? Was her brother here? Who was controlling the creature?

Vaasa almost stumbled over herself as she sprinted down the steps. Mathjin still hollered at her heels. One of the guards tried to step in her way, but she spun, back skimming his shoulder, and flicked her arm out in just enough time to wrap her fingers around the pommel of his sword and tug it out of its scabbard.

Mathjin roared at her as she jumped two steps at a time, her new iron weapon glinting in the sunlight.

Guards flooded the sand. Arrows flew through the air and one ripped through a wing, causing the creature to tilt its horned head and scream in rage. It ripped into the person nearest it, crushing the man between its teeth and throwing his limp body to the side.

It jumped and glided on an invisible wind. The creature's wings blacked out the sun for the briefest of seconds. Shadows fell off it and covered the dusty ground. Magic shot from Vaasa as she reached the interior of the sandy arena and leapt over the last of the walls. The drop was longer than she expected, and she grunted as she tucked and rolled onto the sand. The sword slapped against the ground. Tightness shot up her back, but her momentum pushed her to her feet. Everything Esoti taught her pulsed in her veins. Black magic swirled around her arms and torso as she picked up the sword and kept running.

Reid was there, standing directly in front of the creature, weapon raised. Then his eyes flicked in her direction, widening with anger as Vaasa pushed her body between him and the creature.

"What the *fuck* are you doing?" he yelled.

Panting, she dug her heels into the sand and didn't respond. Instead, she raised her sword.

Crimson eyes sank into a humanlike face. Upon seeing them, the creature's mouth split open to reveal horrifying sharp teeth that dripped with the blood of the man it had just killed. The creature's spine and ribs poked out of its scaled skin, and its oily magic began to creep forward along the sand just in front of them. Reminiscent of a mangled human, this creature was like nothing Vaasa had ever seen before. The rancid scent of its magic moved through the air, sweeping into her nose and down her throat.

Like rotting flesh. Burning hair.

The magic in her stomach churned. It coiled at the memory coursing in her body—muscle memory, in the form of her stomach clenching and nausea tightening her jaw. That scent had haunted her. It had followed her day in and day out in those first few weeks. Memories of it had never once left her.

It had drifted down the hallway where she'd found her mother. That oily substance had slicked across her pale skin, tarnished the green of her dress. She'd thought it was the remnants of Veragi magic. But she remembered then—she'd smelled it on Dominik only weeks prior. Had that just been her mind playing tricks?

Those bloody eyes landed just behind Vaasa.

It cocked its head. Took slow steps toward them.

Her hands tightened on the sword as her entire body prepared to swing.

And then its head whipped to the right, damaged wings rising as it leapt into the air and glided past them, landing firmly on the platform hoisting Ignac Kozár in the air. Vaasa gagged as the creature sank its teeth without hesitation into the general's flesh.

Blood sprayed along the chains and the pole that bound him, the man's final screams not quick enough to be heard. Lost to the air, his inaudible wail emanated around them all.

Especially when the creature turned back to them, just for a moment, before winking out of existence.

Gone.

Nothing but Ignac's limp body remained, and if she dared get close enough, Vaasa knew what she would find. Paleness. Sunken cheeks. Left in its wake would be the oily magic, feeding selfishly upon the corpse. An image that had burrowed itself in her mind so deeply that in that moment, she almost swore she could see her mother's body, the jade of her dress torn and hanging off the platform.

Vaasa dropped her sword.

No one moved.

Not even a guard.

And then, everyone moved at once.

Reid's arm wrapped around her waist and he dragged her from the arena, barking at anyone who got too close. The entire trip into a cold, contained archway was a blur; Vaasa could only smell and see the oily magic.

A wooden door crashed into the sand, cutting off most of the light and sound. They were alone and her breath started to quicken.

Reid pressed her back into cold stone. His hand curled into the fabric of her clothes. She couldn't breathe. Couldn't think.

"Why would you do that?" he demanded.

When she didn't answer, he pushed his body against hers. "Answer me!"

"Shut up," she snapped, then pushed him off her so she could stumble to the left. Bile crept up her throat and she vomited into the sand. Her knees slammed to the ground, stomach wrenching as the contents of her lunch came back up.

Reid cursed from somewhere behind her. He tried to pull back her hair, but she pushed his hands away. "Amalie," she demanded. "*Amalie*."

"You don't have Amalie," he said. "All you have is me."

She wiped her mouth, tears welling in her eyes as she crawled away from the mess. Reid followed her. Leaving enough space to assuage her fear, he dipped to the ground a few paces away. "What is going on?"

Vaasa couldn't sit here in the sand and wail. Using what strength she had left, she lurched to her feet and started into the tunnel. "Where does this lead?"

There was a short pause, then, "Catacombs under the colosseum."

"Can you show me the way out?"

Reid pursed his lips. "Will you tell me what the hell just happened?"

He read her too well. She'd let him get too close. "I know that smell," she confessed. "It was the same one from the night I found my mother."

"Found her where?"

"Dead."

Silence fell around them. She realized she'd never told him that part. He didn't make an event of it. Perhaps he, too, understood the pieces she'd just put together.

Her mother had not lost control of her Veragi magic. Her mother had been murdered.

And whoever had done it had sent that same creature into Icruria.

CHAPTER 20

The city was locked down within minutes.

Reid and Vaasa found their party, few of whom commented on Vaasa's choice to ditch Mathjin. The wise advisor also kept his mouth shut, though something about the anger in his eyes told Vaasa they'd have that conversation later. That there would be hell to pay for not following his plan.

Back at the High Temple, Amalie snuck off to find someone she knew from Wrultho, someone she insisted would have some answers about how they'd gotten Ignac into the arena. Given the creature had targeted him, there had to be a connection. Vaasa bathed, redressed, and kept herself under control.

When Amalie returned, they learned that the rest of the coven was already at the Sodality of Una. It was the only coven that would meet with theirs, despite Melisina's pleas to the other high witches.

Technically, they hadn't been given permission to leave the High Temple. Koen escorted them personally, at Amalie's demand, and it was the only reason they made it down the three blocks to the enormous building. Waiting at the entrance was Brielle, curls bouncing around her face like a halo. Vaasa's heart leapt into her throat, though Brielle only grinned. "Your coven is waiting," she said.

Nodding quietly, they followed Brielle through the dim, golden stacks of the Library of Una and down to the lowest floor, where only a few of the lanterns had been strung far enough to reach. Two women in red acolyte robes stood up straight at their presence, eyeing Brielle first and then eyes widening at Koen and Reid. Brielle smiled at them both, and they nodded their heads sternly to Amalie and Vaasa. Behind the wrought iron barrier of the seventh floor, the stacks were washed in golden light, sconces perched upon each oak bookshelf, the bracket ornamented with different patterns of twisted metal. With a small extension of her palm, light started to grow in Brielle's hand, and Vaasa caught her breath.

She'd never seen one of the witches of Una manipulate light.

As they plunged down a dim hallway, the light almost diminished apart from Brielle's little orb, and then the corridor opened into a catacomb beneath a separate tower. Climbing the marble staircase ornamented with more oak and iron, they found themselves on the first level of their witch's tower. Two more sprawling staircases led to the same balcony and more hallways expanded off the sides, leading to what Vaasa thought were private rooms. In the middle of that second-level balcony was an enormous, long rectangular table, and perched upon it was a small, familiar group of witches.

Vaasa let out a small breath of relief.

"You're alive," Romana said in jest, feet up on one of the tables settled in the center of the enormous room with a book in her hand. Mariana sat at her side, blond hair pulled away from her face. Suma looked up, grinned, and then dug her nose back into her book.

Melisina rose from the table and shuffled forward, down the steps, and then gathered all four of them in her arms. Vaasa tried not to be uncomfortable with so much physical contact, and Reid muttered something to his mother about being overbearing.

An unfamiliar woman watched from next to the table. Short silver hair hung gently over her lean, friendly face. Narrow hazel eyes looked them both up and down, hands lifting to reveal intricate lines of ink upon soft brown skin. Her black robes indicated that she was a sage, though not one whom Vaasa recognized.

"Consort," she said, greeting Vaasa, then turning to Amalie. "And you must be Amalie. I'm happy to see you both safe."

"Pleasure to meet you," Amalie said with a dip of her chin.

"Leanan Day. I'm the high witch of Una."

Melisina's counterpart here in Dihrah, then. "An honor to meet you, Leanan," Vaasa said.

With the strange openness of the witches in the room, Vaasa wondered with a small pang of frustration how easy it would have been to find them all if she'd only bothered to be honest.

"Did you find your soldier from Wrultho?" Leanan asked Amalie. Vaasa wondered silently if this "soldier" was the same man Amalie had told her about weeks ago when they'd eaten lunch; the childhood friend who had been her first love.

Amalie scurried up the steps, towing Vaasa with her, and then gripped the edge of the table. Her foot started to tap. "I did, and I think there's something going on with Ton."

Subtly, Reid moved to the space behind Vaasa, pulling out a chair for her to sit in and then standing behind it, hands on the top. "How do you know this soldier?" he asked Amalie, the undertones of his words sounding a little more like *How do you know we can trust him*?

Amalie paused. She started tapping her foot again. "He is a family friend and a member of the ICF. Just like I do, he has connections to Wrultho's people."

Family friend didn't seem to explain her tone, or the way a small flush crept up her neck as she folded her arms and tried to pretend no one had asked. Shame seemed to flutter on the edges of her mouth, but she lifted her chin and held her ground.

Without a doubt, the same man. The one Ton had sent her away for.

Melisina cut in, uninterested in Amalie's trip down memory lane. "Ton's men are willing to turn on him?"

"I don't know," Amalie said. "But he said something was off. Like they were uncomfortable or divided."

"Who can blame them?" Koen asked.

Between Amalie's taps, Vaasa tried to give the magic breadth. Tried to release little bits of it from her fingertips. The more they spoke, the closer the magic became to a bird of prey feasting on her insides.

"What happened at the colosseum?" Leanan asked. "Let's start there."

Amalie recounted the details to them all, describing the monster with terrifying accuracy and leaving out the part that included Vaasa.

"That sounds like a Miro'dag," Brielle whispered, shifting uncomfortably in her chair.

Amalie stopped tapping, and her lips parted in recognition.

"I suspected," said Koen, who slid into the spot nearest Vaasa. "It is a demon of sorts."

Vaasa's ears perked up at that.

"A Miro'dag requires a very specific sort of magic, a dark and terrible one long extinct," he said. "It is a henchman belonging to a Zetyr witch."

Zetyr, the god of bargains and souls.

It was one of the most infamous sets of bloodlines that had ruled what was now Wrultho for generations. Vaasa had read about it when she'd been searching for information on Veragi. The most prominent family had been slaughtered by one of their own, and then the coven turned on itself fighting for power. At the implications of this, a coldness unfurled deep in Vaasa.

"No one has seen a Zetyr witch in centuries," Leanan argued.

"It sounds like a Miro'dag to me, as well," Melisina said.

"So they aren't extinct?" Romana asked, closing her book and crossing her arms in disbelief.

Melisina gestured for Amalie to continue, giving her the floor. Shifting her weight, Amalie decided to take up the space she deserved, and it was the single moment of relief Vaasa felt. "I've read no records of them for at least a few generations, though we have few records dating past the founding of our coven."

"I've read the same." Koen pushed up his glasses. "You saw it, too, Amalie. Did it seem like Zetyr magic to you?"

Her eyes darted around, lips pursing. Hesitantly, they landed on the foreman of Dihrah. "I've only seen sketches, though the description makes sense. It . . . resembles oil."

"I don't understand," Vaasa said, finally speaking. All the different kinds of magic felt like too much to carry—too much to process. Especially when each coven picked and chose what was acceptable to share. Chances were, even if there was a written history of this kind of magic, it was locked deep in the sodality in Wrultho. And of all the territories, Wrultho was the least likely to offer anything to Vaasa.

There were few times in her life when she wasn't the most informed in a room, wasn't the one with the answers. After everything today, she wanted to fight someone or run the perimeter of the Settara. Anything to work off this energy.

Suma extended a hand to Vaasa's forearm, her large brown eyes gentle. "Just as we get our magic from Veragi, Zetyr witches get their magic from their god. We do many things—and so can they. Their methods were awful and twisted; they could even conjure illusions and pretend to have magic they didn't truly possess. But Zetyr can only bargain the use of their power; it cannot be willed without a trade."

"Which implies there is someone making the bargain and someone else actually using the magic," Leanan said.

"It is always foolish to assume there is only one enemy," Vaasa whispered.

Koen crossed his arms. Reid curled a hand on her shoulder, but she shook him off. She didn't want to be touched, not by anyone. Anything.

That voice in the back of her head blared in warning.

While assumptions were dangerous, she couldn't bring herself to believe Dominik wasn't behind this somehow. The sheer discord it had sown was enough of a reason to presume he had something to do with it. It couldn't be just Ton.

If Dominik was bargaining with people who had far more magic than her, what chance did she stand of surviving this? "I need to think," Vaasa rasped, sliding her chair back from the table in part to stand, but also to put space between her and everyone else. She spun, placing her hands on the wooden banister of the second level.

There must be a way to leverage this information, to gain the upper hand. Secrets were a bargaining piece and pride was often people's downfall.

Dominik wanted the Wrultho forces to stand down, to move out of his way. If he had such magic, why wouldn't he just take what he wanted? Surely someone as brash as Dominik would have decimated entire armies by now if he could.

There must be a limit. A threshold to what his bargainer could accomplish. Looking to Reid, her magic flared again. But it was Melisina who spoke, voice soft and calm. "Let's focus on what we do know."

Vaasa forced herself to breathe. They knew so little, and because of her, they didn't stand a chance at working with the witches from Wrultho.

She looked at Amalie, who gave the smallest of nods, like she understood more than anyone else the guilt and fear that coursed through Vaasa.

But she didn't want understanding. She wanted solutions. She wanted to know she wasn't about to get them all killed.

"Perhaps it was one of the competitors," Koen suggested. "Like Ton. Maybe he set up the entire ambush and killed Ignac to cover it."

"Why would he do something that stupid?" Reid asked. He leaned back against the banister now, only looking to Vaasa when she spoke.

Shrugging, Melisina said, "His competition arrives with a new bride from the very empire Ton is at war with? He of all people has something to lose if you are elected—most notably, his pride."

Koen uncrossed his arms. "It's quite possible Ton has gone to desperate lengths to influence this election."

"If that were the case, why not just attack Reid outright?" Romana said.

"Your city-states are dangerously linked in terms of resource distribution," Vaasa said. "To make a movement of aggression against any of the territories would only further isolate Wrultho, which is something they can't afford."

"Ton isn't a political genius," Koen pointed out.

Reid snorted his agreement.

Vaasa shook her head, brushing both of them off. "He's fighting for Hunt's approval, which means he wants to be a player on the Icrurian stage."

"If he hadn't been the one who started the violence with Asterya, he'd probably be a real contender in this election," Amalie sneered.

Of everything she knew about Ton, one thing was clear: the man wanted power. But Amalie was right. The old-fashioned way, Ton could never win.

"He is ashamed, seeking a way to matter. And I suspect his goals are in line with that motivation," Koen agreed.

"He wants bloodshed. If it was he who summoned that creature, he would have used it against Asterya already," Vaasa said.

"Okay, so then we know nothing," Romana said.

"We know nothing for sure," Koen confirmed.

Frustration crawling over her skin like tiny bugs, Vaasa laid her hands flat against the table. "Can you get me everything you have on Zetyr magic?"

"It isn't much, but I can," Leanan said.

Reid shook his head. "It's late, you should—"

"Don't," Vaasa warned.

The two held each other's eyes for a brief moment before Reid finally crossed his arms and stepped back from his chair. "I'll come find you in a few hours. Kier will come for me and Koen any moment now."

"Go," Melisina said. "This place is safe. No Miro'dag will find us here."

Lips pursed, Reid gave a solid nod, then spun on his heel, descending the stairs without another word. Koen dipped his head to everyone and sprinted after him, the two foremen disappearing into the shadows of the first floor.

All Vaasa wanted was to be alone. To have the space she needed to put together these moving puzzle pieces.

Undoubtedly, they were all connected.

Brielle approached the bookshelf at her right. Plucking out a black leather-bound tome, she slid it across the table. "Start with this. I'll retrieve a cart and bring you everything we have."

"Brielle—" Vaasa stopped, then collected herself as the woman turned to look at her again. "Thank you."

With half a smile and little nod, Brielle sauntered across the room and started pulling books off the shelves.

"There is a room in the back," Leanan said. "A place you can study in quiet."

"I'll go with you—" Amalie said.

"No," Vaasa said, interrupting, knives in her blood.

Hurt flashed across Amalie's eyes, and that dug into Vaasa, too.

There was nothing she could do or say that was right.

Vaasa swept up the book and bowed her head to them all, then quickly disappeared from view.

As the witches gradually left with each turning of the hour, Vaasa's magic flopped back to life and sank like she'd swallowed rocks. Their footsteps and the echoes of doors closing hardly registered. She stayed seated at a table in a room off one of the three hallways, where she could see the expanse of Dihrah through large windows. The City of Scholars glittered beneath starlight, streams of the lights of Una running gold along the oak table and chairs she sat at, playing upon the rivers of crimson and ivory in the marble floors. Alone, she reviewed every detail of the conversation they'd had, of conversations she'd had prior. Of the attack. Of every word she'd said to Dominik. Of the letters she'd reviewed with Mathjin.

A witch was hiding. One who had killed her mother and probably Ignac Kozár in front of every major Icrurian player.

There was only one person who had so much to gain from all this death. One person who had systematically removed every threat to his ascension until there were only two left.

And now she sat here, knowing well enough who those two people were.

She'd learned everything she could about the god Zetyr tonight since there was so little on the magic itself. The mythos surrounding him was laden with cruelty: possessions of mortals, the sacrifice of loved ones, tales of a sinister trickster. There were horrific legends about the bargains he struck and how they were built on twisted words. When she could not find answers about the Zetyr coven precisely, she turned to historical records, but most of them were written in a much older dialect of Icrurian that she could not decipher wholly. In the endeavor for truth, gaps in the context behind certain words and sentences were enough to sink her ambitions. She couldn't uncover a translation that made sense.

Whoever this was, they were infinitely more powerful and far sneakier than Vaasa could hope to be. If this witch had managed to stay hidden this long . . .

The scent of the Miro'dag curled in her nose again, and she dragged her hand through her hair, nails nearly hurting her scalp. The truth was that she had probably never met the witch. Wouldn't even know what they looked like. Someone so powerful—so coveted—was bound to stay concealed.

Then again, she knew better than most that the best way to hide was to blend in.

The sound of the door opening made her jump.

Amalie slid through, hesitation on her charming features. "It's practically morning, Vaasa. You need to sleep."

Gritting her teeth, Vaasa looked down at her books again, the words blurry now. She was a little worn out from people telling her what she needed. "I'm not tired. Go back, I'll come when I'm ready."

"You're burning yourself out. If you don't rest—"

"I don't care," Vaasa snapped, looking up from the tome and squeezing her hands into fists. She knew the witch was right. She was exhausting herself. But what other option was there?

All this death would be on her hands.

Amalie's lips pursed, but she didn't step farther into the room. Nor did she turn and leave, as Vaasa expected her to. "Don't close me out, Vaasa."

Jaw tightening further, Vaasa bit back the angry response that immediately came to her tongue.

Amalie must have seen the poison in her eyes, though. Must have read something in her body language. Her back straightened and her voice lowered. "You're harming yourself. This coldness, it isn't who you are."

Rage was the forefront of what Vaasa felt, irritation like a blade down her back. This coldness was exactly who she was. Why couldn't Amalie see that? Why couldn't they *all* see it?

Vaasa slammed her hand onto the table. "I don't want your wisdom or your advice right now."

Shaking her head, Amalie said, "I am your best friend. Don't do this."

"I don't have a best friend!" Vaasa burst out. "I am here for three years and not a day more."

The moment the words were out, it was as if Vaasa could see them in the air. As if she were reaching for them, but the edges of the letters kept evading her grip.

And then they just hung in the air between them.

Amalie stared at her as if she'd been struck, but then pressed her lips harshly together. Wetness shone in her eyes, but she shook it away.

At the sight of that, regret washed over Vaasa like a tidal wave so powerful it stole the air from the room. This wanting, this foolish desire to throw everything else out the window and make it right. It was ironic how she could see the wrong in what she'd done and yet not do anything about it. Not change her path, as if she was already so far in it would be worse to turn around.

It didn't matter. She didn't get the chance.

"Noted," Amalie said in a clipped tone.

And then her only real friend—her *best* friend—slipped out the door, closing it loudly behind her.

And as she sat there alone, Vaasa wondered if all this work, all this introspection and trial, had been for naught.

If perhaps she hadn't learned anything at all.

CHAPTER 21

By the next day, the madness following the colosseum attack had been tamped. While the number of soldiers around them doubled, particularly those from Wrultho, all seemed as normal as an election could.

Except for Amalie, who hadn't said a word to her.

Vaasa walked with Koen, Kier, and Elijah down the hallways of the High Temple of Dihrah, Reid at her side, gazing upon the artwork of some of Icruria's finest artists. This impressive display happened at every election—*a display of culture*, Kier called it with delight. It was the final daytime event of the election before the actual vote itself. Tomorrow was reserved for negotiations and meetings, though those had been going on in back rooms for two days now, and then Kier's final choice for entertainment for the last night. The following morning, the vote would occur at midday and the celebration of the new headman would begin. The elected headman wouldn't formally take over until three months from now, though the capital would begin the process of moving.

As Vaasa took in the stunning works from all over the nation, she couldn't help but wonder about Freya. Had she placed her work in this traditional exhibit, too? Artists worked for years on what they would display at the election, and out of the corner of her eye, she saw private buyers bickering over their not-so-silent bids.

Behind them, Ton's men shuffled forward, crowding around their foreman like they suspected a fight.

Burly as ever, the foreman of Wrultho stalked forward with his many armed escorts.

Reid went rigid at her side. "Ton."

"Reid."

Kier looked between them, and then Elijah delicately placed his hand upon his husband's arm and led him to a painting Vaasa doubted was more important than the rest of them.

Koen, however, stayed put.

Vaasa raised her brows, but she certainly didn't argue. Especially when Reid gripped his onyx blade and winked at the soldiers waiting by the wall.

Koen stood with a look so neutral he could have been Marc, staring at the colorful painting in front of him. One thing in particular struck her: Hunt of Wrultho was not with Ton, which meant the foreman of Wrultho didn't want his councilor directing him.

"You want to speak in the middle of this exhibit, Ton?" Reid said quietly.

Ton slid his eyes to Vaasa, jaw tight. Her magic swirled in her defensively at the implications between them.

"He believes I had something to do with yesterday's events," she said.

"I've heard the whispers of this *witch*," Ton sneered. "I have experience with her kind."

Vaasa's magic threaded unhappily at the subtle dig at Amalie, even if she had no right. Especially after last night.

Reid froze. "What do you think you know of my consort?"

"The thing did not attack you once she got involved. Why?"

"Maybe it was smarter than you," Reid said fluidly as he pulled Vaasa closer to his side, "and it knew who to be afraid of."

"I am not the only one who has yet to learn that lesson," Ton snapped. He had more knowledge about magic than most, given his authority in his own city, which hosted the very coven of witches Vaasa desperately needed to speak to. The hostility in his body language revealed her request wouldn't be granted, so while it sat on the tip of her tongue, she didn't dare ask.

Koen chuckled, stepping around everyone to cut the tension and casually peer at another painting. "Do you believe you will win this election, Ton?"

"I will be the next headman of Icruria," he confirmed.

Reid pursed his lips, and Vaasa tried not to chuckle.

"Even if you did manage to earn the vote of your predecessor, the drought in your city and the violence along your border makes Wrultho a last choice for the headmanship," Koen said.

"The soldiers who flee to Dihrah share stories of sleeping in your empty waterways," Reid added. "You do know that the councilors have heard such things?"

Ton's large hands tightened on the hilt of his sword. Vaasa's gaze trailed it. All the things she assumed about powerful men had been challenged by Reid and Koen. Yet when she looked at the foreman of Wrultho, she thought them all to be true.

"Luckily for you," Mathjin finally said from the left, "we have a solution to both. Perhaps Wrultho will stand a chance at the end of Reid's cycle."

"Why would I bargain with a man who takes counsel from an Asteryan heiress?" Ton asked sincerely, though the undertone of distaste rode his words.

Vaasa brushed a piece of lint off her blouse as if she were bored. "I know nothing of the magic that struck yesterday. I would ask your city's coven."

"And if I don't believe you?" Ton asked.

"You're wasting much of your energy on something you can neither prove nor barter." Vaasa met Ton's eyes. "If I do know of that monster and you intend to harm my husband's prospects, you'll have no choice but to tell Hunt. How is your councilor going to feel when he learns of your history with Asterya?"

Just the smallest twitch of Ton's left eye, and Vaasa knew she'd hit home. Hunt knew nothing. Given everything Amalie had told them last night, she wondered what exactly was going on in Ton's corps and how it would inevitably play a role in the vote.

Reid began skimming Vaasa's side with his hand, fingers moving up and down in that way of his she now realized was compensation for his nervousness. He touched her like this whenever he was thinking of what to say. Gauging his audience. "I've negotiated with the emperor of Asterya to bring down the dam."

Ton shook his head. "There is no way he agreed to such a thing, and if he did, it is a lie."

"He's asking for a cessation of the violence," Reid continued.

"Asterya *began* the violence," Ton snarled. "They slaughtered our people. They've been decimating the border for half a decade. If you're married to *her*, you know this truth already."

A few heads turned, and as if on cue, some of Ton's corps circled around them closer. Why he'd chosen to have this discussion in public was unclear, but Vaasa wondered if it was because any private discussion would inevitably include Hunt.

Had this foreman made a single decision on his own?

It was Hunt's job to advise Kier, not Ton.

"Which is why we don't want to suggest that you lay down your arms," Reid said. "Instead, you should move your forces farther east and prepare to strike."

Ton started at the words, lips parting then slamming shut.

"And once you've eliminated their company, take down the dam yourself."

Shock tumbled across Ton's face. "So your wife can betray us all?"

Koen entered the conversation again. "You don't have to trust her. Though by my assessment, you don't have much of a choice. Your people are dying, and your territory cannot compete. I know some of your own soldiers who have abandoned their posts and fled."

Ton waited a moment before responding, stubbornness ever present in the tight hold of his shoulders. Finally, he muttered, "Those men are cowards."

What a naive, foolish man.

Koen continued. "Send your dissenters to Mireh, then. We will foster a negotiation with Sigguth to get the ships you need to navigate these shallower waters, at least until the dam comes down. The ships will create jobs for the people you cannot sustain. Reid will set aside plots of land for them to cultivate, and with the new ships, trade should flow without an issue."

Reid started again with that pace along Vaasa's side, neutrality dripping from his lips, no longer even pretending to stare at the painting. "By the next cycle, Wrultho may very well contend for the headmanship. You'd put an end to the dam, to any dissent in your own territory, and potentially to this war with Asterya. You'd have a constant supply of food and a new, working relationship with three foremen. *That* would be your legacy, Ton."

"What's to stop me from endorsing the foreman of Sigguth and bargaining for my own ships directly?" Ton dared ask.

Koen grunted, crossing his arms. "And build them where? There is no water if you don't move those soldiers."

Despite what Ton probably wanted to admit, Koen had a damning point. What Koen didn't say was simple: Sigguth would not bargain with Wrultho unless Mireh helped sanction it—the coastal territory went where the salt was. No port would give Ton access if Mireh didn't.

Reid hadn't been lying when he'd said salt built empires.

The resentment teeming in Ton's eyes told Vaasa the foreman already knew all of this. Turning to him, she said, "My brother will lay waste to you before you can solve this drought. You do know that, right?"

Ton lifted his chin like he didn't believe her. Was he so proud a man he thought himself invincible, or would he not listen just because it was she who spoke?

They'd offered him something any reasonable leader would take. But Ton was not a reasonable leader.

"You want to see your country fail?" Ton asked. "Is that the sort of loyalty you will show Icruria if they are enough of a fool to let you anywhere near the headmanship? You abandoned your own country—"

"It is no longer my country," Vaasa interrupted smoothly, keeping a harsh check on the magic trying to pulse out of her. Instead, she let it bubble along her fingertips and dart away in little whips of darkness, creeping along Reid's arm where he touched her. Ton's eyes dropped to it, practically salivating at its power despite having insulted her for it earlier. "I am the great-granddaughter of one of the most powerful Veragi witches known to this world, and she made her home in Mireh."

Ton's eyes went wide.

"I did not abandon my country," Vaasa said. "I came home."

Reid's lips parted and he craned his neck to look down at her, his expression less readable than it had ever been. She'd never said it aloud—had never claimed Icruria or Mireh as hers. Yet her magic settled confidently in her stomach and hissed out of existence once more.

And she realized that while her show just now had been calculated, it wasn't untrue.

Ton pressed backward and pretended to stare at the painting again, though something new threaded in the corner of his eye. That same inkling she'd seen earlier, and now she knew what to call it.

Lust. Not for her, but for the power he had just seen emanate from her. He'd probably looked just like this the first time he saw what Amalie was capable of. It wasn't safety for his people that Ton wanted for his legacy.

It was blood. Revenge. Violence.

Control.

"Many rulers would give far more than your husband has given for magic like that at their disposal," he said.

Vaasa had to leash what she knew about him, what she *wanted* to say. "And yet you question an alliance with him?"

"I question an alliance with you."

"I translated words, I did not write them. The outcome of your treaty was never mine to decide."

At that, Ton pursed his lips. "I am more interested in how you intend to destabilize your own brother than I am in what your husband offers."

"That would be for you and my husband to decide." She slid her hand over Reid's shoulder. "And that's what you want, right? For my brother to shake when he hears your name? Asterya is not safe from us, and if you are to be our ally, it will not be safe from you, either."

She knew men like Ton, had grown up around them and watched them play with the lives of others across tables and battlefields. They all sought the same thing. It was more than desire and greed that drove their menacing plots; it was a deep-rooted sense of worthlessness that made people crave power.

All she had to do was offer him a slice of value.

She could see it then: the images that danced behind his eyes. The fall of an empire, blood bathing the land he would claim for himself. Ton must have been able to hear the songs they would sing—of the foreman who took his wreckage of a land and turned it into fields of gold.

Because he smiled. "I want to start today. Let us decide where to move these troops. I want negotiations finalized by the vote."

Reid nodded strongly. "I will set up a room this evening."

And though Vaasa stayed silent, for the remainder of the day, she counted the sheer number of Wrultho soldiers walking about the High Temple.

CHAPTER 22

The following hours of the day were spent with councilors and foremen in *private* rooms and negotiations—which meant every councilor from every territory somehow ended up between those four cream-colored walls. Everyone except the party from Hazut. Not only would Hazut lose this election, but they would also be steps behind in economic negotiations at the end of this week. This strange alliance with Ton had assured that.

With a small chuckle, Vaasa thought that Reid had never needed her at all.

Isabel bought herself and Vaasa a way out in the early afternoon, about an hour before Vaasa was meant to report to the Library of Una, so she'd be able to change and enjoy a few quiet moments to herself. She didn't know how to thank Isabel for not following Vaasa to her quarters or wanting to debrief the conversations they'd just been a part of and overheard, but she thought a smile and squeeze of the woman's forearm said plenty.

Vaasa spent the evening at the Sodality of Una practicing for the coven's display of magic at the final event tomorrow evening. Heart thudding against her chest, she anticipated what she would say and do when she finally saw Amalie again.

But Amalie didn't show.

Melisina pursed her lips. "Give her another day or so. I think being here, having to face Ton and all those people from Wrultho is harder on her than she thought. She wasn't going to come."

Vaasa's heart sank. "Then why did she?"

Melisina shrugged her left shoulder. "For you, Vaasa. She thought if you were brave enough to be here, she should be, too."

Immediately, Vaasa hung her head. *Brave* was not the word she would use to describe herself.

Melisina didn't mention it again.

There wasn't a moment Vaasa didn't think about it, though. Not even as Esoti escorted her back to the High Temple. She told her that Amalie was in her rooms and reiterated the same thing Melisina had said: time.

If Amalie wanted to talk, she would come.

So Vaasa left her alone.

At almost the stroke of midnight, Vaasa waited alone curled up on the plush red couch on the patio of their private quarters.

The extension off their first-floor room jutted out into the High Temple's gardens, surrounded by flowering bushes that climbed glass walls, shielding the patio entirely from view. At the top, the glass ceiling kept the cold air in while giving her a clear view of the turquoise night sky. Moonlight bathed the marble floor and played upon the small glimmers of crimson threaded throughout it.

Notebook clenched in her hand, she reviewed the notes she'd copied the night prior—the ones detailing Zetyr lore that the coven had spent all day reading and learning about. Melisina had even tried to capitalize off Reid's tenuous allyship with Ton, but to no avail. When her eyes glazed over, Vaasa switched focus and scanned the route she and Mathjin had discussed, considered which direction Dominik would travel. Without the ability to navigate the menagerie of rivers,

Asterya was outplayed each and every time. It was the reason why Icruria had been impregnable for so many years.

The door opened, and upon seeing Reid amble through, thoughts of war and rivers and blood quieted in her mind.

Reid walked immediately to her, focused eyes on fire and inspecting her thoroughly. He caught the length of her legs across the settee, and the corners of his mouth lifted in a sultry expression. "You won us a nation, Wild One."

Closing the notebook, she gazed at him. At the stunning purple jacket that sometimes strained with his movements. By now, his hair had almost completely rebelled against the leather band, so most of it fell to his shoulders and framed his face. *More than a warrior*, she thought. He looked like a headman of Icruria. It was impossible not to catch his pride and make it her own, or to ignore the thrum of happiness that blossomed when he looked at her like that. When she got to look at him like this. "You would have won regardless. You do know that, right?"

"Perhaps."

She shook her head. Now he chose to be modest?

A little quietly, Reid asked, "What's going on between you and Amalie?"

Vaasa gritted her teeth. Her hands tightened around the notebook in her lap. "Did she say something?"

He shook his head. "Mathjin mentioned that Amalie hadn't come to dinner or to the sodality tonight."

"It's my fault," she whispered. How could Vaasa have been so selfish? "I . . . I'll fix it. I promise."

Sauntering to the seat next to her, Reid leaned back against the velvet arm with more casual ease than anyone should ever be able to maintain. Her hands tightened on the book in her lap as she made room for him. Reid studied the movement, brow furrowing. He blinked as if surprised. "Where did you get that?"

"This?" She looked down at the simple black leather thing and tried to think past the stirring of sadness she wondered if she could ever control. "I chose it a while ago. I've had it for months."

A small, disbelieving sigh pushed out of him. "You chose it?"

She nodded. "It was one of Melisina's tricks. I picked it out of hundreds. I think it was the first time in years I trusted my instinct."

His demeanor changed as he paused, like he was considering. Tentatively, he ran a hand over his jaw and then dropped it to his lap. "I want you to stay past three years."

Vaasa froze.

Dangerous happiness burst forth, replaced swiftly by roaring anger. Anger, which of course was only a disguise for fear. She recognized that now. So she gritted her teeth and reined it in, reminding herself that she didn't want to make the same mistake that she'd made with Amalie.

"I'm not going back on our deal," Reid clarified, probably reading the look on her face. "I'm proposing a new one and hoping you'll consider what I have to say."

She held her composure as well as she could. "I'm listening."

His throat bobbed but he relaxed his shoulders. Reaching for her legs and plopping them into his lap, he started that incessant movement of his finger on her leg. She let him, but only because she needed to pretend, too.

"I don't know how long it's going to take to maneuver your brother and remove him from the equation, but I suspect even if we managed to do that shortly after the election, the stabilizing of Asterya will take longer than three years. Even longer, to have enough influence that I could maintain claim to the throne if you and I were no longer married. So while I do believe myself capable of many things, I'm not stupid enough to think I could manage that situation better than you could."

It didn't matter what his reasons were. She'd gone into this knowing with certainty she never wanted to rule a nation. Never wanted to become what her father had been, what her mother had morphed into, what drove her brother to the point of murder.

So it made no sense, then, that when he asked, each piece of her soul reached for him.

"You want me to stay for political reasons?" she asked.

"Do you suspect it's because of something else?"

"Is it because of something else?"

He shrugged with his usual nonchalance. "This has nothing to do with how much I'd like to have you in my bed, though I do hope you'll find interest in that, too, Wild One."

Her stomach curled in on itself, those words summoning the knots he so easily created. "And you think that's a good idea?"

"I think it's one of our best ideas, actually, which is saying something considering how fucking brilliant I find you."

Vaasa's lips curled up in defiance of everything else she felt. She knew her heart's traitorous wants—that if it could be her choice, that if they could live more regular lives, it would be him. It would be this. So she couldn't help herself from asking, "What is this deal you're proposing?"

Reid adjusted his weight and sank further into the couch, hands still solidly upon her legs. "Stay until you feel Asterya is settled, however long that takes."

"You're removing the time frame?"

"Three years isn't enough."

"What is enough?"

Pausing, his lips pursed. But he never dropped his gaze. "I don't know."

It sounded as if those words held some profound meaning that could not be measured in breath.

"I don't know what else to offer you," he rambled on. "But as it stands, I would be amenable to just about anything you ask for. Give me your list of demands—your wildest dreams."

What did she want, more than what he'd already given her? If she considered the extent of her most unutterable desire, it was exactly what he offered. But she knew him better than she knew herself, and he was lying. "You only do that with your hands when you're trying to decide what to say."

Reid paused the movement on her skin.

"And people who have to decide what to say are hardly ever telling the truth."

Looking down at his hands, he seemed to consciously choose not to move them. Not to break their contact. "Tell me that isn't the truth. Tell me you haven't already discovered there is nothing I won't do or give for you."

All this dripping nonchalance and relaxed demeanor was exactly how he covered himself. It was the wall he put up, similar to her anger and poison.

He knew exactly how much time would be enough, because the answer was simple.

No amount of time would be enough.

She whispered, "And if the truth doesn't matter?"

He looked at her like it was all an excuse. "What is it?" he asked, finally giving up the ruse. "You want to be missed more than you want to be loved?"

Those words tugged at her chest. She had shared more with him than she had with any other person, had given him far more than she had dared to give anyone else. "You know what you are to me."

He shook his head. "I told you once that I don't make assumptions when it comes to you."

Her heart burned with bright fury at his audacity to approach the thing she thought they'd agreed not to approach. But they hadn't agreed, not really. She'd just decided for them both. She knew from the moment she crawled into his bed that there would be a conversation such as this one eventually. And it didn't seem justified to hold it against him for wanting.

Not when he wasn't the only one.

"Dominik is—"

"If he is the only thing standing between you and me, I will go now. Give me the word and he will cease to pull breath."

"It isn't that easy."

"It is." He pointed to the notebook. "It was mine. I bought it a few years ago from one of the artisans in the Lower Garden."

She sat a bit more upright. "It was yours?"

Reid nodded and looked out at the large gardenia bushes that covered their patio, clearly absorbed in whatever thoughts he dragged himself through over and over. "I am driving myself insane with wondering. With guessing. With hoping."

You have grown my capacity for hope.

Had he meant more with those words than she'd let herself believe? Had it been her he hoped for, not just a nation or a title?

She knew him well enough now that the answer was obvious. He had hoped for her, and somewhere along the way she had let herself hope for him, too.

Lying felt like a death sentence. To allow him to go on thinking he would not be her greatest forfeiture was unconscionable. Her voice dropped to a secret's tone. "I have collected a thousand words, and yet I cannot find a single one to tell you what comes alive inside of me when you are near."

"Do you not know the words, or are you just afraid to say them?"

Tears welled in her eyes, and she squeezed them shut. Why was this so hard? She'd thought herself incapable. Thought herself broken. He saw her answer for what it was—a copout. Just another way to hide. "I don't know how to give you what you're asking for."

A tear escaped from the side of her eyes, and even though she didn't see him come closer, she felt him. Felt the soft tip of his thumb as he wiped the tear from her cheek and slid his hand into her hair. "Do you love me the way I love you?" he asked.

Her breath caught. Once again, his transparency pulled the world from beneath her feet. It wasn't lost on her, what he'd just said.

That he loved her.

But they gave affection in two different ways—him with words, her with . . .

With what?

She didn't think she had ever had the courage to look someone in the eye and show them how she felt. Suddenly, it was all the more obvious the mistake she had made with Amalie. The mistake she had been making for months now.

Even though she didn't think for a moment she deserved such a thing as love, she couldn't help herself from *hoping*.

His fingers in her hair tightened like desperation. "Say it for me, Wild One."

Her eyes opened, and she became enraptured by the specks of orange and black in his. Fear lanced through her, the sort of disorienting terror that grabbed courage and snuffed it out. He must have seen her shudder, because he pressed his forehead to hers. "Say it for me and that will be enough."

To say it was to feel it. To say it was to make it real. But she wondered then if silence was real, too. If something could be just as alive in the dark.

Instead of the angry, poisonous serpent she'd known it to be in moments when she was afraid, her magic shifted into that thing it had become recently: white eyes shining in smoky black. It rose in her, fueled her, pushed her forward. To not want him was a futile endeavor. To not need him was a ship that had already set sail.

"Of course I love you," she whispered.

His hand trembled ever so lightly, and he let out a strong breath. "Then it's enough."

He looked at her now in a way no one else had ever looked at her, like all of her sharp edges just softened and glowed. Like to be loved by her was truly enough. And maybe she was destined to lose everything she'd ever loved, maybe it would shatter her into a thousand small pieces, but that single look felt worth breaking for.

So she whispered, "Remind me who I am. Where I am. Because I think you are the only one who really knows."

Reid's lips parted, then he lifted from where he sat to come closer. Assurance coated his stern eyes as he placed one knee on the couch, sinking his weight into the red velvet, looming above her. Gaze darting between her eyes and her lips, he might as well have consumed her. He lowered his mouth to her cheek. His words came soft. "You are here, with me."

Her chest rose at the statement, especially as he sank further into the couch, hand snaking behind her back to lift her and adjust. He settled himself between her legs and lay her back into the cushions.

Their bodies sank together, and the fractured pieces inside of her pulled. In that moment, it was enough to simply love and be loved. "And as for who you are . . ." He ran his lips along the curve of her jaw. The glass above let in just enough light for her to watch the way he moved his fingers over her throat and tilted her face back, his own mouth lingering just above hers.

"You are my wife, and everything begins and ends with that."

Vaasa's heart lurched, and Reid took that very moment to close any remaining space between them, his mouth taking hers. Months of wanting spilled into that kiss and she let it, honesty on her tongue as she swept into his mouth and tasted what those words felt like. He groaned. Tasted her back. They knew each other and the way their mouths moved, and yet it still felt new. Different. Like if she looked through his eyes she would see herself as something discoverable.

It was terrifying, and it drove her forward.

She tugged at the hem of his shirt, and he let her pull it off him, dropping it off the edge of the couch. His bare skin beneath her hands sent desire coursing down her hips. Her lips moved to his jaw. His neck. She remembered what she'd thought the first time they'd ever been close, that she wanted the rough grit of his beard against her skin. Now she passed her lips over it and sighed, her arms tugging him closer.

Reid untucked her white blouse from her olive breeches and pulled it up and over her head, letting it fall next to his own shirt on the floor. Hands lifting to the smooth silk that covered her breasts, he started to descend, his mouth leaving shivers in his wake. This was different from how he touched her before—less hurried and raw, more devastating. He looked up through his lashes and watched her while he pushed the strap off her shoulder, lowering the silk to expose her to the cool air. This time his eyes dropped, and he devoured the sight, pausing for a moment before he dipped his mouth and sucked upon the rosy bud of flesh.

Heat washed over her, and he kissed between her breasts as he moved to the other one, releasing the strap and then licking until she tipped her head back on a moan. More. She wanted more. His fingers found the button of her pants, her hips lifted with his instruction, and he slid the material down her legs, knees pressing into the couch.

Above her, he looked even more handsome than he had the first night they'd met. More handsome than maybe any other moment she'd gazed at him. Her eyes ran over the ink, but she had already memorized every line.

"These, too," he said, dragging the last piece of fabric from her waist and tossing it mindlessly to the floor.

Then he lowered himself again and placed his mouth to her stomach, his hands pressing to her thighs. Curling behind them. Her heart started to race as he crept lower and lower with each press of his lips to her skin.

"You lied about having never been with a man, yes?"

Laughter bubbled in her and heat crawled up her neck. "Yes."

Using one hand, he hooked her leg over his shoulder. "So I don't need to be gentle with you?"

Desire shot down her spine. "No."

"Good."

He pressed a finger inside of her.

She bucked her hips out of instinct.

He only slid back and inserted another, watching how she tried to breathe. Tried to regain control of her hips. He pressed his other thumb to her center and began to circle gently at first, slowly increasing the pressure of his touch.

She started to breathe heavier.

Then he curled the fingers inside of her upward.

A moan broke through her lips. With the pounding need that curled in her stomach, Vaasa said, "Again."

That wicked upturn of his smile could have lit her on fire. He curled his fingers again. She gasped. "Right there?" he said, again pressing to the spot inside of her that sent a wave up into her stomach.

"Yes," she breathed. "Yes."

"And how about here?" He lowered his head between her legs, eyes still locked with hers, his lips pressing to the inside of her thighs. He nipped at her, and her hands pushed into his hair. She felt his warm laughter against her exposed flesh and bumps rose along her stomach and breasts. He curled his fingers inside of her again. "Please," she whimpered. "Please."

The warmth of his breath traveled slowly along her hips and his tongue pressed tentatively against her.

He swiped up. Down.

She sank closer against it.

He licked her again, and again, and again, her legs parting wider as he pushed harder with his weight and his tongue. Every instinct she had bowed to his head between her legs. She couldn't breathe right. Couldn't help but tighten her hands and then raise one to her breast, curling around it herself as he flicked her rhythmically with his tongue.

His eyes darted up through his lashes and he groaned against her at the sight, tongue speeding up and lapping. Her hips started to rise and he used one arm to hold her down, refusing to slow or cede any space, the other still curling up to press against that spot inside of her. A whimper fell from her lips. "Reid," she begged his name, hoping desperately she could hold off until he was inside of her.

He lifted at her wanting and her hands found the buckle and buttons of his pants, ripping them down to his knees before he pushed her back into the pillows and settled himself between her legs. As if he'd already been unleashed and could not breathe until he finally had her. He buried himself inside of her in one thrust of his hips.

She cried out and pleasure spiked within her. He caught her mouth with his and held himself there, kissing her until he slowly lifted his hips. Her fingers pressed into his bare back as she tried to pull him closer. To drag him deeper.

"Fuck," he rasped, and thrust forward again—hard.

Carnal rawness filled them both, and the next time he slid back, she lifted her leg so he could tuck it behind his elbow and thrust deeper. Vaasa moaned as his tongue swept against hers. He pulled back and thrust again. Again. She could feel every inch of him each time he pushed himself forward. She was lost in the moment of watching him—of seeing the moonlight on his brown skin and the way his shoulders tensed with each thrust forward. How his long hair clung to the sides of his face. Desire pooled in her core, and she lifted her hips to his, matching his movements. He slammed into her and pleasure shot up her spine, coiling as he pulled back, then spiking when he filled her again.

Head tilting back, she lost all semblance of the world around her. Of where she ended and he began. All she knew was the depth to which she wanted to take him and the warmth of his breath as he leaned forward and wrapped his mouth around her breast.

He flicked his tongue. Thrust deep inside her.

"Faster," she begged.

His hips pressed to hers quicker this time, sweeping into her and then out. Again. Again. Again. She met his pace with each thrust of his hips and her voice grew louder while he maintained exactly the rhythm and angle that stole all the air from the world.

The muscles in her core tightened ruthlessly.

Pleasure barreled down her spine and through her hips. Her fingers wrapped into his hair and he kept pushing, carrying her through the orgasm, dragging each bit of satisfaction from her that he could.

The muscles in his chest went rigid and he groaned against her skin.

He pulled away at the last moment, finding his release with a string of moans that lit up her chest and made her want to rise again and again and again.

Her head was pressed to his shoulder, and long breaths plagued her while she tried to regain control of her senses, to focus on something more than her longing. Eventually she did, as he rose on his strong legs. Her own couldn't match that stability; she knew that if she stood she would stumble. But it didn't matter because he settled himself behind her, pulling her body up against his chest and saving her from the need to go anywhere.

"We made a mess of this couch," she whispered.

"I'll have Koen send me the bill."

A small, embarrassed chuckle flitted out of her. They lay there for a moment quietly, but the cords tying them together tightened. Against her hair, he whispered, "Will you say it for me again?"

It made no difference if she let herself have him or not. Not in the things that mattered. To not want him would not stop the world from taking him, would not stop the way she would inevitably shatter when the sky righted itself and left her unlucky.

So she turned in his arms, looking him directly in the eye as she told him the truth. "I love you. That will never be untrue."

He shuddered softly at the words, tightening the arms that held her. She looked down at the ink along his shoulder, following the dark lines that depicted a Mirehan pauldron, as if he carried his armor wherever he went.

Reid's voice broke the silence. "I know you don't want a nation or a throne, I know you don't want this life. So if I have to wait until the end of this decade, I will. I will find you and then you can choose what life we live. Any life you want."

All the things he knew she didn't want . . . they were exactly what she wanted, so long as they were with him.

But she could never tell him that. Could never give him that hope and salvation. For if she did, it would be the cruelest thing she had ever done to him. She would turn him into an accomplice of her shattering, and she would break him right along with herself.

Because she did not believe for a moment that the world would ever be safe for her.

For them.

"Shower with me," she whispered, brushing her lips against his. "I want you to have me everywhere in this room, and everywhere when we return to Mireh."

She'd said what he asked of her—that she loved him. That she knew she always would.

And he said it was enough.

But perhaps he saw it in her eyes, though, just as she felt it in her bones.

The thing she did not say. The thing that would actually be enough.

She never told him that she would stay.

CHAPTER 23

Music hummed through the darkness.

The sound of plucked strings and a single violin drifted upon each wall and the floor, filling the darkness with sweet music.

Sitting silently in her seat, Vaasa began to smile as the shadow that covered the enormous theater dissipated. In a brilliant burst of golden light, the witches of Una appeared in white robes at the back. They were the first to enter the theater in the High Temple of Dihrah, people filling the rows of seats at least twenty or thirty across. Their small party of Mirehans sat in box seats framing the theater, crimson and ivory drapes falling from their balcony to line the curving orchestra.

For the show of magic and the final ceremony before the vote tomorrow, the headman's home coven would start and end the evening. Kier had chosen this particular display, and Vaasa wondered if it had been at Melisina's suggestion. She wondered what each coven would leave out, what pieces they were unwilling to share.

The crowd hushed as Leanan, Brielle at her side, led the group of witches down the center aisle. Drifting slowly with little orbs of light in their left hands, the group appeared to be some kind of angels, their robes giving an illusion of floating in time to the music. One by one they reached the stage, their soft hums harmonizing with the tune, and then the crowd began to sing along.

It was beautiful from up here, to see the culture of a nation from this bird's-eye perspective.

Reid reached over and gripped her hand.

She turned to look at him and he watched her, pure contentedness in his eyes, and leaned over. "In ten years, it will be the Veragi who open this ceremony."

Her heart wrenched at the thought. She didn't want to explore the tremor of longing those words elicited. A ball that formed in her throat.

Instead, she tore her eyes away and focused on the witches of Una once more.

But then Melisina tapped her from behind. "Have you seen Amalie?"

Vaasa was supposed to join them at the end of this number behind the stage, so she'd expected Amalie would already be there. That they would finally have the opportunity to speak after the show. "I assumed she was with you."

Melisina shook her head.

She released Reid's hand and stood quietly, squeezing his shoulder. He turned to look at her, questioning, and she gestured toward Melisina.

She didn't know why she remembered that moment so clearly, that subtle upturn of his strong mouth, but it burned itself into her mind.

With one final nod, he looked away.

Vaasa was wearing the most striking outfit she'd been offered: black skintight pants and a bodice with long sleeves, neckline falling off her shoulders. A purple overskirt split at the top of her hips and fell to the floor behind her in a pool of silk chiffon. It was a tad heavy, but it allowed her to wear the boots she'd broken in earlier.

Lifting her long overskirt, she followed Melisina into the hallway. "Where could she be?"

"You check her rooms and I'll check the sodality."

"You need to be here," Vaasa said. "You are the high witch, Reid's mother. Go on without us, I'll search her room first."

"Vaasa—"

"Melisina, this is my fault."

With a small breath, the witch conceded, then set off down the stairs.

Vaasa plunged into the main hall of the theater and then to the doors, nodding at a guard on the way into the gardens. Gardenia immediately wafted beneath her nose, and she took only a moment to appreciate the subtle beauty of the white flower. To remember how she had looked at it the evening prior.

Her stomach knotted at the thought.

Stepping into the main foyer and passing beneath the large, sweeping fans, she scurried up the red velvet stairs and down two halls before curving around the bend that would lead to Amalie's room. Similar to theirs, this one was just above the tower reserved for Mireh.

The oak door was locked.

Vaasa knocked once, twice, and waited.

"Amalie," she said against the door, placing her ear upon the wood to listen.

Nothing.

No sound. No hint of anyone at all.

An acrid sweetness filled her senses, the subtle realization that she wasn't alone only clicking a moment too late.

Her knees went weak.

Her arms and fingers next.

Before she had the opportunity to strike, to fight back, to do something worthwhile of saving her own life, black spots covered her vision. The last thing she saw before she was dragged under was the way his eyes brought out the warm undertone of his brown skin, of that particular smile that lifted both edges of his lips, of the way all of him had looked under muted light. Amber and salt and gardenia, too.

Then darkness swept it all away.

Gone, into nothingness.

Light fluttered behind her eyes before it dared gleam in front of them.

It was the sort of light that burned through closed lids, forcing one to squeeze just to keep it out. To waver on the edge of consciousness without feeling so much as a finger.

Vaasa lifted one lid, then the other, her blurry vision discerning little. She still felt the long sleeves of her bodice, was conscious of the subtle weight of her overskirt.

Slowly she registered the beige of cracked stone, the grand archways with ornate columns, some shattered and crumbling, others holding the weight of something burdensome. Statues of men and women in flowing, sheer robes circled her, the stone now partly consumed by grit and brown. The same erosion coated the faded, raised floor she stood upon, the once-ornate patterns of crimson and gold lost to pink and tinged white. Three steps led off the stone platform into the empty, abandoned room.

This was a catacomb, Vaasa realized with a pound of alarm. And through the cracks, she recognized the stone as that of the colosseum. The breaks in the ceiling let sunlight drench the floor.

Sunlight.

It was *daytime.*

She was standing, feet barely holding her weight, but her bound arms weren't sore. She hadn't been here for long.

Where else had she been?

She started to move, but it caused her wrists to burn, the subtle hum falling down her forearm. Looking up, she saw black-threaded ropes.

The same ones that had been tied to Reid on the boat.

Nowhere inside of her could she feel the snake. Could she feel any trace of the magic at all.

Heart pounding in her chest, she whipped her head around until her gaze landed on something far worse. Something that immediately brought bile into her throat.

Amalie.

The young witch was tied up opposite her, dress torn at the long hem and along her arms, blood in her hair. She'd been hit with something. The same ropes were tied around her torso and held her firmly against a wooden chair. The witch hung her head, and Vaasa didn't know if she was conscious or not.

"Amalie," she croaked.

Amalie lifted her exhausted, tear-stained face.

Vaasa choked.

A bruise coated the left side of her cheek, and white fabric had been tied over her mouth and fastened around her head. Terror painted her brown eyes as they darted around.

Vaasa tugged against her ropes, her eyes filling with tears.

As she tried to form words, footsteps along stone cut her off.

The steps echoed through the catacomb, bouncing off the elegant faces of the statues and stonework around them. Vaasa went rigid. Silvering hair came into view from the corridor behind Amalie. Walking up those three steps, he joined them on the platform, hand on his sword.

Mathjin.

Vaasa's throat started to close in panic, but she tried to calm her heavy breathing. Mathjin?

He did not grin—there was only a stern neutrality in the subtle wrinkles around his eyes.

Vaasa watched as he came to the place right in front of her, gaze moving up to the ropes that secured her wrists. "Ironic, don't you think? I couldn't find the ones you used at your wedding. But those aren't nearly as useful now, are they?"

Vaasa wanted to gag.

He shrugged one shoulder and looked to Amalie, irritation stealing over the features that Vaasa had once perceived as wise. "Of course, she finally did the trick. The young witch goes missing, and everyone falls into a tizzy."

"What are you doing?" Vaasa asked. "Mathjin, why—"

"Why?" He shook his head. "I am not Reid. I am not Kosana. I am not so blind as to believe an Asteryan could ever be worth the seat you have been offered. I would rather see my grave before I allow you to tarnish everything this country has worked for."

Of all the people who had hated her, Mathjin had seemed the lesser. He'd shown her kindness, acceptance, in these months. She didn't know what stung worse: that he'd never meant it, or that she'd allowed herself to believe he did.

"You know, I was only twenty when my daughter was born," Mathjin said, turning from her to walk the length of the platform. Back to a pile of something along one of the stone benches in the right corner. "She had blond hair like me, the same gray eyes. The same features she gave to my granddaughter. My granddaughter, who was eight when an Asteryan soldier stopped her, my daughter, and my wife along the road between Wrultho and Mireh and slaughtered them all. My daughter was more than halfway through her second pregnancy."

With his back to her, he stopped just before the bench.

"You see, when a man becomes a father so young, it is the only identity he knows. It comes before soldier, before advisor, before any other title I have earned. And when I tell you that father, husband, and grandfather were my favorite names to be called, I tell you no lies."

Sympathy tightened Vaasa's throat, pressing on her tongue as she fought impending tears. How could she stand here and cry for this man while he had her kidnapped and bound? She didn't know. But the crack in his voice as he said *grandfather* had nearly torn her in two.

"Do you want to know what Marc of Mireh said when I begged him to go to war?" Mathjin asked, finally turning to look at her, something white folded in his hands.

When Vaasa did not utter a word, he answered regardless.

"He said a war with Asterya would leave the world with far fewer grandchildren."

The cruel truth of the statement wasn't lost on either of them, which she could see plainly written on his trembling face. *A balancing of victims*, Mathjin had called it.

"But here's what they don't tell you." He started forward again, around the statues and up the platform she was hoisted upon. "When it's yours who's taken, you care less for everyone else's. You don't care what it costs, because everything that matters is already gone."

"Mathjin—"

"*Don't* speak!" he boomed suddenly. "You have no right. Instead, you will write a letter."

He marched forward up the steps, boots cracking against the worn marble. She realized then that he held parchment and a pen. He unfolded it, pressing against the flat surface as if to display the blank space.

"You're going to detail in Asteryan the exact movement of Ton's men. The route you and I discussed, the one he and Reid agreed to yesterday. You'll address it to your brother, and you're going to sign it."

Vaasa stopped breathing. "No."

"Yes."

"Why are you doing this? You will sacrifice your own countrymen and start a greater war than—"

"*I want to start a war!*" he screamed, parchment pointed at her as he waved it in his hand. "This letter will be intercepted by Ton's men, who will take it to the foreman this morning. Reid will lose and still have no choice but to agree to war."

Ton's men.

That's why there were so many here. She'd thought she'd spoken smoothly enough, thought she had outsmarted Ton in front of those paintings, but the entire thing must have been an act. A fabrication put together by Mathjin and Ton himself. They'd exchanged information about Wrultho and his soldiers that Vaasa had been privy to—enough that she could betray them all if she were exactly the person Ton claimed her to be.

Her heart constricted. The details of Mathjin's plan took shape in her mind as if she saw them playing out on one of her father's war tables. If she wrote this letter, he'd show it to all of the councilors.

To Reid, who knew her handwriting, her signature. Him losing the election would be only the start of the consequences for this. It would ruin him.

"No," she gasped. "I won't write that letter."

"You will." Another voice came from the darkness, a raw inflection of smooth Asteryan that shot down her spine and demanded an instant, reflexive panic.

No.

Her eyes widened.

He emerged from the right, raven hair delicately in place, twin ocean eyes setting into snow-pale skin. Even the shadows seemed to flee as sunlight passed over his hard, angled features made of sharp bone and malice. His black and bloodred cloak with gold-threaded edging billowed to the floor. He looked sick and brimming with malicious intent, sharp eyes trailing to where the ropes bound her.

Dominik smiled.

CHAPTER 24

Reid waited with hands gripping the wooden chair beneath him, hoping something had changed and that Amalie and Vaasa would join the members of the coven on stage by the end—some spectacular display of their growth in numbers. His wife had always been a fan of dramatic entrances and exits. Each second that ticked by was a testament to his composure.

The crimson curtains closed, and the Veragi witches disappeared upon the enormous theater's stage.

Legs pulling him to stand, Reid turned to Mathjin. The advisor furrowed his brow as if he had the same question. Kosana, who stood at the entrance of their box, stepped forward with a familiar look in her eye. At her side, Esoti was all rigid muscle and concern. "Where is she?"

"She went with my mother," Reid said as he stormed into the hallway and whipped his head around. Panic began to rise in him, but he denied it space, instead focusing on the more logical possibilities. Maybe she was waiting down the stairs; maybe they'd changed their mind about having his consort display such power. Maybe Amalie could not face Ton or the rest of Wrultho, and Vaasa had stayed with her. His mother would know.

Kosana and Esoti trailed him closely as they descended the stairs and walked around the back of the theater, not a guard flinching at their presence or their intrusion. Melisina shuffled out the back door, Romana and the rest of the coven close behind like a flock of birds. Panic started to bubble again as he watched his mother scan the gardens.

"Where is she?" Reid asked the moment they were in earshot.

"She went to find Amalie." His mother plunged into the gardens. "Something is wrong. They should have been back by now."

If she thought something was wrong, Reid knew better than to question it. His mother's instincts had always been far better than his own—he'd learned to listen closely to them, even when he didn't want to. "Scour the property and the sodality. Find her," he said, voice cracking as he turned to Kosana and Esoti.

The latter was already in a sprint, having not waited for an instruction before going after Mireh's consort.

After *his* consort.

"Reid, you may not want to hear this, but is it safe for you to be anywhere unguarded?" Mathjin asked as he walked up to Reid's side, having emerged from the theater at the same time. "If something has happened to the consort and the heir of Veragi, perhaps it is best—"

"I did not ask for your input," Reid snapped at him. Normally, Mathjin's levelheaded frankness was something Reid depended on, but tonight he was in no mood for it.

Mathjin bowed his head and took a step back.

"Fuck," Reid snarled beneath his breath as he trailed after his mother's long robes. He knew more of the dangers Vaasa faced than anyone else. Fear curled in his muscles. "*Fuck.*"

This terror was different from anything he had ever known.

Something was wrong. He didn't know how he knew that, but he did. He knew it.

He sprinted to the main building and started with their room, eyes scanning the length of it. He noted the untouched dressers and armoire, the wooden door leading to the bathroom, still closed as he'd left it. Then he looked to the glass-enclosed patio and the white gardenias creating walls of their own. The starlight sprinkled upon the couch where he'd finally had her. Where he wasn't such a fool that he'd missed her little omission.

She'd never promised him a lifetime.

He'd intended to change her mind.

"It seems you know something I do not," his mother said from behind him.

Reid turned, meeting her stern eyes and feeling for a moment like a child. That same power that surrounded her and had made it impossible not to fear her at times threaded the air. He gritted his teeth. "Dominik . . . he will kill her. He plans to kill her."

"Why?"

"Because Asteryan tradition proclaims that if he is dead, her husband is next in line for his throne. As long as we are married, she and I are the greatest threat to Dominik's reign."

Melisina Le Torneau was impossible to catch off guard. She had always held her composure better than any person Reid had known; every movement, every feeling, was controlled. Even in the wake of his father's death, he had not seen her crumble. He'd resented her for it then, before he had known Vaasa and seen how her emotions ruled her. How they could destroy her.

So, when his mother's face twitched, he felt the gravity of it as if the world had quaked.

"Does she know you plan to kill her only living relative and steal an entire nation?"

"Of course. It was her idea."

"You'd better be telling the truth, Reid Cazden, or I will wring your neck."

His father's last name pounded against his chest, something his mother intended. A small reminder of the expectations his father had placed upon him, and that no matter how large he became, his mother was larger. He'd needed those reminders as a young boy. He no longer needed them. But there was a glimmer of something in his mother's eyes he couldn't ignore, and it lit the determination in him once again. The fear.

His mother loved Vaasa, too, and she would hold him accountable to protect her.

"If I don't find her, I will burn all of Asterya to the ground," Reid assured her as he swept past his mother's dark robes and descended upon the High Temple of Dihrah.

"Kier!" He bellowed louder than the sound of his steps echoing off the stairs. His mother trailed closely behind.

He found the headman and Koen in the main foyer, eyes wide as they took in his rage. At the swirls of darkness coating the stairs.

He didn't stop for condolences. "Lock this entire city down. I want the port armed and every inch of this building searched."

"Reid—" Koen said.

Reid spun.

Lifting his spectacles with that calm demeanor of his, Koen nodded. "It already has been."

Reid could not find her.

It was three hours past the stroke of midnight when he could hardly stand, eyes bleary as he dragged himself along the stacks of books to the table where he'd been told she first spent her time. He'd thought her foolish then not to change her location frequently; to return to the same table on this same floor was the smallest of mistakes she'd made. The one that had allowed him to find her.

Recently he told himself she'd done it on purpose. That she always did everything on purpose. There wasn't a single move that wasn't calculated or planned with some sort of goal in mind. He told himself she wanted to be found. That she'd been waiting for him, had been as hopelessly enthralled with him as he was with her after their wedding night, even if she wouldn't say it out loud. Even if he'd bled quietly on that bed, wondering if the most curious thing in his existence had just slipped out the window.

He knew she hadn't been waiting for him, not really, yet as he stood next to that table in the Library of Una, it was the only comfort he allowed.

His eyes scanned the stacks. Landed on the exact place she'd managed to pull a knife on him again, to the spot where he'd pushed her back against them just so he had a chance to beg her to come along.

He told himself she was still waiting for him. That she was hoping he would come and find her. Because otherwise, he might have to face the treacherous thought starting to form in the back of his mind.

What if Dominik hadn't taken her at all?

What if he'd gotten too close, let his hopes get too high, and she'd run away, like he'd always thought she might?

Fists tightening, Reid darted toward the witch's tower, where his mother and her coven were working. Through the iron gates and down the corridor, he discovered Leanan and Brielle hosting more than just his mother. At the large rectangular table were the high witches from *every* sodality, each gathered around and working together for perhaps the first time in living memory.

His mother's voice floated across the room to him. "You are no good to anyone like this," she said. "Go back to the High Temple, get a few hours of sleep."

Suddenly his knees felt weak. Hot anger and sadness flooded behind his eyes and he choked it down, fingers curling into a fist. His mother eyed his movements. She separated herself from the rest of the witches and grabbed his elbow, leading him down the stairs.

"Zuheia magic takes time," his mother told him. "They are trying to sense life, but this is a big city. It is difficult to narrow it down."

Reid met her eyes, an unspoken concern lingering between them. *Perhaps that sort of magic is contingent upon her still being alive.* It was a thought he would never say aloud.

"She is my wife," Reid finally said.

"And we will find her."

"I am in love with her."

His mother sighed softly, leaning back against the iron railing. "I know."

"She's going to leave anyway."

"I know."

His voice caught, but he forced out the traitorous words. "What if she already has?"

Silence.

Reid turned, a tear escaping the side of his eye as the lump in his throat tightened. "I want—" He stopped, swallowed. "I want what you and Father had."

His mother's face softened. Perhaps she thought of the love he had seen, one that wasn't just true in the rose-colored memories of childhood. A love that was hard at times. A love that meant they chose each other over and over again. One that could look upon the nightmare of mortality and transcend the most brutal laws of nature. One that still existed now in the shadows of grief he saw cross his mother's features. He knew now that just because she had not outwardly crumbled when they'd lost his father, it didn't mean parts of her hadn't chipped away.

He felt those very parts inside of himself now, appearing like eroded stones in the bends of the rivers.

"She has pulled you from a grief," his mother whispered. "One I questioned would ever leave you."

Those years after his father's death were grim. He had not gotten to see Reid ascend to the foremanship or make any of the changes they had spoken about in the east. It was his father who had led him safely through those battlefields. Who had taught him that the most powerful fight was the one a person chose, not the one they fell into. Reid kept choosing the path forward. But no matter what ambition he chased or ladder he climbed, he was not fast enough to escape the past. He was not fast enough to avoid his grief. He'd dedicated every waking moment to this new dream, and Vaasa had come along and changed that.

He saw past the headmanship. Saw past those ten years.

And now he could not see past the hour.

Eyes closing as if she might crack, his mother took a deep breath.

"She went for Amalie, and neither of them can be found. I have learned a lot about Vaasalisa, and one is her affection for that girl. She never, and I mean *never*, would have put Amalie in danger. If she is gone, it is not by choice, my son."

Her words made his heartbeat quicken. Vaasa wasn't the only one afraid of hope. "You believe they are together?"

"I believe it would take a force of nature to rip them apart." His mother lay a nurturing hand upon his shoulder. "I know you don't want to hear this, but if we can't find her, you have a better chance at leveraging an army if you win the election. It is in your best interest to go tomorrow. To win. *That* is what you can do for her."

Reid tapped his finger along the wooden shelf. "You mean to tell me that the councilors haven't already gotten word that my wife is gone?" He shook his head. "I don't know if I stand a chance at winning without her."

"You knew weeks ago that you would win, regardless of her presence."

After Marc had spontaneously arrived with Kenen and Galen. Reid had known then that he'd all but clinched the election—but that was the night she had established herself as necessary, perhaps not for the election, but for him.

"Somewhere along the way, I decided I didn't want to," he whispered.

Sadness coated his mother's brown eyes, but she swallowed and nodded. A fierceness washed over her wise features; while he had inherited his father's brown and gold coloring, it was his mother's determination that he'd spend a lifetime developing. Shuffling forward with her robes dragging along the floor, she stopped on the staircase just long enough to look over her shoulder. "There is still one more thing that I haven't tried."

It was both a promise and a threat. One Reid wasn't sure he could believe in.

But he had begged Vaasa to hope, so it was only right he do the same.

CHAPTER 25

"Mathjin, what did you do?" Vaasa barked in Icrurian. "*What did you do?*"

"I did what I had to," Mathjin said in Asteryan, eyeing each step Dominik took and using Asteryan to ensure Dominik could understand the words between them. Six other people stood at the perimeter—Asteryan guards.

Vaasa's breath started to quicken. Were the Asteryan forces in the city?

"He made a deal, not so unlike our own," Dominik said simply with his hands clasped behind his back as he stepped up the stairs. "If he gave me you, I would kill the general who murdered his family. Tell me, Mathjin, did Ignac Kozár suffer to your liking?"

Mathjin moved away from him and didn't deign a response.

The gift, Vaasa realized. That letter had never been for her; Dominik had known she'd show it to Mathjin. He'd communicated with the advisor through Vaasa, and she hadn't even noticed.

Had she ever had the advantage, or had Dominik outplayed her at every turn?

Dominik stepped closer to Amalie, and fear flooded into Vaasa's trembling hands. "It was a simple deal, really," Dominik said. Running his knuckle along Amalie's cheek, his silver clawed ring pressed into her skin, black stone stark against the pale of it, and Amalie tried to move, but he swiped the ring up to her hairline.

Amalie clenched her teeth to hold back any sound. Blood trickled off her skin in a small thread of droplets, pooling at the white fabric still covering her mouth.

Vaasa knew better than to speak. Knew better than to beg for a life Dominik was more likely to take if he knew it mattered. Instead, she waited with bated breath to see what he would do next.

It was the most powerless she'd ever felt.

"You should have just let the magic kill you." Dominik looked squarely at Vaasa. "You knew you would die regardless."

In that moment, she had a hard time disagreeing.

"You despise Asterya, so you invite its emperor into your capital? Into your *election*?" Vaasa asked Mathjin, falling back into Icrurian, watching as the duplicitous advisor kept a healthy distance from her brother, disgust painting his features. "He gave you one general, delivered on *one* promise, and that was worth betraying Reid?"

Amalie cried out, and Vaasa whipped her head to where her brother stood, ring dripping with Amalie's blood. The cut was a twin to the first one, dragging down her cheek directly next to it. Dominik straightened. "Every time someone speaks in Icrurian, I cut her."

Out of the side of his eye, Mathjin watched the guards. Faint questioning coursed over his features, as if he suddenly debated the deal he had made. "He's agreed to leave peacefully if he's allowed to take you with him," Mathjin responded. "He and I will see each other on the battlefield, and there will be no deal between us then. So you will write this letter, and then you both will go, and whatever war he starts is a war he will lose."

"You are a fool," she spat. But it answered her question: Mathjin wouldn't have let an entire army cross the border, even if he wanted war. There was no way they could've gotten past the scouts along the Settara—unless they'd donned the colors and sigil of Wrultho.

Mathjin had made a fool's bargain, so blinded by grief and revenge that he couldn't see the danger he dealt with. The worst part was that he bargained with the wrong sibling; if he'd told Vaasa of the revenge he sought, she would have done everything in her power to bring him Ignac Kozár.

"I have his advisor. If he makes a move, I slaughter the old man."

Vaasa wanted to laugh, but with her brother that close to Amalie, with her brother *silent*, she couldn't. "You think he cares one moment for Ozik's life?" There wasn't a loyal bone in Dominik's body. "You've gotten into bed with a viper, and you don't know it yet, but you have already been bitten."

"Write the fucking letter," Mathjin growled.

"No."

"I won't kill her," Dominik said from the side, knuckle delicately placed along Amalie's throat. "Not at first. But for every moment you don't write that letter, I will carve another slice into her lovely, delicate skin."

And he did, just below her jawline, as if to make a mockery of the way this had all started for Vaasa. Amalie breathed in sharply through gritted teeth, but let out no sound, as if in defiance.

Mathjin must have told him every intimate detail.

Nausea rolled through her. It was her worst nightmare—for Dominik to know of any moment she'd smiled, of any moment she'd dared allowed herself close enough to these people for them to matter. For him to have a hold on the memories that had etched themselves into her skin and her heart. That vulnerability cut deeper than any blade she'd ever known.

Dominik waited one breath, then dragged a large cut along Amalie's chest.

In exactly the same place Kosana had cut Vaasa.

Amusement glittered in his eyes.

"Stop. You don't have to harm anyone else here," Vaasa said.

Dominik slid his ring down Amalie's inner arm, and this time, she choked out a sob.

"Stop!"

"Write the damn letter!" Mathjin screamed.

Amalie wouldn't raise her eyes. Would never ask Vaasa to give in. She wouldn't start a war, not even if the cost was her very life.

Dominik raised his knuckle back to Amalie's other cheek.

"Stop," Vaasa said. "I'll write it. I'll write the letter."

Dominik cut Amalie anyway.

Amalie let out a whimper and then choked on the gag, holding back tears of terror, no doubt, and anger swelled in Vaasa.

"I told you I would write it!"

"Enough," Mathjin said to Dominik, who raised a brow at the advisor's audacity. On the edge of the catacomb, an Asteryan guard drew his sword.

But Dominik tapped his clawed ring on the crumbling stone and gestured for Mathjin to continue. The sword was lowered. Boredom painted the sharp, angular lines of Dominik's face, which meant he was far more dangerous in that moment than he was whenever he showed emotion. He was thinking, probably about how he would take Mathjin's life.

Looking up at her hands, Vaasa let her shoulders fall. "You'll have to untie me."

"One hand is all she needs," Dominik warned Mathjin, who carefully approached.

Mathjin did not flinch as he touched the ropes at her wrists, the fibers woven within them having no effect on his nonmagical hands. One wrist was released, that of her dominant hand, and it fell like deadweight to her side.

Lifting her knee, she slammed her foot into Mathjin's groin.

He howled in pain and stumbled backward, fury in his eyes, and spat at her feet as he doubled over.

From behind him, Dominik chuckled.

Mathjin forced himself upright and moved forward, lifting his arm and slapping the back of his hand into Vaasa's cheekbone. The echo of the strike reverberated through the room. Vaasa didn't make a sound.

Cranking her head back forward, she curled her lip. "My face will be the last thing you see."

"You won't live long enough."

"You've underestimated me."

"No, I haven't." Mathjin limped back to retrieve the paper and pen on the ground. "I've rightfully estimated him."

Dominik grinned, running the claw of his ring along Amalie's cheek again. She flinched away from him, but he only stepped behind her, leaning to whisper something in her ear, his hands trailing along her throat.

Amalie went utterly still.

Fury swept through Vaasa, and her mind screamed for her to try something, anything, to get Dominik to let Amalie go. Yet she knew the outcome of asking her brother to stop, knew that Dominik would simply drag it out for longer, make it that much worse.

Keeping his distance, Mathjin slid the paper and pen across the bench directly next to her, gesturing harshly with his hand. "Write. And don't forget, I've seen your letters. I know the way you speak. Write it well."

Her arm stretched with the motion, the rope tightening on her wrist and causing her to wince as she reached for the pen. It was cold in her hand, but she took one small breath and began to scribble words that sounded like her own.

She accurately described the route they'd all agreed on, from the dips in the canyons to the curves in the Sanguine River. Mathjin would know if even a single detail was out of place. He was, after all, the one who'd come up with it.

Tears welled in her eyes as she wrote the final line.

Trying not to let out a shaky breath, she signed her name at the bottom of the parchment and dropped the pen.

Mathjin pounced, digging his knee into her stomach and shoving her back so she slammed into the wooden stake she'd been tied to. A yelp slipped through her lips, and her knee buckled. Her shoulder screamed. She caught herself with her free hand upon the bench, leaning against it to try and relieve the weight on her stretched shoulder. "*Fuck. You.*"

"Kill her soon, please," was all Mathjin said as he folded the parchment and put it into his coat. He left her with one hand untied—probably to mock Dominik. "And then get the fuck out of my country."

"A deal is a deal," Dominik purred.

Without looking at her or Amalie, Mathjin disappeared into the shadows of the catacomb, the Asteryan guards parting for him to leave.

Dominik tapped his foot.

Vaasa lifted her eyes, meeting his through the slivers of light filtering through the cracks in the stone around them. She didn't dare make a sound, didn't dare beg for a quick death or for mercy. A part of her had always known the two of them would end up here. That they would someday be across from each other, her death imminent, his grin exactly like this.

It only grieved her that the last face she would ever see would be Dominik's.

Reid, back in the theater with his easy gaze and casual grin, flashed behind her eyelids. And if she hadn't already been on the floor, the thoughts would have brought her there. But in it all, there was a small thread of gratitude: she had this memory, the one of him last night and all the ones before it, too. Her chest ached with gratitude for knowing what it had felt like to have him, even for only a short time.

"Do you intend to die like that?" Dominik asked, looking at her shameful stance.

"Where I die makes no difference to me."

"You know," he drawled from behind Amalie. "There is a part of me that's sorry it's come to this between us."

"No there isn't." She looked to the guards—he'd even brought witnesses. How had he possibly persuaded them all not to speak of what happened here?

"Believe what you will. But you do understand I have no choice in this, right? I thought through the alternatives, you know. I could have simply killed the foreman, but what if you were fool enough to marry again? Plus, this is a much better story: That useless foreman from

Wrultho gets a hankering for power and Asterya's heiress is killed in the crossfire? Our lords will march to war."

For a moment, confusion overtook Vaasa's heartache. She hadn't thought the foreman capable—but he was planning something big, that much was clear. "Have you always talked so much?" she asked.

Dominik snorted, looking down at Amalie, who was still unmoving as she watched Vaasa. Dominik once again ran his ringed finger down her cheek to her neck, then along the neckline of Amalie's shirt.

Amalie squeezed her eyes shut.

"Stop," Vaasa begged. "Leave her alone. She's done nothing to you."

Dominik's hand froze.

Then he swiped his ring over Amalie's chest, one long cut that immediately bubbled with blood. This time, Amalie shook with muffled screams.

Vaasa lurched forward, but the rope caught her and she gritted her teeth, tears welling in her eyes.

Dominik stepped out from behind Amalie and crossed the platform in four steps, even the rays of light leaning away from him. The sharp planes of his face loomed closer with each step he took, but he stopped before getting close enough for Vaasa to strike. Her brother's indigo eyes impeccably measured the distance. "Answer me this: How did you learn to manipulate the curse?"

A desperate laugh came from deep in her chest, a tear escaping with it and rolling down her cheek. "You want answers from me? Like this?"

"Answer the question."

"You can die wondering. I hope it plagues you until your very last day."

He stomped backward, loud footsteps echoing in the chamber until he stopped in front of Amalie. With one long strike, he backhanded her the way Mathjin had struck Vaasa.

Amalie yelped as tears and blood streamed down her face, Dominik's ring now dripping with crimson.

"Answer the question," Dominik snarled as he spun back.

It didn't matter now if he knew—maybe she could at least make death quick and painless for Amalie. "It isn't a curse," Vaasa said in a low voice. "It's magic our mother had in her all along."

Dominik tapped his ring against the wood of Amalie's chair. "Why did she arrange your marriage?"

"Is that why you killed her?" Vaasa countered. It didn't matter what she revealed now, what parts of the puzzle she'd started to put together. She and Amalie were going to die.

"I didn't kill our mother," Dominik insisted, something new flashing in his eyes. It was the only time in her life she had seen it echo in the twin blue: hurt.

Had he . . . loved someone after all?

"Then who did? Who summoned the Miro'dag, who made the bargain with the Zetyr?" she asked.

"I have no clue what you're talking about."

Was that sincerity in his tone, in the curl of his lip? She'd never known what it looked like on him.

He narrowed his eyes. "You aren't the one asking the questions."

It stunned her to see the flash of youth on his face. The impetuous, affronted nature of someone too young not to be susceptible to pain. She'd never looked at him this way, had never had the capacity to. Her shame was like a pinprick. He was still her younger brother. "What do you want, then? What more do you want?"

"I want to *understand*," he demanded. "To know why she gave you the one thing she knew would be a threat to me."

"I don't know, Dominik."

"Oh, but you, sister, you know *everything*." Dominik looked down to Amalie, then back to Vaasa. "You have always known everything. Father's fucking favorite."

"He gave you an empire. He gave me a death sentence."

"*And* she *gave you a way out!*"

There it was again, the hatred. The same emotion that burned in her own eyes when she looked upon him. His cruelty and avarice always came out the moment he felt threatened, and he harmed people for it. He harmed them beyond forgiveness.

And for a moment, she pitied him. How sad to spend a lifetime always afraid.

The moment she thought the words, they struck her. As she gazed upon the paranoid glint in her brother's eyes, she replayed each moment of fear that had coiled in her heart and stomach.

The serpent—the thing she'd thought was a curse. Because it looked like her father. Because it looked like Dominik. And when she'd learned the truth of the magic, she'd thought her brother was the curse. Thought *he* was the affliction that haunted her. The reason she could not love or hope or dream.

She lowered her eyes to the dust-covered ground.

She could no longer feel the snake now, but she knew that if she could, she would be able to hear the soft hum of what her heart had always wanted her to see. It was never the magic, and it was never her brother—her fear was the real curse she'd been born with, one that plagued them both equally. It was the greatest cycle of their lives. And she'd been given a way to break it.

But she hadn't.

How sad to have spent a lifetime always afraid. To have looked upon love and kindness and feared it.

"Killing me is not going to set you free," she whispered.

Dominik remained silent for a moment before his voice sounded along the stone. "What?"

"Father was right. You can never want anything without the chance that it will be taken from you." She lifted her eyes to his, heart pounding. "You will never alleviate your fear, Dominik, because the key is not in taking what you want, but in wanting the right things. And you have *never* wanted the right things."

Dominik's lips parted, but Vaasa no longer looked at him.

She gazed at Amalie, who she knew understood every Asteryan word that had just come out of Vaasa's mouth. And she boldly switched to Icrurian. "You showed me love, and because of that, I learned how to show it, too."

Love. Gratitude.

Hope.

They were the only ways to break the curse. "Close your eyes," she said to Amalie. "Don't watch any of this."

Tears gathered in Amalie's eyes, and then they ran down her cheeks, mixing with the blood. She shook her head in defiance.

"When he kills me, I need you to fight like hell. Your strength is my strength," Vaasa choked. It was perhaps the only kindness she had left to offer Amalie—final moments that were not shrouded in the gruesome image of Vaasa's death, but rather in hope. "And tell Reid . . . that I would have stayed."

Amalie still couldn't speak, but after a moment of hesitation, she nodded. As if it was the promise of fulfilling Vaasa's request—the promise of offering her this one last thing—that truly gave Amalie strength. Wetness shone in her doe-brown eyes, but Amalie swallowed her cries. She lifted her chin in bravery, in what Vaasa could have sworn was *I love you, too*. And the only relief Vaasa felt was when Amalie closed her eyes.

"Kill me, Dominik," Vaasa said, returning her gaze upward. "Kill me and prove me right."

Rage threaded in the coldness of his gaze, and he dragged the gleaming knife from his belt. As Vaasa watched him stalking forward, lip curling, she decided his would not be the last face she saw. Even though she would die here, she would not look at the fear any longer.

She looked to Amalie, and just then, her eyes flew open. Vaasa could have sworn they flashed white.

And then magic flooded the room, slamming into Dominik and cutting off every inch of light and sound.

And there was nothing.

Until the world hummed.

The darkness coating them dissipated in a snap, the sort of control only a trained Veragi witch could accomplish. Mist surrounded the platform. It snaked up the columns and crawled along the fractured ceiling. Through the black mist emerged a stalking cloaked figure, bathed in swirling black, shadows bowing with their steps.

Silvery blond hair lifting with the mist.

Amber eyes glowing in the dark.

Melisina.

Vaasa choked on a sob of relief and railed against the ropes that bound her. Her wrist burned, eyes immediately scanning for Dominik. She found him sprawled on the floor, blood trickling from his head, trying to pull himself up on his arms.

His knife had been dropped in front of him.

Closer to her.

Dominik snapped his head up, ocean eyes locking on hers as he threatened something Vaasa couldn't hear. He sprang toward the blade.

Vaasa threw her body away from the wooden post, her bound arm holding her back, and kicked with every ounce of strength she could still muster. Bone cracked. Blood spurted from Dominik's nose as he recoiled, hands gripping his face. His angry scream pierced the air, and he leapt for the weapon. Using her outstretched foot, she kicked the knife into her hands and could have howled in relief as the blade met her fingers. Quickly, she sawed at the rope tied around her other hand. Dominik began crawling across the floor toward her. Behind him, Melisina was taking on all six guards, black Veragi magic streaming down their throats and noses.

Dominik's fingers wrapped around Vaasa's wrist and slammed it against the wood. The knife clattered to the ground, and Vaasa tried to move her body, tried to kick and get out of his way, but Dominik caught her foot and tugged until she lost her balance. Grabbing the frayed rope above her, Vaasa took one large breath, and then let the weight of her body fall.

A tearing sensation lanced up her arm.

The fringed rope snapped.

Her bound arm fell, and she choked as blood flowed into her fingers, a tingling sensation burning all the way to the tips. She clawed at the tendril of rope still tied to her wrist. If she could get to her magic, if she could—

She rolled as Dominik swung the knife down, iron blade etching into the stone floor. She kicked his side again, causing him to lose his balance. Tossing her weight to the left, she rolled away from him as many times as she could. She hit the hard stone wall. Sharp pieces of granite littered the floor around her. Vaasa dragged one of those stones across the rope still tied to her wrist as she heard Dominik stand, his footsteps echoing on the floor.

She sawed despite the murder in his eyes, despite the blood now streaming down her wrist. Curled on the ground, she had moments before Dominik killed her.

Amalie let out a high-pitched wail. Her hair was strewn along the floor, the chair she'd been in shattered on the floor. The witch was curled on the marble screaming through the gag.

She'd never in her life wanted to picture Amalie broken.

And now Vaasa saw it, the way her friend's entire being seemed to fracture at what had been done. Like a well refilling, like a fire sparking, rage poured into her.

No—not rage.

Magic.

Her nails cut through the last of the rope, and it fell to the floor as darkness shot out of Vaasa, slamming into Dominik and sending him flying backward. Coiled and angrier than it had ever been, the magic slithered in Vaasa's belly and through her veins, rushing to her limbs and out of her fingertips. It swirled up her arms and neck, hissing, mist growing, as she got to her feet.

Dominik's eyes went wide.

"Sister—"

"Don't you dare beg."

He started to shake.

Vaasa took a slow step forward, black mist coating the floor with her fury. Dominik's eyes grew wider. The mist around her shifted. It no longer coiled around her limbs. It writhed on the ground toward him, a collection of serpents with forked tongues spewing, until they reared and piled in on themselves. They wrapped into something new, climbed up into a body and curled around to create four legs. As the creature prowled forward, the serpents that composed it hissed and slithered.

And then the magic inside her grew and shifted, the creature's four limbs stretching, white eyes glowing. In a chorus of screaming shadows, it tipped its head to the sky.

She knew then what it was. Knew with perfect clarity what it had wanted to be this entire time, and what she had not let it. It howled with its loyalty and its outrage.

Her magic sparked, retribution in her blood, and the wolf took form.

It stalked forward with each step Vaasa took, teeth bared, edges of the magic licking the air. This creature of the void was everything inside of her: darkness, pain, fear, and power, too.

"You've spent a lifetime afraid of this moment." She stepped in front of her brother. Looked directly at the horror on his pale face, the way the edges of her magic snapped like whips and bit, tearing at his wrists and clothes. "I have waited a lifetime to watch it. To see each speck of fear dance in your eyes as you come to terms with your greatest nightmare, for you have found every way to witness mine."

Dominik's head whipped back and forth, looking for a way out, in a last display of his cowardice.

"Do you realize that it is you who created your greatest threat?" she asked.

When Dominik laid his eyes upon the magic still swirling around Vaasa, he stopped. "He isn't the wolf," he said. "You are."

The thought crossed her mind to let him live. But despite her unyielding shame, she knew that would never be an option. That he would never stop until the world beneath his feet burned.

The creature of the void struck.

The wolf consumed him, black Veragi mist cutting off every sense of his sight and sound and smell. It cut the air from his lungs and dragged him down into the wicked shadows. Into the void. It drowned him. His gurgling screams could barely be heard, but Vaasa could feel its teeth rip into his neck, taste the metallic blood as it poured, hear the stretching of limbs.

And then the wolf dissipated, snapping back into her with a force she had to brace herself against. Dominik was there, blood pooling on the floor. His head lay a foot away from the rest of his body.

Shock tumbled through Vaasa first. A resistance to what she saw, to what she had just done.

And then she screamed.

Agony shattered her like a broken window, tiny shards of glass piercing each of her organs and ripping out of her skin. Detonating. Black mist exploded around her. From her. Through her. It crashed against the columns and walls, and she wondered for a moment if she might bring down the entire colosseum. If she might shake so hard no foundation could stand a chance.

The last of her family. Dead.

And yet, she could not stop. Could not even slow. There were people still breathing, people who had wanted to take everything from her. People whose selfishness and greed had put her right here, poised her to either kill or be killed. People who right now wanted to witness the shattering of a nation.

It filled her to bursting fullness. Poured into her with the velocity of an explosion: rage.

Faintly she heard Melisina trying to calm Amalie. Trying to undo the knots. Vaasa heard Amalie screaming.

One knee at a time, Vaasa pulled herself from the floor, the void still beating around her and licking the air. She let the torn lower half of her skirt drag through Dominik's blood. The mist scattered where she placed her feet.

Melisina asked, "What are you doing?"

Bending over, one hand gripping Dominik's hair, Vaasa growled, "He wasn't working alone."

CHAPTER 26

The enormous garden hummed around Reid as councilor after councilor filed in. Each candidate sat upon a raised platform at the front of the rectangular space, the white marble statue of Una peering over their shoulders. This main quad built between the building's six cathedrals was the highlight of the High Temple of Dihrah, the smell of gardenias floating through the air and the blooms seeming to shake with excitement. Each sodality had a main quad, and it was there that a new headman was chosen. Headman Kier had been elected in the quad of the High Temple of Sigguth, and now Reid was waiting to make history here in Dihrah. To rule for the next decade. To move the capital to Mireh, where his successor would gaze upon their stones and flowers and make history too.

Headman Kier sat at the front of the platform, brown beard trimmed perfectly and wearing his Icrurian formal wear in the gold, silver, and black of the entire nation. There was no purple, no green, no blue, no yellow, no orange or red—he was a man of all the people. These were the garments Reid hoped to wear when the new term arrived and the exchange of power occurred.

But he couldn't think straight. Couldn't focus on anything but his mother and her coven, who were still scouring the streets to find their two youngest members.

One of whom was his wife.

She had not returned the next morning, though she had in his sleep. It made opening his eyes much worse—morning had always been home to his grief; it was when he felt it most acutely and needed to launch himself into work. It was why he rose with the sun each day and worked tirelessly through it.

As the rays of late-morning light bathed the quad's marble pathways in gold, Reid forced his eyes away from the streams. Every councilor watched him, as they had all morning. Marc's expression showed pity, but not those of the others. They had never grown to truly know Vaasa, had only met her days ago and spent all of those days behind doors debating her loyalty to him and to Icruria.

He hated himself, but there was a small part of him that debated her loyalty, too. Perhaps he couldn't envision a world in which she stayed. In which he got everything he'd ever wanted. All his life he'd been made to choose.

As the music slowed and the councilors took their seats, the gardenias seemed to glare at him, and he struggled to keep his chin up. Kier opened the ceremony with a speech reviewing the progress of Icruria over the years and celebrating the successes of the nation. Reid had imagined himself listening to this speech with Vaasa at his side, considering the one he would give someday. Days ago, he'd pictured her standing there with him ten years from now—the way Elijah now stood with Kier, ready to depart from this phase of their lives. He had clung to the hope that he could convince her in the coming years to make her home and her life with him. That freedom could still be found here. And trust.

Now he couldn't listen to more than three or four sentences. He pictured nothing beyond his grief.

The choir burst into hymns that didn't matter any longer, with music that didn't stir a thing in his soul. Not the way music usually did. He shut it out as he waited for them to end.

As the first councilor rose to speak, a strange murmur filled the crowd. People turned to look, and Reid tensed as someone scurried to Ton, something white folded in their hands. Ton opened it and skimmed it, shook his head, and looked to Reid directly.

"It appears to be a letter my men intercepted. Signed by your wife."

Reid immediately shot up, not a care for decorum, and crossed the platform in a few steps. Ton handed him the letter. Reid instantly recognized Asteryan, recognized Vaasa's script, though it seemed a bit shaken or hurried. But he couldn't read it.

He turned to Mathjin, who sat with the same neutral expression he always wore, and gestured for his advisor to come forward. It took moments for the advisor to arrive, and Reid handed him the letter, pointing. "Can you translate this?"

Mathjin read it carefully, then looked pityingly to Reid and nodded.

"Faithfully," Ton said. "We will have others read it, too."

Reid almost snarled at the foreman, but he reined in his anger. His fear. Instead, he focused on Mathjin. As the advisor spoke, Reid closed his eyes. His stomach dropped. The world seemed to stop turning.

Mathjin read the exact location Reid and Ton had agreed upon less than two days prior. It was a detailed account of where the soldiers would move, which rivers they would take, and the timing they had plotted. It was exactly the plan Mathjin and Vaasa had brought to Reid only weeks ago. It was addressed to her brother. To Dominik.

Anger and betrayal and fear pounded through him as his vision seemed to tunnel and the world shifted beneath his feet with each new word. This would do worse than lose Reid an election; it would spark no less than a civil war.

She'd betrayed them. She'd fled and she'd betrayed—

"Wait," Reid said. "Read that last line again."

Mathjin read the last line in a perfect translation to Icrurian.

"'I told you I would play for you, and I have,'" the advisor said.

The world whirled back on a perfect axis, and Reid straightened his spine. "*Liars*," he snarled, looking to Ton and drawing his onyx blade. His father's blade. "Where is my wife?"

Ton went wide-eyed and drew his own blade, confusion and misunderstanding barreling across the man's features. More swords were drawn, iron slipped from their sheaths, and Kier stood.

And then the crowd began to scream.

Reid spun and looked, and there, at the edge of the garden, stood his mother shrouded in mist. Beside her was Amalie.

And Vaasa.

Reid tried to move, but Mathjin gripped his arm, sword drawn. Like some angel of death, his wife strode forward in the clothing he'd last seen her in, skirts torn and bodice smeared with blood. Black mist trailed around her arms and legs with tendrils of it brushing the ground wherever she stepped. Blood dragged behind her like a wedding veil.

And there at her side, a swirl of glittering darkness, was a wolf.

The edges licked the air and blurred with the swarming of Veragi mist. Sparks of the cosmos—blues and purples and greens—coasted along the edges in veins of constellations. Eyes of pure moonlight glowed even in the sun.

Crimson dripped from Vaasa's fingers. It stained her hands, which gripped something black. All the breath left him when she got close enough for them to see clearly what she held: raven hair. Lifeless blue eyes. Dominik's head was clenched in her hands.

She threw it to the ground at the platform's base. It rolled until it hit the stone. The world was silent.

His wife looked clearly to Reid's left, directly at Mathjin, and said, "You're next."

CHAPTER 27

Every councilor must have gaped, but Vaasa saw nothing past her own misery and rage.

Past Reid, staring at her like she was an omen.

She stared right at Mathjin, and the wolf at her side growled.

Mathjin, sword in hand, flicked his eyes to Reid. Vaasa bared her teeth. Darkness burst from her. Tendrils of magic whipped along the platform, and Mathjin grabbed Reid and spun. Koen moved from the left and dove, slamming into Mathjin, and the two went tumbling to the floor, Reid thrown off balance and rolling on the platform.

Mathjin's body clapped against the stone pavement and he struck down with his blade, but Koen had drawn his sword and deflected the movement. Steel clashed against steel, and the garden erupted.

Men in Wrultho green flooded from all sides, swinging swords burying into bodies, heads tipping back and screaming, and Ton made a move for the platform. He slaughtered a guard on his way, eyes glued to where Kier balked, likely realizing he was the target.

"It's a coup!" someone yelled, just as another man lunged at Vaasa.

Esoti and Kosana were suddenly there. Kosana moved to cover Vaasa's back while Esoti leapt in front of her, stumbling back from the wolf that collided with the oncoming enemy. His screams filled the air, and magic lurched from Vaasa, more powerful than she'd felt it before, as if this new manifestation of her magic had unlocked something in her. Esoti slid a knife into the empty sheath at Vaasa's thigh. With a stern nod, Esoti released her and wrapped her forearm around Kosana's.

The two locked gazes, and then Kosana plunged into the madness.

"Go—" Vaasa said.

"I will not let you out of my sight again," Esoti said, then grabbed her arm. "Now let's go take off someone else's head."

Darkness ripped forth from Vaasa, and she barreled forward with Dominik's knife still in her hand, just as Reid turned around and struck his sword against Ton's. Kier covered Elijah, pushing his husband off the platform and into the waiting mass of their own trusted guards. The men fled with the high consort, and Kier turned, wicked anger gnarling his features.

Vaasa's wolf plunged forward. It struck Ton, teeth bared, and Vaasa tasted the metallic blood, the screams echoing in her ears as she leapt onto the platform.

Reid didn't waste a single breath, burying his sword in Ton's gut and slicing down to his groin. Gore splattered as Ton's large body sank to the ground, no life left in him, and his face cracked on the stone platform. Red bloomed in a pool beneath him.

Vaasa turned as the gardens shook.

The edges of the courtyard were blacked out with mist. Melisina and Amalie stood at the back fighting against the inpouring of soldiers in Wrultho green, their magic creating a circular boundary around the gardens. Kier bellowed orders, the other councilors following suit, instructing the guards to fight Ton's men. Soldiers charged through the void of Veragi magic without sight or sound or smell. Kosana covered both witches, barking orders at her own corps, striking down a man in green as he broke through. Scanning the enormous border, Vaasa saw Romana, Mariana, and Suma, who formed a triangle behind the platform, mist pouring from their hands to enclose the other half of the gardens. It mingled with Melisina's and Amalie's magic, completing a circle enclosing them all. The mist hissed and swirled. Reid barked at Kier's men to defend the witches, leaving the soldiers a choice: side with him, and therefore Icruria, or hesitate and be marked a traitor. Vaasa recognized the faces of the witches of Una, whose light flashed to blind those in green who poured through the magical boundary, and with their display of loyalty, the Icrurian soldiers rallied behind the Veragi coven, too.

But the courtyard was enormous, big enough for five hundred people at least, and there was no way they could stop each person who came out of the mist. Those in Icrurian silver and gold descended upon the interlopers, the screams of runners and fighters echoing off the vines and glass walls of concealed patios like the one Vaasa had slept beneath.

Vaasa spun again, finding herself facing Reid. He reached for the bruise on her cheek, but she knew if she felt anything else, she would crumble. So she gently pushed his hand away, searching once more for her next victim and finding Mathjin still fighting with Koen.

And she moved.

Reid called after her as she stalked forward, the shadow of her wolf whipping at her feet. Mathjin looked up. Terror resided in the blue of his eyes, and she realized that even if she hated herself for it, that terror sustained her. She fed on it. Perhaps she was more like her brother than she'd thought.

Koen landed a blow to Mathjin's side, slicing through his clothing and summoning a line of red. Mathjin stumbled, and Vaasa snapped her head to the foreman, causing Koen to sink backward and lower his sword.

Mathjin dropped the hand gripping his side, his hands tightening around the hilt of his sword, leveling himself in preparation.

"You estimated wrong," Vaasa said. The magic inside her coiled tightly. Only months ago, the tug of her power had been unbearable, but now the sensation was familiar, working with her instead of against her.

Mathjin raised his sword.

The wolf struck.

Vaasa felt each of its movements as if they were her own. Like it was her feet that pounded on the blood-soaked pavement, her teeth that bared, her muscles that coiled. Mathjin swung his sword at the void and the magic flickered, losing some shape as it slammed into the advisor and dragged him backward.

"Vaasa!" Reid yelled as he grabbed her forearm and pulled. She cursed and fought against him, her wolf dissolving and releasing Mathjin.

"He made a deal with Dominik!" she yelled back, spinning and tearing her arm from Reid's hand.

Reid froze. "What?"

"Tell him!" Vaasa screamed as she turned back to Mathjin. Her magic detonated again, lashing out with her fury. It surrounded them in the same way Melisina had surrounded the gardens, a circle that swirled around them all, the void threatening to squeeze tighter. It covered them the way it had covered her that night next to the Settara, except this time, it let her breathe. It let her speak. It expanded around them to a perfect dome, blocking out even the sunlight.

"Tell him what you did to Amalie. How you watched as Dominik tortured her."

Mathjin's eyes blinked furiously as he tried to adjust to the sudden dark.

"Tell him!" Vaasa screamed again, and Mathjin whipped his head forward. "Tell him everything. How you wrote to Dominik in secret. Tell him what you did for Ton and the east."

"Reid—" Mathjin said.

"Is this true?" Reid murmured. The battle raged outside, but in that corner of the garden, in the eye of the storm of her magic, Reid only sauntered to the space next to Vaasa.

"Tell him how you kidnapped me and strung me up. How you forced me to write that letter. How you left me there to die," Vaasa attested.

Mathjin took a step back, desperately searching for a break in the whirling mist.

There was none.

Carefully, he looked to Reid. Their eyes met. "You may not understand now, but you will," the advisor swore.

Reid's composure broke.

Stalking forward like the wolf they'd named him after, not a trace of mercy anywhere on his corded body, Reid descended upon Mathjin with the ruthless ire reserved only for those who touched the ones he loved. It was as if he chose every step, and what he'd said to her that day in his office rang true. He knew when not to fight, and that made his choice all the more frightening.

Reid yelled as he kicked his advisor square in the stomach, sending him flying to the ground and sliding back upon the stone, crashing into one of the many statues that lined the center garden. It cracked and swayed, body splitting, a marble arm sliding and shattering on the ground. Around them, the magic grew wider and darker and louder. It raged with the violence thrumming through Vaasa.

"How dare you," Reid said to Mathjin. Never before had she heard that inflection in his tone—a mix of rage and heartbreak that could only be brought on by the deepest of betrayals.

"How dare *you*," Mathjin yelled back, his body shaking as he stood. "That you would ruin your family's legacy, ruin everything your father worked—"

Reid slammed the hilt of his sword into Mathjin's cheek, sending him back to the ground. The advisor yelped in pain, and blood trickled from his head where it had hit the statue.

Vaasa plunged a knife into his leg.

Mathjin wailed, leg twitching violently and then going slack.

Betrayal seared across Reid's features. Insecurity, too. And then a whisper of resolution as his jaw went taut.

Tears streamed down Mathjin's face, a plea falling from his cowardly lips.

Vaasa watched the stiffness of Reid's motions, the way his arm couldn't lift. Softly, she placed her hand upon his shoulder. He turned to look at her, and silently she absolved him.

She would do this—he did not need to.

But Reid shook his head. Stepping forward, he placed the tip of the sword just beneath Mathjin's chin. Maintaining that same honor she had known of him from the first time she witnessed his protection. It would be he who doled out this punishment—he who carried the weight. "For my wife, and for my father. For failing his only son."

With one long slice, Reid slit Mathjin's throat.

The traitorous advisor gurgled on his own blood, and his head hung forward, concealing the wicked slash that poured crimson onto the man's dust-coated purple coat.

Reid shook.

The magic rose higher and squeezed tighter, the whorls of it picking up tendrils of Vaasa's hair. Quietly, she whispered to Mathjin's lifeless body, "I told you mine would be the last face you saw."

And then the magic hissed to the ground, breaking into a cloud of mist that crept along the bloodied stone.

Reid's body covered hers for the briefest of moments. A single thread of shared rage and sorrow. He brushed his lips against hers, whispering, "*We are not done here*," and left, plunging back into the echoing screams and clash of steel. She thought to follow him, to give him some words of solace, but there were none.

Faintly, she heard the cracking of magic upon the stone, and Vaasa ran with what energy she had left to Melisina and Amalie. To run was all she could do. To fight. Esoti appeared behind her, the two of them coming upon a small cluster of men who'd broken through the shield of mist. Vaasa ducked under the raised arm of one and spun, plunging the dagger into his back at the same moment Esoti sliced the man's throat. Ripping the dagger free, Vaasa whirled and slid the blade into the stomach of another, whose falling sword was blocked by the long blade Esoti wielded.

With each life she took, the well of darkness in her grew deeper, her rage running hotter.

In front of her, the councilor from Hazut gaped and flipped his head around, seeking his candidate. The foreman of Hazut was nowhere to be found. The coward was unfit to have led Icruria anyhow, then.

Vaasa didn't have the time to deliver the righteous remark she felt entitled to about this. Esoti tugged her one way and thrust a blade through the eye of a man wearing Wrultho's sigil. Using his body like a battering ram, she slammed into two more soldiers. Vaasa leapt over a mess of tangled limbs upon the ground and plunged Dominik's dagger into a soldier's thigh. Esoti swiftly executed the other, and they sprinted across the gardens.

By the time she reached Melisina through the swarm of gold-and-silver-clad soldiers, the witch had started to falter. Exhaustion coated Melisina's face as she pushed the limits of her magic. Vaasa gripped Melisina's shoulder, pulling long gulps of air. "You've done enough. You need to rest."

"Not until it's over," she said through gritted teeth.

"It's over," Vaasa assured her. "The tides have turned."

Melisina looked over her shoulder to Vaasa, then past her. Her eyes went wide. Her horrified scream pierced the air and Vaasa spun, ready to sprint. The gardens shook as a familiar awful, nightmarish wail emanated through the grounds.

The Miro'dag broke through the mist. Upon the platform. Directly behind Reid.

Shrieks of fear echoed around the gardens, and people fled, plunging into the void of mist and senselessness, taking their chances in the magic instead of here.

Vaasa did not think. She only ran.

Wings shimmering with dark gray and bloodred, the creature slammed into the statue of Una upon the platform and the marble crumbled, crashing against the stone ground. And then those wings collided with Reid. His knees cracked against the marble. A claw pushed through his shoulder blade and Reid's entire body arched, his bellow of pain echoing off every leaf and vine.

The pound of Vaasa's boots reverberated with each desperate step forward. A scream tore from her throat. But then a figure broke through the mist near the Miro'dag, cloaked in black, and something rippled through the air.

Wind struck her stomach and sent her flying back, skidding across the stone floor, skin tearing on the stone. Vaasa tumbled backward over herself, landing facedown and forcing her palms against the hot ground, head whipping up as she dragged her knees beneath her.

White hair billowing behind him, a sharp-toothed smile on his face, Ozik stood upon the platform, a dark stain against vibrant green and pearly white. Magic roared around him in glossy ripples, the energy translucent yet unmistakable. He clapped and the gardens shook, his mocking applause silencing everything and everyone. Those left jumped into Melisina's shroud of magic, which trembled as she tried to stand.

The ringing sounds of palm against palm echoed off the crumbling stone and washed over Vaasa as dread overtook her. Her father's oldest advisor stepped forward with the Miro'dag, which pinned down a bleeding Reid, at his back.

"A severed head, Vaasalisa?" Ozik said in Asteryan, careless of anyone who was left or whether they could understand. "And I thought I was the one who would make a dramatic entrance."

Vaasa's muscles screamed as she hauled herself to her feet and started forward. She didn't feel the soreness for long; it was swiftly replaced by the coursing adrenaline and magic. Everyone else fled. Soldiers and diplomats alike plunged into the void of Veragi magic to escape the might of the demon. To stand a chance at living.

All Vaasa saw was Reid.

All she felt was the tug to go forward, even as the garden emptied and the witches stood ready, no one daring to strike for fear of Reid's life. The mist around them shivered and hissed. The rest of the coven would fall. Ozik had waited until the end—until they were exhausted from the battle.

He flicked his wrist, and a gleaming thread of power rippled through the air. It pressed against Vaasa's chest until she was forced to a stop by some invisible wall. Yet it trembled as she pushed, and the air was thick, as if Ozik struggled to maintain it. Her eyes locked on Reid, on the Miro'dag that held him down, and she didn't dare move.

Golden eyes inspected her, staring out of an ancient face that strained against its own bones. Ozik did not look polished and smooth, as he was in her memories; no, he was ragged and torn at the edges. She wasn't the only one who was tired.

"What are you doing?" Vaasa dared ask.

"Start by dropping that pesky little knife." Ozik gestured with his head toward Dominik's severed one, which hadn't been buried beneath other bodies yet. His lifeless eyes faced the platform, raven hair still sticky with blood that now shimmered in a way it hadn't before. "I don't trust what you might do with it. The blade at your thigh, too."

Esoti growled from behind her, and Reid tried to speak, but his stifled cry was enough to fracture Vaasa once more. The Miro'dag dripped oily blood onto his shoulder. First Amalie. Now him. On the verge of breaking, Vaasa dropped her knives, which clanged as they hit the ground, one by one, Ozik watching each blade as it fell to Vaasa's feet.

"Kick them away."

Using the tip of her blood-soaked boot, she kicked the weapons to the left.

Ozik merely chuckled. Adjusting his stance, he moved to the edge of the platform, his black cloak dragging behind him and through the blood of those fallen. He kicked a body over the edge of the stage. "Your brother and I made a deal, you see. A *bargain*. But now he is dead, and I am left with an empty promise."

Of course. She had never even considered it. "You're the Zetyr," Vaasa croaked. Had Dominik even known who he bargained with? The power he had summoned?

Ozik leapt off the platform and walked forward. Boredom threaded each of his wary features and he stopped a healthy distance away. The hem of his cloak swept the ground. "Yes. Very good."

The maniacal gleam of his eye told her he had suspected Dominik would never have walked out of their altercation alive. She realized Ozik had been pulling strings for far longer than her brother had drawn breath.

But she had never once suspected him.

An oversight on her part, blinded by her own pure hatred of Dominik. Her overestimation of his mind. With Mathjin and Ton, Ozik had also been privy to every discussion, to every letter, to each move on the chessboard between her brother and her, yet she had never questioned if Ozik could actually be the one making the moves. The callous advisor who had stood at her father's side and helped him win an empire. Who had overseen her tutelage, always demanding more of her, always on the inside of everyone's secrets.

"How many bargains have you made, Ozik?"

"Vaasa—" Reid gasped in warning, but Ozik lifted his hand and the Miro'dag pushed its long, pointed claw further into Reid's shoulder. Through the tattoo she'd memorized. Reid gasped in pain and Vaasa started forward again, faster now, though Ozik jumped between her and the platform.

"How many bargains?" she demanded, refusing to slow.

"How much time do you think we have?" He raised his hand, directing her to stop where she was.

She paused, Esoti still a pace behind her, cautiously following.

"It is best if your guard backs up," he instructed.

Esoti bared her teeth.

Vaasa could feel the shadows and the mist dancing up her wrists. Could see the brutality in Ozik's eyes as he turned toward Reid once again, and the Miro'dag coiled to strike. "Step back," she commanded over her shoulder.

The warrior cursed but listened.

Ozik smiled and tilted his head. "Should I start at the beginning, or just with the little trade your mother made me? Your father's life, to finally have her all to myself. To sit upon the throne with the only other witch I knew and be done with your father's foolish reign. To finally have one of our own. No one ever suspected more than a flu."

Vaasa's breathing faltered. Ozik had loved her mother? Had they been having an affair?

He'd killed her father for his throne and his wife.

"I should have listened more closely when your father droned on about how love is useless. Your mother left for that *one* pesky summer. Came here of all places, and I suspect that's when she put her little plan in motion. Persuade me to kill her husband. Give her son the throne. Send her daughter to a stronghold of Veragi magic, one that would protect you against me, against your brother, against the rest of the world." He shook his head. "Well, can you guess what happens to a bargain broken with a Zetyr witch?"

As the oil dripped upon Reid's drape, his eyes stayed locked to hers. Then the sequence of events and motivations all fell into place. The pieces of the puzzle finally seemed to settle, finding their curves and edges and resting neatly upon the table in front of her.

"Death," Vaasa said. Zetyr magic was an exchange—that much she had gleaned from reading about the god himself. That was the caveat, the reason it was either the most powerful force in existence or the least accessible. It was based on a bargain, subject to someone else's desires. And so the consequence made sense; if the source went back on their end of the deal, they forfeited their life.

Vaasa's mother knew she would die. And yet she did not cede the throne to Ozik. In a way, she had given each of her children their birthright—Dominik a throne, Vaasa a coven.

Vaasa took a strangled breath, fighting against the fresh grief that poured into her. "You killed my parents. You pitted me and Dominik against each other. All to clear your way to the Asteryan throne."

Ozik gave an amused chuckle, then furrowed his brow at the body nearest him. Ton of Wrultho. He snorted, kicking him aside with the toe of his boot. "Useless. Though he did plan this little coup d'état all on his own. So messy, these eastern Icrurians."

"*Enough.* What do you want?" she pleaded.

Ozik flicked his wrist, and the Miro'dag struck. Its webbed wings opening on a howl, the beast ripped its claw from Reid's shoulder.

And plunged it directly through his back, lifting him into the air and piercing his heart.

Melisina's scream could be heard from the other side of the gardens, and the Veragi mist fell to the stone floor, dissipating on the wind. The curved claw ripped from Reid's tendons and cracked through his shoulder blade, dripping blood as the Miro'dag yowled and Reid's body fell to the platform.

"No!"

Vaasa's scream was bloodcurdling as she ran to Reid. Her magic hissed against the ground, and Ozik barked a warning at her. She leapt onto the platform, the Miro'dag lingering above them, oil leaking onto the white marble around his body, mixing with the mist and the snakes and her cries. She could smell it, the rot. The death. The same scent that had haunted her all these months.

The Miro'dag's bony spine curved as it retreated backward, crimson eyes animated and glowing. It didn't strike again, didn't drain the life from Reid. It only watched.

Waited.

And all Vaasa had was the smell. The unwanted images. Amalie, covered in blood. Dominik's head, inches from his body. Mathjin's slit throat.

Blood poured from the wound and Reid's breaths came shallow, ragged, and Vaasa didn't care if the Miro'dag took her, too. Didn't care if she had survived Dominik only to die here, on her knees, at Reid's side. But the bleeding was too much. It pooled around them, and her hands shook, barely touching his body, his eyes no longer moving.

"Reid!" she shouted. She watched with horror as the skin around his mouth paled.

As his rigid jaw went slack.

As the life dimmed from his expressive golden eyes.

And she felt it.

Felt his breathing cease.

Felt him leave this life.

Felt her insides crack.

A piercing wail broke from her chest, and she hauled his heavy head into her lap, tears streaming down her face as her magic whipped around her. "No," she breathed. "No, you can't go. You can't go!" Her forehead fell to his. Her fingers ran through his disheveled hair, through the strands that had broken from his leather tie. She searched for signs of life, for a pulse, for something, and found nothing but the slick of his blood and the shattering of her heart.

Melisina's cries broke through stillness of the garden. The most miserable keening rang around them.

A lifetime flashed before her eyes—Mireh, and the villa, and the places he would show her in stunning oranges and yellows and blues. The way his body would curl against hers at night. How they would be sleepless and tired in the morning, no regrets about how they'd lost themselves in each other.

The laughter of children; the patter of their feet.

She secretly hoped they would have her eyes.

That he would teach them his kindness.

She saw his hair turning gray and his beard threading with it, too. How time would wrinkle the skin of his hands. And how they would sit upon the veranda, and he'd place his forehead against hers, whispering of the life they had lived and how the world was not made of mountains and adventurous horizons, but of living room floors and the quiet flicker of candlelight.

The future haunted her more than any memory, than any ghost. The heart-wrenching realization not of what they had, but of what they never would.

She should have told him sooner. Should have begged him to keep her.

All that time she had wasted.

"It isn't enough." Her clawed whisper floated around them, his still-warm skin against hers. "It isn't enough."

And through the elegy of her own heart, she heard Ozik's voice in the haze. "Are you ready to make a deal?"

Slowly, she lifted her head. Her magic jostled her insides and snapped from her, the wolf coming back to life, looming next to her as if prepared to strike.

Ozik remained still. "Kill me and he stays dead."

The wolf paused.

Fingers shaking, she looked down at Reid's lifeless body and realized exactly what Ozik had planned. The extent of what Zetyr magic could do when called upon.

He wanted a bargain. And he'd found the one way to make her desperate enough to give him anything he asked for.

"Bring him back," she stammered. "Whatever you want, it's yours. Just bring him back."

They were supposed to have time. She had killed her brother. She had *survived*. But it didn't matter what she lost, what the world demanded of her now. The only thing that mattered was that Reid 's lungs pulled breath, that goodness like his still lived.

Ozik stepped onto the platform and approached slowly, inspecting the places she touched Reid. For only a moment, Ozik eyed the wolf, but with Reid dead in her arms, assurance played upon his smile. Vaasa wouldn't strike—not when he held the one thing she wanted most in his hands. "*Surrender your magic*," he growled.

A warning coiled within her, deep and low, a small whisper of possession that might have found a voice if Ozik hadn't cut her off at the knees. There was no debate, no question she had to ask herself. "It's yours."

"Tell me you surrender your magic to me. Do that, and in exchange, I will renew his life."

"Fine."

"Say it."

Her heart leapt into her throat, but she choked down the magic and the rage and the fear. "I surrender my magic to you. In exchange, *you must renew his life.*"

Ozik took a large breath, the air around them stirring with something wicked, and then the muscles inside Vaasa's abdomen went taut. Like a well run dry, she felt her power—that new, powerful wolf—being pulled from her very bones. It clung to her insides on its way out. Clawed at her throat. The force rebelled against their parting, teeth sinking into her so brutally she screamed, but then it was ripped from the tissue it had burrowed into, like the roots of a tree yanked violently from the ground. Something broke within her. Vaasa heard the howl of the wolf as it disintegrated, saw the glittering black ashes of what once was hers floating around Ozik. She had earned that magic. Conquered that darkness. The emptiness she had once craved became a hollow pit. Cold. And though her fingers itched to reach back out and reclaim what was hers, they remained on the lifeless body beneath them.

Ozik rolled his head from side to side, eyes closed with the kind of relief that only came when a deep, dark pain abated. When he opened them, he nodded, then knelt next to her, pale hand falling to the wound on Reid's chest. Black veins ran along the back of his hand and dipped beneath his cloak. After a few moments, Reid's wound began to mend. The air around them fizzed with raw, startling magic unlike anything Vaasa had ever seen. It was as if Ozik had been born a Zuheia witch with the ultimate power of healing and could direct it to fulfill any command he wanted. As if with her words he had unlocked a potential greater than she could even begin to fathom.

Vaasa screamed in agony, her stomach twisting, the empty pit now full of fire. Flames licked the caverns of where her power had been. They rose and burned and—

Just as quickly as it came, it disappeared.

Color bloomed on Reid's face.

And then he gasped.

Vaasa sobbed, strength abandoning her, and she slumped. She

dropped her head to his chest. There, her cheek pressed to him in both duty and powerlessness, she heard a quickening rhythm.

A heartbeat.

Another sob burst from her lips. She didn't care what she'd given up, didn't care that Asterya would fall to the hands of a madman or that the continent would be ravaged. All she cared was that Reid filled his lungs.

A hand landed at the base of her hair and pulled, causing Vaasa to cry out as she was dragged away from Reid. His body slipped from her arms. In the cold absence, she registered the rough scrape of rope against her throat. Vaasa stopped breathing.

Her hands flew to the rope, fingers scraping to get beneath it. She kicked her legs and flung her body to the side, finding the hard press of an unfamiliar chest as her arm was pulled behind her back. Then the other. Soldiers she did not know, all dressed in Wrultho green, dragged her across the platform, someone still tugging her hair. Rope circled her wrists and pulled tight before Vaasa had the opportunity to fight. Instinctively, she reached for her magic—but there was no answer. She choked on her sobs.

"Let her go!" Vaasa heard Esoti's desperate call, then heard her grunt. She flung her head to the side to see Esoti plunge her knife into the abdomen of the man who attacked her. All around, men dressed in the old uniforms of Wrultho descended into the courtyard, forcing the witches back into a fight. Asteryans, all here and prepared to murder, who had been hiding in plain sight.

The world reoriented as the soldiers threw Vaasa forward, the hand in her hair not letting go as her knees cracked against the platform. Ozik stood in front of her. They craned her neck so she had no option but to look at him. His face was gnarled with magic, the black veins she'd seen on his hands suddenly gone. The tiredness disappeared. Then he looked like a new man: youthful and endlessly wicked. "Walk, or I'll kill every single person in this courtyard," he whispered in her ear.

Vaasa didn't need to calculate her odds; with their lives, she would no longer gamble. She stood as she'd been instructed, and the hand in her hair released.

She walked.

Soldiers flanked all sides of her, one holding firmly to the rope tied like a noose around her neck, the others preventing her from being able to turn around. She tried. They blocked her view—of the courtyard, of the witches, of Reid.

Of the pounding footsteps she swore echoed behind them.

She saw nothing. No one. Not as they led her off the platform and dove straight through the circle of Veragi mist that rose like a border around the bloodshed. For a moment the familiarity of it brushed her, but then it staggered, angry and betrayed.

Something covered her mouth and nose, and inhaling the acrid scent of poison, Vaasa fell into nothing.

CHAPTER 28

Fire burned in Reid's chest.

He tried to sit up, and suddenly there was a hand on his shoulder. Above him, his mother loomed. "Don't," she warned him, pressing lightly to push him back down.

Around him were faces—his mother's, carved with misery and exhaustion, dirt-caked and tearstained. The other Veragi witches. The high witch of Zuheia. People he did not know. Their worried frowns floated in and out of his consciousness.

Colors burst behind his eyes. Black and white. Red. Purple. Shades of yellow.

The pain ebbed.

Distantly, he heard voices. Crying.

This happened over and over—the waking and the subsequent sleep. Each time he looked. He listened.

For a face and a voice he did not hear.

Until he heard nothing at all.

Reid woke to a quiet room and an empty bed.

A pillow seemed to swallow his head. He scanned the room: the reflection of broken glass beneath the doors at the edge of his quarters, the patio marred by petals and broken vines. Glass covered the left side of the room. The patio window had been blown to bits.

He knew a few things in increasing order. If he was here, he was likely alive. The city still stood, and the High Temple remained Icruria's.

But it was his mother sitting beside his bed, not his wife.

"Tell me she is alive," Reid croaked. He held his breath. So much of the day came in flashes and blurs—but he remembered little. Like watching his life in still sketches and paintings, he could not grasp anything real.

"She is alive," his mother confirmed.

He turned his head to look at her, and then tried to sit up. He could. His muscles worked for him as they had before. His mother shuffled forward and gripped his arm, but he brushed off her hands. He needed to know what he was capable of. Reid rose all the way, bringing his knees up to his chest and resting his arms upon them. He rolled his wrists, then his ankles, and wiggled his toes. Everything worked. Nothing hurt.

Then he was up on his feet. Squeaking from his mother's chair emanated around him, but he moved with alarming speed right past her, making for the armoire. He started to pass the mirror, but then he stopped. Stared. He no longer cared about the broken glass or the state of the High Temple. He looked ragged and dirty. Unkempt. His hair stuck to his cheeks and he swiped it away, his beard overgrown.

"What. Happened," he demanded, enunciating both words not at all like a question.

"You were . . ." His mother paused. "You were dead, Reid. I felt it. Vaasa made a bargain to bring you back."

Reid turned and finally looked at his mother, who seemed more tired than he was. Had she slept? He remembered the intensity of the fight—of what she had put herself and her magic through in order to hold the border around the gardens. All at once, Reid felt useless. How many days had it been since the election? Faintly, there was a part of him that cowered in terror at the words his mother had just spoken. Dead. He had been *dead*. He didn't remember what happened. But he didn't have the time to consider that, not yet. "Her magic?"

His mother nodded, her tired eyes looking like shattered stones. "I cannot feel it. It is still there, but veiled in something entirely different. A shadow."

Vaasa had saved his life, had saved all of their lives, and yet it was still she who suffered the consequences. "How did this happen?"

"Dominik's advisor is the Zetyr witch, and his demon is a manifestation of that power, much like my horse and Amalie's fox. He—" His mother stopped, swallowing what Reid assumed was the urge to cry. "The creature impaled you. It killed you almost instantly. Vaasalisa struck a bargain with Ozik—her magic for your life."

Reid's head whirled, and though he knew he could stand, he feared his legs would fail to hold him. "Surely he cannot simply *take* her magic?"

"The Zuheia have written histories about his kind—about their traditions of human sacrifice, their twisted bargains. They have offered me access unlike anything the Veragi have known before. I will be going to Wrultho next." Then Melisina bit her cheek, and her shoulders dropped. "But right now, I know nothing for certain, other than that there is something terrible at play."

Reid took a careful account of his mother: based on the knowing purse of her lips and the soft tap of her finger against her knee, he suspected she was holding something back. "What do you know?"

Melisina looked down, and he wondered what she would not say—always keeping him just at the edge, because he was not a witch, not a part of her coven.

"Mother," he warned.

Melisina looked up at him, perhaps reading the desperation in his gaze, and nodded. "Vaasalisa's mother . . . she was running from something. I had always believed it was the emperor. But . . ." She shook her head. "Now I'm not so sure."

"What do you mean?"

"On the day she left, she did so despite my pleas. I asked Vena Kozár to stay, told her we would protect her. But she said it was already over for her, that any chance she may have had was long gone. She asked me for one thing, and one thing only."

Reid paused, his body frozen as he watched his mother recall a memory she'd likely never mentioned to another soul.

"She asked me to protect her daughter." Melisina raised her gaze to meet his. "To bring her here however I could."

"The marriage agreement," Reid whispered.

"It was the only sure way I could think of."

He closed his eyes, remembering the day his mother had asked him to take Vaasalisa Kozár, their greatest enemy's daughter, as his bride. He had trusted her implicitly, had barely bothered to ask questions. She'd made it sound like the perfect political move, and by all means, it was. He'd never been good at politics, never possessed that particular, cunning ability to see behind the curtain of people's words into their intent. Not the way his mother did. Not the way his wife did. "You believe her mother was running from the advisor?"

"I believe there is more to this story than we have even begun to uncover," Melisina whispered, standing on tired, wobbly legs. She reached for the chair next to her, leaning her weight against it. Melisina's eyes started to water, and she pulled in a ragged, exhausted breath. "He did not just take Vaasalisa. Amalie, she . . . she abandoned her post. Went after them. I could not stop her."

Reid swallowed back tears. In every way that mattered, he had failed the two witches. His mother had lost *two* of her coven, and he could all but see the tears she held in. The high witch of Veragi, with what must feel like a limb missing. To keep the coven safe was her life's goal. Now she could barely hold her weight against the world, and he had nothing to make a difference. "The Zuheia witches, they've healed me?"

"They didn't even find a trace of injury."

Reid flexed his feet, then bent his knees. Lifted his arms. Everything worked. He felt as though he had never tasted death—as though he could walk right into battle. "How many days has it been?"

"It's been a little over a week."

Reid's jaw tensed. *A week?* It somehow struck him as both a blink and an entire lifetime. He opened the armoire and began to gather his things, no plan coming together in his head yet, but he was certain he'd have one by the time he reached the docks. "I need a ship."

"You can't go," his mother said.

"Try to stop me."

"You are headman elect, Reid."

Reid paused and stared at his hands, now curled around Vaasa's clothes. He couldn't look away. "They held the election?"

"Once you were given a clean bill of health, yes. They voted you headman. We need to figure out how we're going to utilize that to get her back. Until we know where they are, you'd be traveling blind."

Reid lifted his gray shirt from the drawer in front of him, and a dangerous spark of violence ignited in him. "Where is Koen?"

"In a rage, waiting for you," his mother said.

Reid threw a shirt over his head, tucking it into the breeches he wore, and started for the door.

"Reid."

He paused, his mother's voice sounding weaker than he'd ever heard it. "I will take the witches. We will scour every book that has ever been written. You have my word. But you cannot march into that empire without a plan."

"I command armies. Entire fleets—"

"Your armies are no match for what is to come, Reid Cazden," she exclaimed, and hearing his father's surname, the one he had exchanged for his title, made his entire body freeze. He could count the few times since his adolescence that she'd called him by it. Melisina shook her head, as though Reid was missing an integral piece of information. And he *always* was. She sat, the chair groaning beneath her. For the second time, she looked fragile to Reid. She had always seemed so large, so otherworldly to him. "She has spoken to me for the first time in years. For the first time since the day Vena Kozár walked into my sodality."

"Who?" Reid asked.

"Veragi," Melisina murmured, raising her eyes to meet his with purpose. "She told me where to find Vaasalisa when she was down in the catacombs, but since the gardens, I cannot hear her. All I feel is pain—immeasurable, insurmountable pain."

Reid's heart beat faster, the pounding reaching his ears.

"This is beyond even us," Melisina told him. "This is much more than a war between mortals. This is about a wrong committed many, many years ago, one I think the goddess intends to right."

"I don't understand," Reid said.

"There is one question we must ask ourselves, something you must consider with every move you make. If we have a goddess on our side, my son, then who—or what—is on Ozik's?"

Reid grasped the handle of the door, every muscle telling him to go forward now, to tear apart the continent and cut down anyone in his path. To find Vaasa, and to finally set her free. "There's something you're forgetting. Something even Ozik himself can't deny."

His mother tilted her head. "What?"

"Dominik is dead. I am married to Vaasalisa Kozár, the last remaining heiress to the Asteryan throne. So though I am the headman elect of Icruria"—Reid opened the door, looking over his shoulder once more at where his mother sat—"I am the emperor of Asterya, too. And I'm going to get my wife back."

ACKNOWLEDGMENTS

Debuting a book is a whirlwind of a process, and sometimes I still can't believe I've had this opportunity. Interestingly enough, Vaasa began as a therapeutic exercise for me—to write a character whose grief, dysregulation, and anger matched my own at the time. Her story blossomed, and with it, I did, too. To give this story to the world has been such a surreal experience, and it takes a whole lot of people other than just an author to bring a book to life. I'll do my best to thank everyone and to get this right.

Firstly, to Samantha Fabien, agent extraordinaire, who believed in this novel and believed in me. From our first phone call I felt the magic—you are an amazing support system in this crazy publishing world. Without you, I never would have gotten to this place. I'm so grateful to have you on my side and for you to be the champion of my words. To the entire Root Literary family and to Team Samantha: your support has made all the difference. To Heather, who took this work abroad, and to everyone else working with the Root Literary team—thank you.

Thank you to my editor, Amara, for seeing the heart and soul of this novel. Your vision for this book fit so perfectly with what I wanted this manuscript to turn into, and your expert eye elevated the story to the incredible work we put out. To everyone on the Saga Press team, thank you for your time, energy, and answering my questions as I navigated this publishing season as a debut author. Caroline and Savannah, you both rock!

Noémie—what a blessing to know you and to be your friend. You are my CP Soulmate for life, and there are no words that see the light of day that you don't read first. Your feedback is incredible, and you're the only person I trust enough to flat-out tell me *this sucks* because it's always followed with an *I know you can make it perfect.* A big thank-you to Catherine for reading an early version of this manuscript and helping me push character development even further. Your feedback was integral in the process, and I'm so grateful for you.

Tiffanie—your guidance, thoughtfulness, and kindness is what spurred the work necessary to write this novel. You were the first person to encourage me to create this character, and it was through your strategies that I began the difficult work of looking inward. Thank you for supporting me through a very difficult time.

To Jacob, who I owe a whole page of this acknowledgment, but who I will do my best to keep it simple: you are one of the best friends I could ever have, and the fact that you'll build a whole world with me for just one good glass of bourbon (or four) is only a perk. Without you as a creativity partner, this novel would not have seen the light of day. I hope you always know how important you are. Thank you for running over when I hit a wall, for drawing an enormous map on poster board to help me make sense of this, and for always broadening my mindset. I appreciate you endlessly and my life would be infinitely worse without you in it.

To Erin, who read even the earliest of my works and has encouraged me every step of the way. From colleagues, to roommates, to wives, to mothers, we have spent the better part of my adulthood in the same place and for that I am forever grateful. And to Spencer, who has been an amazing friend and the best partner for my best friend I could ask for. Thank you both for my little nephew and for supporting me through this crazy process.

Roomz, who is one of my dearest friends and my SSR buddy for life, your friendship makes me a better person. Thank you for always talking books with me, for eating soup no matter the season, and for reading this novel. I'm so thankful our high school friendship blossomed into this lifelong connection. To DeeDee, who was with me for some of the darkest parts when the snake was at its worst—thank you for being my friend through it all. And for Marissa, who loved me even when you weren't obligated to, who read early copies of this work and provided a reader perspective. Without your time and encouragement, I may never have been brave enough to query this manuscript.

Emma, you've been there since the start and I know you'll be there until the end. Thank you for reading even the roughest, earliest words I put on paper so many years ago. Thank you for always supporting me and for being there in the blink of an eye, always. I love you so much.

To Aunt Julie and Uncle Manrique, Sam and Luis, thank you for sharing in this excitement and encouraging me to keep the path. To my grandmother, who told me to never settle—to never accept less than what I deserved. You are an incredible woman with fortitude, and I am deeply grateful for you.

Thank you to Lisa and Chris, who have loved me like their own daughter since I was merely eighteen. You have always supported my writing, even when it meant I was typing instead of watching the family movie or helping finish the puzzle. I am so blessed to have in-laws I can't wait to call and spend time with. The way you opened your life to me is a big part of what inspired the feeling of belonging in this novel. I thank you for that.

To my father, who gave to me his steadfastness and determination. The hard choices you have made for your family don't go unnoticed, and it is because of them that I am able to make choices for mine, too. I have never related to you more than I did while I wrote this book, especially when it meant I was away from my child. I understand now. To my mother, who bought me an embossed binder for the first manuscript I ever wrote, never knowing if my words would see the light of day; it is rare that people have a woman like you who always picks up the phone, who gives kindness like it's breathing, and who always sees the best in others. Even if they don't deserve it. Even when I don't. You are exceptional.

Thank you to Ben, who listened to my senseless plotlines and let me read scenes aloud until they made sense in my mind. You are the landing place for all of me—the joy, the sadness, the creativity. It is in the silent evenings with you that I find myself most at home and most able to tap into the love I have for this craft. I could write forever about what you mean to me.

To Lucas: you gave me the motivation to keep looking within, even if what I found was sometimes difficult. For you, I will always try to be the best mother—which means being the best *person*—I can be. You carry a wolf, my son. Just like your father. Just like your mother.

And finally, I want to express a little gratitude to myself. It was incredible work to write this novel and to navigate a debut year while raising an infant, starting a new day job, and drafting the second novel in this duology. I never should have questioned my own strength—and I'm proud of myself for finding it. Next is balance. Next is self-love.

Thank you.

ICRURI
Sigguth
Dihrah
Irhu
The Settara
Mireh
CISAL
UTHIBA